My Baby My Baby!

By

Earl S. Kratzer

This book is a work of fiction. Places, events, and situations in this story are purely fictional. Any resemblance to actual persons, living or dead, is coincidental.

© 2002 by Earl S. Kratzer. All rights reserved.

No part of this book may be reproduced, stored in a retrieval system, or transmitted by any means, electronic, mechanical, photocopying, recording, or otherwise, without written permission from the author.

ISBN: 1-4033-2656-8 (E-book)
ISBN: 1-4033-2657-6 (Softcover)
ISBN: 1-4033-2658-4 (Rocketbook)

Library of Congress Control Number: 2002091821

This book is printed on acid free paper.

Printed in the United States of America
Bloomington, IN

1stBooks - rev. 09/18/02

CHAPTER 1

"MY BABY, MY BABY, SHE'S GONE!" Marylou Barnes screamed as she ran back into her apartment on the lower West Side of Cleveland, Ohio.

Marylou Blankenship Barnes was born February 21, 1947 to Walter and Stella Blankenship in Logon County West Virginia.

She was the youngest of nine, two brothers and one sister had already gone to the Promise Land. That's what her daddy used to tell Marylou as he sat at the kitchen table swigging from a fresh-made jug of moonshine. That's about all there was to do back in the hills of West Virginia, make some moonshine, sell some, but drink most of it yourself.

Marylou was only eight when her mother died. Stella died at the old age of thirty-nine. She endured three years of pain from cancer and twenty-four years of plan and abuse from Walter.

By that time, the three living brothers had run away. It was anybody's guess where they were, but who cared? One sister was married and living in an old shack, down the road, with her three kids and husband. Her husband was a carbon copy of her daddy, Walter. There was no doubt the sister was headed down the same road as her momma.

The other sister was living at home with Marylou and her father. She was six months pregnant. Everyone knew it was Walter's Baby, but who cared?

She had the baby and moved down the road to her sister's shack and Lord knows what was in store for her. That's when the sexual abuse by Marylou's father started. Marylou took her mother's place, not only in the kitchen but in the bedroom as well. She wanted to leave but that would not happen for two years.

On December 18, 1959, Aunt Millie, Walter's sister, came from Cleveland, Ohio to visit over the holidays. Two days into the visit, Aunt Millie found Walter drunk and in bed with Marylou.

Aunt Millie said nothing, she packed up Marylou's few clothes and whisked her off to Cleveland, Ohio.

Aunt Millie and her husband had moved to the lower West Side of Cleveland in the early fifties. Her husband had gone to work for Republic Steel. But died a few years later.

Aunt Millie had had one daughter, who was living on the East Side of Cleveland. Mille saw her daughter once in a while when she needed money.

Aunt Millie was living on Welfare and a few dollars she made under the table working for Mr. Barnes, who owned the corner store.

Marylou was enrolled at William Dean Howell in the Seventh Grade. It wasn't very long before she was very popular at school, for all the wrong reasons.

Marylou was fourteen years old and five month's pregnant. She had no idea who the father was.

Marylou had little Billy at City Hospital and then dropped out of school. She signed up for Welfare and stayed at home to care for her baby.

Aunt Millie was working afternoons at the store, and Marylou was getting bored staying at home and caring for the baby. She began inviting her friends over to the house. Soon Marylou's house became the place to be. "Bring beer and get some" was the motto of Marylou and her friends.

Word of the party house spread fast. Soon, the most frequent visitor was Nate Barnes, the eighteen year old son of Mr. Barnes, the store owner.

Nate was tall and good-looking; but better yet, he could get the beer and the price was right. Free!

By the time Marylou was sixteen, she was pregnant again. Marylou was much smarter now, so she told Nate the baby was his.

Nate's mother and father were very upset to say the least, but Nate said he loved Marylou and wanted to marry her. Marylou seeing a good opportunity, lied and said she loved Nate and also wanted to marry him.

They were married in a simple ceremony at the City Hall in Cleveland.

Nate's father gave Nate a full-time job at the store. He told Marylou and his son they could move in with Nate's mother and him.

Marylou liked the idea of Nate working full-time, but refused to move from Aunt Millie's house.

My Baby My Baby!

Nate moved in with Marylou, little Billy, and Aunt Millie.

A short time later, Marylou gave birth to a little boy. They named him Joey.

It wasn't long before Aunt Millie's house again became the party house. Nate was working most of the time, but was still supplying the beer.

In a short time, Marylou was pregnant again. She told Nate this was his baby, too although she knew different.

Aunt Millie thought this was about enough and told the couple to pack their bags and git!

Marylou found a cheap apartment not far from Aunt Millie. Nate and she bought some furniture from the Salvation Army and set up housekeeping.

Not long after they moved to the apartment, Marylou gave birth to a little girl. She was also born at City Hospital, and they named her Susan.

Nate was working longer hours at the store and Marylou was busy taking care of the three babies. The partying slowed down, except on the weekends.

The apartment Marylou and Nate lived in had six suites. Each suite was occupied with young mothers, all of whom had little children.

There was a large backyard where all the mothers took their children to play. While watching their children, the mothers discussed their problems, mostly relating to their husbands. They were always comparing one husband with the other.

Here Marylou met Debbie Thompson. Debbie was married to Jimmy Thompson. They had a little baby.

Jimmy was about ten years older than Marylou, but Marylou wanted him. Marylou started a little campaign to get Jimmy.

Becoming good friends with Debbie, Marylou invited Debbie and Jimmy over to her apartment on Saturday night. She had Nate bring home a case of beer and two bottles of cheap wine from the store. Now, her trap was set.

From the beginning Nate did not like Jimmy. Jimmy was bigger, older and louder, making Nate feel like a little boy. Jimmy was always looking at Marylou as though she was naked, and that made Nate mad.

That Saturday night when they were all sitting at the table, Nate didn't have much to say. He sat there drinking beer and wine as fast as he could.

Jimmy, on the other hand, was having a great time, telling dirty jokes, all the time while winking at Marylou and drinking the beer and wine.

Debbie sat at the table scowling at both Jimmy and Marylou. She had had but one glass of wine, mainly because she could see what was going on between Marylou and Jimmy. Also, she had left her three-week old baby across the hall in their apartment and was listening for him to cry.

Marylou was not drinking at all, that was not part of her plan.

They had been there about three hours when Debbie heard the baby crying.

"Come on Jimmy, let's go home. The baby is crying," she said to Jimmy, "And, you have had enough to drink."

"Hey bitch, who do you think you're talking to?" Jimmy yelled. "Get home and take care of the kid. Fuck, there's still beer and wine here. I'll be home when it's gone!"

Debbie ran from Marylou's apartment crying. She got across the hall and slammed her apartment door.

Jimmy laughed and yelled, "Go home bitch, I'll be there when I'm good and ready." Jimmy grabbed his crotch and yelled, "And, you better be ready for some action when I get home!"

Marylou started giggling. Nate groaned, threw back his head, drank a half-glass of wine straight down, and headed for the bathroom gagging.

Marylou was laughing out loud at what Jimmy had said and at poor Nate.

Jimmy hollered after Nate, "Hey boy, that stuff ain't made for kids. It says so right on the bottle." Jimmy stretched back in his chair and was laughing.

Marylou reached over and grabbed Jimmy between the legs and whispered in his ear, "If you want some action big boy, meet me out in the backyard in about a half hour."

Jimmy grabbed Marylou by the neck and pulled her face down to his. He put about a yard of tongue in her mouth and then said, "I'll be there."

Marylou's plan was working better and faster than she had planned.

While Debbie lay in her bed crying and nursing her baby, Nate was lying in his own vomit passed out on the bathroom floor. Marylou and Jimmy were getting their action in the backyard under the bushes.

It was around seven o'clock the next morning when Nate woke up. He was still on the bathroom floor, and all he could hear were three babies crying. He got up from the floor, his head pounding and his mouth tasting like rat shit.

He staggered to the bedroom and saw Marylou lying on the bed sound asleep.

Nate smacked her across the face and yelled, "Get out of that bed you fucking whore and take care of those brats!"

Marylou jumped from the bed screaming, "Don't you ever hit me again or I'll kill you!"

"Go take care of those kids, shut them up now!" Nate yelled. Marylou ran out of the bedroom and Nate crawled into the bed. He was asleep in no time.

Nate woke up about three o'clock that afternoon. The apartment was unusually quiet. Nate listened for some sound, but heard nothing. He got up from the bed and walked to the kitchen. On the way, he checked the living room, the other bedroom, and the bathroom, and found nothing.

The kitchen door was open and Nate could see across the hall into Debbie's apartment. Her door was also open. Nate walked across the hall. He saw his three children playing on the floor. Debbie was sitting in a chair holding her baby and crying.

Nate yelled, "Where the hell is Marylou?"

"They left!" Debbie whimpered.

"Who left? What do you mean they left? What the hell are you talking about?" Nate was screaming now.

"Jimmy and Marylou left in Jimmy's truck. They left about an hour ago. He took all the money, told me to watch the kids, him and Marylou were going out to party. He told me if I woke you up, he would kill me." Debbie told Nate all this between sobs.

Nate took the kids back to his apartment and waited for Marylou to come home.

Jimmy and Marylou didn't come home that night. They didn't come home Monday night or Tuesday night. They were only a few blocks away, staying at the Sleepy Bear Motel and drinking at all the bars on West 25th Street.

Monday morning, Nate was due to go to work. He asked Debbie to watch the kids.

"Fuck you," she said. "I ain't watching that whore's kids while she's out with my old man!"

Nate called his father to tell him what had happened and to see if he could take the day off work to look for Marylou.

Nate's father started to scream over the phone, "Get into work right now or you won't have a job! This is the best thing that can happen to you! You know she ain't nothing but a slut! None of those kids are yours anyhow! You come back home! Come back to work! Leave that whore and those babies! Your ma and me don't want no part of her or them! You come home, now!" His father slammed the phone down.

Nate knew his father was right. He knew the children weren't his, and he knew Marylou had been cheating on him any chance she could get. Jimmy wasn't the first guy she had slept with.

Now was his chance to get out of this mess. Nate took the children over to Aunt Millie's house. She wasn't at home. Nate left them on the front porch.

Wednesday night, Nate left work and went to the apartment to pick up his clothes. He knocked on the door of the apartment before he went in. He didn't want to find Marylou and Jimmy there. He thought if anyone answers the door, he would leave. There was no answer. Nate put his ear to the door, nothing.

Nate opened the door, reached in, and turned on the lights. He watched as the cockroaches dove for cover. He looked at the mess; dirty dishes stacked on the sink, empty beer bottles and cans thrown on the floor, mouse or maybe even rat shit on the table and counters. I'm going home, Nate thought to himself. Man, I don't need this shit. Just then, the phone rang.

The drunken voice on the other end was Marylou. "You still there shithead?" She mumbled.

Nate could hear Jimmy laughing in the background.

"Where the fuck are my kids?" Marylou asked.

"I took them to Aunt Millie's," Nate told her.

"Good, and you leave them there!" Marylou slobbered over the phone. "None of them are yours anyhow. They all have men for fathers, not some punk like you!"

Nate could hear Jimmy in the background again, egging Marylou on.

Marylou started screaming over the phone, "Get out of my apartment, get out, me and my man, Jimmy are coming home, get out and get out now! Jimmy is going to take me in your bed and ___" Nate slammed the phone down.

Nate took his clothes to the car. He came back and looked around the apartment. She can have everything else in her, and with a sigh of relief, he closed the door.

Nate walked across the hall to Debbie's apartment. The door was closed. Nate knocked, but there was no answer. He knocked louder, still no answer. Someone from upstairs yelled down. "She and the baby left yesterday, she took the kid to her mama's house, they're gone!"

Nate walked away from the door. Well, thought Nate. Maybe three lives saved.

CHAPTER 2

Marylou had planned, set the trap, and caught God only knew what.

There's an old saying: Don't wish too hard for something, you just might get it! Well, Marylou got it!

Marylou and Jimmy had come back to the apartment late Wednesday night. They were drunk and broke.

By late Thursday morning, Marylou was feeling guilty about her kids and maybe a little guilty about Nate; but, Oh Well! Nate was getting to be a pain in the ass.

Marylou shook Jimmy awake. "Let's go to Aunt Millie's and get my kids," she said.

"Fuck you and those kids," Jimmy mumbled. "Get back in this bed, I got something that will make you forget all about them kids."

Marylou walked to Aunt Millie's alone while Jimmy was still in bed half-drunk. She knocked on Aunt Millie's door.

Aunt Millie answered the door screaming, "Marylou, I'm sick and tired of you, sick and tired of these kids, and sick and tired of life! I should have left you with your father and been done with it. I don't want to see you or your kids anymore! Take them away now, don't you call or come here anymore!" Aunt Millie sent the children out on the porch and slammed the door.

Marylou started walking down the street. All the kids were crying, they all wanted to be carried. Marylou started crying, too. Shit, shit, shit, that's what life is all about, she said to herself.

Marylou got back to the apartment, and she saw Jimmy walking up the street carrying a six-pack of beer.

"God Jimmy, there's no milk or food in the house of the kids, but you find enough money to buy beer," Marylou moaned.

"Well honey, I got credit down at the store from Nate's father," Jimmy laughed. "Ditch them brats and let's you and me get drunk."

Marylou slapped Jimmy across the face and ran into the apartment slamming and locking the door behind her.

Jimmy stood on the street staring after the fleeing four-some.

Jimmy walked slowly to the back porch of the apartment, carefully setting the six-pack down on the porch, and kicked down the apartment door.

Jimmy walked inside the apartment, punched and kicked Marylou unconscious.

Jimmy then walked outside, sat on the back porch, and went to work on the six-pack.

Marylou was slowly waking up on the kitchen floor. The kids were all crying, "Mommy, Mommy get up! Get up!"

Painfully, Marylou got up. She looked around. Jimmy was gone. The six-pack lay empty on the back porch. Jimmy was probably at Duke's Bar. She knew that was always where he went to drink.

Marylou took the kids and headed down the street to the only friend she had left, Patty Davis.

Patty lived down the street from Marylou. She had one little boy named Rick. Her husband had left a few month's ago. He said he was going to look for a job. Patty always said he must have found one traveling, because he never came home again. Patty always laughed when she told that one.

Patty let Marylou and the kids in, and she helped Marylou clean up her face. Patty put some coffee on, and she and Marylou sat at the kitchen table.

Patty told Marylou she thought she was pregnant. Patty said she had gone out one night and got half-drunk, well, maybe more than half. She had gone to a bar on West 25th where her sister and her husband hung out. "Well, guess what?" Patty told Marylou. "My sister wasn't there, but her husband was. Well, I always said, keep it in the family. Well, I guess he put the family in me!" Patty laughed. Marylou even smiled at that one.

Patty told Marylou she and the kids could stay with her until Marylou got things straightened out, no problem.

Marylou got Jimmy out of her apartment after calling the police a few times. Jimmy got an apartment up on Lorain Avenue. He also rented a garage for his pick-up truck. Marylou settled down taking care of the kids and seeing Jimmy only on the weekends. Marylou knew she was pregnant again. Was it Jimmy's or Nate's? Marylou took the easy way out and told Jimmy he was going to be a father.

CHAPTER 3

It was lunch time on a hot August day in 1970. Marylou Barnes was fixing lunch for her four children, her friend Patty Davis, and Patty's two children.

Billy, Marylou's oldest boy, now eight, was playing outside with Patty's son, Ricky, now five.

Joey, six, and Susan, five, were playing in the living room.

Noreen, Marylou's youngest daughter, three, and Sally, Patty's youngest daughter, also three, were taking a nap in the bedroom.

Marylou went into the bedroom to wake up Noreen and Sally for lunch. She came back into the kitchen and told Patty to call the two boys in for lunch.

Little Noreen came running from the he bedroom and yelled, "Mommy, Mommy, let me go get them!"

"O.K." Marylou said. "But come right back into this house."

"O.K." Noreen said, "I'll come right back."

Marylou dished up the stew and sat down at the table. Five minutes later, Marylou got up from the table and went to the door to look for the children. She saw Billy and Rick still playing in the dirt in the backyard.

Marylou yelled out the door, "Get in here and eat, and bring Noreen."

Billy yelled back, "We ain't seen Noreen."

Marylou ran outside. She could see the entire backyard from the porch. There was not a sigh of Noreen.

Marylou ran to the corner of the street looking up and down. There was not a sign of Noreen. Marylou ran back to the yard and looked again. Nothing.

Marylou yelled for Patty, "Patty, Patty, help me, call the police. My baby is gone!"

CHAPTER 4

The zone car in the area got the call from the radio at 1:35 p.m. The call came over, "Car 211, missing three year-old female at 4800 Franklin Avenue, Apartment #1."

The uniformed men in Car 211 got there at one forty-five p.m.

Marylou came running out into the street screaming that her daughter was missing. The street was full of people by now, all trying to talk to the police. The police got Marylou back into the apartment and tried to get information from her. Marylou was hysterical, and the police tried to calm her down. Not succeeding, they questioned Patty.

Patty told them the story about getting lunch ready and not being able to find Noreen. While Patty had been calling the police, Marylou had been running up and down the street screaming for Noreen.

The police wanted a description from Marylou, but they had to get it from Patty.

Patty told the police Noreen was three years old, white female, blonde hair, blue eyes, about three feet tall. She was wearing a pink short-sleeve blouse, blue jeans, and tennis shoes with red socks.

The police immediately got the description on the radio and called for a supervisor to meet them at the apartment.

Lieutenant Smith of the Second District met the patrolmen at the apartment and told them to call the detectives right away. The Lieutenant also told the officers to stay on the scene until the detectives arrived. The Lieutenant got into his car to check around the neighborhood.

A team of detectives arrived at the scene at about three-fifteen p.m. Detectives Don Fox and Dick Bender talked to the Zone car men, but were unable to talk to Marylou because she was hysterical. The detectives called the policewomen and had them take Marylou to the hospital.

The detectives told the zone car men to search the neighborhood while the detectives interviewed some of the people on the scene.

The patrol car returned about an hour later and reported that they could not find any trace of the little girl.

The detectives had gathered as much information as was possible from Patty and the neighbors, and had decided that this was very possibly a kidnapping. It was time to call in their supervisor and let him decide what course of action to take.

CHAPTER 5

Detective Sergeant Jack Hunter had just finished the four o'clock roll call and was sitting at his desk thinking about last night. It had been one of the all-night drinking bouts at Rose and Jerry's, a policeman's hang-out, where drinking and lying was the rule and not the exception.

Jack's phone rang. It was Detective Fox. "Hey Sarge, we've got a problem here." Fox told the Sergeant the story so far.

"I'll be right there," Hunter said.

Sergeant Hunted arrived on the scene at about five o'clock p.m. "O.K. boys, what have we got here?" Sergeant Hunter asked as he got out of his car.

Detectives Fox and Bender told the Sergeant that a little three year old girl was missing for about three hours.

"What's been done so far?" Hunter asked.

"Well, Sarge," Bender said, "the zone cars have searched the area and some detectives are going from house to house interviewing neighbors."

"Where are the mother and father?" Hunter asked.

"The mother just got back from the hospital and is in bed under sedation." Bender said. "We don't know where the father is yet." Bender continued, "We have some information that he doesn't live here and is the common-law husband of this Marylou, the mother."

"Let's see if we can find him." Hunter said. "With any luck, the kid is with him and we can wrap this up."

"In the meantime," Hunter said, "let's use this apartment as a base until we can get organized."

"Oh, oh Sarge, you're not going to like this" Fox said, "This is a bad place; there are more cockroaches than Carter's Little Liver Pills in this joint, and is it dirty!"

"Is there a phone in there?" Hunter asked.

"Yes," Bender answered, "but, I sure as hell would hold it away from my ear."

The three detectives walked into the apartment. "Who the hell are all these people?" Hunter asked.

"Friends and neighbors." Fox said.

"Get them all out of here, now!" Hunter yelled.

Hunter and Fox walked through the apartment with Fox leading the way. "This is the living room," Fox said. "This is the bedroom, the kitchen, and the shithouse."

"The whole place is a shithouse," Hunter said. "The only difference is this room has a toilet in it."

"Sarge" someone yelled from the kitchen, "the phone's for you."

Hunter walked to the kitchen and grabbed the phone. "Holy shit!" Hunter yelled. "Get something to wipe this phone off, it's full of scrambled eggs."

The call came from one of the uniformed men. They had found the father at Duke's Bar, a wino place on Bridge Avenue. The officer told Hunter the guy was all juiced up and had told them he did not know the little girl was missing.

"Get him over here!" Hunter told the officer.

Jimmy Thompson was a six foot, four inch two hundred sixty-five pound hillbilly and drunk as a skunk. "Where the fuck is my little girl?" He bellowed. "You cocksuckers had better find her, and when you catch the motherfuckers that took her, I'm going to kill em!"

"Hold it!" Hunter said. "Who told you she was taken by anyone?"

"You just find her, and I'll take care of the rest of it," Thompson yelled.

Marylou came running from the bedroom screaming, "Jimmy, Jimmy, our baby is gone. What did you do with her?"

Bender and Fox grabbed Marylou and took her back into the bedroom. One of the uniformed men pushed Jimmy down into one of the kitchen chairs.

"Get some coffee into that slob and find out where he was today," Hunter said. "Now let's get down to business."

"Fox, get hold of radio." Hunter started to bark out the orders. "I want the Command Bus set up in the parking lot across the street as soon as possible. I want personnel here by five a.m. to start searching al the vacant and condemned buildings in the area. Call the K9 and get the dogs out here. I want all the News media notified. Get this kid's picture in every newspaper and on all the TV stations. We'll start treating this like a kidnapping until we find out different. I don't want any bullshit from the Chief about why it took so long to get moving."

By daylight the next morning, the Command Bus was set up and the neighborhood was swarming with police. They were interviewing the neighbors and searching every nook and cranny in the area.

"God damn Sarge!" Bender said. "This is crazy, we've got over one hundred calls from people that claim to have seen this kid from one end of the city to the other."

"I know," Hunter said. "All we can do is check each and every lead as best as we can. By the way, how did the dogs do?"

"Well," Bender said. "I think it was kind of a joke. The two dogs ran around the apartment for a while; then, they dragged the handler, Duffy, out the door, ran to the nearest telephone pole and took a piss."

"That's better than usual," Fox said. "The dogs piss on Duffy's leg most of the time."

"Fox," Hunter said. "What did you and Bender find out about the whereabouts of Thompson yesterday."

"He had a busy day," Bender said. "He started drinking about ten o'clock yesterday morning. He hit about four wino joints, and then the uniformed men found him at the Duke's Bar on Bridge Avenue."

"I want that guy's story checked with a fine-tooth comb," Hunter said. "Now let's go get some rest, but I want you guys back here at five a.m."

Fox and Bender headed for home. Hunter headed for Rosie's Bar.

Yes, home for Sergeant Jack Hunter was Rosie's Bar. At forty-two years old, Jack Hunter had three daughters, twenty years on the department, had been divorced ten years, married two months ago, and was working on that divorce. His new wife had already left him and wanted a divorce.

Oh well, Hunter thought. Hit Rosie's. Pop a few caps on some Millers, maybe quite a few, maybe a couple shooters. With any luck, Rosie will make some pork chop sandwiches. Good old Rosie.

Jack knew there would be some other copper there. There always were. They would discuss this case, compare it with others. Jack thought I should turn in an overtime card every time I go down there. After all they only talked police work.

Jack knew the program by heart. Get half shit-faced, tell some lies, go home to bed, get up and start all over.

I better drink fast tonight, Jack thought. Five a.m. comes early.

CHAPTER 6

"It's been forty-eight hours and we don't have a decent lead to follow up on," Hunter said. "The Chief says we can't keep all the troops here." Hunter sat back in his chair in the Command Bus thinking. Then, he said, "Fox, Bender, send all the men back to their zones, send this bus back to wherever they hide it. Bring all the logs and meet me back at the station. I bet a thousand dollars that girl is long gone from here!"

Hunter was no sooner back at the station when he had a phone call from the Chief.

"Here's the way it is," Hunter said to Fox and Bender. "The Chief assigned us full-time to the case. All leads and reports concerning the case will come to us, and we have to follow-up the best we can. Now, let's sit down and see what we have so far."

"I'd say the kid was picked up by someone right in the yard," Bender said. "If she had just walked away, someone would have seen her."

"That's right," Fox said. "Someone had to pick her up. If she was just lost, she would have shown up by now."

"You think some pervert was watching her and snatched her from the yard?" Hunter asked.

"I don't know about that Sarge," Fox said. "That doesn't seem to fit. The chances of some pervert walking down the street at the same time the kid came out of the house are pretty slim."

"Well, let's go on the assumption the girl was gone longer than the mother thought and was snatched off the street," Hunter said. "So, go through the records and get the names of all the assholes in the area. Also, get me full reports on the mother and father, record checks, the whole nine yards."

Bender and Fox got busy gathering the info Hunter wanted.

"Hey Sarge," Fox yelled from across the room. "Wait until you see the record on Thompson!"

"Bring it over and let's take a look," Hunter said. "Holy shit! In six years, he has nine intoxication arrests, nineteen traffic arrests, three assault arrests, one aggravated robbery and attempted murder arrest, and three shoplifting arrests."

"Aw Sarge, just sounds like your everyday citizen," Fox laughed.

"Thompson is still on probation for the attempted murder rap," Hunter said. "Get the reports on that case and let's see what it's all about."

Bender brought all the reports back about an hour later. "Got the reports Sarge," Bender said. "Thompson was with another guy they call Nate 'The Real' McCoy. They were robbing some old bum outside Duke's Bar, and the bum started to run away. Either Thompson or McCoy shot the bum in the back, but the bum lived. Thompson turned states witness, put all the shit on McCoy, and then got probation. McCoy is still in the can serving time."

"How about the mother?" Hunter asked.

"Not bad at all," Bender said. "Ten intoxication arrests. By the way, one of the assault arrests on Thompson was made by Marylou, but she dropped the charges."

"Fox, I want you to go down to Columbus and talk to McCoy," Hunter said. "See how McCoy feels about Thompson. Maybe, he had someone on the outside snatch the kid for revenge. In the meantime, Bender and I will follow up some leads. I think it's about time we talk to the mother and get her story."

CHAPTER 7

Two days later, Detective Fox returned from Columbus with a very interesting story from McCoy.

McCoy told Detective Fox about the robbery and the shooting. He told him that Thompson had the gun and had shot the bum. McCoy told Fox the following about Thompson: "That man is crazy, and when he drinks, he gets worse. He wants to fight all the time, and the more he drinks, the more he wants to fight. Everyone at Duke's Bar is afraid of him, that's where he hangs out, and everyone buys him drinks and gives him money. He just shot that bum for no reason, just for the fun of it. He didn't' have to shoot him to rob him. I was with him when he shot the bum, but I didn't do anything. He told the cops I shot the bum, and he told me if I said I didn't, he would shoot me, and man, I believe him! Fuck it! I'll take a short rap, and when I get out of here, I'll stay clear of that crazy son of a bitch."

Detective Fox said he asked McCoy about Thompson and his daughter and got the following reply: "One time Thompson had talked about selling his daughter, because he needed some money for drugs he had bought. Thompson told me that he had talked to two guys at Duke's Bar. They had offered him money for the kid, but Thompson said he was afraid to do it. But then, he said Marylou treated him like shit and this would piss him off. He would start screaming 'I don't even know if that kid is mine, that Marylou is cheating on me all the time.'" McCoy said, "I think he might get drunk enough to sell the kid."

"I don't know," Bender said. "This McCoy may just be pissed off at Thompson and making up this whole story."

"We'll see," Hunter said. "We'll see."

"Sure," Bender said to Fox, "you get to go to Columbus and have a good time, I get stuck working with the Sarge."

"Hey, hey," Hunter said. "Didn't I take you out for lunch every day Fox was gone?"

"Oh yeah, Rosie's for lunch, a pork chop sandwich, the highlight of my tour of duty," Bender replied. "No, I take that back, the highlight was the interview with Marylou Barnes."

My Baby My Baby!

"Tell me about it," Fox said.

"Me and the Sarge went over to the apartment from hell, about ten in the morning," Bender told Fox. "Marylou had all the neighbors and a minister from some storefront church there. They were getting posters made and passing them around the neighborhood. They also had set up a fund for the family at the neighborhood bank. I'm telling you it looked just like a board meeting, and Marylou was Chairman of the Board. They already had fifteen hundred dollars in the fund, and it looks like they will be getting plenty more. Anyway, we got Marylou away from the meeting, and this is what we found out."

Marylou told us it was true she didn't know if Noreen was, in fact, Jimmy's daughter, but once told Jimmy that when she was drunk. Jimmy did not live in the apartment anymore, but lived in one rented room upon Lorain Avenue. He stayed at the apartment sometimes, but when he did, he slept on the living room floor. Jimmy did some handy-man work when he could get some. He had an old pick-up truck he used. He rented a garage on West 32nd where he kept the truck and some materials he used on the job.

Bender then told Fox, "Marylou said she didn't let Noreen go over to Jimmy's apartment anymore. She thought Jimmy was fooling around with Noreen. We asked her what she meant by that, and Marylou told us that Noreen had said that her daddy had touched her on her wee-wee and wanted to hug her all the time. Marylou said that one time when Jimmy had stayed at the apartment, she had found Jimmy sleeping on the front room floor with Noreen. Jimmy was naked and was holding Noreen in his arms. She screamed at him and told him to get out of here. Jimmy said he had come home drunk and was going to come into her room for some action. He took his clothes off in the front room and then passed out. 'Ain't that a crock of shit!' Marylou said. "I told him to get the hell out of here with his lies, and if he ever came into my bedroom when he was drunk, he would get some action, but not the kind he wanted."

Bender continued, "I asked Marylou if she thought Jimmy would ever take, or have someone take Noreen for money." "You know," Marylou said. "Jimmy asked me one time if I would take twenty-five thousand dollars for one of my kids." I said, "Where the hell would you get twenty-five thousand dollars?" And Jimmy said, "Don't worry about it." "I thought he was kidding, but maybe if he got drunk enough, he could do something like that. He can be a real pain in the ass when he drinks. Come to think of it, he doesn't even have to drink to be one."

CHAPTER 8

Duke's Bar seven months before Noreen is missing. Jimmy Thompson is sitting at the bar on a stool, his head laying on the bar, one hand still wrapped around a bottle of Strohs beer.

Duke, the owner, slaps Jimmy up along side the head. "Wake up you drunken bum!" Duke hollers. "Either drink or get out of here. I ain't running no God damn hotel here!"

Jimmy looks at Duke through red, bleary eyes. "Gimme a break will ya? I've been here three days buying drinks for everyone in the place," Jimmy moaned.

"So what?" Duke said. "That was then, this is now. Get some money on the bar, or get out!"

"You son of a bitch!" Jimmy screamed back. "You stole all the money I had on the bar last night."

"Get out of here," Duke yelled.

Jimmy staggered towards the front door. Duke hollered after him. "Why don't you sell that kid like those two guys told you to do last night? She ain't yours anyhow. Marylou told me all about it!"

"Fuck you!" Jimmy screamed as he slammed the door.

Thompson headed for his old pick-up truck. He got in to start the truck, but there was no noise. He tried the horn. Silence. The battery was dead. "Motherfucker!" Jimmy screamed as he beat on the steering wheel with his fist. "God damn it, I need a drink! Maybe I should sell that little brat. She ain't mine, none of them are. That bitch Marylou, she's got a boyfriend, maybe more than one. Who the fuck were those guys? I can't remember what I said to them. Maybe Duke knows who they are." Jimmy slammed the door of the truck and staggered down the snow-covered street headed for Marylou's apartment.

CHAPTER 9

"Fox, Bender!" Sergeant Hunter called across the squad room. "Get down to that bar; Duke's or whatever it is, on Bridge Avenue, and talk to the owner. Both McCoy and Marylou came up with that story about selling the kid, and the figure of twenty-five thousand dollars. Maybe, there is something to it."

The detective car with Fox and Bender pulled out of the district. The air conditioning was on full-blast. It was hot and humid outside. It was a typical August day in Cleveland.

"You ever been to this joint?" Fox asked Bender.

"Not socially," Bender said. "We had a stakeout a couple times when I was working Vice. Had a lot of complaints about drugs being sold and gambling inside; but, we never came up with anything. It's a real red-neck, low life joint. But one thing, the owner fits right in," Bender laughed.

The two detectives pulled up in front of Duke's Bar.

"Christ, I hate to get out of this car," Fox said.

"Yeah," replied Bender. "I see a little air conditioner above the door of the bar, and I don't see any water dripping from it. You know what that means?"

"Broken," Fox said. "But, let's do what we got to do."

Fox and Bender walked into the bar. They were right. The air conditioning was broken. It was dark and smelled of stale beer, sweat, and other disgusting odors. There was a sloppy fat barmaid in a dirty tee shirt and jeans behind the bar.

There was one customer sitting at the bar. The bar was filled with dirty glasses from the night before.

The barmaid looked at Fox and Bender, smiled, all front teeth missing, and said, "What do you cops want?"

"The owner," Fox said. "What's his name?"

The barmaid still smiling said, "His name is Duke, but you gotta wait, he's taking a dump. Can I get you guys a drink?"

Bender said, "No."

Fox gagged.

"Don't sit down!" Bender said to Fox. "Unless you want to take some pets home."

My Baby My Baby!

Fox looked down at the barstools and saw the shadowy forms of cockroaches moving around on them. "Just keep your feet moving," Fox said to Bender.

They heard the toilet flush. The door to the men's room opened, and out came a beer-bellied, unshaven, shaggy-looking hillbilly.

"Must be Duke," Fox whispered.

"Yeah, I'm Duke, and I just sent a message to your Chief," he laughed. "What do you coppers want? A free drink?" Duke slapped his belly laughing.

"No, we don't want anything," Bender said. "Just some information from you."

"Maybe, that don't come free," Duke said. "Maybe, I don't have nothing to tell you. Maybe, I don't want you in here, and maybe, I'll throw your asses out the door."

"And, maybe, we'll just kick your fat ass!" Fox said.

"Hey man, relax," Duke said. "Just kidding, can't you guys take a joke?"

"Look, we're not here for a social, and we don't want to hear your jokes," Bender told Duke.

Duke walked behind the bar and poured himself a shot of whiskey. "O.K., what the hell do you guys want?" Duke gulped the whiskey.

"Let's knock off all this shit and get down to business," Fox said. "Tell us about Jimmy Thompson."

"Who?" Duke sneered.

"Please," Bender said. "We told you no jokes. Jimmy Thompson, tell us."

"Oh, oh," Duke said. "You mean that guy whose kid was kidnapped? Hey, I hardly know the guy."

"That's about enough," Fox said. "How would you like the Health Department to check this place out?"

"Hey, threats ain't gonna do it man," Duke said. "Look all I know is this guy comes in here once in a while, and I heard his kid was snatched. That's all I know. Look, I got a poster here about the kid, and there's that jar on the bar to collect money for the kid's mother. There's about ten bucks in it already."

"O.K." Fox said. "Did Thompson every talk to you about selling his kid?"

23

"What?" Duke said. "Are you crazy? Nobody sells their kid!"

"Come on," Bender said. "We know there were two guys in here that offered Thompson twenty-five thousand bucks for his kid!"

Duke poured himself another shot. "Man, are you guys crazy? I don't know what you're talking about. Look, if this is all you want to talk about, I'm done talking."

"That's it then?" Fox said. "You don't know anything about it?"

"That's right," Duke said. "I don't know nothing, so there's the door. Don't let it hit you in the ass on the way out."

"Come on," Fox said to Bender. "Let's get out of here before I smack this asshole!"

Bender and Fox walked out the door.

Duke yelled after them, "Hey, when there's a reward for that kid, come back and talk to me."

Back at the station, Bender and Fox told Sergeant Hunter what had happened at the bar.

Hunter thought for a while, then said, "Let's let him sit for a while. We'll get back to him later. We need to concentrate on what we have so far. We'll look over all the calls and reports we have. Fox, I want you to set up an appointment for the lie detector test."

"For Thompson?" Fox asked.

"For Thompson and Marylou," Hunter said. "I don't believe either one of them," Hunter said. "Also, check on that fund they have for Marylou. I want to know where the money is going and who is going to distribute it. Bender, check with Vice and see if they have anything on that Duke guy. Maybe, they know or have some ideas about who hangs around that joint."

"You know Sarge, the calls have really slowed down," Fox said.

"That's why I think the kid is long gone from here, and I think she was gone from the area before we were called," Hunter said. "I also think the mother and father are involved, or maybe just one of them. But, I don't think that the kid was snatched by some pervert. I think she is safe and sound some place, and whoever has her, paid for her. So, get those two on the lie box and maybe we can nail at least one of them."

Hunter went back to his paperwork thinking, God damn it, I know one of them sold that kid. I wonder if it could be the mother?

"Well Sarge, how did the lie tests go?" Fox asked.

"Shit, the same God damned thing we always get, inconclusive, whatever the hell that means. Either you're lying, or you're not. I just don't understand this shit."

"Easy Sarge," Fox said. "You know that box never works."

"I talked to the guy that gives the test," Hunter said. "He told me Marylou was cool as a cucumber. Seemed like she didn't have a care in the world. Jimmy, well, that's another story. He was so high and nervous, that according to the machine, he was lying about every question they asked."

"You know, Sarge," Bender said. "I'm starting to get the same feeling you have. That kid was sold and the mother or father or both of them know who took her."

CHAPTER 10

Nate Barnes was still working in his father's store. He had to work long hours, but he had a clean house to live in. His mother kept their house spotless, had good meals, and his father was off his ass, at least for now.

Nate had not thought about Marylou for a long time, until he saw her on television begging for the return of her little daughter, Noreen. I wonder if that kid could be mine, Nate thought.

Some woman came into the store. "Can we put this poster in your window?" She asked Nate.

"Sure, no problem," Nate told her.

The woman left. Nate took the poster down and looked at it. Blonde hair, blue eyes, light complexion. A cute kid. But no, it can't be mine, Nate thought with relief. I'm just glad I'm out of that mess, he thought.

Nate put the poster back into the window of the store. Just then, the door opened and slammed. Nate's father stood there fuming.

"Get that poster out of my window! I don't want you to have anything to do with that whore or her kids! You didn't have anything to do with this, did you?" His father screamed.

Before Nate could answer him, Detectives Fox and Bender walked in the door.

"Wow Sarge, you should have been on the interview with Nate Barnes and his father," Fox said. "We walked into the store just as the old man was screaming at the kid. When the old man saw us, he nearly shit his pants. Before we could every say anything, the old man started whining, "My Nate, he's a good boy. He don't have nothing to do with that whore no more, he works for me all the time. Then, he goes home to help his mother. That whore, she tricked my Nate, right Nate? But my Nate, he's a good boy now, he don't got nothing to do with taking that kid. That kid's not his, he don't want it, right Nate?"

Bender continued the story. "It was quite a job to get the old man away from the kid. Fox took the old man into the back room, and then I talked to the kid."

"The old man didn't have much to say," Fox said. "He just carried on about the same old thing; that whore tricked his Nate, but the kid saw the light now and was saved. But, wait till you hear what the kid told Bender!"

"Come on Bender, let's hear it," Hunter said. "This is no mystery story."

"All right, Sarge," Bender said. "You're going to like this."

"God damn it Bender," Hunter said. "Just tell me what the kid said."

"O.K., O.K., I started by asking the kid how he felt about Marylou. It was just like a dam breaking," Bender said. "I didn't have to ask any more questions, he just kept talking."

"Bender, please tell me what Nate said, please!" Hunter said.

"Gee Sarge," Bender said. "I'm just trying to set the stage."

"Save that shit for Rosie's," Hunter told him.

"O.K., O.K., Nate told me the whole story; how he met Marylou, how she tricked him into getting married. He told me he knew she was cheating on him, but he didn't know what to do. But, the last straw was the Thompson affair. Nate told me about the night Marylou left with Jimmy and didn't come back, and how he saw Jimmy's wife crying. Nate said he was glad it worked out that way because it made it easier for him to leave Marylou, with his father's help. He also told me that his father gave Marylou one thousand dollars and told her never to bother Nate again. Even though Marylou lived only a few blocks from the store, Nate never saw her or the kids. But, wait till you hear this."

"Bender stop it!" Hunter said.

"O.K., O.K, Bender said. "Nate never saw Marylou again, but guess who he saw all the time?"

"Bender, I'm only going to tell you one more time." Hunter said.

"O.K. Sarge," Bender said. "When Nate's father was gone from the store, Jimmy Thompson would come into the store. Nate asked us not to tell his father about this. Jimmy would bully Nate and Nate would give him free beer and cigarettes. But, that's not the kicker," Bender said. "Sarge, ready or not, here it comes. One day Thompson comes into the store and says, 'Nate, I think I'll sell your kid Noreen!'"

CHAPTER 11

At Duke's Bar about three months before the kidnapping, Jimmy came in the door. "Hey, Duke gimme a shot and a beer. You have one, too, and give everyone in the joint a drink." Jimmy puffed out his chest and threw a fifty dollar bill on the bar.

"Hey, Jimmy is that real?" Duke asked. "I don't' want no funny money in here."

Jimmy laughed and said, "I bet you ain't got no change for that big boy."

Duke looked at Jimmy and said, "By the time you pay your bar bill, ain't gonna be no change." Duke grabbed the fifty and said, "I'll tell you when it's gone."

"Shit, shit, shit!" Jimmy moaned. "I knew it, I knew it. Gimme another drink, make it a double, and I ain't buying you one!"

Duke smiled. I got this asshole again he thought to himself.

At two o'clock in the morning, Duke and Jimmy were the only ones left in the bar. "Am I out of money yet?" Jimmy asked Duke.

"Hey man, you've been out of money for about four hours," Duke told him. "But not to worry, I been running a tab for ya."

"Thanks," Jimmy said. "Man, you're a real friend Duke."

After a while, Jimmy lifted his head up from the bar and said to Duke, "Duke, you gotta loan me some money. That fifty was to buy some materials for a job I got…I'm supposed to start tomorrow."

"Jimmy, I ain't got no money to loan ya," Duke said. "You know if people like you would pay their bar tabs, I'd be a rich man."

"You know someday, I'm going to stop coming in here!" Jimmy said.

"Where else you gonna go?" Duke asked Jimmy. "Who else is gonna give you credit? Tell me!"

"O.K.," Jimmy said. "I'll tell you, only the Duke, man, only the Duke."

"If my credit is so good, pour them for both of us," Jimmy said.

Duke walked behind the bar smiling. His ass belongs to me, Duke thought. Hey, maybe, this is the time to hit him with the kid deal.

"Hey, Jimmy, how are you and Marylou getting along?" Duke asked.

My Baby My Baby!

"Are you kidding?" Jimmy said. "That bitch kicked me out again. I went to her apartment one night from here and passed out naked on the front room floor. Marylou woke up and found me lying on the floor with Noreen. Man, was she ever pissed off!"

"Jimmy, tell me the truth," Duke said. "You ever fuck around with that little girl? Here have another shot, Well?"

Jimmy smiled and said, "It's not as if she's mine you know. Hey, man, I don't hurt her or nothing like that."

"It's O.K." Duke said. "I know how it is." I got him now, Duke thought.

"Hey, look Jimmy," Duke said. "Remember a few months ago when those two guys were in here?"

"What two guys?" Jimmy slurred.

"Come on Jimmy," Duke said. "Those two guys that wanted to buy a little kid."

"Oh yeah," Jimmy said. "Twenty-five thousand dollars. Shit, I'd be a millionaire."

"Almost," Duke said. "Look, maybe we can get a hold of those two guys, and you and me and them can sit down and have a little meeting."

"I don't know, Duke," Jimmy said.

"Come on Jimmy, it won't hurt to talk to them. Have another beer, Jimmy. Hey, what the hell, have a shot, too, it's on me." Duke said. "O.K., Jimmy. I'm gonna get a hold of those two guys, what do you say?"

"I don't know, Duke," Jimmy said. "This shit scares me."

"Jimmy, believe me, it will be all right. Look here's fifty dollars for the materials."

Jimmy looked up at Duke and said, "You mean you're gonna lend me the money?"

"Sure, Duke said. "What the hell, you're gonna be a millionaire pretty soon!" Duke slapped Jimmy on the back. Come on, I'll walk you to your truck. Be here tomorrow night around eleven or so."

"O.K. Duke," Jimmy said. "Thanks a lot Duke. Man, I knew you would help me Duke." Jimmy got into his truck and drove away.

What an asshole, Duke thought as he walked back into the bar. Duke made the phone call to set up the meeting.

"We'll be there," the voice on the other end said.

Tony and Big Al were at Duke's Bar about eleven-thirty the next night. Jimmy was there, had been most of the day. "Duke, why the hell didn't you keep him sober? How can we talk to him?"

"Don't you worry about it," Jimmy said. "You're buying, I'm selling."

"Shut up stupid!" Big Al said. "Or, I'll knock your head off! Duke, get this asshole some coffee. Let's try and sober him up."

About an hour later, Tony and Big Al thought they could talk to Jimmy.

"O.K. Jimmy," Big Al began. "We're going to make this as easy as possible. All you do is bring the kid to us. We take her out of town. We got a buyer in New York. When we get back, we give you twenty-five thousand dollars. Nice and simple."

"Wait a minute, wait just one minute here," Jimmy said. "You want me to give you the kid and wait for you to give me the money? I don't even know you guys, are you crazy?"

"Hey, hey," Duke said. "These are my friends, you can't talk to them like that."

"Hold it, Duke," Big Al said. "Listen Jimmy, we understand how you feel. Now, we got a lot of expenses in this deal. But how about if we give you some money now, a little more when you bring the kid to us, and the rest when we get back from New York?"

"Gimme some money now!" Jimmy said.

"Hold it, Jimmy, when are you gonna bring us the kid?" Tony asked.

"Gimme some time," Jimmy said. "I'll do it, just gimme some money now."

"I'll tell you what," Tony said. "Here's a hundred dollars, just to show we trust you. When you bring us the kid, we'll give you a lot more."

"What's a lot more?" Jimmy asked.

"Maybe half of the twenty-five thousand." Big Al said.

"How do I get a hold of you?" Jimmy asked.

"Just call Duke when you are ready, and he will tell you what to do," Tony told him.

It would be almost three months before Jimmy called Duke.

CHAPTER 12

"Time is going by and we're going no place." Sergeant Hunter said to Fox and Bender. They were sitting in the district, reports spread all over the table. "We hear all this talk about Jimmy selling the kid, but we can't get any proof. We've followed all these leads and we've come up with nothing," Hunter said.

"Maybe, we should put more pressure on that Duke guy and Jimmy," Bender said.

"Bender, what did you get from the Vice guys on that Duke?" Hunter asked.

"Well, not too much. Vice knows Duke does some booking, buys some hot stuff, and sells it to the guys that come into the joint." Bender continued, "He buys a small amount of dope; they think, and sells it to a few people that come into the place. The Vice guys say that if there is any dope sold, it is very little. Most of the people that come in the place are drinkers. Vice doesn't like to go near the place; it's so crummy, and they figure Duke's not hurting anyone. Plus, he's not big enough for Vice to bust. Oh yeah, one more thing, the two guys that pick up the bets. Vice says they are working a few small bars mostly booking for the owners, picking up policy slips, stuff like that. Vice thinks they could be selling a small mount of drugs, but that's it. That's about all they know about those two except their names: Tony and Big Al."

CHAPTER 13

One month before Noreen is missing, Jimmy heads for Duke's bar. Jimmy had been staying away from the bar because Duke was on Jimmy's ass about not taking the kid yet. Duke wouldn't let up. All that shit about Duke's friends saying if Jimmy didn't come through; Duke would have to give Tony and Big Al their money back. That would hurt Duke's reputation. Oh man, what kind of reputation did Duke have? Shit, Jimmy thought. That crummy hundred dollars was gone the same night he got it. Jimmy didn't remember spending all of it; but when he woke up at the bar a few hours after he got the money, it was gone. Duke had told him, "Man you bought drinks for everyone in the bar, and boy were we crowded that night. I'd call it a hundred dollar plus night!"

"What do you mean a hundred dollar night plus?" Jimmy asked.

"That one hundred dollars you spent, plus the tab you ran up," Duke roared with laughter.

Jimmy stayed away from the bar for about three weeks after that; but tonight, he needed a drink. The other places he hung around had cut him off. Jimmy's credit was no good anywhere except Dukes, so Duke's it was.

Jimmy walked through the door of Duke's Bar. Duke yelled from the end of the bar, "Welcome back asshole, get down here."

"Oh man, give me a break, will you?" Jimmy said.

"The only break I'll give you is when I break your fucking neck!" Growled Duke. "Where have you been? Tony and Big Al are looking for you, and man are they pissed!"

"Yeah, yeah," Jimmy said. "Just gimme a drink."

"You got money?" Duke asked. "You ain't paid your tab in over three weeks. What the hell do you think I'm running here? Come on, you want a drink? Come up with some dough!"

"Man, don't worry about it" Jimmy said as he reached into his pocket. "Here's a ten for the tab, and I got another ten for the drinking."

"Good, good, a shot and a beer for you, and I know you want to buy a drink for me," Duke smiled. "All kidding aside Jimmy. Those two guys are looking for you. They can be nasty if they don't get what they want." Just then, the door opened.

Jimmy looked up, "Oh shit, oh shit!" He exclaimed.

Tony and Big Al walked towards the end of the bar where Duke and Jimmy were sitting. "Well, well," Tony said to Big Al. "Looky, looky, who's here."

"I told you guys I'd get him here for you guys, I was just going to call you!" Duke whimpered.

"Thanks a lot," Jimmy said to Duke. "You're a real son of a bitch!"

"Look Jimmy. You ain't come up with the goods yet, so we want our money back," Tony said as he glared at Jimmy.

"I can't do the job! I'm too scared! I tried!" Jimmy said. "I just can't do it! I'll give you your money back next week. Honest, I will. I got a job for next week remodeling, and I'll have the hundred then!"

"What do you mean, a hundred dollars?" Tony said. "You owe us five hundred."

"What, what? You only gave me one hundred?" Jimmy said.

"Interest," Big Al said. "Interest, and by next week, it will be eight hundred. And, in two weeks, it will be twelve hundred. Get the idea?"

Tony reached over and slapped Jimmy on the head. "Get the goods and our deal is just like before. Don't get the goods, and we got a deal you ain't gonna like."

Tony and Big Al walked out the door. Tony turned and yelled back to Duke. "Duke, you ain't out of this either. You hooked us up with that asshole. So, you owe us, too. What he don't pay, we get from you one way or the other!" Tony and big Al walked out the door.

"Aw shit, look what you got me into!" Duke said to Jimmy. "I don't need no problems with those guys. You better do something Jimmy; and don't forget, you owe me money, too. Fifty dollars, plus that tab. So come on man, do something!"

"Come on Duke, you got to help me. I'm scared!" Jimmy said. "I don't know what to do! You got to help me Duke!"

"Look Jimmy, you're right. I do have to help you. Now, I gotta help you to save my own ass! Jimmy, you gotta take that kid! You're in too deep! Those guys will never let you off the hook! They want that kid and that's that!" Duke said. "I'll buy the drinks. You and me gotta make some plans."

At four in the morning, Jack Hunter had just crawled into his bed. He was working the afternoon shift and had gone to Rosie's after work for a few beers. The phone rang. Hunter knocked it to the floor as he reached over to pick it up. He could hear Bender's voice on the other end. "Hello, hello, Sarge! It's me, Bender."

"Yeah, yeah," Hunter said as he tried to pick up the phone.

"Sarge, you have to come into the station right away" Bender told him. "We might have something on the Barne's case!"

"I'll be right in!" Hunter told him.

Hunted took a quick shower and headed for the District. This case is a real pain Hunter was thinking as he drove. That kid just disappeared from the face of the earth. I know she's alive and with some family; and I know one of them, either Jimmy or Marylou sold her. Well, that little girl is probably better off wherever she is, but our job is to find her. Bender sounded pretty excited. Maybe, this is it. Hunter parked his car and went into the district.

Bender and Fox were both in the office. Fox was on the phone.

"What's up Bender?" Hunter asked.

"We may have a lead in Detroit." Bender said. "Some security guard called here and said an older couple just rented a trailer there last week, and they had a little girl with them. The guard told us the little girl fits the description of Noreen. Fox is on the phone with Detroit Police now. They want to talk to a boss here."

"Here Sarge," Fox said as he handed the phone to Hunter. "There's a Sergeant Jones on the line. I filled him in on the case, but he wants to talk to you."

Hunter took the phone. "Hello, Sergeant Jones. This is Detective Sergeant Hunter, Cleveland Police."

After the call, Hunter filled Fox and Bender in. "Here's the deal," Hunter told them. "The detectives in Detroit are going over to the trailer park to talk to the guard. Then, they will call us from the park and give us the information."

"You know, Sarge. We had that one report of Noreen being taken by four gypsies from behind the Lawsons store. The clerk said it was a black caddy with Michigan license plates that he saw a little girl get into. I thought we followed that lead up pretty good," Bender said. "I talked to Miller, the King of the gypsies here, and he told me none of his family was here from Michigan, and no one he knew had a black caddy. We checked the neighborhood to see if there were any store fronts rented out to the gypsies. We found two families had been living in the area, but had left about two weeks before the girl was reported missing."

Just then, the phone rang. The Detroit detectives told Hunter they had talked to the guard, and it sounds as if they might have something. No one was home at the trailer right now, but they would stake it out and call Cleveland when someone gets home. Hunter thanked them and hung up the phone. He told Bender and Fox about the call.

"This could be a long day," Hunter said.

It was a long day. The Detroit Police never called back until nine o'clock that night. When the call came, Hunter told Bender and Fox to pick up the extensions. The Detroit Police told them the people that lived in the trailer had been out of town for a few days. The little girl did look a lot like Noreen, but it is not her. The couple that lives there are her grandparents, and they have had the little girl for about two years. Her mother and father had been killed in a car crash. We checked out the story, and everything they told us is true. Sorry.

"They're sorry!" Hunter said. "I thought this was it. I thought we had the kid and would find out the true story. Now, we have to start all over. Tomorrow, I want that Marylou in my office, and we'll put the squeeze on her but good!"

Hunter left the office and went right to Rosie's. All the time he sat there drinking, he was thinking about what he would do with Marylou in the morning.

CHAPTER 14

Fox and Bender went to Marylou's apartment the next morning. They knocked on the door, but there was no answer. They talked to one of the neighbors, and she told them Marylou and the kids had not been staying at the apartment. Marylou was paying the rent, but only stopping by to pick up the mail. She got a lot of mail.

"Do you know where we can find her!" Fox asked.

The neighbor looked down at her feet and turned red. "I think she might be staying at the Reverend Weather's place."

"Pray tell," quipped Fox. "Do you know the address?"

"No, but the church is down the street about two blocks on your right-hand side. It's called THE MASTER'S TOUCH," the neighbor told them.

"Man, this case is turning into the soap opera," Bender said.

It was about noon when the two detectives got to THE MASTER'S TOUCH. The place looked like the typical store front church from the outside. Fox and Bender tried the front door of the church, but it was locked. Knocking did not arouse anyone.

There was a small walk at the side of the building. "Let's try the back," Fox said.

In the back of the building were a small porch and a door. "I guess these are the living quarters," Bender said.

They knocked on the door, no answer. "Knock louder," Bender said to Fox.

"You want me to knock the door down?" Fox said as he banged on the door.

"I'm coming, I'm coming!" A yell came from inside the house. Marylou wrapped in a robe, hair messed up, and yawning answered the door. "Oh, it's you guys. You got news about my kid, or are you just spying on me?" She asked.

"Hey Marylou, give us a break. We didn't know you were here. We came to talk to the Reverend," Fox said.

"Go to hell!" Marylou hissed. "Who told you I was shacked up here?"

A yell came from inside the house, "Hey baby, who the hell is at the door? Get back in here!"

Fox smiled at Marylou and said, "The Master is calling. I think he wants to be touched."

"Fuck you!" Marylou snarled.

"Nice talk in church," Fox said. "Call the Master out here."

The Reverend Herman Weathers was about five feet six inches tall and weighed about one hundred and ten pounds. He looked as if he hadn't shaved or bathed for at least a week.

"Why don't you two get dressed?" Fox said. "The sergeant would like to see you at the station."

"Tell him to come here!" Marylou yelled. "It's cold out. Why should we go down there?"

"Take it easy Marylou," the Reverend said. "Let's get dressed and go down there. It never looks good if you don't cooperate with the police."

"O.K., Hermy," Marylou purred. Then, she glared at the Detectives and said, "I still don't like it. I'll go. You get dressed first, Hermy. Then, come out here and watch them so they don't steal nothin."

Bender and Fox walked into Sergeant Hunter's office. "We have Marylou waiting outside with a friend," Fox told Hunter.

"What do you mean a friend?" Hunter asked. "Who's with her?"

Bender started to laugh. "Wait until you hear this." Bender told the Sergeant the story.

"I'm telling you," Hunter said. "These people have the morals of alley cats, bring Marylou in here."

"O.K., Marylou, the Sergeant will see you now," Fox said.

Marylou got up from her chair. "Come on, Hermy," she said. "Let's see what this is all about."

"Wait a minute," Bender said. "The Sergeant wants to see you alone."

"Oh no, Hermy goes with me, or I don't go. Hermy is my Minister. I need him at my side for support. Come on Hermy," Marylou cooed.

"Have a seat," Hunter said as he gestured to two hard chairs in front of his desk. "How are you Marylou?"

"I'm fine, Sergeant. I want you to meet my friend and minister, the Reverend Herman J. Weathers," Marylou smiled.

"How do you do Reverend," hunter said politely.

"I'm fine, but please call me Herman. Before we start, Sergeant," Herman said. "Would you join us in a little prayer?" Herman took Marylou's hand as he bowed his head and began to pray.

Oh man, thought Hunter. He's probably praying for more money to go into the fund for Noreen.

"Amen," Herman said. "Now, Sergeant, what can we do for you?"

Sergeant Hunter had given a lot of thought as to how he was going to handle this, and had decided to play the accuser.

Hunter leaned across the desk, looked right into Marylou's eyes and said: "How much did you sell Noreen for?"

"What! What did you say?" Marylou gasped. "What did you say?"

"How much! Tell me how much you got for her!" Hunter yelled. "I know you sold Noreen, just tell me how much did you get?"

"You son of a bitch!" Marylou screamed back. "Who the fuck do you think you are? Hermy, did you hear what that bastard said?" Marylou and Hunter were both on their feet. Hunter came out from behind the desk. "I know you sold her, or you know who sold her! Tell me! Tell me!" Hunter screamed into Marylou's face.

Marylou slapped Hunter across the face. "You bastard!" Marylou screamed at Hunter.

"Stop it! Stop it!" Hermy pleaded as he grabbed for Marylou.

Hunter walked behind the desk and asked very calmly, "would you like some coffee?"

Marylou stared at Hunter through blank eyes. "Yes, she said. "I'd like some, how about you Hermy?"

"Sure" Hermy said, "I'd like mine with cream and sugar."

"I'll be right back," Hunter said. He left the office to get some coffee.

"What the hell is going on in there?" Fox asked Hunter.

"Oh, it's called getting to know you," Hunter said.

"I'm going to get some coffee. Bender, run a check on that little weasel, Hermy. When you get the information, call me out of the office." Hunter poured three cups of coffee, two from the stale pot, and one for him from the fresh pot. With a smile on his face, he went back into his office.

My Baby My Baby!

Hunter served the coffee, then sat down behind his desk and began. "Marylou, this is a hard job, and I try to do the best I can. Most of the time, it isn't fun. But, I know it's not fun for you either, grieving for your daughter." The sarcasm was lost on Marylou. Hunter continued. "We have run out of leads, we have no clues as to where Noreen is. You have to think back, Marylou, think of everything that happened before Noreen disappeared. Think of everything that happened after she disappeared. Marylou, you have to help us, please help us!"

Hunter wasn't prepared for what happened next.

Marylou's eye went blank, her whole body relaxed, she stared right through Hunter. In a voice free of expression, she said, "I know where my baby is, and she's dead, she's all cut up in a building near the lake, upstairs in an old abandoned building. There's a bed in that room covered with old blankets. My baby is under the blankets, pieces of her. It's bloody there, if you help me, we can find her."

Hunter felt a cold chill going up his spine. He felt as if he was going to wet his pants. Hunter slowly got up from his chair, never taking his eyes off Marylou. Marylou stared straight ahead still in a trance. Hunter opened the door to his office and said to Bender and Fox, "Get the car, we'll be right down." Hunter walked over to Marylou and took her hand and helped her from the chair. Weathers took Marylou by the other hand, and they walked her from the building to the car.

Bender and Fox got into the front seat of the car. Marylou sat between Hunter and Weathers in the back seat.

I don't know where the building is," Marylou said. "But, I think it's near the lake."

Hunter thought. Down by Lakeside Avenue, there are a lot of abandoned buildings there. "Head down to East Fortieth and Lakeside," Hunter told Fox.

Fox looked into the rear-view mirror. Marylou was sitting up, straight up, staring straight ahead, her eyes blank. Fox felt the chills. He shivered and put his eyes back on the road ahead.

They drove up and down Lakeside Avenue slowly. "No, not here. No, not here," Marylou whimpered. "I know, I know!" Marylou shouted. "On the West Side. My baby is on the West Side!"

The only place Hunter could think of was the tennis courts off Clifton Avenue. He told Fox to head over there.

They started to check the abandoned buildings near the tennis courts. Marylou stared straight ahead and told them, "No, not here" as they stopped by building after building.

Hunter was just about ready to give up. He was thinking, t his is a bunch of crap. Hunter had received a phone call from a psychic at the beginning of this case. She had told Hunter the little girl was in the back seat of an old Ford. The car is in an alley on the West Side. The psychic had told him. The car is up on blocks and all rusty. Noreen is in the back seat of the car under some dirty blankets, dead. Hunter had spent two days and nights driving the alleys of the West Side finding nothing. God, had Marylou talked to the same psychic? The story was so close. Only this time, it was a building, not a car.

Marylou screamed, scaring the shit out of Hunter.

"I remember now, I remember where it is!" Marylou screamed. "I know where by baby is. Go to the bottom of West Fourteenth Street, upstairs of the building. That's were my baby is!"

Fox didn't need anyone to tell him were to go. He turned and headed for West Fourteenth, driving as if he were under the influence of Marylou's spell.

Fox turned down West 14th. As they started down the hill, they could see it. There was a vacant building at the bottom of the hill. It seemed like the only building on the street.

Jesus Christ, thought Bender, this is just like the Twilight Zone. Bender could feel himself starting to shake.

Fox pulled the car up to the front of the building. Everyone got out of the car, not a sound from any of them. Hunter saw a door on the side of the building. Marylou said, "The side door upstairs, that's where she is!" Marylou fainted and fell to the ground.

"Fox, call for an ambulance!" Hunter said. Bender, you come with me!"

Hunter opened the side door of the building. Sure enough, there was a set of stairs leading up into the dark. Hunter took out his flashlight and started slowly up the stairs. Bender following. The steps were steep and dust-covered. Hunter showed the light on each step looking for footprints. So far, there was nothing. Hunter and Bender moved up the stairs as if they were in a trance. Were they afraid of what they would find? In the background, they could hear the wail of a siren. It must be the ambulance Fox called, thought Hunter.

Shit, Bender thought to himself. How long have we been climbing these stairs? I'm not even here, he thought. It feels like I'm outside my body watching this.

Hunter's head came above floor level. There was just one room at the top of the stairs. In the middle of the room was a bed covered with blankets.

"Oh shit!" Hunter whispered to Bender. "We were wrong. I think this is it, we found her!" They walked over to the bed. The blankets were piled up. It looked as if something or someone was underneath them. "Don't even touch the blankets. Call the evidence boys right now!" Hunter said to Bender. Bender ran down the stairs. He was released from the trance. It was all business now!

Hunter listened as Bender ran down the stairs. Was she under the blankets all cut up? Hunter stared at the blankets on the bed. He couldn't see any blood. The blankets were covered with dirt and dust. Hunter had waited all this time. I can wait a longer, he thought. Hunter stood by keeping his mind almost blank. Then, he heard the evidence men coming up the stairs. This is it, he thought.

Hunter thought wrong. The evidence men removed the covers on the bed one by one until the mattress shown bare.

"Take all those blankets to the lab and check them out for blood," Hunter said. "Check this whole place out, see if you can find anything to help us."

CHAPTER 15

Hunter started down the steps. He felt relieved but at the same time, pissed. Had that Marylou conned him? How had she known about this place? God, was there no end to this case?

Outside, Fox and Bender were leaning against the car. "Holy shit! What a show that was!" Fox said. "I can't believe the way I felt."

"Me, too!" Bender said. "I believed her. Man, did I ever believe her!"

"Don't feel pregnant," Hunter said. "She had me all the way! Where are Marylou and Hermy?"

"They both went to the hospital," Fox said. "Let's get over there. I bet you want to talk to that Marylou, right Sarge?"

When they arrived at the hospital, Marylou and Hermy had already left. "Treated and released; she had just fainted," the doctor said. "No one said anything about holding them. Sorry."

"Let's go check the apartment and the church," Hunter said. They had no luck at either place. Hunter called the district and told them to have a car check both places every hour so, and to call him when Marylou or Hermy showed up.

"O.K. boys, it's Rosie's for dinner. I'm buying," Hunter said.

"Are we drinking or eating dinner tonight?" Fox asked.

"Both," said Hunter. "But I'll meet you there. I have one stop to make."

Fox and Bender were sitting at the bar at Rosie's having a beer when the door opened. Hunter walked in carrying a large grocery bag. Fox and Bender both knew where the Sarge had stopped. HOT DOG INN!

CHAPTER 16

It was the beginning of August. Jimmy had been working fairly steady over the last few weeks. Today, he is putting a new roof on a garage at West Thirty Second and Bridge Avenue. It's a hot day. As Jimmy climbs down the ladder, he thinks, it's lunch time. It's awful hot, only one block from Duke's Bar. Hum, Duke's it is for lunch.

Right at noon, Jimmy walked into the bar. "Hey Duke," Jimmy yells. "Fry me up one of those greasy burgers, some fries, and gimme a cold one. Man, it's hot in here. Why don't you get the air conditioner fixed?"

"Jimmy, I don't make enough money in this joint to have luxuries. Anyhow, the hotter it is, the more beer you guys drink," Duke laughed.

While Jimmy was waiting for his lunch, Duke went to the phone. Tony and Big Al had been in about two days ago looking for Jimmy. They had told Duke he had better get Jimmy moving on their deal. Duke told them Jimmy hadn't been around for a few days. That's when Big Al grabbed Duke by the back of his neck and slammed his face into the bar. "Call us when Jimmy comes in. My people want a kid, now!"

Duke knew how rough those two guys could be. There was no sense in taking any chances. The phone rang once and a voice said "yeah?"

"He's here," Duke said.

"Be right there," the voice responded.

Jimmy just finished the last of the greasy burger and lifted the beer to his mouth. The door of the bar swung open. Jimmy put the beer down. Oh shit, Jimmy thought, not them again. Tony and Big Al walked towards Jimmy.

They sat on either side of Jimmy. "Long time, no see," Big Al said. "Come outside Jimmy. We want to talk to you."

Jimmy got up from the stool and headed for the door. Tony and Big Al followed. Big Al threw a dollar bill on the bar. "For his lunch, and keep the change, Duke."

Duke knew this was going to be big trouble for Jimmy. Maybe, I shouldn't have made that call, he thought.

Tony and Big Al took Jimmy to the alley behind the bar. "Well?" Big Al asked. "Where's the kid?"

"I've been trying," Jimmy said. "But, Marylou won't even let me come over to her house."

Tony grabbed Jimmy from behind, and Big Al started to punch Jimmy in the face and stomach. Jimmy didn't even try to fight back. He knew it would be useless. Jimmy could feel himself going out. Tony let him slip to the ground and began to kick him.

Big Al said, "Jimmy, we want that kid by the end of the month!" Big Al and Tony walked out of the alley. On the way to their car, Tony yelled in the bar. "Hey Duke, your buddy needs some help in the alley. Oh by the way, Duke, take a good look at him. Because if the deal doesn't go through, you get just what he got!"

Duke ran back to the alley. I should have never made that call, he thought. Jimmy was lying on his side with blood running from his mouth and nose. "Man Jimmy," Duke said. "You got to do something and soon! These guys are going to kill you and me!"

CHAPTER 17

Marylou and Hermy left the hospital and headed for Hermy's place. They could walk the distance in about ten minutes.

"Marylou," Hermy said. "What was that dream all about? Was it real?"

"Hell no!" Marylou said. "Did I fool you?"

"Yeah, for sure," Hermy said. "I sure thought you was telling the truth. You should be in the movies. How did you know about that place? How the hell did you ever come up with that story?"

"That's for me to know and you never to find out!" Marylou said. "Right now, let's go back to your place. I got some plans."

Once back at Hermy's, Marylou went into the church to a panel behind the make-shift altar and pulled out a fireproof box. Marylou opened the box and pulled out a wad of money. She counted it. There was three thousand dollars. "Come on Hermy, let's buy a car," she said. "I want to go to West Virginia and see some old friends of mine."

"But, Marylou," Hermy whined. "That money is for your kids."

"Hell with them kids!" Marylou said. "Come on, let's go."

"But, Marylou, what about the police? That Sergeant is going to want to see you," Hermy said. "I bet he's mad as hell."

"We'll see him when we get back," Marylou said. "Come on. We'll get a car and stop by Patty's house. I'll give her a couple hundred bucks, and she'll keep my kids there. Come on, Hermy. Let's go before that goofy Sergeant gets here. He's probably on his way here now."

CHAPTER 18

It was two days and Hunter hadn't heard from Marylou. Fox and Bender had checked around and found that Hermy and Marylou had bought a used car from the car lot down the street. They had paid eight hundred dollars for the car and had headed for West Virginia. On the way, they had stopped at Patty's house. Patty had been watching Marylou's kids. Patty told them that Marylou had given her two hundred dollars and said she would be back in about two weeks.

"Oh Sarge," Bender said. "Marylou left a note for you with Patty." He handed the note to Hunter.

Hunter opened the envelope.

Dear Sergeant Hunter,

Hermy and I need a vacation. We will be back in about two weeks.

See you then.

Marylou

"I'll say one thing about that broad," Hunter remarked to Bender and Fox. "She sure has a lot of guts. When she gets back, I want her on that lie box again. I really don't think it will do any good, but I still think she and Jimmy are involved in this thing. You never know. The more pressure you put on, maybe something will snap. By the way, what's happening with Jimmy?"

"Not much," Fox said. "We try to talk to him about once a week. He's working off and on, and drinking at Duke's Bar. He never likes it when we talk to him. We just tell him we're keeping him posted, but we don't have anything new to go on. Last time we talked to him, Jimmy said, "Maybe in a few weeks, you'll have some leads.""

CHAPTER 19

Sergeant Hunter was sitting at his desk in his office going through the reports on the Barnes case. This case was about all he ever thought about lately. Hunter really felt that Noreen was alive. He just knew that she had been sold. I just can't get anywhere with this, he thought. There was a knock on the door. "Come in," Hunter said.

Bender came in the door. "Look Sarge, I've got that record check on Weathers."

"Good," Hunter said. "Let's see how bad this guy is." Hunter took the report. "One D.W.I., a couple of parking tickets, and no warrants. That's it?"

"That's all there is to it," Bender said. "Not bad, eh?"

"O.K., so what did you guys find out about his personal life?" Hunter asked.

"He works at the Chevy Plant, but is laid off now. He came here from Logan County West Virginia about ten years ago. He was ordained as a minister through some magazine, some deal about not paying taxes if you are a minister. He opened up that store front church, THE MASTERS TOUCH, about a year ago. The most members he has ever had were about fifteen or twenty. Fox and I talked to the members we could find and got the same story from all of them. They started going to THE MASTER TOUCH when it first opened, but it seemed Weathers just kept asking for more money. The more they gave, the more Weathers spent at the pub. Then this thing with the Barnes kid came up, and that was the last straw."

"What happened with the Barnes case? Hunter asked.

"Well," Fox said. "It seems Weathers and Marylou didn't know each other before the kidnapping. The first night Noreen was missing, it seems Weathers just came over to Marylou's apartment to see what was going on. Someone there introduced him as a minister, and he just took over at that point. He elected himself to handle all the funds Marylou got. But, you know Marylou. After a few days, she took over the money and Hermy."

Fox took a sip of his coffee and went on. "Hermy is married, but soon after he met Marylou, he sent his wife and three kids back to her mother's house in West Virginia. Marylou moved right in. That's when people stopped going to THE MASTERS TOUCH. Now, Hermy doesn't even open the doors on Sunday."

CHAPTER 20

Two weeks had gone by and Hunter still had not heard from Marylou. He had Bender and Fox check every day at Patty's house, but Patty said she had not heard from Marylou. "I'm getting tired of watching her kids while she is out playing. This is the last time she sucks me into baby-sitting!"

They asked Patty if she knew where in West Virginia Marylou could be.

"Hell, I don't know," Patty said. "Who knows if they even got to West Virginia. Hell, the two of them could have driven to Akron, stopped at some joint, and been drunk for two weeks. Who knows about them? I'm getting tired of watching her kids. I'll watch them for a few more days and that's it!"

Three weeks later, Hunter heard the Marylou and Hermy were back in town. "Get her in here!" Hunter told Fox and Bender. "Get the guys to set up that lie box again. I want to see if I can get her to take a test right now. Tell them to set up for two tests. Let's see if we can get Hermy to take a test. Perhaps Marylou told him something. It won't hurt to try."

First, "Fox and Bender went to THE MASTERS TOUCH. There was no one there. They asked the neighbors if they had seen Marylou or Hermy. There were told no one had been around for about three weeks or so. Next, they went to the apartment. No one answered the door, but one of the neighbors told them that Marylou and Hermy had left the apartment about an hour or so ago. They went to Patty's house. Sure enough, there they were.

Marylou and Patty were arguing about Marylou leaving her children there, but when Fox knocked on the door, they stopped. Patty answered the door and told the detectives to come in. When Marylou saw the detectives, she started yelling, "I told you if they came looking for me to tell them I wasn't here, and you don't know where I am. Goddamn it, Patty! I told you, but no what the fuck do you do, but let them walk right in here. Shit!"

Patty yelled back, "Shut up Marylou! You left these kids here for three weeks and never even called me! You don't give two shits about these kids!"

"I paid you to watch my kids!" Marylou yelled back.

"Come on girls," Hermy said. "Let's be nice in front of company. Officers, would you like to sit down?"

"No," Fox said. "We just dropped by to tell you Sergeant Hunter would like to see you down at the station right now."

Marylou started screaming, "What the hell does he want now? Am I the only one he talks to? No wonder you guys can't find out nothing!"

"Marylou, take it easy," Hermy said. "The man is only trying to do his job. Detective, we'll follow you down to the station. Come on Marylou. Let's go."

"O.K., O.K., Marylou said. "Will you watch my kids Patty? I'll come right back from the station."

"You better!" Patty said. "Cause if you don't, I'm going to call your social worker and turn these kids over to her!"

"O.K., O.K., Marylou said. "Come on Hermy. Let's go!"

They followed the detectives down to the station.

The office man came into Hunter's office. "They are all set for the tests Sarge. They want to know if there are any special questions you want to ask Marylou or Weathers."

"No, I don't think so," Hunter said. "Just tell them to go over the tests right away. I'll try to keep Marylou and Weathers here until they have the results."

"O.K., the office man said. "I'll go tell them."

Fox walked into Hunter's office. "We got them here," he said. "But, Marylou is bitching about you. She's mad, but Weathers is trying to calm her down."

"O.K., I'm ready as can be," Hunter told him. "Bring them in."

Marylou and Weathers walked into Hunter's office. Weathers was smiling and Marylou was scowling. "Hello," Hunter said. "Have a seat. Can I get you anything?" Hunter thought to himself, I'll be nice for a while. Maybe, I can catch them off guard.

"No, no," Weathers said. "We're fine." Marylou just shook her head no.

"Good," Hunter said. "I hope you two had a nice vacation. Now, maybe we can get down to business and help each other out." Marylou started to say something, but Hunter held up his hand to quiet her. "Look Marylou. I want to find Noreen, but you keep fighting me. I want you to take another lie detector test right now!"

Marylou looked at Hunter with her eyes wide open. "You mean right now! I don't know, I'm not ready yet. Why do you want me to take another test? I took one before, and I passed it!"

"Well, Marylou," Hunter explained. "Sometimes, we forget to ask a question or two, but I'm not trying to trick you. It's just that maybe we can find something we missed before, maybe something that will help us."

"I don't know, Hermy. What do you think I should do?" Marylou asked. "Should I call a lawyer? What do you think?"

"I don't know, Marylou," Hermy said. "I don't think you have anything to hide. If the Sergeant wants you to take the test, take it."

"O.K.," Marylou said. "If you think it's all right, I'll do it, but it doesn't make me happy."

"Oh by the way, Mr. Weathers. When Marylou is finished with her test, would you please take the test?" Hunter asked.

"What?" Hermy asked. "Me take the test? Why in the world would you ask me to take the test? I don't know anything about Noreen. Why would you give me that test?"

"We just want to follow up on everything," Hunter replied. "You know, just to tie up any loose ends. This way, my boss won't get mad at me, or ask that you come back down here. What do you say, Hermy? Will you take the test?"

Hermy thought for a minute, then said, "Well, o.k. But, I'll tell you one thing right now. If I don't like the questions they ask me, I'm going to stop the test right then and that's final!"

"No problem," Hunter said. "Let me get Marylou upstairs, and I'll be right back." Hunter escorted Marylou out the door. Bender was in the outer office. "Take her upstairs for the test," Hunter told him. "I'm going back to my office to talk to Hermy."

Hunter walked back into his office. Weathers was standing looking out the window. "Sit down Hermy," Hunter said. "Let's you and me have a little talk without Marylou."

"Sure," Hermy said. "What would you like to talk about Sergeant? You know, you are making me a little nervous about taking this test. What is it you really want Sergeant?"

"Listen, Hermy, how about if you let me ask the questions?" Hunter asked. "For openers, why don't you tell me how you know you met Marylou?"

"That's simple enough," Hermy said. "The day Noreen disappeared, one of my flock came to the church and asked if I would go to this poor woman's home to comfort her. I went immediately and found Marylou very distraught. I began to talk to her, and she started to quiet down."

"That was the first time you ever saw her?" Hunter asked. "I mean, you never saw her in the neighborhood or talked to her before that day?"

"No, never. I Mean, I never saw her or talked to her anytime before that night."

"How about Jimmy, her husband? Did you ever see him?"

"Yes," replied Hermy. "He did some work on the church when I first opened it."

"How did you get him, or rather, how did you find him to do the work on the church?" Hunter asked Hermy.

"To tell the truth," Hermy said. "Before I was saved, I used to hang around this bar on Bridge Avenue called Duke's Bar. I met Jimmy there. I remembered he did handy-man's work. So when I needed some work done on the church, I asked that when Duke saw Jimmy, he send him up to see me, and I'd give him some work to do. Jimmy came up a few days later and did the work for me. But, I swear I never met or saw Marylou until the night I was asked to help her."

"I really believe you, Hermy," hunter smiled. "Now, I want you to think back and tell me anything you can remember about Noreen's disappearance that Marylou told you."

Hermy told Hunter pretty much the same story Hunter already knew. "Hermy," Hunter asked. "Did Marylou every say anything about Jimmy being involved in Noreen's disappearance?"

"I just don't know if I should say anything about this. I mean, Marylou confided in me as a minister. I don't know if it would be right to tell you this," Henry said. "But if it will help, I'll tell you."

Come on, come on, thought Hunter. Tell me!

"Well, here goes. I hope Marylou won't get mad at me," Hermy said. "She told me she thinks Noreen is alive and that some family has her. She thinks Jimmy took the kid away."

"Hold it a minute, Hermy," Hunter said as he walked to the door. "I'll be right back." Hunter walked out into the office and grabbed Bender. "Get upstairs and tell the guy giving Marylou the test to ask her if she knows who took Noreen. Also, ask her if she thinks Jimmy had anything to do with Noreen's disappearance." Hunter walked back into his office feeling good inside. I knew it, I knew it, he thought to himself. Everyone said I was wrong, but I know that kid is some place, and alive!

"O.K., Hermy, can you think of anything else that might help?" Hunter asked.

"No, that's about all. Do you think I did the right thing?" Hermy asked.

"So far, you did just fine," Hunter told him. "But, let me ask you one thing, Hermy. Why didn't Marylou ever tell us what she thought?"

"Because." Hermy turned red and looked down at the floor. Then, he whispered, "She wanted the money to keep coming in."

"What money?" Hunter asked.

"The donations, that money," Hermy said. "Please don't ask me any more questions. I've said enough. Do you have to tell Marylou what I told you?"

"Relax, Hermy, I won't say anything to Marylou," Hunter said. "What I want you to do now is relax. Just sit by yourself and rest before you take the test. "I'll leave you alone for a few minutes."

"Can I pray?" Hermy asked.

"You can do whatever you want," Hunter said as he walked out the door.

"Bender," Hunter said. "When Fox calls from upstairs to tell you Marylou is done, have him bring her to my office and you take Hermy up the back way. I don't want them to see each other until after he takes the test. I've got some questions I want them to ask Hermy." Just the, the phone rang. Marylou was through.

Fox brought Marylou into Sergeant Hunter's office. She was visibly shaken. Fox was holding her arm and walked her to the chair in front of Hunter's desk. Hunter thought, This is the first time I've seen her shook up. She's pale and shaking, good. Maybe, I'll get some place with her now. "Marylou, can I get you some coffee or anything?" Hunter asked her.

"Get me a can of pop you son of a bitch!" Marylou spat. "You tricked me. Where's Hermy? What did that little rat tell you? I'll kill him the first chance I get!"

"Marylou, what are you talking about? What do you mean I tricked you?" Hunter asked trying to keep his voice calm.

"You know what you did, those questions you asked. They weren't fair. I saw that Bender come up there and tell that guy something. Then, he came back and asked me those questions," Marylou said. She was close to tears now. "I don't care what that box says. It don't work anyhow, and that's the last time I go near that thing. That's the last time you ask me any questions without my lawyer. You hear me!" She screamed. Bender walked through the door and help out a can of pop. Marylou grabbed it, opened it, and drank half of it right down. She wiped her mouth with the back of her hand and stared at Hunter.

"Sure, Marylou I hear you. But I don't hear the truth from you, and that's what I want to hear?" Hunter said.

Marylou slammed the can of pop down on the desk. "I told the truth to every question you've asked me," Marylou yelled. "What more do you want from me!?"

"I want to know what happened to Noreen. I want to know where she is. I want to know who took her," Hunter said calmly.

This seemed to have some effect on Marylou. She sat back in her chair and said. "One thing Sergeant, I think she's safe, but that's all I know. I don't want to talk about it anymore."

Hunter's phone rang. He picked it up. "Yeah?"

"It's me, Bender." She answered 'no' to both those questions, and the box says she's lying. No question about it. They just put Weathers on the box now. I'll call you when he is done."

"O.K., sure," Hunter said as he gently replaced the receiver.

Hunter looked at Marylou. "You lied on the last two questions, didn't you?"

"I told you, I ain't answering any more questions, and I'm not going to," Marylou told him. "If you want anymore from me, arrest me, and I'll get a lawyer. So that's it, Sergeant." If looks could kill, Hunter knew he would be dead. They sat there in silence. Hunter waiting for the phone to ring, and Marylou staring straight ahead.

My Baby My Baby!

Hunter kept staring at Marylou hoping to break her, or at least, make her nervous. He got no place. Marylou just sat there looking right through Hunter.

Finally, the phone rang. Hunter picked it up.

"Sarge, Weathers is done with the test. Those questions you gave him. He told the truth, and he passed everything else."

"O.K.," Hunter said. "Bring him down."

Hunter knew what he was going to do now. Marylou was already mad at him. So, if Weathers got mad too, that was the breaks. Hunter knew he had to keep the pressure on Marylou. That was the only way to break her. But, just enough. He didn't want her to get a lawyer yet. No, not yet.

Bender brought Weathers into Sergeant Hunter's office. He helped Weathers to a chair. Weathers was visibly shaken. "How did it go?" Hunter asked Weathers.

"Oh, not too bad," Weather answered. "But, I would like to talk to you about something. Sergeant and I want to do it now and with Marylou out of the room."

Hunter looked at Weathers and thought to himself. Here goes nothing.

Hunter jumped up from his desk. "I'm tired of all this bullshit! Marylou, Weathers told me you know Jimmy took Noreen, and he also told me that all you want is the money that's coming in as donations? You don't give one little shit about that kid, and don't tell me Weathers is lying. He passed that test with flying colors!"

Marylou turned a bright red. She was holding her breath and looked as if she was ready to blow up. Then, to everyone's surprise, she let out a long sigh. "Well, he's partly right," Marylou said. "But Hermy, I didn't expect you to tell on me!"

"What part is right?" Hunter asked. And, don't try to con me again, Marylou. Not like that bullshit about knowing where the kid is and taking us on wild goose chase, which we will talk about later. Now, tell me what the hell is going on?"

"O.K.," Marylou said. "I'm going to tell exactly what I know."

"I told you before that Jimmy had asked me if I would ever sell one of my kids for twenty-five thousand dollars, but he never said anymore about it. But one night after Noreen was gone, I was at the apartment by myself, and Jimmy came over. He had just left Duke's

Bar and was drunk. We started talking about Noreen, and then Jimmy started crying, and he said to me. 'Don't worry, honey. Noreen is O.K., and if I don't get what's coming to me, she will be back here.' I asked him what he meant, and he told me, 'Don't worry about it."
Marylou sat back in the chair for a minute before she continued. "Then, I said, 'Jimmy, did you have anything to do with Noreen being gone?" Jimmy got all upset then, and he told me he would make sure that I would never see Noreen or find out what had happened to her. "Then, he started crying again and said 'Just don't worry, Marylou. It won't be long until we're all together again, and we'll have a lot of money.' After Jimmy left, I thought about telling you, but I thought. What the hell, if Jimmy is telling the truth, maybe Noreen is better off. She never would have a chance in this neighborhood, nobody ever does. So, I made myself believe that she is living with some rich people and that they love her."

Hunter looked at her and said. "Sure, I believe most of what you are telling me, but what about the money that Jimmy got for the kid? I know you would want your share of that!"

"God damn it, Sergeant, this is hard enough for me to tell the way it is," Marylou started crying. "But, Jimmy said that so far, he had got no money, but when he did, we would go away. I ain't heard a word from Jimmy for a long time. I ain't lying Sergeant. I feel better already just telling somebody about it. That's why I ain't mad at Hermy for telling you. I told him part of the story, and I think I was just waiting for him to spill the beans. I just didn't have the guts to tell you."

"Marylou," Hunter said. "I don't know if I'm doing the right thing, but this time, I do believe you. What I want you to do now, is go home and get some rest. Come back here at noon tomorrow, and we can really get started on this case."

"Thank you, Sergeant," Marylou said. "I'll try to think of anything else that Jimmy told me, and we'll be back tomorrow."

Marylou and Hermy walked out the door. When they were gone, Hunter said. "Bender, you and Fox follow them. Sit with them all night. I don't want them out of your sight until they come back here tomorrow. I'll bring you guys some lunch later, so you won't have to leave them. Get going!"

About midnight, Hunter found Fox and Bender sitting in front of Marylou's apartment in their car. Bender said, "they came right here Sarge, and they haven't left. We can see the phone in the kitchen from here, and so far, no one has used it."

"Good," Hunter said. "I don't want her to be talking to Jimmy. Here's what I want you guys to do. Go by Duke's Bar and see if Jimmy is there. Don't go in. Just check from the outside for me. If he is there, follow him. If not, go home, grab some sleep and meet me back here about seven in the morning and bring some black coffee."

Bender and Fox headed right for Duke's bar. First, they checked the front, and then the back. They did not see Jimmy's truck. They parked down the street, and Fox walked back to look through the window. Nobody was in the place. They headed for home and some sleep.

Hunter sat outside Marylou's apartment watching the lights inside. Sometimes, he needed to be alone to think, and he had a lot of thinking to do. The lights in the apartment went out and Hunter prepared for a long, boring night. He wasn't disappointed.

CHAPTER 21

Bender and Fox returned to meet the Sergeant at seven o'clock the next morning. "No luck," Fox told Hunter. "We didn't see Jimmy's truck at Duke's bar. I looked in the window, nobody was in the place. As a matter of fact, the place may have been closed. I didn't see anyone behind the bar; but, I didn't try the door in case someone would see me."

"Good," Hunter said. "I've been doing some thinking. Do you guys know where that Duke character lives?"

"Yeah," Fox said. "He lives above the bar."

"O.K., here's what we are going to do," Hunter said. "You two follow me to the bar. Let's see if we can roust this Duke guy and find out where Jimmy is. Then, we get Jimmy and take him down to the station while Marylou and Weathers are there. We put them all in one room and see what happens."

"I don't know about that," Bender said. "All hell may break loose."

"So what," Hunter said. "I know we're close to getting some place. We have to make something happen. So let's take a chance!"

"I think your right," Fox said. "But you know, the Captain is going to be mad. He told you before about spending so much time on this case."

"The hell with it!" Hunter said. "Let's go down to Duke's Bar."

The two cars pulled right up in front of Duke's Bar and the detectives got out. Bender went over to try the front door of the bar, but it was locked. He tried the door that lead upstairs. It was also locked. Bender started to pound on the door. The upstairs window opened and Duke stuck his head out. "What the fuck do you guys want? I don't open the bar until I get up. You can wait that long for free drinks!"

"Get down here and open this fucking door before we kick it down!" Fox yelled. "And if we have to do that, the next thing we kick will be your fat ass!"

"O.K., O.K.," Duke said. "I'll be right down. Man, you guys can never take a joke."

My Baby My Baby!

They could hear Duke coming down the steps talking to himself. He was trying to open the door, but couldn't get it unlocked. Finally, after considerable swearing and pounding, the door flew open. Out came Duke looking and smelling like some old wino. "What the hell do you guys want? Are you crazy waking me up this early in the morning! Man, I just got to bed a few hours ago. Come on in the joint, and I'll fix us all some coffee. Don't worry, it will be free," Duke laughed.

Hunter whispered to Fox, "Give that asshole some time to keep busy; then sneak upstairs and check his place out." Fox shook his head yes and stepped off to the side as Duke, Bender, and Hunter walked into the bar.

As usual, the bar was covered with dirty glasses, and the place smelled like piss. Hunter started to gag and pulled out his hanky to cover his mouth. Duke looked around smiling. "Sounds like you could use a cup of coffee, too. I'll have her perking in a minute. Hey, where's the other guy?"

"He went down the street to make a phone call," Hunter lied.

"He could have used my phone," Duke said. "But, it's out of order anyhow."

"Look, Duke," Bender said. "We don't have time for coffee and small talk. The Sergeant has a few questions to ask you, and then we can be on our way."

"O.K., but if I don't like the questions, I won't answer them," Duke grinned.

"These questions will be simple enough," Hunter said. "Where's Jimmy?"

"I don't know," Duke said. "As a matter of fact, I ain't seen him in a couple of days."

"When was he in here last?" Hunter asked.

"The last time I saw him was about three days ago, honest," Duke said. "I was supposed to meet him last night, but he never showed up."

"Does he have a phone?" Bender asked.

"Hell no. If he gets any calls, he gets them here. Shit I'm like his secretary," Duke grunted.

Just then, Fox walked in the door. He shook his head and said to Hunter, "Nothing there."

"O.K.," Hunter said. "Duke, if Jimmy comes in here, tell him to call me right away, and I mean right away." Hunter started towards the door.

"Come on you guys, stay and have some coffee with me," Duke laughed. Bender slammed the door.

Hunter got into his car. "Meet me at the station. I can't stand being even this close to this creep." Hunter pulled away.

Hunter, Bender, and Fox were sitting around the desk in Hunter's office. "Man," Fox said. "You should have seen that place upstairs. It smelled as bad as the bar. Dirty clothes were all over the place. The sheets on the bed were gray from dirt. The kitchen floor is covered with garbage, and there are maggots crawling all over."

"That sounds right," Bender said. "After all, that guy is the king of the maggots."

"I've got some paper work to do before our awesome twosome gets here," Hunter said. "How about if you and Fox hop in the car and go check out Jimmy's apartment? Then, come right back here."

Bender and Fox drove up to Jimmy's apartment and knocked on the door, no answer. "Let's try the house next door. Maybe, they saw Jimmy around," Bender said. The people next door told the detectives they hadn't seen Jimmy for three days or longer.

"Well, let's head back to the station and see what the Sergeant has planned for the awesome twosome," Fox laughed.

CHAPTER 22

The day before Noreen disappeared, Jimmy walked into Duke's bar. "Hey, Jimmy come over here. I need to talk to you now!" Duke hollered. "Big Al and Tony are looking for you. They left a message for you." Duke reached into his pocket and pulled out two .38 caliber bullets. He set them up on the bar. "One is for you, one is for me. Now Jimmy boy, let's get this show on the road. Tony says you got one week to get the kid to them or you and I get killed. I'm going to help you Jimmy. We have to take care of this as soon as possible!"

"But, you don't understand Duke," Jimmy whined. "I'm scared to even try to do this thing. What if we get caught? Man, people hate guys that fool around with little kids! Marylou will tell the cops about me and Noreen. I'll go to the can for sure! Duke, you know what those guys in jail do to guys that fool around with little kids!"

"God damn it Jimmy. You're big enough to take care of yourself; and besides, would you rather be dead? Well, not me," Duke said. "Look Jimmy, if you don't do it, I'll get someone else to do it, and I'll find a way to blame you. So, you might as well do the job and at least get the money. Besides that, we won't get caught. Trust me. Now come on Jimmy, let's make a plan."

Duke and Jimmy sat around for a couple of hours drinking and talking, trying to come up with some kind of plan they thought would work.

"You know, Jimmy. What you could do is tell Marylou you want to take Noreen to the zoo, or some place like that; and then, you could bring the kid here. Give her to Big Al and Tony, then tell Marylou the kid got lost at the zoo."

"No, no," Jimmy said. "Marylou won't let me take that kid any place. That idea won't work, think of something else."

"Sure," Duke said. "But, I'm doing all the thinking, and you're doing all the drinking. Now, I'm going to get us another beer and start putting these drinks on your tab."

"That figures," Jimmy said. "You're always trying to screw me."

"I'm going to screw you alright if you don't come up with some idea," Duke said. "Either that, or I'm going to kill you myself."

"Get serious, will you?" Jimmy said. "How about if I tell Marylou I'll give her ten thousand dollars for Noreen, and then she can make up her own story about the kid being gone."

"Don't be stupid, Jimmy. You just said she won't let you have the kid; and anyway, those two guys said they would give you the money after they had the kid. You know Marylou ain't gonna go for that shit. Besides," Duke said, "How many fucking people do you want to split that money with?"

"What the fuck do you mean, split the money?" Jimmy said. "Do you think for one minute I'm going to split the money with you. I'm going to pay you what I owe you and maybe a little more, but that's it!"

"Bullshit, that's it!" Duke said. "We're partners and partners we'll stay. Now, let's come up with a plan partner, and we'll do this job together."

"O.K.," Jimmy started laughing. "O.K., partner. But, let's start with you buying the drinks, and let's go some place nice."

Jimmy and Duke left the bar and started to hit all the joints around the area. Around three in the morning after they were as drunk as the proverbial skunk, they stopped for breakfast on Detroit Avenue. They had proceeded to get plenty drunk; but so far, had not come up with one good idea. They finished breakfast and headed back to Duke's place. The only idea they had now was to keep on drinking.

Jimmy and Duke got back to the bar around four-thirty a.m. Duke unlocked the door, and they both went in. Duke headed right behind the bar for more drinks and Jimmy tried to sit on a bar stool. Jimmy fell on the floor and Duke roared with laughter. "Get over to a table and sit there. You're getting my floor all dirty with your clothes."

In less than an hour, both Duke and Jimmy lay on the table in a drunken stupor.

Duke's barmaid, Fatty, came in about ten in the morning. She found Duke and Jimmy passed out at the table. She shook Duke. "Wake up you drunken' bum! What's the matter with you? The fucking doors are wide open and you're sleeping! Man, anyone could come in here and rob you!"

"Get away from me ya fat slob!" Duke mumbled. "What the hell are they gonna steal, Jimmy or me? Just get your ass behind that bar and get to work. That's what I pay you for!"

"You don't pay me very much asshole," Fatty retorted "Come to think of it, I want a raise."

"I'll give you a raise," Duke yelled as he grabbed his crotch.

"Now get me and my friend, Jimmy, some breakfast."

"Yeah, what do I look like, a fucking cook?" Fatty asked.

"You look like a fucking asshole, that's what you look like!" Duke laughed. "You don't have to cook us breakfast! Just pour it from the bottle."

That woke Jimmy up, and he said, "And, Duke's buying my breakfast!"

Duke and Jimmy sat at the table. Fatty kept bringing them shots and beers one after another until about twelve fifteen in the afternoon.

Jimmy said to Duke, "Let's take some booze over to Marylou's place. Maybe, it will be like the good old days. Maybe, Patty will be there, and we both can get lucky."

"Good idea," Duke said. "Hey Fatty, gimme a twelve pack and a bottle of that cheap whisky. Let's go get lucky, Jimmy!" Out the door they staggered.

Jimmy and Duke got into Jimmy's truck and headed for Marylou's apartment. They were both laughing and had opened a couple of beers from the twelve pack. "Today, might be our lucky day," Duke said. "I ain't been laid for a month of Sundays. I feel good man, I feel good."

"Me, too!" Jimmy said. "This is gonna be just like the old days."

It was about twelve fifty in the afternoon when they pulled across the street from Marylou's apartment. Noreen was just walking out of the door to call her brother when she saw Jimmy's truck pull up. She had not seen Jimmy for a long time and ran right to the truck. Jimmy opened the door of the truck. "Hi Noreen, I haven't seen you for a long time." Noreen jumped into the truck and onto Jimmy's lap and started to hug him.

Duke's eyes got as big as saucers as he looked on. All of a sudden, he was stone sober. "This is it!" Duke yelled. "This is it! Jimmy let's go! Hurry up, let's go!"

"What, what are you talking about?" Jimmy asked.

"We got her! We got her! Let's go! Let's go!" Jimmy slammed the door on the truck and drove away.

"Where are we going to go?" Jimmy asked. "Shit, I'm scared!"

"Just drive to my place. We'll take her to my apartment. Hurry!" Duke said as he looked out the back window of the truck. He saw nothing except the two boys playing in the yard. They had not even looked up. They had not seen Noreen.

Jimmy pulled up in front of Duke's bar and Duke jumped out. "Let me go inside and make sure Fatty doesn't look out the window. You take the kid upstairs to my place, and I'll be right up!"

Duke went into the bar. "Hey Fatty, what's cooking!"

"I am, you fat slob. When the hell are you going to get that air conditioner fixed?" Fatty asked.

"Mighty soon," Duke said. "Mighty soon. Sooner than you think. Hell, I might even buy a new one."

"That will be the day," Fatty said.

"Hey Fatty," Duke said. "I'll be upstairs in my place in case anyone wants me."

"That will be the day," Fatty said. "Yeah, go upstairs. You bother me down here."

Duke went out the door and up the stairs to his place. Jimmy and Noreen were in the kitchen. Noreen was asking Jimmy for some lunch. "Mommy was just fixing lunch when you came and took me. Can I have some lunch?"

"Sure thing," Duke said. "How would you like a hamburger, some fries, and a coke?"

"Only if it's from McDonald's," Noreen told Duke.

"Jimmy stay with her. I'll run up the street and get some chow. Jimmy, keep the noise down. They can hear you downstairs at the bar."

"But, Duke, what are we going to do now?" Jimmy whined.

"Just shut up and play with the kid until I get back." Duke ran out the door and down the stairs. He felt like he was walking on air. Man, this was his lucky day! And, he was going to make some money, too. Duke was already trying to figure out a way to get Jimmy's share.

I have to talk to Jimmy before I call Big al and Tony, Duke was thinking. We have to make some plans. Man, I don't want to get caught in the middle of this thing. I have to think of a plan, so if we get caught, Jimmy will get all the blame. Duke brought the hamburgers and fries back to the apartment just in time. He could hear Noreen whining for lunch. I have to move fast and get this kid out of my apartment. He opened the door and went in.

Noreen sat at the kitchen table eater her burger and fries. Duke and Jimmy sat on the couch in the living room talking about what they would do now. They were both sober now; Jimmy because he was scared, and Duke because he could smell money.

"Duke, I just don't know if I can go through with this," Jimmy whined.

"God damn it Jimmy!" Duke exclaimed. "This is the perfect time, no one saw us take the kid, and we couldn't have planned this any better. Let me call Big Al and see what he says."

"I don't know," Jimmy said. "Do you think those guys will hurt Noreen?"

"Jimmy. They told you they have a nice family who will take care of her. Come on let me make the call," Duke said.

Duke went out to make the phone call. I better use the phone down the street, thought Duke. As he walked down Bridge Avenue, he saw the cop cars going up and down the streets looking between the houses. Man, they can't be looking for her already. "Hey buddy," the copy yelled from the car that had pulled up to the curb next to him. "You seen a little girl walking around her?"

"No, no," Duke stuttered. "I'm just going to make a phone call."

"Keep your eyes open, will you?" The cop asked. "She's a little girl. We think she is lost."

"Sure will," Duke answered. The car pulled away. Oh shit, Duke thought as he made the call. I gotta get that kid out of my place. Man, Big Al and Tony better come through and help me out.

CHAPTER 23

Duke stepped into the phone booth and shut the door. He dug into his pocket for changed, pulled out a dime and started to put it in the slot. Oh shit, I can't remember the number, he thought. I gotta relax; then, it will come to me. Duke took a couple of deep breaths and felt a lot better. He put the dime in the slot and dialed the number. One ring, two rings. Man, oh man, any other time, they answer on the first ring. There were four rings, and then an answer. "We got her!" Duke shouted.

"Who, the hell is this!"

"It's me! It's me!" Duke yelled, "And we got her!"

The person on the other end asked: "Look, who is this and who do you got?"

"Is this Big Al?" Duke asked.

"Maybe it is, and maybe it ain't. Who the hell is this?"

"God damn it, it's me, Duke. Duke. Christ, don't give me all this bullshit. We got Jimmy's little girl. She's at my place. Will you get over here? Man, we're scared!"

"Hold tight!" Big Al said. "We'll be right there!"

"Hurry, just hurry!" Duke hung up the phone.

Duke walked slowly back to his place. A few times he saw patrol cars driving slowly down the side streets. He was afraid to walk too fast, afraid he might attract some attention and be stopped by the police again. Man, if they stopped him again, he just knew he would have a heart attack. Big Al and Tony better get that kid out of my place. What the hell did I get myself into, and how did I end up being partners with that asshole Jimmy? He thought. This seemed like such a good idea before. Now, oh man! And, I thought this was my lucky day. It's more like my unlucky day!

Duke walked up the stairs of his apartment. By now, he was wet with perspiration. Man, I need a drink. No, maybe that ain't such a good idea. Yes, it is! Duke ran back down the steps and into the bar.

"What the hell's wrong with you!" Fatty asked.

"Just mind your own business and pour me a shot," Duke told her. He downed that one and she poured another. He drank one more. "Ah, I feel better." God, he thought. Let me sit here and relax for a

My Baby My Baby!

while, then I can get this shit together. Maybe, it's not as bad as I first thought. Just then, there was a big bang from upstairs, and then he could hear Jimmy yelling.

"What the hell is that?" Fatty asked. "Who you got up in your place?"

"Oh that's Jimmy," Duke said. "He must have fallen off the couch. You know how drunk he was this morning." Duke headed out the door and ran up the steps. He opened the door and yelled at Jimmy. "Be quiet, will you man? If they know that kid is up here, we've had it! The cops are already cruising the neighborhood looking for her!"

"What are we going to do Duke?" Jimmy asked. "Let's just take her back, and I'll tell Marylou I just took her to McDonald's for lunch."

"You know, she ain't gonna believe that shit!" Duke said. "I called Big Al and Tony. They're on their way here, so just keep her quiet and we wait."

"O.K., Jimmy said. "But Duke, I need a drink!"

Duke thought. Maybe, he's better off with a few drinks. He could be easier to deal with. I'll give him a couple of beers, but no whiskey.

Duke went back down to the bar. "Hey Fatty, gimme a twelve pack, will you?"

"Is that to go, or are you going to drink it here?" Fatty asked.

"Just gimme the beer. I ain't got time for your smart mouth."

"Oh, sure you and your buddy, Jimmy, are going to party all day again. Well, let me tell you this. I ain't going to work all night again. I got a life, too," Fatty said.

"Sure, sure," Duke said. "Don't worry about it." Duke went back upstairs. "Here, Jimmy, have one," Duke said as he handed Jimmy a beer. "Where's the kid?"

"She's out playing on the back porch," Jimmy said.

"What? Get her back in here. What if somebody sees her out there? What if those coppers see her? Jimmy, you got to be the biggest asshole I've even seen!"

Jimmy yelled at Noreen, "Get in here, now!"

Noreen came in crying, "I want to go home, I want my mommy!"

"Shut her up!" Duke said. "They'll hear her downstairs."

Jimmy picked Noreen up. "Noreen, be quiet, honey," he said. "I'll take care of you now, and we can go home in a little while. I'm going to put you in bed for a little while, and you try to take a nap, O.K.? Then, when you wake up, I'll take you home to mommy." Jimmy took Noreen into the bedroom. In a few minutes, he came out. "She fell asleep," he said. "But, I don't know for how long." Jimmy sat on the couch and opened a can of beer. "What do we do now, Duke?" He asked.

"Well, Big Al and Tony are on their way," Duke said. "Let's just wait for them and let them decide what to do."

"Do you think they will take good care of Noreen?" Jimmy asked. "I mean, they won't hurt her or nothing, will they Duke?"

"I don't think so," Duke said. "Let's just wait for them, and then we'll find out."

Duke and Jimmy sat on the couch waiting, each thinking different thoughts and sipping beer.

There was a knock on the door, and both Jimmy and Duke jumped up from the couch. "Who is it?" Duke yelled.

"Open the God damn door!" A voice shouts back.

"I think its' Big Al," Duke whispered to Jimmy. Duke opened the door to peek out. Big Al slammed into the door knocking Duke back and down on the floor. "Jesus, Al, what the hell are you trying to do, kill me?" Duke moaned as he picked himself up from the floor.

"What the hell took you so long to answer the door?" Big Al asked.

Tony and Big Al came in and sat on the couch. "Where's the kid?" Tony asked.

"She's in the bedroom taking a nap. She should be up soon," Jimmy said.

"Hey you guys," Duke said. "What should we do now. I mean, what's the next step?"

"The next step is for you to shut up," Tony said. "We have some phone calls to make. But first, we see the kid and see if she fits the bill. Our customers are very choosy." Big Al looked in the bedroom and checked the kid. He walked back into the living room and said: "We've got a deal."

"You guys sit tight here with the kid, and we'll get a hold of you," Tony told them.

My Baby My Baby!

"Wait a minute!" Duke said. "We can't keep her here. Shit, somebody might come here looking for Jimmy. Everyone knows he hangs around my place!"

"That's your problem, not mine," Bit Al said.

"Hey look," Jimmy said. "I can quit this thing right now and take the kid home!"

"Really?" Tony said. "Maybe, you should listen to the radio or watch television. They are already talking about the missing kid; and besides that, you know our deal, the kid or we kill you and your friend, Duke."

"But if we keep her up here, how can we keep her quiet?" Duke asked.

I got just the thing for you," Tony said. He pulled out a small packed from his pocket. "When she wakes up, give her a couple of these pills, and she'll be quiet." Big Al and Tony headed for the door.

"We'll be in touch," Tony said as they left.

Tony slammed the door as he left, and Noreen started to cry. "See what I mean," Duke said. "How the hell are we going to keep her quiet?"

"What did Tony give you?" Jimmy asked Duke.

Duke looked in the packet that Tony had given him. "Hmm, looks like some downers, seems a waste to let the kid have them. But, we have to keep her quiet," Duke said.

"I don't want to give Noreen no dope," Jimmy said. "Man, she could die from that stuff."

"We have no choice," Duke said as he walked towards the bedroom. "Come on and help me give her one of these."

"Not me," Jimmy said. "Not me. I don't want no part of this."

"O.K., O.K., Duke said. "I'll do it myself."

About five minutes later, Duke came out of the bedroom smiling. "She's out like a light and should be for a long time. Now, let's me and you talk," Duke said to Jimmy.

Duke and Jimmy sat on the couch and opened a couple of cans of beer. O.K., Duke said. "The way I figure it is the cops will start to look for you, just to tell you the kid is missing. We can't stay up here, because your truck is parked outside. The cops would see it right away, and if they don't find you downstairs in the bar, the first thing they will do is dome up here."

69

"So what can we do?" Jimmy asked. "We can't leave her up here alone, can we?"

"Sure we can. Here's what we do," Duke said. "We keep her doped up and tie her to the bed. We put some tape over her mouth, and we check on her every hour or so."

"Jesus, I don't know about all that tying up and everything. I don't want to hurt her," Jimmy whined.

"Hell, you've done enough to hurt that kid already," Duke said. "So, just shut up and help me tie her to the bed."

Duke and Jimmy tied Noreen to the bed and put a piece of tape over her mouth. Jimmy was not too happy about all this, but Duke persuaded him that this would be the best thing to do. "What if we were both downstairs at the bar and she started crying? She could be heard, and that would be the end of us," Duke told Jimmy.

"What if just one of us goes down to the bar? Then, we wouldn't have to put that tape on her mouth. Shit, she could suffocate!" Jimmy said.

"Look, it would look suspicious if one of us was up here. Just do what I tell you," Duke said.

"O.K., O.K., let's go down to the bar now," Jimmy said. "I'm thirsty." They left the bedroom and went down to the bar.

When they got down to the bar, Duke told Fatty she could go home. "Big deal," Fatty said. "You think you can save an hour's pay by sending my home early?"

"God damn it, Fatty," Duke said. "I'll pay you for the hour."

"O.K., O.K.," Fatty said. "I'm going. As a matter of fact, I'm going down the street to a bar where the air conditioning is working. See you bums in the morning."

"Now," Duke said. "Let's just sit here and wait. I doubt if any customers will come in on account of the air being broken. So, let's just wait."

"Sounds good to me," Jimmy said. "But while we wait, start pouring."

A couple of hours later, the door to the bar opened and two policemen walked in. "Hey, are you Jimmy Thompson?" One policeman asked Jimmy.

"Yeah, so what?" Jimmy said.

My Baby My Baby!

"Come with us," one of the policeman said. "We have to take you to see our boss."

"For what? I ain't done nothing!" Jimmy said.

"Come on man, your kid, Noreen, is missing. We got to take you to the apartment on Franklin."

Jimmy got up from the stool and walked out the door with the policeman. He turned and winked at Duke. "See you later man," Jimmy said.

Duke watched as Jimmy walked out the door. Man, I hope he doesn't blow this thing. Duke poured himself a double.

Jimmy got outside the bar and said to the cops, "Hey, I'll just get in my truck and meet you guys there, O.K.?"

"No, not O.K.," one of the cops said. "Get in the car. We'll take you there. Hell, you're so drunk now, I don't even think you should walk there, let alone drive."

Jimmy got into the back seat of the police car. Man, this is easy, Jimmy thought. When I get to the apartment, I'll really put on a show for them.

Jimmy put on his little show when he got to the apartment. He stopped after Marylou came out screaming, asking what he had done with Noreen. Man, that kind of scared the shit out of him a little, but it didn't seem like anyone paid much attention to Marylou's outburst.

Jimmy stuck around the apartment until about three in the morning. He was getting kind of nervous, and he needed a drink. Well, he thought, no one will miss me if I go. I can come back later. So, he headed for Duke's Bar on foot. No sense telling anyone where he was going.

Jimmy tried the door of the bar, it was open. Duke was sitting at the bar all alone. He turned as Jimmy came in the door. "Well, how did it go, Jimmy?"

"Pretty good," Jimmy said. "But, I sure could use a drink."

"You got it," Duke said. "Do you think they suspect anything?"

"Hell no," Jimmy said. "Everybody is running around looking for her. They don't even know I left. How is she doing?"

"Fine, just fine," Duke said. "I just checked on her an hour ago. Big Al called about an hour ago, also, and said they would be here at ten in the morning to pick up the package. He said they got a buyer."

"That's good," Jimmy said. "I can go back to the apartment about eight in the morning to see if they missed me, and if the cops know anything. I can be back here by ten, so don't let them take her until I get back. I want to talk to them."

"No problem," Duke said. "We want everything to do right."

"Now, let's have a couple drinks," Jimmy said. "Then, I'll check the kid and head back to the apartment."

Duke and Jimmy sat there and drank for a couple of hours. Maybe, it was more than a couple of hours, because when Jimmy asked Duke what time it was, Duke told him it was seven thirty. Jimmy never went to check on Noreen, but headed straight for the apartment.

The minute Jimmy left the bar, Duke ran to the phone and called Big Al. "Look," Duke told him. "You better get right over here and get his kid before Jimmy gets back. I'm afraid he might change his mind, or at least, give you a hard time."

"He ain't gonna give me no hard time!" Big Al snarled. "He's in this all the way!"

"But, just to be on the safe side, I'll get Tony and we'll come over right away. Have the kid ready to go." Big Al hung up.

Forty-five minutes later, Big Al and Tony pulled up in front of the bar. Tony went upstairs, and Big Al went into the bar to get Duke. "Come on," Big Al told Duke. "We ain't got all day."

"O.K., O.K.," Duke said as he came out from behind the bar. "I got the kid all tied up and ready to go. She's out like a light." They both went up the stairs where Tony was waiting for them.

Noreen was still tied to the bed and asleep. "O.K.," Tony said. "Wrap her in a blanket. We'll take her downstairs to the car and put her in the trunk. But, be careful. There are still a lot of cop cars all over the place." Big Al went down to start the car and opend the trunk. Duke checked up and down the street and waved to Tony, who was carrying Noreen down the steps. Tony put Noreen in the trunk, shut the lid, jumped into the car, slammed the door, and they were gone.

Thank God, thought Duke. Now, all I have to do is tell Jimmy something happened, and they had to pick her up right away and get out of town. Duke went back into the bar and poured himself a drink.

Jimmy got back to Marylou's apartment about eight. The place was packed with people. Outside, there were reporters, television, radio, and newspaper people. Across the street, the police had set up a big bus, and there were policeman constantly going in and out. It gave Jimmy a good feeling. He could tell these coppers where Noreen was anytime he wanted to. Hell, those coppers were so dumb when they came to the bar. The kid was right above them. They ain't as smart as they think they are.

Jimmy walked around the outside of the apartment, but it seemed no one paid any attention to him. He walked inside the apartment and saw Marylou sitting at the kitchen table with a bunch of people. They were talking about getting posters to pass around the neighborhood. There was some guy sitting next to Marylou that everyone was calling Reverend Weathers. Marylou was hanging on every word he said, like it was gospel. That was a good one, Jimmy thought. Just then, Marylou looked up and saw Jimmy standing there with a stupid grin on his face. She jumped up from the chair and screamed, "What the hell do you want? Get out of here, now! Don't you ever come back here, and if I find out you have anything to do with Noreen being gone, I'll kill you!"

Jesus, Jimmy thought. Let me out of here. If she keeps hollering like that, someone will start asking me questions. Jimmy slipped out the door as quickly as he could. I'm going back to Duke's place to talk to those guys before they take Noreen. Maybe, they will give me some money now. Maybe, I'll raise the price of the kid. Man, this is easy. Jimmy walked to his truck that he had parked down the street.

"What do you mean they took her!?" Jimmy screamed. "I told you to wait until I got back!" He grabbed Duke by the neck and started to strangle him. "I'll kill you, you son of a bitch!"

Duke was choking. Let me go! Let me go!" He screamed. Jimmy threw Duke to the floor. Duke crawled behind the bar. Man, Duke thought. I ain't never seen him this mad. Christ, he could kill me. Duke grabbed the bar and pulled himself up.

"Take it easy, Jimmy," Duke pleaded. "They just came and told me they wanted the kid now. I told them no, they had to wait for you, but Tony grabbed me and Big Al started to punch me! Honest, I tried!" Duke lied. "Then, Big Al pulled a gun on me and Tony went upstairs and got the kid. Honest Jimmy. If Big Al didn't have that gun, I would have grabbed him and made them wait until you got her! Come on Jimmy. Here, have a drink." Duke put a glass on the bar and reached for a bottle of whiskey.

"O.K.," Jimmy said. "I believe you. I know you would have stopped them if you could have. Gimme a beer, too."

"What should we do now!" Jimmy asked Duke. "When are those guys going to give me some money! Did they give you any money Duke?"

"No," Duke answered. "But they said they would see us in a few days." Duke was lying again, but he had to keep Jimmy happy for a while."

CHAPTER 24

Jimmy spent all his time now either with Duke or just sitting at the bar alone. He was not working at all, but still found money to drink with. He was running a large tab at Duke's and Duke did not seem to care. He was also living with Duke upstairs from the bar. This did not seem to bother Duke, either. Duke had plans to get Jimmy's money, if he ever got any from Big Al and that gang.

The only thing that Duke did not like was the constant whining from Jimmy. "Where are those guys? When are they going to give me some money? I'm going to the cops if they don't give me my money."

Duke was afraid that someone in the bar would hear Jimmy. Jimmy whined more when he was drunk, which was most of the time. Duke stayed as close to him as he could to try to control what Jimmy said, and who he said it to.

One day, Duke was just about fed up with Jimmy's whining. He went to the phone and called Big Al. "Look Al, this Jimmy is talking too much. I'm afraid he might spill the beans. Why don't you guys come and talk to him?"

"When will he be there?" Big Al asked.

"He's here all the time, just come over," Duke told Al. "Come early so he can talk to you. If you come too late, he'll be passed out."

"O.K., see you tonight." Big Al hung up.

About one-thirty that night, or really early the next morning, Big Al and Tony walked into the bar. As usual, the only people in the bar were Duke, standing behind the bar, and Jimmy, sitting on a barstool. Of course, they were both drunk. Big Al sat on one side of Jimmy, and Tony sat on the other side of him. "What seems to be the problem?" Big Al asked Jimmy.

"Well," Jimmy said. "You guys told me you would give me half the money when you got back from giving the kid to someone, and I haven't seen you since you took the kid. I need some money, and I need it now!" Jimmy was getting braver as he talked. "I did my part of the deal and you guys ain't doing your part! If you don't give me the money, I'm going to the police or else, I want my kid back!"

"Look here, Jimmy." Big Al was talking very low. "This is a hard business. Sometimes, it takes longer to get things done. But me and Tony are all right guys, ain't we Duke?" Big Al didn't wait for an answer, but kept on talking to Jimmy. "When me and Tony give you our word, it's like gold. Now listen Jimmy. There are a lot of people involved in this deal. It ain't easy to get something like this done right away, so bear with us for awhile. I can tell you this, Jimmy. The kid is in a good home and the people have a lot of money, so that should make you happy, right Jimmy?"

"Sure," Jimmy said. He had tears in his eyes. "That makes me happy, but where is she?"

"Now Jimmy, we can't tell you that. All we can tell you now is that the kid is happy. Now here is what Tony and me are going to do," Big Al said. "Here's five hundred dollars, just for now. Me and Tony are going back to our boss and tell him to try and get the rest of the money as fast as he can. So, you just sit tight until we get back to you."

"O.K., Jimmy said. "Can I buy you guys a drink?"

"No thanks," Big Al said. "Maybe, next time." Big Al and Tony got up from their stools and walked out the door. Big Al and Tony got into their car.

"I think we're going to have to get rid of that asshole," Tony said.

"I think you're right," Big Al replied. "But, let's wait and see how long before we do it. We don't want it to look suspicious; so we feed him a little money until we get the chance, and then we whack him." That made Tony smile. He always liked this part of the job.

As Big Al and Tony walked out the door, Jimmy said to Duke: "You know, those two guys are all right. I trust them now. Gimme another drink. Hey, give us both a drink and take it out of here," Jimmy said as he pushed a one hundred dollar bill to Duke. Duke smiled to himself as he took the money. Duke thought to himself, I think old boy Jimmy is in a shit load of trouble. I just hope I ain't in it with him.

Jimmy and Duke sat at the bar drinking. Jimmy was telling Duke how great Big Al and Tony were, and Duke was trying to figure out how to get the five hundred dollars from Jimmy. "Look Jimmy, you got all that money now," Duke said. "How about paying your bar bill. I thought you and me was partners? So, you owe me some of that money."

"Sure," Jimmy said. "How much is the bar bill?"

"O.K., Jimmy," Duke said. "The bill is two hundred dollars. I'm not going to charge you anything for staying at my place. Then as a partner, you owe me half of that five hundred, so you owe me four hundred and fifty dollars."

"Are you fucking crazy?" Jimmy yelled. "Here's two hundred for the bar bill, and I know you fucked me on that. Here's fifty bucks for you! And, I ain't paying you for staying in that shit hole upstairs!"

"O.K., O.K.," Duke said. "That's o.k. I'll have the rest of your money by tomorrow night." Duke was right.

By the next afternoon, Jimmy was asking Fatty to put the next round of drinks on this tab. Fatty looked over at Duke. "Sure," Duke said. "Anything for my best friend."

Jimmy put his arm around Duke and said, "Duke you're my best friend, too. I don't know what I would do without you."

In just a few days, Jimmy was back to his whining. "I'm serious this time. I'm going to the cops. Those guys ain't never going to give me no more money! Get a hold of those guys Duke. I want to talk to them, and soon. You call them Duke and tell them I want more money, and I mean it!"

Duke tried to calm Jimmy down. "Look," Duke said. "I can call them, but why not wait a few days. They were just here and you don't want to get them mad, do you?"

"I don't care if they get mad or not, I want more money or I want my kid back. They got their choice, that's it!" Jimmy said.

Duke got a few more drinks for Jimmy and finally persuaded Jimmy to wait a couple of days. Duke was really beginning to worry about what might happen if they bothered Big Al and Tony too much. Duke wasn't too worried about what they might do to Jimmy, but he didn't want to get hurt or even killed. Man, I'd be happy just to get out of his deal now. Just let them forget me and I can forget all of this.

The next morning, Duke got up and Jimmy was already drinking and whining. "I need to see those guys now, Duke. Call them, will you?"

"Not now!" Duke said. "Why don't you try to get a few jobs and take your mind off this for a while?"

"Hey, why the fuck should I work?" Jimmy asked. "Big Al owes me a lot of money, and I want it! I'm not going to work!"

"Look at it this way," Duke said. "If you come up with a lot of money all of a sudden, the cops will get suspicious and have you in for questioning right away. The longer we wait, the better off you will be. When the cops start giving up on the case, we'll call Big Al and put pressure on him."

"O.K.," Jimmy said. "Maybe you are right. I'll go see if I can get some work just to make it look good."

Jimmy looked around the neighborhood and found a few odd jobs to do. Maybe, Duke was right. He felt better, but he wasn't going to wait too long before he would have Duke call those guys. He'd get the money and maybe get out of Cleveland. He could live down home like a king with all that money. He could hang around the General Store, drink some shine with the boys and tell some lies. Oh boy, could he live good. Just a little more time, and then watch out Big Al and Tony. Here I come and you better have my money ready!

Duke was trying his best to keep Jimmy quiet. He kept Jimmy working odd jobs during the day and kept him drunk at night. So far, it was working. But, Duke was getting greedy, too. He wasn't satisfied with getting all the money Jimmy made during the day. He wanted some of the big money Big Al had promised Jimmy. Maybe, they would pay, and then again, maybe not. But, it was worth the chance and the aggravation to take care of Jimmy for a while. Hey, if it worked out, he'd have some big money; if it didn't so what. He had made enough money off Jimmy all this time, so he was ahead of the game no matter what.

One thing Duke didn't know about. One night after Jimmy had been drinking, he had left the bar and had gone over to Marylou's apartment. He had almost told her that he knew who had taken Noreen and that those people owed him money. If Duke thought he could write Jimmy off, he was right. If he thought he could handle Marylou, that might be a horse of a different color. Maybe, more like a mule of a different color.

Three months had gone by since Big Al and Tony had given Jimmy the five hundred dollars, and it was getting harder and harder for Duke to keep Jimmy quiet. The more Jimmy drank, the more he wanted to see Big Al and get the money. Duke knew that some of the people in the bar had heard Jimmy bitching. Good thing most of them were winos and only paid attention to where their next drink was coming from.

One night when Duke's bar was busy, Duke overheard Jimmy telling one of the regulars that two guys owed him a lot of money and if he gave Jimmy a couple hundred dollars, Jimmy would pay him back double.

Duke came around from behind the bar, grabbed Jimmy, and dragged him outside. "What the hell are you doing? Do you want to get us both killed? If word gets back to Big Al that you are talking about what happened, he'll kill us! Jesus Christ, Jimmy, what the fuck is wrong with you?"

"Fuck you, Duke," Jimmy yelled. "This ain't your problem anyhow. It was my kid they took, and it's me they owe the money to, and I want it."

"Jimmy," Duke said. "Tell me the truth, did you tell anyone else? Believe me Jimmy. I'm your friend, and I'm just trying to help you. Come on, tell me! Who else did you tell?"

"Well," Jimmy looked down at his shoes and shuffled his feet. "Well, I didn't really tell anyone except…"

"Who, God damn it, who?" Duke shouted.

"Well, maybe I kind of told Marylou," Jimmy said.

"What? Of all the people to tell," screamed Duke. "Jesus, what did she say?"

"She didn't really say much of anything," Jimmy said.

"What exactly did you tell her?" Duke asked.

"I just kind of told her that Noreen was all right and with a good family," Jimmy said.

"What about the money!?" Duke asked. "What about the God damn money? What did you tell her?"

"I kind of told her…"

"What the fuck did you tell her? I'm getting pissed off here, Jimmy. Now, tell me what you told her!"

Jimmy said, "I just told her that I would get the money, and me, her, and Noreen would be together again."

"Man, are you crazy?" Duke asked. "What do you think those guys are going to do, give you the money, and then tell you where the kid is? Or, do you think they are going to give you the money and give you the kid back? You must be going off your God damn rocker!" Duke was screaming by now.

"Hey, Duke. Take it easy, will you?" Jimmy said. "Marylou ain't gonna say nothing yet, and I haven't heard from the cops or her, so everything must be all right. Relax, Duke. When I get the money, maybe Marylou and me will just leave this old town, and we'll be happy."

Jesus, Duke thought. This guy is really cracking up. If he told Marylou that much, maybe, he told her about me. Shit, I'm not even going to ask him. I gotta call Big Al. Man, I think it's time for me to bail out of this shit. Hell with Jimmy Thompson, I gotta save my own ass. Man, I hope there's still time. Duke went to make a phone call.

Duke met Big Al and Tony at a bar on West 65th and Detroit Avenue. He told them what Jimmy had said and left nothing out. Big Al looked at Duke and said. "Look here asshole, you put us on to this guy Jimmy, and you said you could handle him. Do you think we're stupid? We know you've been bleeding the guy. Now, you really got a problem. Let me tell you where you stand. Jimmy tells the cops anything and you go down the tubes with us. You tell the cops anything, or pull that 'turn over state's witness' and we kill you for sure. But maybe, we can work this out. We take care of Jimmy and you forget all about the deal that went down."

"You mean that's it?" Duke said. "You mean that's all I gotta do?"

"That's it," Tony said. "That's all there is to it."

"Wait a minute!" Duke said. "Do I have to do anything to Jimmy?"

"Don't you listen?" Big Al said. "I told you we would take care of Jimmy and you get the bad memory."

"O.K.," Duke said. "It's a deal." Duke held out his hand. Big Al and Tony looked at his hand like it was a piece of shit. Duke slipped his hand into his pocket and said, "Well, I guess I'll see you guys later."

"Wait just a minute," Big Al said. Oh shit, Duke thought. Here it comes now. "Where's Jimmy?" Tony asked.

"Why, he's upstairs in my apartment sleeping off a drunk," Duke told him.

"O.K.," Big Al said. "If I was you, I wouldn't go home for a few hours."

"O.K.," Duke said. "I got it."

Big Al and Tony got up to leave. "Oh by the way, Duke. Don't forget your bad memory."

"I already forgot," Duke smiled.

Duke left the bar about one hour after Big Al and Tony. Big Al had told Duke not to go home for a few hours, and Duke was not about to do anything Big Al had told him not to do. Well, he thought. Tonight would be a good night to hit a couple of bars that he hadn't been to for a long time. He could see a few old friends, and who knows, maybe get lucky.

Things did not go quite that way. The more Duke drank, the more he thought about what he had done. He had turned Jimmy in to Big Al. He had ratted on Jimmy. But then again, Jimmy deserved it by telling people what was going on. But then again, he would get no more money from Jimmy. Wait a minute, who said Big Al and Tony were going to kill Jimmy? Maybe, they would just rough him up a bit, well maybe, a lot. That wouldn't be so bad. Duke would nurse Jimmy back to health and be his good friend again.

Duke had breakfast at a restaurant and thought. What a waste, all that drinking and not even stiff. Oh well, I'll just go home and get some sleep. Maybe Jimmy will be there. He might need some help. Man, I hope they didn't hurt him too bad.

Duke got back to his apartment and tried the door. It was open. He went in and yelled for Jimmy. No answer. Duke checked the floors and the walls for blood. None could be seen. So far, so good thought Duke. Maybe, they just took him for a ride to talk to him. Duke felt relieved. He took his clothes off and went to bed. It seemed like he had just fallen asleep when he heard pounding on the downstairs door. Duke went to the window and looked out. Shit! Those two detectives. Duke opened the window and shouted out. "What the fuck do you guys want?"

CHAPTER 25

Fox and Bender got back to Hunter's office before Marylou and Weathers got there. They told Hunter that they had checked Jimmy's apartment and talked to the neighbors. It seemed no one had seen Jimmy for a while. Hunter decided to wait until Marylou got there and ask her about Jimmy. If she knew nothing, they would have to look for him. Both Bender and Fox agreed with Hunter.

Weathers and Marylou arrived at the station about twelve-thirty, late as usual. Hunter took them into his office and got right to the point. "Marylou," he asked. "Have you seen Jimmy lately?"

"No Sergeant, I haven't seen him for about a month or so," Marylou said.

"You told me before that you thought he was involved with taking Noreen and even offered to take you away with him when he got the money. Is that all true?" Hunter asked.

"Well, kind of true, but..."

"God damn it Marylou! Hunter yelled. "Quit bullshitting me. All I'm asking you is to tell the truth."

"I'm telling the truth. You just get me confused with all your questions," Marylou whined.

"Marylou, will you just tell me what Jimmy said about taking Noreen."

"O.K., O.K., here it goes again," Marylou said. "But, when I tell you this time, will you leave me alone? 'Cause if you don't, I'm going to get a lawyer and sue you."

"Please Marylou, I'm giving you all the breaks now, but you never want to help me." Hunter told her. "So, don't threaten me. You know I can make it a lot worse for you." Hunter continued, "So, why not help me with this thing?" Just then, the phone rang.

"Yeah?" Hunter said as he picked up the phone. He turned white. Let me call you back. Hunter told Marylou he would be right back, and he left the office.

Hunter walked out of his office. Bender and Fox were sitting at their desks. Fox looked at Hunter. "What's the matter Sarge? You look like you just saw a ghost."

Hunter dialed the phone and told Bender and Fox to pick up the extensions. Fox and Bender heard one ring. "Homicide, Butcher speaking."

"Butcher," Hunter said. "Tell me what happened again."

"Sure Sarge, I thought you might like to know. We just received a call from one of the zone cars. Seems they found a body in a garage over on West 32nd. They think it's Jimmy Thompson. We sent a team out about fifteen minutes ago."

"O.K.," Hunter told Butcher. "Make a call on your radio and tell them we'll be right out. Tell them not to move anything until we get there."

"O.K., Sarge," Butcher said. "You got it."

"Jesus Christ, Sarge. What do you think?" Fox asked.

"I don't know," Hunter said. "Let's wait until we get there. Meanwhile, I've got to tell Marylou. You guys get ready to go. As soon as I'm done, we'll hit the road."

Hunter went back into his office. Marylou and Weathers were sitting there talking. Hunter walked into the room. "Something wrong Sergeant?" Marylou asked.

"Yeah, well I hate to be the one to tell you this," Hunter said. "But, the police have just found a body over on West 32nd Street, and it may be Jimmy."

Marylou's expression did not change. "That's the breaks," she said. "Who killed him?"

"We don't even know for sure if it's him," Hunter said. "And besides that, what makes you think someone killed him?"

"I doubt if he died from natural causes!" Marylou shot back. "He was always in some kind of trouble. What, with his drinking and always shooting off his mouth. Nobody liked him, except that asshole Duke that he was always hanging around with. He just hung around Jimmy to get any money he could from him. Come on Hermy. Let's get out of here," Marylou said.

"Marylou, where are you gonna be later?" Hunter asked. "When we find out what's what, I want to talk to you."

"You always want to talk to me," Marylou said. "Remember what I told you about getting a lawyer? Anyhow, I'll be at Hermy's. You can tell me if it was Jimmy or not, and that's all I want to talk to you about." With that, Marylou grabbed Hermy's arm and out the door they went.

Hunter waited until he thought they were gone, and then he walked out of his office. Fox and Bender were already waiting to go.

They walked down to the garage and got into the car without saying a word. Fox drove out of the garage. Hunter asked, "West 32nd, is that where Jimmy kept his truck?"

"You're right," Bender said. "He rented a garage there to park that old truck of his."

When they arrived at the scene, the Homicide team was already there along with the ambulance and the zone car. The uniformed men had marked off the perimeter and were keeping the crowd away.

One of the Homicide Detectives waved Hunter and his men over to the garage. "Hey Sarge, how are you doing?"

"Doing O.K. Weaver, how about you?" Hunter asked.

"O.K., we saved everything for you, ain't touched nothing yet. Come on in, let's take a looksee."

Weaver led Hunter into the garage. Jimmy's truck was parked facing out to the street. The garage was filled with what was left over from different odd jobs that Jimmy had done. They walked to the back of the truck. Sitting on the floor about two feet from the back of the truck was a body. The legs were stretched out towards the truck. Both arms lay to the side of the body. The hands were laying palms up and open. The head was lying on the left shoulder, but against the wall. His eyes were open. The mouth was open with some reddish black stuff congealed on the chin. Hunter looked at the body. There was no question about it, it was Jimmy.

Jimmy was dressed in a pair of jeans, a tee shirt (even though it was cold out), and a pair of blue and white tennis shoes. Next to Jimmy was an empty fifth of Seven Crown and six empty Miller beer cans. The truck was not running, but the ignition was on. The gas gauge read empty.

"So far," Weaver said. "It looks like a possible suicide. Of course, we can't tell yet. We haven't even moved the body yet. When we got the call from the office, we just waited for you guys to get here."

My Baby My Baby!

"Thanks," Hunter said. "We appreciate it." Just then, Hunter saw Lieutenant Hurd from Homicide coming towards the garage. "Uh, oh," Hunter said. "Here comes trouble."

"What the fuck are you doing here Hunter?" Hurd yelled. "I heard Butcher tell these guys to wait until you got here. Since when do you give orders to Homicide? You should have enough to do on general duty. So my advice to you is to leave here and get back to your own work!"

"Hey Lieutenant," Hunter said. "Wait a minute, this guy is from a case we are working on!"

"Hunter, I really don't give a shit. Homicide will handle this. Any information you need, you get from the reports. So hit the road and let my men get back to work, understand?" Hurd said.

"Come on Sarge, let's go," Bender said to Hunter as he grabbed him by the arm. "We got another call anyway."

Hunter turned and walked to the car. No sense in starting anything with that asshole Hurd now. Hunter was in enough trouble with the Captain anyway. The Captain was getting pissed about all the time Hunter was spending on this case now. Well, Hunter thought, I can get the info from Weaver.

Hunter got into the car and said, "Let's go to Hermy's. I'll tell Marylou it was Jimmy, and then we can go to Rosie's for lunch."

"O.K.," Fox said. "Man, Sarge, we had to get you out of there before you punched that Hurd. He doesn't like you too much, does he?"

"He doesn't like anyone he can't suck ass with," Hunter said. "He really worries about his job."

"You know he's going to give us a hard time about seeing the reports," Bender said.

"I know, but we'll take Weaver out for dinner and get the information from him. No problem," Hunter said.

By now, they were at Hermy's place. "Wait here and I'll go tell Marylou," Hunter said. Hunter got out of the car and went to the back door of Hermy's. He knocked and waited. He knocked again.

"Yeah, who is it?" Marylou yelled from inside.

"It's me, Sergeant Hunter." Marylou opened the door a crack.

"Well, was it him?" Marylou asked.

"Yes, it was. I'm sorry," Hunter said.

"Don't be," Marylou said and slammed the door.

Hunter walked back to the car. "She took it pretty hard," Hunter said to Fox and Bender. He started laughing and said, "Just kidding. Let's go to lunch, and let's make it a long one."

CHAPTER 26

Big Al and Tony had left Duke at the bar and headed for Duke's apartment. "We got to get rid of this asshole Jimmy," Tony said.

"I know," Big Al said. "But, we got to do this cool-like. I don't want to get Duke scared of us to a point that we got to get rid of him, too. So let's stop and think this over for a while. As a matter of fact, we got a bottle of Seven Crown in the car. Let's stop and get a six-pack of Miller's." They stopped at Matt's Deli on Bridge Avenue and picked up the six-pack. They pulled the car into the back of Duke's place, had a drink from the bottle and popped the caps on a couple of beers. "O.K., let's think about this," Big Al said.

They each came up with a couple of ideas, but nothing seemed to fit the bill. Then, Big Al said, "Hey, does that Jimmy do any dope?"

"Yeah, I think so," Tony said. "Remember one time, we got some shit for Duke and he said Jimmy wanted some?"

"That's right, I remember," Al said. "You got anything?"

Tony opened the glove compartment. "I got two good hits of LSD and about ten or twelve downers."

"That will do it," Al said. "Bring the bottle and the rest of the six-pack. Let's get this show on the road."

Big Al and Tony went up the stairs to Duke's apartment. They knocked softly on the door, no answer.

"Try the door," Big Al said. Tony pushed the door and it swung open. They went into the apartment. They could hear Jimmy snoring in the bedroom. "Let's get him up," Big Al said. "When we get done with him, he'll be sleeping for a long time."

Tony shook Jimmy. "Come on, wake up Jimmy." Jimmy opened his eyes.

"Hey guys, you got my money for me?" Jimmy asked. "I need it."

"You got it," Tony said. "But first, let's talk and have a little drink."

The three of them sat in Duke's front room. Jimmy was taking a drink of beer and then a sip of Seven Crown. Big Al and Tony were just sipping on a beer. "Well," said Jimmy. "You got the money?"

"Sure," answered Tony. "We got it. But first, we need a favor from you."

"Sure," Jimmy said. "Anything you want, you got."

"You got a truck don't you Jimmy?" Tony asked.

"Yeah, I sure do," Jimmy said. "Got it parked up in a garage on West 32nd Street."

"Good," Tony said. "We need t his stuff moved tonight and you're going to get paid plenty for helping us."

Big Al smiled and said, "But first, let's finish up this here booze. You want some more, don't you Jimmy?"

"Sure, sure," Jimmy laughed. "The price is right, and I'm always thirsty."

"By the way, man," Tony said. "How about a couple downers? Think you could do a few?"

"Sure man," Jimmy said. "Gimme a couple of them, too. Man, I feel good."

Big Al and Tony got Jimmy down the stairs and into the car.

"Man, we got to keep him awake to show us where the garage is," Tony said.

"Hey man, don't worry about me," Jimmy said from the back seat of the car. He took them right to the garage.

Jimmy unlocked the garage door and said, "Well boys, there's the old truck and here are the keys. "Let's go pick up the shit."

Standing right inside the door of the garage was a piece of pipe about three feet long. Tony picked it up and smacked Jimmy right in the back of the head. Jimmy fell to the ground and was out like a light.

"Jesus, Tony, why the hell did you do that?" Big Al asked.

"I don't know. I just saw the pipe there and that was it," Tony said.

"O.K., let's get him to the back of the truck," Big Al said. "Sit him up in the corner. Tony, get the bottle and all the empties from the car."

Tony got all the empties and the bottle that was almost empty. "We might as well finish the bottle," Tony said. "I think Jimmy boy is done drinking." The two of them finished the bottle off.

"Wipe the cans and the bottle clean," Big Al told Tony. "Good! Now, let's see if we can just wrap his hands around these cans and the bottle. Ah, perfect. Now, his prints are on all of them. Now, Tony give him a nice big shot of that LSD."

Big Al took the keys and got into the truck. The truck started right away. Big Al got out of the truck. "Come on Tony, let's go." They pulled down the door of the garage and walked to their car.

Big Al started the car and pulled away from the curb. "What do you want to do with this stuff?" Tony asked.

"What stuff?" Big Al looked at Tony.

"The needle and this here pipe?" Tony said.

"Jesus Christ, why the fuck did you take the needle? You should have left that there."

"I never thought about that," Tony said.

"Oh well, let me pull down this alley," Big Al said. "You throw the stuff out the window. Nobody will think anything about seeing shit like that laying in his alley, but make sure you wipe your prints off. Tony picked up a rag from under the front seat of the car. He wiped off the needle and the pipe and threw them both out the window.

"Now, let's go home and get some sleep," Big Al said. "We have to keep an eye on that Duke guy just in case he gets nervous. Maybe, we'll go see him in a couple of days, after they find Jimmy and see how things are going with him. If he doesn't hold up, he can be taken care of, too. Let's just hope those dumb cops think it's a suicide and we'll be home clear." Tony and Big Al headed for home, well satisfied with the work they had done that night.

CHAPTER 27

After the detectives left, Duke went back up to his apartment. I wonder if Big Al and Tony took Jimmy from here? I got to call them and find out what is going on. I want to know the story so I don't get screwed up. First, I'll check with Fatty. She always knows what's going on, or so, she things she does. But, she may have heard something going up in my place last night.

Duke went out to call Fatty. Fatty answered the phone sleepily. "Yeah, who is it and what do you want?"

"It's me Duke. Listen Fatty. When I left last night, Jimmy was up in my apartment sleeping off a drunk. When I got home this morning, he was gone. Did you hear or see him last night?"

"You mean you woke me up just to ask about that bum friend of your? Are you crazy?" Fatty was pissed.

"Fatty, don't give me a bunch of shit. Just tell me if you heard or saw Jimmy," Duke said.

"I don't know," Fatty said. "I heard someone moving around in the apartment; and if you say Jimmy was up there, then that's who I heard."

"O.K.," Duke said. "But did it sound like there was more than Jimmy up there?"

"I don't know, ask Jimmy when you see him," Fatty slammed down the phone.

"Bitch," Duke hollered as he slammed the phone down.

Oh well, thought Duke. I better call Big Al. Maybe, he can tell me something. Duke dialed the number. The phone rang three times before Big Al answered it. "Yeah, who is it?" Big Al asked.

"It's me Duke. When I got home last night Jimmy wasn't here. Can you tell me what happened to him?"

There was a moment of silence, and then Big Al said, "Look Duke, maybe you better forget this number. We not nothing to talk about. Oh, by the way, you gave us a bum steer last night. We went to your apartment and Jimmy wasn't there. So, the next time you see him, tell him we're looking for him." Big Al hung up.

Duke hung up the phone. He felt relieved. Jimmy must be o.k. Maybe Jimmy just left to go back to his own apartment. He had told

My Baby My Baby!

Duke he needed some clean clothes. That was good. Jimmy probably would show up in a few days. They could go out, and I'll buy Jimmy some drinks. Duke felt guilty about calling Big Al and telling him about Jimmy. Oh well, that was over with. He'd make it up to Jimmy and maybe they could get a few more bucks from Big Al. Duke was already scheming to get more money from Jimmy. That Big Al and Tony ain't such big deals. Man, they never got to Jimmy, and they don't seem too excited about finding him. When I see Jimmy, I'll have a long talk with him. Get him to keep his mouth shut and we'll be o.k. again. No problem. Duke felt like a million dollars. I think I'll just go back to the joint. Fatty will be in pretty soon. I'll just give her the day off. Man, I feel good.

Duke went back to the bar and unlocked the door. I think I'll clean the place up. Fatty won't be here for about two more hours. She'll be surprised when she gets here, and I got the place nice and clean. Duke started washing the glasses. He was even humming a little tune. Duke was polishing the bar when the door opened. It was Fatty. "Hey, how you doing Fatty?" Duke yelled out cheerfully.

Fatty looked at him with a shocked expression. "How can you be so happy when your best buddy is dead?"

"What? Who? Who's dead?" Duke asked looking at Fatty.

"Oh man, I guess you didn't know. I just heard it on the radio before I left home. I'm sorry Duke, but they said on the radio that Jimmy Thompson was dead. They say he committed suicide in that garage where he keeps that old truck of his. Here, Duke sit down. Let me get you a drink."

Duke felt like he was in a trance. He watched as Fatty reached for a bottle of whiskey and a glass. It looked like she was doing it in slow motion. Jesus Christ, thought Duke. What the hell happened? Man, I can't figure this out. Jimmy committing suicide, why? Oh no, Big Al and Tony must have found him last night. But, wait a minute. Big Al said they couldn't find him here. Maybe, the found him walking down the street. No, Big Al just told me to tell Jimmy they were looking for him. Oh shit! Was Big Al lying to me? Maybe, they found Jimmy upstairs and took him to the garage and killed him; then made it look like suicide.

Duke was scared. He was afraid those two guys would come back to see him. But then again, Big Al had told him to forget the number.

That's one thing I'm going to do, thought Duke. If I ever get out of this mess, I'm going to be one of the good guys. Duke drank half a glass of whiskey, then filled the glass to the top again.

I know the cops are going to come here to ask me a lot of questions. I'll just tell them I ain't seen Jimmy for a while. I'll tell them the last time I saw him, he was real drunk and said he was going to his apartment for a few days. That's it, that's what I'll tell them.

The whiskey was making Duke feel better. When those cops come here, maybe they'll tell me it was a suicide. If it was, maybe I can get some money from Big Al. Hell, if they didn't kill Jimmy, maybe they ain't such tough guys. We'll see about this. Yeah, it wasn't over yet. Maybe, I can get all the money they owe Jimmy and maybe some more. Man, they ain't playing with no dummy here. Duke drank down the glass of whiskey and poured some more.

CHAPTER 28

The three detectives were sitting at the end of the bar at Rosie's. Most of the talk was about the case and if Jimmy had committed suicide or not. All three of them felt that Jimmy had been murdered, but they could not decide who would have killed him. They all wondered if Marylou and Hermy could have anything to do with it, but they all thought not. "You know whoever is involved in this thing, I'll tell you one guy that's sure as hell got a hand in it," Bender said. "It's that Duke."

"Yeah," Fox said. "Jimmy and Duke were always hanging around together."

Hunter thought for a while and said: "How about those two guys, those bookies or whatever they are? The ones that come into the bar every once in a while. Has anybody checked them out?"

"No," Fox said. "All we know is that they're some small time hoods. But, we'll check them out."

"O.K.," Hunter said. "I'm going back to the office and you guys go talk to Duke. See what you can come up with."

Back at the office, Hunter was trying to see if he could get some of the pieces to fit in this puzzle. It seemed like it was getting more complicated as time went on. One thing for sure, there were still a lot of pieces missing. Oh well, maybe Jimmy did commit suicide! But, that still didn't help the puzzle.

Noreen was still missing and Hunter thought Jimmy had had something to do with it. But what? Weaver should be calling him by tomorrow night. Maybe, he would give him some information that would help. Hunter turned on the TV in his office to catch the six o'clock news.

The reporter was just telling about the body of Jimmy Thompson found in a garage on West 32nd. He was the father of the little girl, Noreen, who was still missing. So far, it looked like a suicide. Hunter shut the TV off. We'll see. We'll see, Hunter thought to himself.

Bender and Fox pulled up in front of Duke's Bar and sat there for a couple of minutes. "Boy, I hate to go into that rat hole again," Fox said.

"Yeah, I know," Bender said. "And on top of that, you get to listen to all that bullshit from Duke. That's probably the worst part of it." They both laughed and got out of the car.

When they went in the door, they saw three customers sitting at the bar. Fatty, the barmaid, was behind the bar, and Duke was sitting at a table passed out. "Well, one thing," Fox said. "We don't have to listen to any bullshit from him. Let's talk to the barmaid."

Fatty looked at the two detectives and said, "Man, can't you leave him alone. His best friend just died. Anyhow, he's passed out now, and there ain't no way to talk to him now."

"That's o.k.," Fox said. "But we can talk to you."

"Sure, sure," Fatty said. "You guys want a drink?"

"No, we'll pass this time. When's the last time you saw Jimmy?" Bender asked her.

"Well," Fatty said. "I didn't really see him for about two days, but I think he might have been upstairs last night in Duke's apartment."

"Where was Duke?" Fox asked.

"Oh, I think he was out all night," Fatty said. "Because, he asked me this morning if I had heard Jimmy moving around upstairs."

"Well, did you?" Bender asked.

"Well, did I what?" Fatty replied.

"Did you hear Jimmy moving around upstairs?" Bender asked.

"I don't know if it was Jimmy or not," Fatty said. "But I heard somebody up there."

"Look," Fox said. "Why don't you try to get Duke over there sobered up and then have him give us a call."

"Sure," Fatty said. "But he ain't gonna be sober for a while. He was tossing them down pretty good."

"Just have him call us later," Bender said. "Here's our card."

"You guys got it. I'll just get him some coffee," Fatty said. "You guys want any?"

"No, thank you," Fox said. "We have to get back to the station."

Bender and Fox got into the car and headed for the station. "This case sure seems confusing," Fox said to Bender. "It seems like we're getting nowhere fast."

"I know," Bender said. "We got a lot of pieces, but nothing fits. Well, let's go back and talk to the Sarge. Maybe, he's heard something about Jimmy."

My Baby My Baby!

When they got back to the office, Hunter's door to his office was open. "Well," Hunter yelled from the office, "what did you guys find out from Duke?"

Fox and Bender went into Hunter's office. "Well Sarge, it's this way." Fox told Hunter what had happened at the bar.

"That puts us no place," Hunter said. "But when that Duke guy calls, I want you to bring him in here on our turf and question him. I'm sure he knows something about this deal. If Jimmy was involved with taking his kid, then, I'm sure Duke was, too. By the way, did you guys hear anything on the news?"

"No," Fox said. "We didn't hear anything."

"I did," Hunter said. "At this point, they're calling Jimmy's death a suicide."

"Did you hear anything from Weaver yet?" Bender asked.

"No," Hunter said. "But, it's still too early to call him. I want to make sure he has all the reports. No sense in bothering him too much."

"You think he'll give you everything on the case?" Bender asked.

"Sure," Hunter said. "He owes me some favors, and besides that, he doesn't like Hurd much. If he doesn't call by tomorrow night, I'll call him and have him meet us for dinner. Let's call it quits for the night, and tomorrow, we'll start with Duke. In fact, on the way into work tomorrow, stop by the bar around seven o'clock and pick him up. If he won't come with you, tell him he's under arrest. See you in the morning."

Hunter left the office and headed to Rosie's Bar. He was hungry and thirsty. Hunter had nothing to eat at his apartment. There were a few beers in the fridge and a hunk of pepperoni that had probably turned green by now. Anyhow, Rosie cooked much better than he did. I'll make it an early night, Hunter thought. But as usual, it was about three in the morning when Hunter got back to his apartment and into bed. That would give him only a few hours of sleep before the alarm went off. But, that was all the sleep he ever seemed to need.

Bender and Fox were supposed to pick Duke up around seven in the morning and bring him into the office. Hunter went to sleep and started to dream of Noreen.

The alarm went off at six in the morning. Hunter lay in the bed for a few minutes thinking about what he was going to say to Duke.

Hunter knew when he was face to face with Duke, he would know just what to say. Interrogation was one of Hunter's strong points, and he enjoyed it. He seemed to get more answers from people than most of the other detectives.

Hunter jumped into the shower. He recalled the dream about Noreen. Don't worry little girl, he said to himself. We'll find you.

CHAPTER 29

Bender met Fox at the station at six-thirty in the morning. They were going to pick up the police car and then go and get Duke. "Well, what kind of night did you have?" Fox asked Bender.

"Nothing much," Bender said. "I went home. The old lady was bitching about my working late again. I had supper, a couple of beers, yelled at the kids, and fell asleep in my chair watching the television. It was just the regular night. How about you?"

"Well," Fox said. "I stopped at Rosie's for a few beers and got home around ten-thirty. My wife wasn't home yet, she had some kind of meeting after work. Same thing though, I started to watch television and fell asleep in the chair. The old lady got home around midnight, and we went to bed. That was it."

"Was the Sergeant at Rosie's?" Bender asked.

"Does a bear shit in the woods? Sure, he was there," Fox said. "By the time I left, he was really starting to roll. Rosie kept telling him to eat and the Sarge kept saying 'in a minute.' Well, as usual, I'm sure he never did eat."

Bender and Fox got into the car and headed to Duke's Bar. "Do you think that slob will be able to talk to us this morning?" Fox asked.

"Who knows? If he got up and started drinking again, we won't be able to wake him up," Bender said. "Man that guy sure is a slob, even when he's sober, he's still an asshole. Oh well, let's go get him."

Bender and Fox would have been surprised if they had known what had happened after they left Duke the day before. Fatty had poured coffee into Duke and would not let him have another drink.

She told Duke the cops had been there and told her to have him call them when he sobered up. Fatty told Duke, "I don't know what's going on, but I don't want to see you get in any trouble."

"You're right," Duke said. "I got to get straight before I have to talk to those coppers."

Duke thanked Fatty and headed upstairs. He shaved, showered, and put on some clean clothes. He went into the kitchen to fix himself something to eat. Duke found a couple of eggs and some bacon in the refrigerator. He looked in the bread box and found two slices of bread. The bread was a little green, but he scraped that off and made some toast. He made a big pot of coffee and fried up the bacon and eggs.

Duke was sitting at the kitchen table thinking about what he was going to tell the cops when it hit him. Jesus, if those two guys killed Jimmy, he might be next. If they did kill Jimmy, they must have picked him up here. The place looked in order. There didn't seem to have been a struggle or anything like that. But, there could be fingerprints or something they had left behind. Duke started cleaning the place up.

When he finished four hours later, the place looked like a million bucks. Duke felt good. He was all cleaned up, and the apartment was all cleaned up. The place looked pretty good. All right, bring on them fucking cops, I can handle anything now.

Bender and Fox got to Duke's about seven-fifteen. They knocked on the door, and Duke yelled down to them. "Hey, come on up."

"God, I hate to go back in that rat trap," Fox said. When they got to the top of the steps, Duke was holding the door open. The two detectives could not believe their eyes. Duke was all dressed up in slacks with a sharp crease in them. He had on a freshly pressed shirt and a clean sport coat. "Come on in for a minute," Duke said, and showed them the way into a nice tidy apartment.

Fox looked at Bender, and then they both looked at Duke.

"Hey man, I saw the light," Duke said. "I got to get myself in order. How about a cup of java boys?"

"No thanks, Duke, we just had some. But listen, the Sergeant would like to see you at the station. He'd like to ask you a few questions about Jimmy," Bender said.

"Why don't he come here?" Duke asked. "I mean, I ain't under arrest or nothing like that, am I?"

"No, no," Bender said. "It's just routine. The Sergeant is so busy. It's hard for him to get out of the office. He just wants to clear up a few things."

"Sure," Duke said. "I'll go along with you fellows, no problem. I ain't got nothing to hide. After all, Jimmy was a good friend of mine, and anything I can do to help, I'll do. Let's go. I want to get back here. I got a business to run, you know."

My Baby My Baby!

Hunter was sitting at this desk when the three men came into his office. He took one look at Duke and whistled. What have we got here?" Hunter asked. "I thought I told you to bring that guy in that owns Duke's Bar. Who the hell is this guy?" Hunter had on his best smile.

"Oh come on Sarge, gimme a break," Duke said.

"Sure," Hunter said. "Have a seat Duke. How about some coffee? Hey Fox, get us some coffee, will you?"

Duke sat down in the chair and said, "Well Sarge, what can I do for you?" Duke still felt good, he thought to himself. I can handle this guy anytime.

Hunter looked at Duke. He could tell just about what Duke was thinking. He thinks this is going to be easy, Hunter thought. Well, let's make it that away for a while.

"O.K. Duke, tell me a little about you and Jimmy," Hunter said.

"What do you mean Sergeant?"

"Where did you guys go? You know, stuff like that."

"Oh yeah," Duke said. "Well, Jimmy was my best friend and we did a lot of things together, like drinking and staying out all night. I would try to get Jimmy some work through the people that came into the bar and stuff like that. Sometimes, he would stay at my apartment, and I would give him some work to do around the bar."

"So, if Jimmy was your best friend, he probably told you things that he wouldn't tell other people, right?" Hunter asked.

"Sure, Sergeant. He told me everything. Me and Jimmy were buddies," Duke said.

"Yeah," said Hunter. "And that bitch Marylou never did like him very much, did she Duke?"

"That woman is one son of a bitch!" Duke said. "She was always giving Jimmy a bad time. I don't know what the hell he ever saw in her; and those kids, shit, none of them was Jimmy's. Hell, she screws anything that walks and some that don't."

"Do you think Jimmy knew about all this?" Hunter asked.

"Well," Duke said. "Enough people told him about it. I mean they told Jimmy she was out screwing around. Jimmy would get all drunk and start crying. Then, he would go to Marylou's apartment and she would tell him everyone was telling him lies. Sometimes, she would scream and holler at him. Sometimes, she would give him a little

99

loving. It didn't make no difference. Jimmy would be happy for a while and then, it would start all over. You know, I think that Jimmy was what you call, pussy-whipped." Duke and Hunter both laughed.

"Did Jimmy fool around with other women?" Hunter asked.

"Not too much," Duke said. "Oh, once in a while me and Jimmy would get lucky; but for the most part, Jimmy was happy to get drunk and pass out."

"Yeah, I bet you two guys had some good times," Hunter said.

"Oh yeah," Duke said. "That Jimmy and me was a team. Yes sir, we could really party."

Hunter was watching Duke. Duke was relaxed now, sipping on his coffee with a smile on his face. Hunter thought, let's hit him a little bit harder and see where we get.

"Duke, do you think Jimmy knew that Noreen wasn't his kid?" Hunter asked.

"Well," Duke said. "Sometimes he would say that Noreen was his and sometimes, he would say she wasn't. It all depended on what kind of mood he was in. Jimmy was pretty mad when Marylou wouldn't let him take Noreen with him anymore."

"Why wouldn't she let Jimmy take Noreen anymore?" Hunter asked.

Duke looked at Hunter for a minute before he said, "Well, Jimmy told me that Marylou thought he was touching Noreen."

"What do you mean by touching?" Hunter asked.

"You know what I mean," Duke said. "Touching her on her privates. You know."

"What you mean is, Jimmy was molesting Noreen, right?" Hunter asked.

"No, no, not like that. Hell, Jimmy told me he fooled around with her, but he never hurt her." Duke said it before he thought. Shit, Duke thought. I should have never said that.

Hunter could see by the look in Duke's eyes that what he had just said slipped out. "So what you are telling me is that Jimmy was molesting his daughter, right?" Hunter asked again.

"No, God damn it, he never said that!" Duke said. "What the fuck are you trying to do? Get me mixed up? I said he never hurt her."

"You mean he just touched her? Did he make her touch him?" Hunter asked Duke.

"Hey, I don't know?" Duke said. "I wasn't there. The man's dead. Let's just forget about it!"

"Tell me," Hunter said to Duke. "Did you ever fool around with her? Did you touch her a little or have her touch you?"

"Hey, who are you talking about?" Duke shouted. "Have who touch me?"

"Noreen, that's who I mean, Noreen!" Hunter said. "You and Jimmy were such good friends. Maybe, he told Noreen to make you happy."

"Jesus Christ," Duke said. "Maybe Jimmy liked to have the kid make him happy, but I ain't that kind of guy. Man, what's wrong with you, Sergeant, are you crazy or something? Man, I'll give you some girls to talk to. They'll tell you I don't fool around with little kids."

"O.K., take it easy, Duke," Hunter said smiling. "I'm just trying to do my job, you know, get the facts straight."

"Yeah," Duke said. "But, man, that's a hell of a thing to say about a guy when it ain't true."

"What did you think about Jimmy doing that kind of thing to a little girl?" Hunter asked Duke.

"Well, he never done it in front of me," Duke said. "And, he only told me about it once. I kind of just let it slide. What the hell, I wasn't going to say anything to him."

Hunter thought Duke had relaxed again. Let's see what he has to say about this. Hunter watched Duke's face and said: "Duke, did Jimmy ever talk to you about selling Noreen?"

Duke's eyes starting blinking and he turned white. "I, I, don't think so," Duke stammered. Duke could not remember if he had mentioned anything about that to the cops. Shit! This lying is hard to do. "No, he never said anything about that to me."

"Tell me Duke," Hunter asked. "What do you think happened to the kid?"

"Hey man, I don't know. That's your job to figure that stuff out."

"Come on, Duke," Hunter said. "Just give me an idea of what you think. It might help me a lot."

"Well," Duke said. "I would figure that some pervert got her and killed her, that's what I think."

"Only one thing," Hunter said. "What happened to the body? What do you think about that, Duke?"

"Forget it man, I don't want to talk about it." Duke sat back in the chair.

"Yeah, Duke, I don't like to talk about it either," Hunter said, "But I have to. What did Jimmy think happened to Noreen? You two were such good friends and all, I mean you must have talked about it. Tell me Duke, what did Jimmy think happened?"

"Hey man," Duke said. "I told you, I don't want to talk about it. I told you what I thought had happened, and I don't know what the hell Jimmy thought. Those two coppers said you wanted to talk to me about what happened to Jimmy. Why all these questions about Noreen? I told you all I know about Jimmy, and that's it."

"Sure," Hunter said. "I guess you're right. I guess I just got a little carried away. Sorry Duke."

"Yeah," Duke said. "I know you're just trying to do your job."

"Now, Duke," Hunter said. "Did Jimmy ever talk about committing suicide?"

"No, not that I can remember. I never heard him say anything about that. I was thinking," Duke said. "Do you think it could have been an accident? You know, maybe he fell asleep in the garage, something like that. What do you think Sergeant?"

"Anything could have happened," Hunter said smiling. "Anything, Duke. You know maybe he was murdered. How do we know for sure? Did Jimmy have any enemies, Duke? Was there somebody that might have killed him?" Hunter was watching Duke closely for any reaction. He got it.

Duke turned white as a ghost. "What? What? Do you mean murdered? They said he committed suicide! Why you even said it Sergeant."

"I did," Hunter said. "But then again, who knows for sure?"

"I'm going Sergeant!" Duke said. "I don't like the way things are going here. You talk to me like you think I know something about this case. Man, I just mind my own business. I had nothing to do with nothing. I don't know about the kid being gone, and I sure as hell don't know about no suicide or murder or whatever you want to call it!"

"Maybe so, Duke," Hunter said. "Maybe so, but then again, maybe you ought to ask those two hoods that come into your joint. You know, the ones that collect the book."

"Get lost Sergeant," Duke said. "I don't know no bookies. If you want to talk to me anymore, call my attorney!"

Duke slammed the door of Hunter's office as he left. Man, I need a drink, Duke thought. What the hell does that Hunter know? He was playing cat and mouse in there with me, and I was the mouse. Next time, he ain't talking to me until I get a lawyer. Shit now, I don't know if those guys killed Jimmy or not. Shit, I don't know if I want to know. Man, I'd just like to be done with all this bullshit. Those assholes didn't even offer to drive me home. Oh well, I can always walk. It ain't too far, and there's a couple of joints on the way I can stop at.

Hunter, Fox, and Bender sat at Hunter's desk drinking coffee. "What do you think Sarge?" Fox asked.

"I think we got him thinking," Hunter said as he laughed. "I think he's involved in this thing up to his neck. He knows what happened to Noreen. It just takes time, he'll screw up."

"Or he might turn up dead," Bender said.

"We can't watch him all the time," Hunter said. "But you two, keep tabs on him. Let him see you every once in a while, just enough to keep him on his toes. Get the names of those two hoods and find all you can about them. I don't want you to bring them in yet," Hunter said. "But I know they have everything or something to do with the missing girl or Jimmy dying."

Just then, the phone rang. "Yeah," Hunter said. "I'll be right in." Hunter hung up. "Shit, the Captain wants to see me and he doesn't sound too happy!"

Hunter was right. The Captain was not happy at all.

Hunter walked into the Captain's office. The Captain waved him to a chair in front of his desk. Hunter sat down and the Captain did not say a word for a while. He just stared at Hunter. Then, the Captain said, "Hunter, what the hell is your problem? I just got a call from Homicide, and they said you were interfering with one of their cases."

"What case would that be?" Hunter asked.

"Don't' give me any shit Hunter," the Captain said. "You know God damn well what case!"

"Oh, you must mean Jimmy Thompson," Hunter said. "The suicide."

"Yeah," the Captain said. "That's the one. You know, Hunter. That's why we have different departments. They handle the homicides, and you handle your work. Now if you continue to interfere with Homicide, I'm going to pull you off this case altogether. I told you before, you, Bender, and Fox are spending way too much time on this case."

"But Captain," Hunter said. "We have a few good ideas and some possible leads we are following up on. All we need is a little time, and I really think we can find the little girl."

"Look Hunter," the Captain said. "I told you before and this is the last time I'm going to tell you! Leave it alone!"

"But Captain," Hunter said. "What if Thompson was murdered?"

"Hunter," the Captain said. "The Homicide guy said it was suicide and that's what it is. Now go back and do the work you are supposed to do, and it's not homicide. Do you understand? Now get out of here!"

Hunter went back to his office where Bender and Fox were waiting. "What did he say?" Fox asked.

"The same old shit," Hunter said. "He wants us to lay off the case, and he claims we're bothering the Homicide guys with their investigation."

"Well, what do we do now?" Bender asked.

"We call Weaver and find out what's going on with the investigation," Hunter said as he picked up the phone.

Hunter lucked out. The phone in Homicide rang and was answered by Weaver. "Hey man, what's happening?" Hunter asked.

"Nothing," Weaver answered. "I shouldn't even be talking to you. The Lieutenant up here is really pissed at you. He thinks you're trying to get his job."

"I don't want his job," Hunter said. "All I want to do is find that little girl. So, tell me what the reports say about Thompson."

"Man, are you crazy, over the phone? I'll meet you for dinner tonight and tell you what's going on," Weaver said.

"Good," replied Hunter. "Meet me at seven o'clock at Rosie's Bar."

"Sarge, if I'm going to give you all this information and take a chance on the Lieutenant finding out and giving me hell, I ain't going to do it for a pork chop sandwich and a couple of beers at Rosie's Bar.

I'll tell you what Sarge. Meet me at the Steak Joint on East 30th and St. Clair. You can buy me a couple of martinis and a nice big steak, and I'll give you the info. Believe me Sarge, it will be worth it." Weaver hung up.

"That man drives a hard bargain," Hunter said to Fox and Bender. "Damn Homicide guys always want to go first class when someone else is paying. Oh well, Weaver says it will be worth it. So, seven o'clock, we meet him at the Steak Joint, and don't be ordering the best steaks there because I'll be picking up the tab!"

"Give us a break Sergeant," Bender said. "We know you have plenty of money."

"What do you say we have a couple of martinis, too?" Fox asked.

"Sounds good to me," Bender said. "They taste so much better when the Sarge is buying."

"Yeah, yeah," Hunter said. "You guys are a riot. But I'll tell you one thing. If that check is over a hundred dollars, you guys are paying."

"Don't worry Sarge. We'll make sure the bill is ninety-nine, ninety-nine with the tip," Bender said.

The three detectives were at the Steak Joint around six-thirty. "It's cocktail time," Fox said as he looked at Hunter and laughed.

"Remember what I told you about the bill," Hunter said, "and I ain't kidding."

"Sure Sarge," Bender said. "We know. Hell, I can't pay anyway, the old lady didn't give me any money. She told me if I have to eat out, the good Sergeant can pay. She told me to eat good and eat plenty, because she ain't fixing me no dinner tomorrow night either. As a matter of fact, she said if I'm going to spend so much time with you, I better start sleeping with you because dinner ain't the only thing she ain't gonna give me."

They were all laughing when the owner, Dan, came over to the table. "How are you doing Sarge? I haven't seen you for a while," Dan said.

"I'm doing good, Dan. How about you?" Hunter asked.

"Oh, just fine. What can I get you fellows?"

"Well, Dan. We'll have a couple of martinis with two olives for starters," Hunter said. Then, Dan, I got another guy coming for dinner; so once we order, make sure nobody bothers us."

"No problem," Dan said as he went to get the drinks.

"Oh by the way," Hunter yelled after him, "make sure the bill is over one hundred dollars will you?"

"No problem," Dan said smiling. "But the first round is on me."

"I knew it," Fox said. "We might as well drink and eat good and not worry about the bill."

"Right," Bender said. "He got us again."

Just then, Weaver walked in. He came over to the table and yelled to Dan, "Bring me a martini. Hi boys, what's happening?" Weaver said as he shook hands with everyone and sat down next to Hunter.

The four men made small talk and drank two martinis each before they ordered. Tina, the waitress, came over and took their orders. All four ordered the big New York strip steak well-done, a salad, and baked potato. "Bring us four Heinekens to wash down that steak," Hunter said. The four men ate without saying much. They had plenty of time to talk, so they enjoyed their meal.

When they had finished eating, Hunter called Tina to clear the table. He ordered four coffees and four amarettos on the rocks. Tina brought the drinks, and the men settled back to talk.

"Well Weaver, give us the low down," Hunter said.

"Sure will," Weaver said. "But let me tell you, if the Lieutenant finds out I gave you all this info, I'll be in some deep shit."

"Don't worry, Weaver," Hunter assured him. "Anything you tell us stays right here."

"O.K.," Weaver said. "Here's what we have. The coroner was going to rule it as a homicide, but the Lieutenant stayed on him and badgered him into calling it a suicide. There were a few things left unanswered, enough to be able to rule either way."

"Like what things?" Hunter asked.

"Well," Weaver continued, "we have a couple of things. You know if this guy had been anyone else, there would have been more of an investigation. But, we're so busy now that we just don't have time to investigate, so take the easy way out and close the case."

"Yeah, we all know about that shit," Bender said. "The little guy always get the shaft."

"Well, that's the way it is," Weaver said. "You get used to doing things that way and that's it."

"All right, that's enough of the philosophy," Hunter said. "Let's get down to this case. What thing? I ask again."

Weaver began to tell his story. "On the surface, this could very well look like a suicide. Thompson's blood showed a high alcohol content and enough dope to OD him. We found empty bottles of beer and an empty whiskey bottle in the garage. We didn't find a note any place in the garage. But then again, he could have left the note somewhere else. Another thing we didn't find in the garage was a needle. Now, Thompson had needle marks on his arm. He could have shot up someplace else, but it would have had to be close by. So far, we have been unable to trace his whereabouts for the last few days. So until we do that, we still have no reason to think it was not a suicide. Except for one more thing."

"What's that?" Fox asked.

"Well," Weaver said. "There was a big gash on the back of Thompson's head. The coroner thought Thompson could have been hit on the back of the head with a blunt instrument. Perhaps, it was a lead pipe or something like that. But, the Lieutenant convinced the coroner that Thompson hit his head on the leg of the work bench in the garage. That's the part that looks fishy to me. Thompson didn't look like he had fallen on the floor. I think he either sat down behind the truck if he committed suicide. Or, if not, he was placed in a sitting position behind the truck. I've been investigating homicides for over twenty years, and this sure looks like one to me. But, the verdict is in. Suicide, end of story, end of investigation. That's it." Weaver drank down his drink, smiled, held his glass up and said, "I think I'll switch to scotch and water. I know you guys want to ask me some questions and that always makes me thirsty."

Hunter called Tina over and everyone ordered drinks. "Keep them coming Tina," Hunter told her. Hunter then turned to Weaver and said, "If you were investigating this case, give me an idea of where you would start."

"Sure," Weaver said. "The first thing I would do is check all the garbage cans in that alley around the garage. The garbage men don't come for another two days."

"Yeah, but what would we be looking for?" Bender asked.

"I'd be looking for a piece of lead pipe and a needle," Weaver said. "The next thing I would do is find out where Thompson was before he died and who he was with. He had to get the dope and the booze from someone. That's how I would begin the investigation. I'd bet money you would find you have a homicide on your hands."

"Why do you think someone would kill him?" Fox asked. "I mean it's not like he's some drug dealer or something like that. He's just a drunk and works part-time as a handyman. Hell, he's got no money or nothing."

"I don't know why," Weaver said. "Who knows? I've seen people killed over a dime, so who knows that the motive could have been?"

"I think I know," Hunter said. "It's the kid, he knew where the kid was, and maybe he was causing waves. We have to find out where he was and who he was with. That asshole Duke should be able to help us."

"Bender and Fox. You guys get busy and start to dig through the garbage cans. I'll meet you later. I want to talk to Weaver for a while."

"Great Sarge," Bender said. "I always like to dig through garbage cans right after I eat a big steak with all the trimmings."

"That's just what I thought," Hunter said. "That's why I told you to do it. So get going!"

On the way out, Fox stopped at the bar. "How much is the bill Dan?"

"Oh, about one hundred dollars and one cent," Dan smiled.

"Give it to the Sarge," Fox said as he and Bender walked out the door.

Hunter and Weaver sat at the table and ordered another drink. "Sarge," Weaver asked. "Why are you so interested in this case?"

"Really, it's easy to explain," Hunter said. "From the beginning of the case, I had this feeling that Marylou and Jimmy had something to do with Noreen's disappearance. Then, the more we found out about the case, the more I felt I was right. It just seems like we can never prove anything we come up with. But, all we need is a break. Just one person to talk, and the case is solved. Maybe, that Duke guy knows more than he is saying. If I can scare him enough, maybe he'll tell us what he really knows."

My Baby My Baby!

Hunter and Weaver ordered another drink. "Tell me Weaver," Hunter said. "Why do you think your lieutenant is so set about making this case a suicide?"

"For one thing," Weaver said. "Hurd is worried about how many homicides we've had so far this year, and most of them aren't solved yet. So, it makes him look bad. Second of all, he has no use for you and thinks you are trying to show him up, especially on this case."

"But, he never had anything to do with this case until Jimmy's death," Hunter said.

"I know," Weaver said. "But the way he figures it, if you solve this case, you'll get all the publicity and that makes him jealous. I guess all it amounts to is that the guy is afraid of losing his job."

Hunter thought for a while. Then, he said, "It sure is a shame when a guy will give up his morals to make statistics look good. But, I guess everybody spends more time looking at the statistics and not at the people that make them."

"That's right Sarge," Weaver said. "But, you have to roll with the flow, and with that, I have to go. My wife is waiting up for me. Thanks for the meal Sarge, and good luck." Weaver left Hunter sitting at the table.

Dan came over to Hunter's table and sat down. "Well Sarge, is the meeting all over?"

"Yeah," Hunter said. "Good steak, Dan."

"Thanks," Dan waved Tina over to the table. "Give me and the Sarge another drink." Dan sat back in his chair and said, "You know Sarge, sometimes a man just has to sit back and relax. Sip on a good drink and just let the mind wander. Then sometimes, you can get a better look at things."

Hunter sat back in his chair. "Maybe you're right Dan, but it never seems like you have the time to do that."

"Make the time," Dan said. "Because if you don't you're going to have a heart attack."

"I don't even have time for that," Hunter said. "By the way Dan, give me the bill. I have to meet Bender and Fox."

"Hey Sarge, the dinner is on me," Dan said. "And, don't stay away so long, hear me?"

"O.K. Dan. Thanks, and I'll see you later." Hunter left. He got into his car. Well, he thought. Rosie's is right down the street, and I'm not in any hurry to go help those guys go through garbage. So, I'll just stop by Rosie's and see what's happening.

CHAPTER 30

Bender and Fox were in the alley not far from the garage where Jimmy had been found. They were going through the garbage and bitching to each other. "Man, I'm glad we stopped home and got these coveralls to wear," Fox said.

"Yeah, but I had to take a lot of grief from the old lady," Bender said. "She thinks I'm going out to fool around. I told her what kind of girl do you think I'm going to fool around with in coveralls?" She said, 'Those clothes better have plenty of garbage on them when you get home." Just then, they saw the headlights of a car turn into the alley. "Maybe that's Hunter," Fox said. "Oh shit, it's a zone car."

The zone car put on the bright lights and called through the loud speaker. "You guys, put your hands up and walk over to that garage door."

"Hey," Fox yelled. "We're policemen!"

The voice on the loudspeaker said, "Sure, you are. When you get to the garage, assume the position; hands and legs spread and lean against the garage."

"Will you guys wait a minute?" Fox yelled.

"Get over there and now!"

"Let's just do what they say," Bender told Fox. "It could be a couple of rookies, and we'll end up getting shot."

"Yeah," Fox said. "I guess you're right, that would be just our luck."

Fox and Bender got up against the garage door and waited. They heard the doors of the zone car open and close. Then, it was quiet. "O.K., Fox said. "What the hell are you guys doing back there?" There was nothing, but quiet.

Suddenly, there was a flash. Both Fox and Bender hit the deck, and then they heard the zone car men start to laugh. "You got them. They couldn't detect shit on a door knob. Now, we got them covered with it!"

Now, Fox knew who one of them was, his old partner, Sam Star. Sam always carried his camera with him, sneaking up on lovers parked and snapping pictures through the car windows. He had a collection of photos. Some were very unusual. "God damn you guys," Bender said. "You scared the shit out of us."

"Hey man," Sam said. "We got a call of prowlers in the alley. You're lucky we didn't shoot first and take pictures later." Both zone car men laughed. "We never thought we would find two detectives moonlighting as garbage men."

"Ha, ha Star, you really are funny," Fox said. "Now leave us alone, we have work to do."

"Sure will," Star said. "We have to get back and have this picture developed. It will be at all the roll calls starting tomorrow." They jumped into the zone car and took off laughing.

"That's just great," Bender said. "You know Star wasn't lying. He'll have that picture at every roll call in the city by morning."

"You're right," Fox said. "But, who cares? Not me, that's for sure. I'm just sick of going through this garbage. And, by the way, where the hell is Hunter?"

"Easy man," Bender said. "You know he's at Rosie's now, and you also know that rank has its privileges."

"That may be so, but we have the rank job now!" Fox said. They both started digging in the cans again.

After another half hour or so, Fox said. "You know, maybe we're going this all wrong."

"Why? What do you mean?" Bender asked.

"Well," Fox said. "If someone left the garage with a pipe or whatever, I don't think they would walk to the back of the garage to dump the stuff. Look, if they had a car parked out front where we're parked, they would get into the car and drive away right?"

"Sounds right to me," Bender said. "Let's do it."

Bender and Fox walked out to the car and got in. "O.K.," Fox said as he started the car. "You're holding the stuff and we want to dump it right away. So, we pull away from the curb and start down the street."

"So far, you got it right," Bender said. "Unless they were parked on the other side of the street or headed the other way."

"Let's just try this way first and if it doesn't work, we'll do it from the other side of the street," Fox said. They drove about one hundred yards down the street and they saw a side street that cut through the alley.

"Turn right down this side street," Bender said. They came to the alley, and Fox stopped the car.

"O.K., which way?" Fox asked.

"I doubt if they would head back towards the garage," Bender said. "So turn left." Fox turned left and started slowly down the alley. "Now," Bender said. "I'm on the right side with the stuff in my hands. I want to get rid of it right away, so I roll down the window. Hmm, do I throw the shit out the window or do we stop and put it in a garbage can? Stop the car." Fox stopped the car. Right there by Bender's door was a garbage can filled with garbage. Fox and Bender got out of the car and shone their flashlights around the can.

"Bingo!" Fox said. "Here's a lead pipe lying right next to the can." Fox knelt down to look at the pipe. "Hey, it looks like there might be some dried blood and hair on this pipe."

"Don't touch it," Bender said. "Let's see if we can find the needle."

The two detectives slowly sifted through the garbage. They found nothing. "Do you think they could have thrown it out farther down the alley, or even farther back?" Fox asked.

"Yeah," Bender said. "This is the needle in the haystack trick."

"Let's look further away from the can," Fox said. "Maybe it hit the edge of the can and bounced out."

A few minutes later, Bender said, "Here it is, over here." Fox went over to look. Sure enough lying on the ground part way under a garage door was a needle.

"It could be the one we're looking for," Fox said. "But in this neighborhood, who knows?"

"It's the only one we see here," Bender said. "So let's wait for Hunter and see what he wants to do."

Bender and Fox got back into the car and settled down to wait for Hunter.

It was about an hour wait when they saw Hunter's car turn down the alley. They both got out and walked over to Hunter, who was just getting out of the car. "What the hell are you guys doing up here?" Hunter said, "I've been looking all over for you." Fox told him how they had thought about what might have happened and took Hunter over to show him the pipe and needle.

"Great," Hunter said. "You guys do nice work. Now call for S.I.U. We'll have them take some pictures and bag this evidence. I'll tell them just to take it back to the station for now and sign it to us. We don't want anyone to know what we have. Not yet, at least. Let's just wait to see if it's what we think it is. If it is connected with the case, we can drop the bomb on that asshole Hurd and really make him worry about his job. You guys call for the car, then go home and get some sleep. I'll wait here for the S.I.U. car and tell them what we want to do."

"Sure Sarge," Fox said. "It's been a long day. See you in the morning."

Bender and Fox left. Hunter sat in his car to wait for S.I.U. Hunter felt pretty good. If the pipe and the needle are the ones we are looking for, and I know they are, Hunter was thinking to himself again, we might be getting closer to finding that kid. More, than someone wants us to. Damn, all we need is for someone to start talking. Soon, soon, thought Hunter. The S.I.U. boys took about half an hour to get things done. "Thanks," Hunter told the crew. "And, don't forget, don't tell anyone about this."

"You got it Sarge," they said and they drove away. Hunter looked at his watch. It was four a.m. Hunter headed for his apartment.

CHAPTER 31

The next day Bender and Fox got to work a little late. Hunter was already in his office. "Well boys, stay out too late last night?" Hunter grinned.

"Nope, but it took a little longer in the shower this morning."

"You mean you waited until this morning to take a shower?" Bender asked. "I was in the shower last night before I even had all my clothes off. Man, I'm glad it was dark when we were going through that garbage last night. That way, we didn't have to see half the things we were touching."

"You got that right," Fox said.

"O.K., if you guys are done making all the small talk, we have a lot of work to do here. When we were talking to Weaver last night, he told us to first check those garbage cans. We did that and might have come up with a winner. Then, he told us to check to see where Thompson was before they found his body. That's what I want you guys to do today. Try to track him down to the minute before he died. I'd say the best place to start would be Duke's Bar. The barmaid should be in by now. Check with her first and find out what she knows."

Bender and Fox headed for their car and drove to Duke's Bar. "Do you think we're getting any closer to this thing?" Bender asked Fox.

"Yes, I do," Fox said. "I think the Sarge is right about this case. That girl is alive and is with someone. The more tangled up it gets and the more people involved, the better it is for us. Sooner or later, someone will make that one mistake we need, and we will have a solved case."

Bender and Fox pulled up in front of Duke's. "Looks like it's open," Fox said. "Just our luck." They got out of the car and went inside.

"Man, this place never changes," Bender said. "It looks like the same glasses sitting on the bar since the last time we were here."

"Yeah, maybe this place is in a time warp," Fox said. Fatty was standing behind the bar.

"What do you guys want now? Duke's not here. So unless you came to drink, beat it!" Fatty told them.

"Wait a minute," Fox said. "We were just in the neighborhood and stopped by to see our favorite barmaid."

Fatty smiled at that and said, "Hey, maybe you guys ain't so bad after all."

Bender pulled a ten dollar bill out of his pocket and said, "Look Fatty, we ain't drinking now because we're on duty; but the next couple of guys that come in, buy them a drink on us."

"Sure will," Fatty said, as she put the ten down the front of her tee shirt. "Now, what do you guys really want?"

"What we are trying to do, Fatty," Fox said, "is find out exactly where Jimmy was before he died and who he was with. That's all. Now you told us you heard someone moving around upstairs the night before they found Jimmy, but you don't know for sure who it was. Right?"

"That's right," Fatty said. "The only thing I do know is that it wasn't Duke because he asked me if I had heard anything. Besides that, he told me later that he had gone out to some bar on West 65th and Detroit that night."

"Did it sound like there was more than one person upstairs?" Fox asked Fatty.

"I couldn't tell you that," Fatty said. "But, if you are trying to tie Duke into any of this, I can tell you you are wrong. Duke and Jimmy were the best of friends. Believe me on this one!"

"Sure, we believe you, Fatty. We just have to check around," Bender said. "You know how it is."

Bender and Fox left the bar and got into their car. There were four bars on the corner of West 65th and Detroit. "Just park the car, pick one, and we'll start there," Fox said. "By the way, Bender. I think you're starting to like that Fatty. Maybe if you hang around that joint long enough, you could get lucky.

"That's not all I would get," Bender said. "And, don't let me catch you hanging around there, I saw Fatty first." They both laughed as they got out of the car.

The two detectives tried the first bar without any luck. They were lucky at the second bar. The bartender knew Duke and said he had been in a few nights ago. "He came in by himself and sat in the corner. Later, two dudes came in and sat with Duke. They talked for a while and then left. Duke stayed, had a few more drinks, and then told me he was going out drinking and to see a few old friends.

Bender and Fox got back into their car. "The pretty much sounds like what Fatty told us," Fox said to Bender.

"Right," Bender replied, "but, let's stop back at Duke's and see if he is there. Let's just ask him who the two guys are that were with him at the bar."

Duke was just walking out of his apartment door when Fox and Bender pulled up. "Hey Duke," Bender said. "Come over here for a minute, will you?"

"What do you guys want? Man you're getting to be a real pain in the ass," duke said.

"Listen Duke, we've been checking up on you to see where you were the night Jimmy was killed. I mean died," Fox said. "All we want to know is, who were the two guys you get at the bar on West 65th and Detroit?"

"What two guys are you talking about? I didn't meet anybody at that bar. I was there by myself," Duke told them.

"Look Duke, we talked to the bartender. He told us two guys came over to your table and talked to you for a while. Then, they left. So, who were they?" Fox asked.

"Oh yeah, you guys mean the two fellows that walked over and talked to me. I never saw those guys before. All they did was ask me for some directions. All they wanted was directions," Duke said.

"Directions to where?" Fox asked.

"Hey man, I forget to where, but I can give some directions to you guys. Go to hell!" Duke said as he walked away from the car and into the bar.

"He's a real smart ass, don't you think?" Fox said to Bender.

"Not smart," Bender said, "just an ass." They pulled away and headed for the station.

Duke walked into the bar. "Fatty," he yelled. "Gimme a shot and a beer," Duke mumbled to himself. What the hell did those guys want now? That one asshole was pretending he slipped up when he said Jimmy was killed. What the hell, do those guys think I'm stupid? Man, playing that old trick on me, shit! Fatty brought the shot and beer to him. "What did those two guys ask you?" Duke asked Fatty.

"What guys?" Fatty asked him. "What the hell are you talking about Duke, or are you talking to your self?"

"God damn it Fatty," Duke yelled. "The cops, that's who. Did they ask you anything?"

"About what?" Fatty asked Duke.

"Quit the shit!" Duke said to Fatty. "Did they ask anything about me or Jimmy?"

"No, I haven't talked to them," Fatty said.

"That's good," Duke told her. "And, I don't want you talking to them, got it!"

"Sure, Duke. I got it from now on if they come in here I won't talk to them. Jesus, I think you're cracking up, Duke. Now, just leave me alone," Fatty said as she walked away.

Duke yelled after her, "Just bring me a bottle of whiskey and then you clean this damn place up, you hear me? Do those damn glasses."

"Sure Duke, sure," Fatty said.

Duke sat there thinking. Damn it, I know those guys killed Jimmy. They ain't fooling me. I hope I never see them again, that would be too soon. Just leave me alone everybody! Just leave me alone! Duke took a big swig out of the whiskey bottle and washed it down with a sip of beer.

Fatty stood behind the bar watching Duke. She thought, it won't be long before he's passed out. Well, that's all right. He can be such a pain in the ass when he's talking. Something's going on here, Fatty thought. I wonder what the hell it is? Whatever it is, Duke sure is shook up about it. Maybe, it has something to do with that girl of Jimmy's. Hey, maybe I can make some money off this deal. Let me think about this. Maybe, I shall talk to Marylou. Yeah, her and I did some drinking together. I'll just stop by and see her. With that thought in mind, Fatty started to do the glasses.

Duke was still drinking and thinking, although he was just barely able to lift the whiskey bottle up to his lips. Life is so shitty, he thought. Just when I thought I had a good deal going, that asshole Jimmy fucks up. Shit, if Jimmy would have got that twenty-five thousand dollars, it would have been as good as mine. Man, I could have gotten rid of this joint and headed for Florida, or some place warm. Yeah, I would have had it made in the shade. Now, all I have to look forward to is this God damn bar and sitting here, shit! Oh well, the more you drink, the less you remember, and there ain't too much I want to remember. One thing, I have to remember. Jimmy's funeral is tomorrow. Duke's head fell on the bar. He was out like a light.

CHAPTER 32

Bender and Fox were headed for the station when Fox said, "You know we never did check out those guys that were with Duke. I bet those are the two hoods Hunter wanted us to find out about."

"Right," Bender said, "but nobody seems to know who they are. But, I have an idea. Remember that little snitch we used to deal with? What the hell was his name? He used to hang around that playground by Lawn School."

"Hey, I remember," Fox said. "His name is Porky. Yeah, Porky. That's it. Come on. Let's take a ride up to the playground and see if he's there."

The two detectives pulled up to the gate of the playground, and there big as life was Porky sitting on one of the swings. "Man, things never change do they?" Fox said.

"I guess not," Bender answered. "Let's go talk to him. By the way, Fox. It's your turn to give him ten bucks."

"Man, we ought to have an expense account," Fox said. "Maybe, on the next contract we get."

Porky saw the two detectives walking toward him. "Hey you guys, long time no see. What's shakin'?"

"Same old thing, Porky, same old thing. What's new with you?" Bender asked.

"Well, I ain't been working much. Things are a little too hot around here right now. But, I found me a little old lady. She's got a couple of kids and gets welfare, so I got a roof over my head and food. That's about it."

"Listen, Porky, maybe you can help us," Fox pulled out a ten and held it out to Porky.

"Ten don't go far these days," Porky said. "Not like the good old days. But, maybe I can help. Shoot!"

"You know where Duke's Bar is?" Fox asked.

"You mean that joint down on Bridge Avenue? Hey, I know the joint, and I know the asshole who owns it, too. Man, what a creep!"

"Yeah," said Bender. "We know. Anyhow, there's two guys that have been seen around there. They look like two hoods. They might be small time bookies or at least bagmen for somebody. You got any ideas who they are?"

"Sure," Porky said. "I know exactly who they are."

"Well," Bender said. "Who are they?"

"Hey man, I told you things are bad. You know what I mean. One guy, one ten. Two guys, two tens. Come on boys, give old Porky another ten, and I'll give you all the info."

"This better be good," Fox said, "or you could lose both tens."

Porky grabbed the ten from Fox. "Shit man, easy money. Both the guys are small potatoes. All they are is collection guys, you know bagmen. They pick up bets at a few bars, sell a little dope, and buy some stolen shit. Nothing big."

"That's great," Bender said. "Now give us some names."

"Sure, no problem. One guy's name is Big Al and the other guy's name is Tony."

"Last names," Fox said.

"Hey man, I don't know no last names, but they're easy to find. They hang around some joint on West 117th and Clifton Avenue. Everyone in the joint knows them. Just ask around."

"Who do they work for?" Bender asked Porky.

"You know better than that. Don't ask me that kind of question," Porky said. "You find that out for yourself. I ain't mentioning any big names. Man, you get dead that way. Now you guys got your twenty bucks worth. Now, I ain't got no more to say but bye." Porky got off the swing and walked towards the playground gate.

"Nice fellow," Bender said.

"Yeah," Fox said. "Why don't you invite him to your house for dinner?"

"Funny, come on, let's go see if we can get some last names on those guys. Then, we can run some record checks." They got into the car and headed for West 117th and Clifton Avenue.

"Well, well," Fox said. "Nice place. Do we want valet parking, or should we park in the rear?"

"Valet, if you pay," Bender said. "In the rear, if I pay."

"In the back it is," Fox said.

Bender and Fox walked into the restaurant. "Check your coat?" Fox asked Bender.

"Fox, will you give me a break?" Bender moaned. "I can't stand all this comedy."

"What a grouch you are," Fox said. "Lighten up a little." They walked into the bar.

"The bartender looked at them and asked, "May I help you?"

"Sure, two cokes," Fox responded.

The bartender looked at them and said, "Really?"

"Really," Bender told him.

The bartender brought back the two cokes and set them on napkins in front of the two detectives. "That will be four dollars please."

"Do we get to keep the glasses?" Fox asked.

"No, but you do get a free refill if you order dinner," the bartender told them.

"No dinner, but we would like to ask you a few questions," Bender said as he reached into his pocket and flashed his badge.

"I don't do questions," the bartender said, "but, I'll get the manager for you." The bartender pushed a button under the bar and walked to the other end.

Almost immediately, a well-dressed man came from the back room. The bartender whispered in his ear and glanced over to the two detectives. The man shook his head and walked towards the detectives.

"Can I help you gentlemen?"

"Yes, you can," Bender said. "We'd just like to ask you a few questions."

"Fine, would you like to go back to my office?" The man asked.

"No, I think we can take care of it right here," Fox said. "We're looking for Big Al and Tony."

"Well, as you can see, they are not here. If that's all you want, you can probably find them at the car lot they own, he told them.

"And where might that be?" Fox asked.

"West 126th and Lorain Avenue. It's called B.A.T. Auto Sales." With that, he turned and walked away. He then stopped and looked back. "The cokes are on the house."

Bender pulled a five from his pocket and threw it on the bar. "Keep the change," Bender and Fox walked away.

Bender and Fox got into their car. "Man, both those guys pissed me off!" Bender said.

"I could tell when you threw that fiver on the bar," Fox said. "But, we did get our information. Well, part of it anyhow. They sure don't talk much, do they? Let's go up on Lorain and look for this car lot, B.A.T. I can't believe that's the name of the lot!"

When they got to West 126th and Lorain Avenue, they saw the car lot. B.A.T. BUY HERE PAY HERE. The office was an old trailer and there was one junk car parked in front of the office. Bender and Fox pulled into the lot, got out of the car, and walked over to the office. A sign on the door said OUT TO LUNCH. Bender looked in the window. There was one desk, a couple of chairs. That was about it. "It doesn't look like they do much business here, at least not car business," Bender said. They checked the mailbox on the front door and found a bunch of circulars, none with any names on them.

Next to the car lot was a brick building with two apartments up, a barber ship, and a real estate company down. "Let's try the barber shop and see if the barber knows who these guys are," Fox said.

The barber was watching out the window as they walked to the door. Fox and Bender walked into the sop. "Can I help you?"

"Is that car lot even open?" Fox asked the barber.

"Well," the barber responded, "I've seen the two guys that own it there, but I've never seen anyone buy a car there."

"Do you know who owns the lot?" Bender asked.

"Yes, I do," the barber said. They all stood there. The barber was looking at the two detectives and the two detectives were looking at the barber.

Bender shook his head and sighed, "Well, could you tell us?"

"Sure," the barber said, "Big Al and Tony own the lot."

"Do they have any last names?" Fox asked.

"No, I don't know their last names. They stop in here once in a while for a haircut, but they never told me their last names," the barber told them.

"Do you know where they live or anything else about them?" Bender asked.

"Sure, I know where they live," the barber said and looked at the detectives.

Bender shook his head again and asked, "Where do they live?"

"They live upstairs in Apartment #1. But, I can tell you that they are not home now." The barber went on. "I can tell when they are home though."

"How can you tell that?" Fox asked.

"I can hear them up there for one thing," the barber said. "The other way I can tell is that their car is parked in the lot."

"Hey, that's pretty good," Fox said. "Maybe, you should be a detective like us."

"Ha," the barber said. "I knew you guys were cops."

"How did you know that?" Bender asked.

"I saw you pull up in that unmarked car. I can tell those detective cars a mile away," the barber told them.

"I bet you can. Thanks for the information," Fox said.

"Anytime," the barber said. "Stop back for a haircut sometime."

"Let's check the mailbox for the apartments," Bender said. They lucked out. There were some letters in the Apartment #1 box. Some were addressed to a Albert Welsh, and some were addressed to an Anthony Russo.

"Good, that takes care of the last names," Fox said. "Now, we can go back to the station and run some record checks on those guys."

They headed back to their car. "Wait a minute," Bender said. "I want to tell the barber something." Bender went back to the barber shop and said to the barber. "You sure could help us if you didn't mention us being here to Big Al and Tony."

"Sure," said the barber. "Mum's the word."

"One other thing," Bender said. "When's the last time you saw those two guys?"

"Oh, I'd say at least three or four days ago," the barber told him.

"Thanks," Bender said.

Fox pulled the car up in front of the barber shop and Bender jumped in. He looked back and saw the barber watching out the window and waving. Bender waved back. They headed for the station.

When Fox and Bender got back to the station, Hunter called them into his office. "How did you make out?" he asked Fox and Bender.

Fox and Bender told Hunter the story of what had happened. "Good," said Hunter. "Maybe, we are getting some place now. These pieces have to fit somewhere in this puzzle. Now, give those names to the office man so he can run the checks on them. You guys pick up that pipe and needle from the evidence room and take them to the morgue. Talk to Dr. Levi. I already talked to him about what I want and he will do it. Then, he'll keep the papers in his desk for a couple of days until we see what we can do. Jimmy's funeral is tomorrow, so Levi has to run the tests today before he releases the body."

Fox and Bender left to go to the morgue. They were gone for about an hour. When they got back, the office man had the reports on Big Al and Tony. "O.K., Hunter said, "let's take a look at the records on these two bums."

Big Al's report was first. Albert Welsh, white male, forty-three years old. AKA Big Al. one D.W.I., three Disorderly Conducts, three Assaults, five Traffic. "Not too bad," Hunter said. "The charges on all three assaults were dropped.

Anthony, Tony, Russo, white male, forty years old, five Assaults, one Disorderly Conduct, one Traffic. That's it," Hunter said. "All the charges on the assaults were dropped. We'll get back to these guys later," Hunter said.

"Right now, I want to talk to you about tomorrow. Jimmy's funeral is going to be at one p.m. at the, if you can believe this, THE MASTER'S TOUCH, the Reverend H. Weathers presiding."

"Oh, Jesus," Fox said. "I bet that would make Jimmy real happy." Just then, the phone rang.

Hunter answered it. "Yeah, no kidding, thanks a lot Doc. That was Doc Levi from the morgue. He said the blood type on the pipe matches Jimmy's but there was no hair on the pipe."

"How about the needle?" Bender asked.

"He didn't run the test on that yet," Hunter said. "He did tell me the funeral home picked up Jimmy's body, Sauers Funeral Home. They are going to make all the arrangements to have the body cremated. We'll all go to the service tomorrow just to mix in with the crowd and see if we hear anything that might help us. I don't want you to ask any questions," Hunter continued. "Just listen and look around."

CHAPTER 33

Hunter, Bender, and Fox arrived at the storefront church about ten to one. They walked inside the place and saw about fifteen card table chairs set up in front of a makeshift altar. In front of the altar was a small table with an urn sitting on it. Behind, and on either side were two sprays reading: My Beloved Husband; the other read, Our Beloved Father. "I think I'm going to puke," Fox said.

There were not many people there. There might have been about fifteen people or so. There was Patty, Marylou's girlfriend; Duke and Fatty; a couple of old winos from Duke's bar, about four guys who helped Jimmy now and again whenever he had enough work; the three detectives; the funeral director; and, of course, Hermy.

At exactly one o'clock, Hermy went up to the altar and motioned for everyone to be seated.

Hermy gave a short eulogy, and the service ended with the singing of Rock Of Ages, everyone off-key. Then, Hermy said, "The family wishes everyone to stay and partake of cookies and beverage."

"Do we have to stay?" Fox asked Hunter.

"Yes, you both have to stay," Hunter said. "I told you I want you to mix with the crowd."

"Sure," Bender said. "It's a nice crowd. We might be able to make some friends to hang around with." Fox and Bender each moved off in different directions.

Marylou came over to Hunter. "Thank you for coming today. That was nice of you and your two men. As you can see by looking around, Jimmy didn't have many friends. But, he must have had one good friend."

"Why? What makes you say that?" Hunter asked.

Marylou replied, "Mr. Sauers called me and said that he had received a phone call from someone who said they would pay for the funeral bill."

"Is that right?" Hunter said. "That's good for Jimmy. At least, he left here without owing for his own funeral!" Hunter walked away looking for Mr. Sauers.

Hunter saw Mr. Sauers standing over by the door. Hunter walked over. "Hello Mr. Sauers, I'm Sergeant Hunter from the Police Department."

Mr. Sauers held out his hand. "How are you Sergeant?"

"Fine," Hunter said. "I wonder if you can help me with something."

"Sure, what is it?" Mrs. Sauers asked Hunter.

"I understand someone other than the family is paying for the funeral bill," Hunter said.

"That's right, Sergeant," Mr. Sauers said. "It was rather unusual the way it was arranged, but there are times when people wish to remain anonymous."

"Just how was this arranged?" Hunter asked.

"Well, yesterday morning I received a call, and the party asked about the arrangements for the Thompson funeral. I told them, and then they asked me if payment had been arranged yet. I told them no, there were no payments yet. They then said if the body was to be cremated, they would pay the bill. I told them that I could not guarantee that, but I would call Marylou and advise her of our conversation. I asked if he would leave his name and number so that I could contact him with Marylou's answer. He said no, but he would call me back in an hour. I said fine and hung up. I immediately contacted Marylou and told her what the man had said."

"Well," Hunter asked. "What did Marylou tell you?"

Mr. Sauers cleared his throat. "Marylou said if someone would pay for the funeral, I could burn the body in the backyard, just bring the ashes to the church. Then awhile later, the man called back. I told him the family would be pleased to have the funeral paid for and that they did not object to cremation. The man asked me how much. I told him, and he said the money would be there in an hour. Sure enough, about an hour later, my bell rang and there was a man at the door who handed me an envelope. Inside was a cashier's check for the full amount."

"Did you recognize the man who delivered the check, or the voice on the phone?" Hunter asked.

"No, neither one," Mr. Sauers said.

Hunter made some small talk with Mr. Sauers and then excused himself to get some coffee. He looked around the room and saw Fox and Bender talking to some people. He also saw Fatty and Marylou talking together. They sure looked like two old buddies talking over good times, Hunter thought. Marylou was shaking her head up and down, and Fatty was talking like crazy. I wonder what they have to say to each other that could take so long. Maybe, I'll work my way over there and eavesdrop a little. As Hunter was starting over to them, he saw Duke headed for them. He was near enough when Duke got there to see him grab Fatty by the arm and say to her, "Come on, let's go, you got to get back to work!" Duke led her out by the arm never saying a word to Marylou.

Marylou yelled after them, "See you later, Fatty."

Fatty looked around and shook her head yes. Hunter walked over to Marylou. "Duke's not too friendly, is he?"

"That fat slob," Marylou said. "I hate that guy. I never could see why Jimmy hung around with him. He makes my skin crawl!"

"Do you know Fatty?" Hunter asked Marylou.

"Sure, her and I go back a long way. It was long before she started working for that slob Duke."

Hunter told Marylou he was leaving and she thanked him again for coming.

Hunter motioned to Bender and Fox. They followed Hunter out the door. "Any luck?" Hunter asked Fox and Bender.

"Naw," Fox said. "Just those old timers bitching because there was no booze in the place. They said, 'Jimmy wouldn't have been too happy about that.'"

"I didn't hear anything either," Bender told Hunter. "At least I didn't hear anything that might help us."

"It was just a shot in the dark anyhow," Hunter said. "The only thing I saw that was interesting was the long talk Marylou and Fatty were having. While they were talking, Duke came over and dragged Fatty away from Marylou, telling her she had to get back to work. He never said one word to Marylou, which I thought was a little odd."

"Remember Sarge, we're dealing with some pretty odd people here," Bender said.

"Let's go back to the station and see if anything new popped up on those two hoods," Hunter told them.

CHAPTER 34

After the service, Marylou and Hermy were cleaning up the church and talking about the day's events. "Hermy, go in the back and get us a couple of beers, will you?" Marylou asked.

"Sure will," Hermy said. "I think we deserve a few beers. As a matter of fact, I got a bottle hid in the back that I was saving for a special occasion, and I think this is it!"

"You sure are a good boy, Hermy, now get going on the double." Marylou sat down by one of the little tables and waited for Hermy.

Hermy came back with the beer, a couple of glasses, and some ice. He poured each of them a glass of whiskey and opened up two beers. Hermy and Marylou each drank a good shot of whiskey and washed it down with a swig of beer. "Man, this hits the spot," Hermy sighed and then said, "Marylou how much money did we get?"

Marylou looked at him and said, "You greedy little son of a bitch. My husband just died and all you can think of is money?" Then, she started to laugh. She got her purse and pulled out the cards she had received. "Here Hermy, help me open these cards, but mind, I'm watching you. If you try to short change me, I'll break your God damn arm!"

Hermy laughed, "Marylou, the way you carry on, and in church, too, my, my."

It didn't take them long to go through the cards and Marylou wasn't too happy. "Son of a bitch!" She hollered. "Those cheap bastards. What the hell is this world coming to? A lousy sixty bucks, that's all we got? Look at this, that God damn Duke, a card with five dollars in it. After all the money he stole from Jimmy, I can't believe this. And another thing," Marylou bitched, "those fucking cops didn't even give me a card. What the hell did they want here? Well Hermy, fuck all of them. Let's you and me get good and drunk!" And, that's just what they did. Marylou and Hermy finished the beer and the bottle of whiskey. The only thing left was some ice. Marylou woke up at three-thirty in the morning still sitting at the table. She looked over and saw Hermy lying on the floor with his pants down around his ankles. What a sorry sight, Marylou thought as she got up. I wonder if we did anything last night. Well, it won't do any good to ask him. He would never remember. That's the way it always is. Let the little bastard sleep on the floor, I'm going back to bed.

Marylou went to bed, but couldn't get to sleep. I have to talk to that bitch, Fatty. I wonder what she knows. The way she was talking; she thinks I know more than I do. I'll have to be cool with her. Maybe, I can find out what the hell is going on. She said something about getting money. Well, that always interests me. I'm sure I can outsmart that Fatty. She never was too bright. With that on her mind, Marylou fell asleep.

She felt Hermy crawling into bed. "What the hell time is it, Hermy?" Marylou moaned.

"It's almost eight o'clock in the morning. How come you let me sleep on the floor? It was getting cold out there. Did we do anything last night?" Hermy asked.

"We sure did Hermy, we sure did," Marylou told him. "And, it was great for me. How about you Hermy?"

"Yeah, now I remember," Hermy smiled. "No wonder I'm so tired!"

"Hermy, don't get into this bed now. I'm hungry, and I want some breakfast now. So go fix me some bacon and eggs, and put the coffee on, all right?"

"Oh come on, Marylou, give me a break, will you?" Hermy asked.

"You got your break last night Hermy," Marylou lied. "Remember? Now, go fix my breakfast."

"O.K., Marylou, you win," Hermy said. "Do you want breakfast in bed or in the kitchen?"

"In bed," Marylou cooed.

While Hermy was out in the kitchen fixing breakfast, Marylou picked up the phone at the side of the bed and dialed Fatty's number. The phone rang five times she hear a sleepy voice.

"Who the hell is this? Do you have any idea what time it is?"

"Fatty, it's me, Marylou."

"Oh yeah, but why did you have to call so early in the morning?" Fatty asked.

"You said you wanted to talk to me. Tell me where and when," Marylou said.

"How about meeting me at the bar?" Fatty asked her.

"I don't want to go there," Marylou said. "I'd hate to run into Duke; I hate him. Why not your place?"

"No," Fatty said. "I have to be at work at ten, so I won't have time to talk to you before that."

"We can't talk here," Marylou told Fatty. "I don't want Hermy to know I'm meeting you. The less he knows, the better."

"Listen," Fatty said. "Why don't you meet me at the bar around two o'clock this afternoon? Usually, no one is in there then, and Duke was so drunk last night, he probably won't come down until later at night.

"That sounds good to me," Marylou told her. "I'll meet you around two this afternoon. See you then." Marylou just hung up the phone when Hermy came in with some coffee.

"Breakfast will be served shortly," Hermy said.

Hermy and Marylou were sitting on the edge of the bed eating and Marylou said, "You know Hermy, I got to go see my kids. I haven't seen them in a couple of weeks, and you know how pissed off Patty gets. I'll go see them and give Patty fifty bucks. That way, I can leave them there for a while longer without any bullshit from Patty."

"Sure," Hermy said. "I'll go with you and after that, we can go for a few drinks."

"No, no," Marylou shook her head. "I'm going to go alone; that way, I can spend some time with my kids and Patty and I can talk for a while, you know, some girl talk."

"I guess that would be all right," Hermy said in his whiny voice. "But don't be too late, will you?"

"No," Marylou said. "I'll be back early."

Marylou finished breakfast and got up to get ready to go. She took a bath and got dressed. All the time, Hermy was moping around. He was not happy at all. "Why do you have to get all dressed up to go see your kids?" he asked.

"Hermy, will you relax? I'm just going to Patty's, that's all. Man, I can't be with you all the time. Don't you have anything to do while I am gone? Why don't you clean this place up and maybe when I get back, I'll have a nice surprise for you!"

"O.K.," Hermy grinned. "You know how I like surprises."

Marylou left the house and got into her car. First, I'll go to Patty's just in case that little weasel checks up on me and I know he will.

Marylou got over to Patty's and knocked on the door. Patty looked out and open the door swearing. "Where the hell have you been? Marylou, you know I'm sick of watching these kids for you. You haven't been here for weeks! Hell, I couldn't say anything to you at Jimmy's funeral because I didn't think it would be right. But, God damn it Marylou, you're taking advantage of me again."

"I'm sorry, Patty," Marylou said. "But come on, let's talk and get things fixed up." Patty and Marylou went into Patty's kitchen.

"I can't stay too long Patty," Marylou told her. "I have to meet someone at two o'clock."

"Oh, don't tell me you're cheating on little Hermy already?" Patty said.

"Not yet, but in due time," Marylou said. "He's such a little piss pot." They both laughed.

About an hour after Marylou got there, the phone rang. "I'll bet money Hermy is calling to check up on me," Marylou said. "I thought he would call before now."

Patty answered the phone, "Yeah, she's here." Patty turned to Marylou. "It's him," and she giggled.

After Marylou talked to Hermy, she gave Patty the fifty dollars and told her she would pick the kids up this weekend. "If Hermy calls, tell him I can't come to the phone right now, and then call me at Duke's Bar. Thank you, Patty. I owe you one. See you later."

Marylou got to Duke's Bar about two-thirty that afternoon. She was more than satisfied with her talk with Patty, knowing that all Patty needed was a little attention once in a while, and then Marylou could leave her kids with Patty for another week or two with no problem.

Marylou parked her car in the back alley. In case Hermy came driving around the neighborhood, maybe he wouldn't see it. Marylou really dreaded going into the bar because she hated Duke so much and didn't want to run into him.

Marylou opened the door to go in. She stopped and looked around. One customer was sitting at the bar. Fatty was standing behind the bar. It had probably been at least three years ago when she had been in here, and she had been with Jimmy at that time.

Fatty looked up and saw Marylou standing by the door. She walked from behind the door and waved Marylou over to a table near the back.

"How are you doing Fatty?" Marylou asked.

"I'm fine," Fatty said. "Can I get you some coffee or something?"

Marylou laughed and said, "Now Fatty, you know I'd rather have the 'or something' so get me a beer for starters."

"Good," said Fatty. "That's what I'll have too, and this afternoon will be on Duke." They both laughed as Fatty went to get the drinks.

Fatty came back with the beer and two glasses and set them on the table. Marylou picked up her glass and held it up to the light to see if it was clean.

"Don't worry," Fatty told her. "These two glasses I keep for my friends and me! I don't let anyone else use them."

The two women sat at the table making small talk for a while and then Marylou said, "Look Fatty, what did you want to talk to me about?"

"It's kind of hard to tell you because I only pick up bits and pieces here and there; you know, things that I've heard Duke say and things I heard Jimmy say. It seems to me like they had some kind of deal going on."

"What the hell are you talking about?" Marylou butted in. "I really don't care about any deals those two had, they never panned out anyway!"

"Marylou, I don't know if you are bullshitting me or not, but I know something about what was going on. Now, if you know about it, I want a cut in it. If you don't know about it, then maybe there's a chance we can make us some money."

"God damn it, Fatty. That's all well and good, but will you please tell me what the hell you are talking about?" Marylou asked.

"Damn it, Marylou. I'm talking about your girl, Noreen. Did you forget about her or what?" Fatty was getting mad.

"No, I didn't forget about her, but I still don't know what the hell you are talking about! Do you know where she is or something? Tell me, will you?" Marylou was starting to yell.

"O.K.," Fatty said. "Let's calm down. I'll get us a couple more beers and then we can talk about this."

Fatty went to get the beer and Marylou sat there thinking. What the hell does she know? If it's some deal to make money, I have to find out what the hell is going on. If that Duke and Jimmy were involved in this thing, it's probably all fucked up by now. Jesus, maybe Jimmy wasn't lying to me about Noreen, maybe, they did sell her. That would be good. I know he was talking about that twenty-five thousand dollars. Man, I could do a lot with that kind of money. Her thoughts were interrupted with the return of Fatty with the beers. Fatty set the beers down on the table and then pulled her chair over closer to Marylou and sat down.

"I don't know what you know, Marylou. I'm going to tell you what I've heard, and what I can put together," Fatty said. "Then, I hope you will do the same with me and not lie to me."

"O.K.," Marylou said to Fatty. "You got a deal."

"Well," Fatty said. "The best I can figure out is that Duke and Jimmy were in partnership to collect some money from two guys that took Noreen. Now, I think that the two guys were those two that come in here in suits. They come here to collect the bets that Duke takes. They look like real hoods, you know the type. I think their names are Big Al and Tony. Now, I never really heard them talking about taking Noreen, and I really don't know who took her or where she is. The best as I can put together is what I just told you. Now, tell me what you know, and let's see what we can do together."

Marylou thought for a minute then said to Fatty, "I really don't know more than that. As a matter of fact, I didn't know as much as you just told me. All I know is that one time Jimmy had mentioned selling Noreen, but that was all he ever said. Oh yeah, he once said after Noreen was gone that someday him and me would be together and move away from here, but nothing came of it."

Fatty reached across the table and grabbed Marylou's hand. "How about being partners?" Fatty asked.

"Good idea," replied Marylou. "Let's make some plans and that planning can start with that asshole Duke. You leave him to me Fatty, I owe him."

"That sounds good to me," Fatty said as he squeezed Marylou's hand. "And I'd like to take care of you some day."

My Baby My Baby!

Marylou laughed and said, "Fatty, that might not be a bad idea, someday."

The two women sat at the table drinking beer and talking about old times. After a couple of hours, they switched to shots and beers. Then after a few of those, they switched to whiskey and coke. By eight o'clock, they were both pretty drunk. That was about the time Duke made his entrance.

Duke had been sleeping most of the day up in his apartment. He had not gone to bed until about nine that morning. After Jimmy's funeral, he got drunk, drinking with a few of the old timers that had gone to the funeral. He was talking to them about the times Jimmy and he had had, the good and the bad. Now, it seemed like all the times were good ones.

When Duke walked in the door of the bar and saw Marylou and Fatty sitting together, his first thought was; What the hell are they planning? I know those two are up to no good. He went over to the table and said, "What the hell are you doing here?"

Fatty laughed and said, "I work here you dummy!"

"Not you," Duke yelled. "I mean her!"

"Hey Duke, how are you?" Marylou said. "Me and Fatty are just having a few drinks and talking about the old days."

"First of all Marylou. You don't care how I am," Duke said. "And second of all, if you want to talk to Fatty, talk to her on her own time!"

"Oh come on Duke, sit down," Marylou said. "I'll even buy you a drink." Well, Duke never was one to pass up a drink, so he flopped down in a chair and told Fatty to bring him a scotch and soda. Hell, if this dumb broad was buying, he was drinking top shelf.

Duke watched Fatty go to get the drinks and could tell that she was done working for the night. Shit, in about half an hour, the place would be busier than hell with the guys coming in from playing ball. Duke backed a softball team and they came in once a week after the game to drink.

Oh well, let Fatty get him a drink or two, and then he would tend bar. He was thinking; if Fatty and Marylou drank enough, maybe they would get drunk and he could get a shot at that bitch Marylou. Jimmy was always bragging about what a good piece she was. She looked a little too fat for Duke, but hell, fat broads need fucking, too. Duke laughed a little to himself and grabbed his crotch.

"What the hell are you laughing about?" Marylou asked Duke.

"I was just thinking about us sitting here having a drink together," Duke said.

"Well don't think too much about it," Marylou said to him.

Fatty came back with the drinks. Duke lifted his glass to Marylou. "To us," he said.

"In a pig's eye," Marylou shot back and all three of them laughed as they drank up.

They had a couple more drinks and Duke could see Fatty and Marylou were well on their way. Marylou was even joking with Duke. Duke got up from the table and told the girls he would keep the drinks coming and to have a good time, he would work the bar.

Fatty said, "Thanks Duke," and Duke went behind the bar.

"Hey Fatty," Marylou said. "Maybe that Duke ain't such a bad guy after all."

"We'll see," Fatty said and started to laugh. "Maybe him and you can get together."

"Maybe, we will have to," Marylou said. "That is if we want to make some money."

"I just hope it's worth it," Fatty said.

"Hell," Marylou said, "I've been giving it away all this time for nothing. Now maybe this time, I can get paid for it, and I'm sure it's worth twenty-five thousand dollars."

"I bet it is," Fatty leered.

"We better have another drink," Marylou said to Fatty. "I got to get my mind on Duke."

It seemed to Duke that the bar was busier than it had been in years. The softball team and all their friends had come tonight and they had won, very unusual. Everyone was buying drinks and replaying the game inning by inning. Duke was feeling good; not only from the drinks, but because the bar was doing a great business. He kept glancing over at the table where Marylou and Fatty were sitting. The more he looked at Marylou, the more he thought about getting her in bed.

In the meantime, Marylou and Fatty were doing all right by themselves. The guys from the team were crowding around the table buying the girls drinks. Soon, the money was flying into the juke box and the songs were rolling out. Marylou and Fatty were dancing with all the guys, those that were not dancing were singing.

CHAPTER 35

It was one in the morning and the joint was starting to slow down a bit. Most of the guys from the softball team had left, just a few hard-core drinkers were hanging on. Marylou and Fatty were sitting back at the table talking and the juke box was playing slow country ballads. Duke was sitting behind the bar having a drink with the boys. Every once in a while he would glance over at Marylou and smile. If Marylou happened to be looking at Duke, she would smile back. Fatty did not miss what was going on and said to Marylou, "Do I see a trap being set here?"

"That you do," Marylou said. "That you do, Fatty, a trap to catch a rat worth twenty-five thousand dollars!"

"Well," Fatty said. "If you were the bait, that rat should be biting pretty soon. Oh boy, I wish I were the bait!" Fatty winked at Marylou.

The quiet didn't last too long because just about the time Fatty finished winking at Marylou, the door burst open and in come Hermy!

Hermy ran right to the table Marylou was sitting at, grabbed her by the hair, and pulled her out of the chair screaming, "You dirty rotten whore. Where the hell have you been all night? I've been looking all over for you! You son of a bitch, I should fucking kill you! I knew damn well right I couldn't trust you! I have to stay with you all the time! Why did you lie to me?" With that, Hermy punched Marylou right in the face. The blood flew from her nose like water.

Duke ran from behind the bar and grabbed Hermy by the shoulder, spun him around, and punched him in the face. He gave him a right to the stomach and an upper cut to the jaw, and old Hermy was out for the count. Duke picked Hermy up and threw him out the door in the middle of Bridge Avenue. Duke went back into the bar and locked the door.

Fatty had given Marylou a wet rag and was holding it to Marylou's face. "Get some ice," she told Duke, "and bring it over here!" Duke ran to get the ice.

"I'll be all right!" Marylou said.

"Sure, she will," Fatty said. "Just get the ice so we can keep the swelling down!"

Duke brought the ice back to Fatty, who put it in a rag and gave it to Marylou to hold on her nose. "Can you imagine that little bastard hitting me like that?" Marylou mumbled through the rag. "I just can't believe him!"

"Duke, go get us some drinks," Fatty said. "Me and Marylou got to have us some women talk here."

Duke got each of them a shot and a beer and went back behind the bar. He poured the guys that were still there a drink and said, "Look boys, this one is on me. Then, you got to hit the road cause I'm gonna close up."

"Here's to you, Duke." The boys drank up and Duke let them out the door and locked it back up. When Duke let them out, he didn't see Hermy anywhere.

Duke headed back to the table to sit down, but Fatty stopped him and told him to get more drinks for Marylou and her. Duke brought the drinks to the table and Fatty said, "Duke, will you please go clean up the bar or something? Marylou and I want to be alone for a while."

Duke went behind the bar and poured himself a drink and started to wipe up the bar. Duke finished cleaning up the bar and doing all the glasses; all the time pouring himself drinks and looking over at the table where the two girls were deep in conversation.

About three-thirty, Duke took drinks over to the table for himself and the girls. "Well, how's it going?" he asked them.

"O.K., Duke, but I really wish you would leave us alone," Fatty said.

"Hey, listen!" Duke said, "This is my place and it's past closing time. So if you want to sit here and talk, I sit with you. I mean, I saved your life Marylou. The least you could do is sit here with me and have a few drinks."

"Sure," Marylou said, "no problem, but I better not stay too long. I want to go home and kick the shit out of Hermy!" Duke and Fatty both laughed.

"You know, you can stay here with me if you are scared to go home," Duke told Marylou.

"Scared!" Marylou said. "If anyone is scared, it better be poor little Hermy!"

The three of them sat at the table for a few more drinks. About four-thirty, Marylou said, "I better get going. My car is out back; maybe you could walk me out there. What do you say Duke?"

"Sure, no problem," Duke said. "Where are you parked Fatty?"

"My car is in the back, also, so you can walk us both out," Fatty said.

"Oh, lucky me," Duke said as he took a girl on each arm and walked out the door.

Duke, Fatty, and Marylou came around the corner of the building where the cars were parked. They all stopped at the same time. There sat Marylou's car, or what was left of it. The windshield was broken out along with all the other windows of the car. All four tires were flat. The headlights and taillights were smashed out.

"That little son of a bitch!" Marylou screamed. "I'll kill that little fucker!"

"Easy, Marylou, take it easy," Duke said. "You stay the night with me."

"Don't be such an ass," Fatty said to Duke. "She can go home with me. At least, she'll be safe there."

"I don't know about that!" Duke replied. "You might be just as dangerous as me if you get this pretty thing alone!"

"Get lost Duke. Is that all you ever got on your mind? Come on Marylou, honey. Old Fatty will take care of you." Fatty took Marylou to her car, helped her in, and they pulled out of the parking lot.

Duke watched them go and headed back to go up to his apartment. Shit, I almost had her staying here, Duke thought. I have to work on her. Yeah, I've got to find out what makes her as good as she says she is. Hell, Jimmy would like me taking care of his widow. I mean after all, what are friends for? Duke got undressed and crawled into his bed. He went right to sleep thinking about the good luck he was having with the business at the bar being so good, and then having Marylou stop in. Yes, yes, lucky me, Duke thought. Little did he know what was in store for him. Well, maybe it was better he didn't know.

Marylou sat in Fatty's car with her head against the window and her eyes closed. She was thinking about Hermy. He had never shown her a mean streak before. Maybe, he was just drunk. Even so, look at

My Baby My Baby!

the damage he did to my car. It looked like a madman had done that. Marylou turned to Fatty and said, "Fatty, let's drive by Hermy's place and see if he is at home."

"I don't know about that, Marylou," Fatty said. "Suppose he sees us and starts some more trouble? Maybe, we should just let him sleep it off and then you can talk to him in the morning."

"We'll just drive by and see if he is there," Marylou said.

"Well, all right, but I'm not going to let you go in the house," Fatty said to Marylou.

Fatty pulled up in front of THE MASTER'S TOUCH.

"Stop right here," Marylou said. "I can see if the lights are on in the back." Marylou rolled down her window and stuck her head out. "I can hear loud music on the TV. He must be in there." Just as Marylou finished saying that, she felt something grab her hair! Jesus!" she yelled. She was being pulled through the window of the car!

Hermy was yelling, "You son of a bitch! You whore! I got you now, and I'm going to kill you!"

Marylou was hanging part way out the car window and Hermy was still pulling her. "Fatty! Fatty help me!" Marylou screamed.

At first, Fatty just sat there with her mouth hanging wide open. She could hear both Marylou and Hermy screaming. Marylou's feet were kicking the seat of the car.

Fatty grabbed one of Marylou's feet and gave the car the gas. Fatty almost lost Marylou out the window, but then she heard a loud scream and Marylou flew back into the car!

"God damn it, Fatty, you almost ripped me in half!" Marylou screamed.

They could hear Hermy screaming, "Get back here you bitch! I'm going to kill you!"

"Should we go back?" Fatty asked Marylou, and they both started laughing hysterically.

Fatty had to pull the car over to the curb because she was laughing so hard. "I'm sorry, Marylou. I can't help it. All I could see were your feet hanging on the seat and hear you screaming like a hurt cat."

"Jesus, he scared the shit out of me!" Marylou said. "I didn't even see him. Hell, I think he pulled my hair out! Man, that son of a bitch is crazy! I think I will go to your house and stay, if that's o.k.? That

Hermy just might kill me. To tell the truth, I'm afraid of him right now. When he sobers up, I'll get even with that little shit! I have a good idea. As soon as we get to your house, I'm going to call the police!"

Sure enough, when Marylou got to Fatty's house, she went straight to the phone to call the police. She gave the police Hermy's address and said she was a neighbor. She said, "There is a crazy man here, and he has a gun! He's threatening to shoot anyone that comes near him! Uh, oh! He's shooting now!" Marylou hung up the phone. "That will get him," Marylou said. "The cops come right away if they think someone has a gun." Marylou and Fatty started to laugh again.

"Boy, what a night!" Fatty said. "Let me get us a couple of beers just for a night cap. We need them!"

Fatty and Marylou had a few night caps and talked about Hermy and a little about Duke. "It's getting late," Fatty said. "How about if we hit the hay? We are going to have plenty of time to talk, but I think we could both use some sleep now."

"Right," Marylou said. "Get me a pillow and some blankets and I'll camp out on the couch."

"O.K., but you really could sleep in the bed with me. It would be a lot cozier," Fatty cooed.

"I bet it would be," Marylou smiled. "But right now, I need some sleep. So let's do it this way."

"Sure," Fatty said. "But it never hurts to try."

CHAPTER 36

Hunter had come to work early this morning. Actually, he had just left Rosie's. There was no sense going home at five thirty in the morning. What the hell! He could get off work early and go home to catch some sleep. Of course, if he wasn't tired, he could get off work and go to Rosie's for lunch…Good idea, he thought. That way, he could leave Rosie's early and get a good night's sleep. That's exactly what he had planned last night. Oh well, the best laid plans, etc.

Hunter was walking down the hall when one of the patrolmen going off duty from the night shift hollered, "Hey Sarge, hold on a minute, will you? I have something that might interest you."

"Sure," Hunter said, "what do you have?"

"You know that Hermy from THE MASTER'S TOUCH?" The patrolman asked.

"Yeah, what about him?" Hunter asked.

"Well, we got a call last night; man with a gun shooting. So, we get there, and all we find is this Hermy sitting in the doorway crying." The patrolman went on, "He had a handful of hair in his hand, and he kept crying over and over again, 'she left me, she left me for that fat slob Duke.'"

"Are you sure that's what he was saying?" Hunter asked.

"Yeah, for sure," the patrolman said. "He said it over and over again. So, we took old Hermy in the back to his house and put him in bed. We tried to take the hair out of his hand, but he had a death grip on it, so he went to bed still holding on to it."

"Was Marylou around?" Hunter asked.

"You mean that girlfriend of his? No, nobody was there but poor Hermy," the patrolman said.

"O.K., thanks a lot," hunter told him. "Anytime you guys have any calls involving any of those people, let me know."

"Sure Sarge," the patrolman said, "no problem."

Hunter went back to his office and told Fox and Bender what the patrolman had told him.

"You know," Fox said. "Maybe something is going to happen here and give us the break we need."

"Could be," Hunter said. "But right now, I want you two to go and talk to Hermy. See if you can find Duke. Maybe Marylou will be with him."

"We're on our way," Bender said.

Fox and Bender got into the car and headed for THE MASTER'S TOUCH to see Hermy. "I'm telling you," Bender said. "This is like one of those soap operas."

"It sure is," Fox replied. "It's not the average case."

"Yeah," Bender said. "Someone should write a book about this one."

"Hell, every copper says he is going to write a book," Fox laughed. "But, they never do."

"Maybe it's just as well," Bender said as they pulled up to THE MASTER'S TOUCH.

Fox and Bender walked to the back door. They could hear some music playing, some western song about losing my girl.

The door was wide open, but Fox knocked anyway. They waited at the door, but got no response. Fox knocked louder and hollered, "Hey Hermy, are you in there?" There was no answer. "What do you think?" Fox asked Bender. "Think we should go in?"

"What the hell," Bender said. "The door is open." They walked into the kitchen and looked into the living room. There was no one. They crossed the living room and pushed open the bedroom door. There lying across the bed was Hermy, fully dressed and snoring away.

"What the hell does he have in his hand?" Fox asked. "It looks like a wig."

"It's a handful of hair," Bender said. "But for sure, it ain't his."

Fox leaned over Hermy. "Man, he smells like he drank a ton of booze. We may not be able to wake him up." Fox shook Hermy and called out his name. Hermy didn't move. Fox shook him harder and yelled, "Hermy wake up!" Hermy woke up all right. He grabbed Fox, pulled him onto the bed and started kissing him!

Hermy was saying; "Oh Marylou, I knew you would come back to me, I love you, I love you."

Fox was yelling, "Let me go you son of a bitch! Let me go!"

At first, Bender thought that Hermy had attacked Fox and he reached for his gun. When he saw what was happening, he started to laugh. By now, Hermy had Fox pinned beneath him. He was kissing Fox and telling him how much he loved him.

"Help me! Bender, God damn it, help me!" Fox yelled from underneath Hermy.

Bender couldn't help anyone. He was leaning against the wall and laughing so hard, the tears were running down his face.

Fox got one hand free and slapped Hermy across the face.

"Don't hit me Marylou," Hermy said. "I'm sorry, I'm go glad you're back."

Fox kicked Hermy in the groin with is knee, and with his free hand, he shoved Hermy off the bed and onto the floor. Fox jumped up from the bed spitting and rubbing his face.

"If you give me any kind of germs, I'll kill you!" Fox yelled.

Hermy looked up from the floor. "What happened to Marylou! He asked. "I just had her in my arms and now she's gone again!"

Bender let out a hoot, he could not stop laughing.

Fox grabbed Hermy and yanked him up from the floor. "Get out in the living room you little shit."

Hermy, wide-eyed, ran for the couch. Fox looked over at Bender, who was still leaning against the wall holding his stomach and laughing.

"God damn it, Bender. Why the fuck didn't you help me!" Fox exclaimed.

"You looked like you were enjoying it!" Bender howled. "At least, Hermy was."

"Bender, this is not funny, and if you tell anyone about this, I'll kill you. Bender, quit laughing!" Fox said. "I'm not kidding!" Fox stormed from the room and went outside.

Bender walked out to the living room where Hermy was sitting on the couch. "Man, you are in some big trouble with that man. You better be nice to him when he comes back, but not too nice." Bender started laughing again.

It was a full ten minutes before Fox walked back into the house. Hermy was still sitting on the couch staring and Bender was sitting in a chair. Bender looked at Fox, put his hand up to his mouth, and started giggling.

"Bender, will you give me a break?" Fox said, but he didn't sound as angry as before.

"O.K.," Bender said, "I'll try my best. Perhaps you should talk to Hermy. I don't think I can." Bender got up from the chair. "I'll go talk to the neighbors while you talk to Hermy."

"Thanks," Fox said and turned to Hermy. "O.K., Hermy, let's hear what happened last night."

Hermy looked up at Fox and said, "You ain't gonna hit me or anything like that, are you?"

"No, I'm not," Fox said. "But let me tell you something, Hermy. If you mention this, what happened here now or ever in your life, you will be dead one minute after you tell, got it."

"I got it," Hermy said.

"Good," Fox said to him. "Now, tell me what happened last night."

Hermy told Fox the story. Fox looked down at Hermy's hand and saw he still had Marylou's hair wrapped around his fingers. "Where do you think Marylou is now?" Fox asked him.

"I don't know," Hermy said. "To tell you the truth Detective, I don't even know who was in the car with her. I just grabbed her. She started to scream and the car pulled away. That's all I remember."

Bender walked back into the house. "Nobody saw or heard anything," Bender said. "How did you guys make out? OOPS, wrong choice of words," Bender smiled.

Fox pretended he didn't hear him and said, "Let's go see if we can find Duke."

"O.K.," Bender said. "You can tell me what Hermy had to say on the way."

Fox turned to Hermy and said, "Would you like to go with us?"

"No, no," Hermy said. "Look if Marylou is there, I don't want to see her. I'd just rather not. But, if you guys see her, would you please tell her to call me, or just come home. Tell her I love her no matter what!"

"Sure, we'll tell her all those things," Fox said. The two detectives left and headed to Duke's Bar.

On the way, Fox filled Bender in on everything that Hermy had told him.

"I bet that Marylou is with Duke," Bender said.

"No bet," Fox replied. "I have the same feeling."

My Baby My Baby!

It was about eleven o'clock when Fox and Bender pulled up in front of Duke's Bar. The Miller sign was on in the front window and the door was open.

"I can't believe the place is open," Fox said. "Fatty must be in there. You know Duke is never in this early."

The detectives were in for yet another surprise. The bar was clean and the place smelled clean, well more like Pinesol. Duke was behind the bar polishing the glasses and humming a tune. Duke looked up as the two detectives walked in the door.

"Can I help you gentlemen?" Duke asked.

Fox and Bender looked at each other. "We must be in the wrong place," Bender said. "Can you tell me where Duke's Bar is?"

"Funny, very funny," Duke said. "But you are at the new Duke's Bar. Can I get you anything?"

"Nope, all we want is some information about last night," Fox said. He still wasn't ready to be drinking coffee or anything else for that matter in this place, no matter how clean it looked.

"Sure," Duke said. "What do you guys want to know about last night?"

"First of all," Bender said. "Where is Marylou?"

"Hey man, as far as I know, she's at Fatty's," Duke said.

"You sure she's not upstairs?" Fox asked Duke.

"Hell no," Duke said. "Go look if you want to. I told you that she is with Fatty."

Fox looked at Bender and rolled his eyes, "Good thing we didn't bet the house on this!"

"Will wonders never cease," Bender said shaking his head.

"What the hell are you guys talking about?" Duke asked.

"Oh nothing," Fox said. "Just tell us about last night?"

Duke told the detectives the story, leaving out the part about throwing Hermy out on Bridge Avenue. He told them the last he saw of Marylou and Fatty was as they were driving away to go to Fatty's house. Duke finished the story and said, "Come on in the back. I want to show you Marylou's car." All three of them walked to the back of the building and looked at the car.

"Man," Fox said. "Whoever did this must have really been pissed off."

"It looks worse in the daylight," Duke said. "Wait until Marylou sees it."

"Who do you think did it?" Fox asked Duke.

"Hermy, who else would do it?" Duke asked.

"That could well be," Fox said. "But didn't one of you call the police?"

"Well," Duke said. "It was late. Marylou was all shook up and to tell the truth, we never even thought about it."

"Do you think Marylou will want to make a police report?" Bender asked Duke.

"Hey man, how do I know?" Duke answered. "I mean, what good would it do? Hell, she ain't got no insurance and Hermy ain't got no money. So tell me, what is the object of making a police report?"

"Yeah, you're right," Fox told Duke. "Good idea, if no one makes police reports. It saves us a lot of work." Fox winked at Bender.

"That's right," Bender said. "It gives us more time to drink coffee and eat donuts."

"Hey, I'm glad I can help you guys," Duke patted Fox on the back. "Yeah, any time I can be of help to the police, I'm more than glad."

"That's good," Bender said. "So if you want to help us, tell us where Fatty lives."

"She lives on Seymour Avenue. But, it's no use going over there now. It's almost time for her to come into work. Why don't you come back in the bar, and I'll fix some breakfast for you," Duke told them.

"No, I think we'll pass, but thanks," Fox said. "We will come back later to see Fatty."

"O.K.," Duke said. "I'll see you guys later." Duke went back into the bar. Fox and Bender looked at the car.

"We might as well look through the car. All they found were McDonald wrappers and the usual junk found under the seats of cars.

"Let's head back to the station and tell the Sarge what we have," Fox said.

They walked out of the back alley and looked in the window of the bar as they headed for their car. Duke was behind the bar polishing glasses and singing. Fatty wasn't there yet.

"I wonder what Duke is so happy about?" Fox asked.

"I don't know," Bender said. "It's sure hard to believe it's the same guy, all cleaned up and shaved, and the joint with the floors and glasses cleaned. It's almost safe enough to have a beer in."

"I don't know about this," Fox said. "I bet Hunter will want us to keep tabs on this situation."

"We better not bet on anything today," Bender said to Fox. "We haven't been doing so good lately."

That would have been a good bet for the detectives because when they got back to the station and told Hunter what was going on, he was very interested.

"You know," Hunter told the detectives. "The Captain still does not want us to spend too much time on this case. Besides that, we really have not come up with anything new for some time. But, I think we can justify working a little overtime on this. What I want you two to do is get back there and talk to Fatty. See if you can find Marylou and talk to her, too. Also, we haven't been doing anything about those two hoods. Did you guys ever find them?"

"No,' Bender said. "The barber never called us, but we'll stop by and talk to him."

"Good," Hunter said. "I want you to keep an eye on that Duke guy. Try to get to know him a little better, you know, stop in every once in a while, be nice to him. He might tell you something, or make a slip with some information we can use."

"That's not a bad idea," Fox said. "But, I'll tell you one thing Sarge. We're not going to make that place one of our watering holes. That place gives me the creeps whenever I go in there. Every time I leave, I feel like taking all my clothes to the cleaners!"

"Give it a break, will you Fox?" Hunter said. "I've seen you and Bender in some worse places than that, and you were both having a good time."

"Hey Sarge," Bender said. "Those places you are talking about are the places you told us to meet you in. That's the only reason we would be in those bad places."

"Get out of here you two and do some detective work," Hunter laughed. "And, by the way, you know I only meet you guys in high class places. So tonight, meet me around seven at Rosie's!"

Bender and Fox left the station, debating where to go first. Should they see if Big Al and Tony are around, or go to Duke's and see if Fatty was there. They decided to go see about Big Al and Tony first. After all, Fatty would be at the bar all night.

The detectives drove pass the car lot. It looked vacant as usual. The same junk car was parked there, but no other cars were in view. As they drove by, they saw the barber looking out the window.

"I wonder if that guy makes a living in that place. It looks like there is never anyone in there," Bender said.

"Let me go around the block and park on the side street," Fox said. "That way if those two guys are around, they won't see our car."

They parked the car and walked down Lorain Avenue. The barber was smiling at them as they walked into the shop.

"Hey, nice to see you guys again. I see you drive by every now and then. How come you don't stop in?"

"We're pretty busy," Fox told him. "We just drive by to check the car lot to see if anyone is around. So far, the place always looks vacant. Have you seen Big Al or Tony around?"

"I haven't exactly seen either one of them, but I have heard them moving around upstairs," the barber said.

"When did you hear them?" Fox asked. "I mean was it like yesterday or a few days ago, what?"

"I think it might have been three days ago," the barber said. "I was just getting ready to close up when I heard someone moving around upstairs."

"Look," Fox said. "The next time you see or hear them, will you call us?"

"Sure," the barber said. "Let me have your number."

Bender gave him one of his cards. The two detectives started to walk out the door when the barber said, "You know both you guys could use haircuts. I give the police half price."

"Next time," Fox said.

They walked back to their car. Fox said, "Before we go to Duke's, let's have some lunch. I know a nice little diner up the street. They make good veal cutlet sandwiches."

After they had had lunch, Bender and Fox headed for Duke's Bar. On the way, they were making small talk in the car. Fox suggested

My Baby My Baby!

that they contact the zone car in the area of the used car lot and see if the patrolmen know about or ever see Big Al or Tony around. Bender thought that was a good idea, and they decided to stop at the district.

When they got to Duke's Bar, Fatty was there working. They went in and sat at the bar.

Fatty said, "Hi boys!. Duke said you might be back to talk to me. What can I do for you?"

"Just tell us about last night for openers," Fox said.

"Sure, no problem." Fatty told them about what had happened the night before. It was just about word for word that they had gotten from Hermy and Duke. Except Duke was the only one that didn't tell about Hermy being tossed out on the street.

"Sounds like everyone had one hell of a night!" Fox said. "Do you know where Marylou is now?"

"She borrowed my car," fatty told them. "She said she had a few errands to run. She said she would be back around five o'clock or so."

"Do you think she went to see Hermy?" Bender asked Fatty.

"I don't know about that," Fatty said. "I think she might be a little scared of Hermy yet. She said something about letting him calm down. Then, she was going to kick the shit out of him."

Bender and Fox started to laugh. "I don't doubt she could do it," Fox said.

"You bet your sweet ass she could!" Fatty told them.

"We're not betting on anything," Bender told Fatty. "Our luck hasn't been too good lately."

"Hey, maybe I can help change your luck," Fatty winked.

"We better go," Fox said. "Tell Marylou that we will stop by later tonight."

They got back to their car. "Change our luck from bad to worse!" Bender said. They headed for the district to talk to the zone car men.

Bender and Fox walked into the First District and talked to the Officer in Charge. He told them they were in luck; the patrolmen that worked that zone were in the report room making reports. Fox and Bender walked back to the room.

"Hey Fox, how are you doing?" It was Patrolman Baker. He had started on the job with Fox.

"Hey Baker, doing good, how about you?" Fox asked.

"Good," Baker said. "What brings you detectives into the trenches? Are you slumming, or do you need to know something about real police work?"

"Always the kidder, Baker," Fox said. "But, this time you're right. You're working that zone with the B.A.T. Auto Sales in it?"

"You mean the one on West 126th and Lorain Avenue?" Baker asked.

"That's the one," Fox said. "What can you tell me about it?"

"Really not too much," Baker said. "Two guys called Big Al and Tony run the place if it's ever open. I don't know who owns it. The two guys live in an apartment next door above the barber shop. Last month when me and my partner were working nights, we had a few complaints of them running a card game in there. It was supposed to be pretty high stakes from what we heard. We drove by a few times and saw some cars parked in the lot and lights on in the trailer, but the shades were pulled down.

"Didn't you ever go knock on the door, or bust the place?" Fox asked Baker.

"Man Fox," Baker said. "What do you have your head in the sand or what! Man, you don't know shit about district work. We turned it over to the vicemen, and the next night we got a note from the inspector to mind our own business. If the viceman needed any help, they would let us know."

"Thanks Baker, but one more thing," Fox said. "If you see those two guys around there, would you give us a call right away?"

"Hey man, you got it," Baker said. "Is there a reward in it for the poor zone car men?"

"Baker, you never stop, do you?" Fox thanked Baker again and he and Bender were on their way.

CHAPTER 37

That morning after Marylou had gone to bed on Fatty's couch, Marylou awoke to the smell of fresh coffee brewing and bacon and eggs frying. She stretched, got up, and slipped on a robe Fatty had put out for her. She walked into the kitchen. Fatty looked up from her cooking. "Well, good morning sleepy head. Did you sleep well?"

"Sure did," Marylou said. "And, I'm as hungry as a bear."

"Breakfast will be ready in a minute. Sit down and let me pour you a cup of coffee."

Marylou sat down at the table and looked around the kitchen. Everything was very neat and in order; very homey and cheerful. The guys down at the bar would be real surprised. This was a different side of Fatty, and a nice side, too.

Fatty brought Marylou a plate of scrambled eggs and bacon.

"The toast will be ready in a minute," she told Marylou. "I scrambled the eggs because I wanted them to be ready when you work up. I hope that's o.k.?"

"My favorite," Marylou said. "I feel like a queen being waited on like this."

"You are honey, you are," Fatty smiled and said. "And after breakfast, you can take a long hot shower. If you need anyone to wash your back, just call old Fatty. She's willing and able."

"I believe that, Fatty," Marylou winked at her and said. "But, I think I'll pass this time, but don't give up."

Fatty cleaned up the kitchen while Marylou took a shower. After they were done, they got into Fatty's car and headed for the bar. Fatty had to go to work, so Marylou had asked if she could borrow her car for a while to run some errands.

"Sure," Fatty told her. "When you get done, come back to the bar. It will be time for cocktails, on Duke." They both laughed. Marylou dropped Fatty off at the bar and left.

Marylou's first stop was the junk yard on Fulton Road. She talked to Junkyard Jack and told him to come down to Duke's Bar and get her car. She told him she didn't have any money right now. She asked if he could look at the car and see if it could be fixed cheap. They might be able to work something out in payments or whatever.

Junkyard said he'd like to take the whatever. "Maybe, that's what you'll get, Marylou told him. She left there and went to her old apartment to check the mail. Good, the Welfare check was there. She went to the money exchange and cashed the check. Next, she stopped at the landlords, paid her rent, and told him she would be moving out. Marylou was already thinking about moving in with Fatty. Perhaps that was planning too far ahead. After all, Hermy wasn't counted out yet, and then, there was always Duke. She would have to see. But one thing, she could move out of the apartment. After all, she hardly stayed there anymore.

Marylou stopped at the store and picked up some things for the children, some groceries for Patty, and then headed for Patty's house. She had to stay on the good side of Patty now because she needed a lot of time to work on Duke. She would have to leave the kids with Patty a while longer. Someday, she might have that twenty-five thousand dollars and all her children and move into a nice place and live happily every after. Oh shit, she thought, that's not the real world. Everything is all fucked up and not looking like it will get any better.

Marylou arrived at Patty's house. The children were still in school, so they had a little time to sit and talk. Patty spent most of the time laughing as Marylou unfolded her story. When Marylou told Patty about Hermy grabbing her by the hair and almost pulling her out of the car window, Patty almost fell from her chair laughing. "Marylou, Patty said. "You must lead the most exciting life in the world!"

"I don't know about that," Marylou said. "But, I'll tell you one thing, it ain't boring!"

"Oh Marylou, you are such a card!" Patty said to her.

"I have a good idea, Patty," Marylou said. "When's the last time you were out?"

"Hell," Patty said. "I can't even remember. I think it was the time my brother-in-law knocked me up! Yeah, that was it!" Patty started to laugh.

"Look," Marylou said. "Get a baby sitter and you come with me."

"Gee," Patty said. "I don't know about that. It's been so long since I've been out. I don't know."

My Baby My Baby!

"Come on," Marylou said. "We'll have a good time. Anyhow, I owe you. Patty, come on. I'll take you for dinner and then we'll have a few drinks. It's all on me, including the baby sitter."

Patty looked at her and said, "You're on. Let me call the girl next door and see if my friends will baby-sit these little monsters!" Patty made the call and they said yes. "Let's go," Patty said. "And let the good times roll!"

Marylou and Patty jumped into the car and Marylou pulled away from the curb.

"Where to?" Patty shouted as she turned the radio up to full volume. Oh boy, Marylou thought. I hope I didn't make a mistake talking old Patty out. Oh well, I owe her, so here we go!

"Let me drive by Hermy's place first," Marylou said. "I just want to check and see if the place is till standing. In the meantime, you think about where you want to eat." They drove by Hermy's. Marylou was driving very slow. The place looked fine, no one was around and there was no noise. I wonder if I should go in, Marylou thought to herself. But, she was still shook up from the night before. Maybe, I should call that little weasel first. I don't trust him.

"Hey," Patty screamed above the roar of the radio. "Want to stop in and see Hermy?"

"Really funny, Patty," Marylou answered. "Maybe, I'll drop you off and you can go see him!"

"Scratch that idea?" Patty yelled. "Let's go eat!"

"O.K.," Marylou said. "It's your choice. Where would you like to go?"

"Well," patty frowned. "It's been a long time since I've been out. I don't know what kind of food I want. Wait, I know. How about that little Chinese restaurant on Madison Avenue. Do you think it's still there?"

"There's only one way to find out," Marylou said and headed for Madison Avenue.

The restaurant was still there, so Marylou parked the car, and she and Patty went in. They enjoyed an excellent dinner, a few glasses of wine, and a long chat. After dinner, the waitress brought the check and fortune cookies. Marylou's fortune told her; her finances would be looking up. Patty's said; she was going to have a new love in her life.

"Wow," yelled Patty. "I sure could use some new love. As a matter of fact, I could use some old love." They were giggling.

Marylou paid the check and the girls walked to the car. Marylou told Patty she was going to Duke's Bar and asked if Patty would like to come along.

"Are you kidding?" Patty said. "Hey, this is my first night out in a long time. Let's make a whole night of it."

"O.K., and its' all going to be on me," Marylou told her. As Marylou was driving to Duke's, she kept thinking about what the fortune cookie said. Her finances would be looking up. Hmm, she thought. Duke, your ass is mine.

Marylou parked Fatty's car into the back lot. She saw her car was gone. Good old Junkyard Jack. He was on the ball. Marylou knew this would cost her, but at least, the car would be fixed. It was about nine o'clock when they walked into Duke's. Fatty was still tending bar, but Duke was nowhere to be seen.

Fatty looked up, "Hey Marylou, I thought you were coming back around five."

"Me and Patty went out to eat," Marylou said. "You know Patty, don't you?"

"Oh yeah," Fatty said. "But I ain't seen her in a long time. How are you?"

"Just fine," Patty said, "and ready to party!"

"You're in the right place," Fatty said. "It's always party time at Duke's Bar!"

Fatty turned to Marylou sand said, "I got some news for you. Hermy called. He was crying and told me to tell you he loves you and is sorry for what he's done. Will you please come home?"

"The little weasel is back to his whimpering self," Marylou said. "But, that's good. He can just wait for a while."

"Also," Fatty said. "The police were here looking for you."

"Which ones? Those detectives?" Marylou asked.

"Yeah, that Fox and Bender," Fatty said. "They said they wanted to talk to you about last night. They already talked to Duke, me, and Hermy. They said they would be back here later, but they ain't showed up yet."

"Well," Marylou said to Fatty. "Pour us a drink, and let's wait for the dicks."

"That's a good one," Patty said. "I'm ready for them, don't forget what my fortune cookie said!"

Fatty was pouring the drinks and all three of them were laughing. "By the way," Marylou said. "Where is Duke?"

"Oh, he went out for a while," Fatty said. "But, he told me to tell you to wait for him and he would buy you a few drinks."

"Hell," Marylou said. "That dummy is buying them right now. So, pour us some more!"

"You got it," Fatty said and thought. This may prove to be quite a night.

About an hour after the girls had started drinking, the phone rang. Marylou yelled to Fatty, "If that's for me, I ain't here." Marylou saw Fatty answer the phone and hang up right away.

"It was for you," Fatty said. "It was Hermy."

"Oh no," Marylou said. "I hope he's not going to start any shit!"

The phone rang again. "She's not here! I told you!" Fatty said and then hung up the phone. The phone rang again.

"Let me answer it," Marylou said. Marylou picked up the phone and said in her sweetest voice, "Duke's Bar, may I help you?"

"Oh thank God," Hermy said. "It's you. I knew you were there."

"What do you want Hermy?" Marylou asked.

"I just want you to come home. I love you so much! Please come home Marylou. I'm so sorry for what happened last night. Please come home. I miss you! I don't know what to do without you here!"

"You should have thought about all that shit last night Hermy," Marylou told him. "And by the way, I want my car fixed and you better come up with the money Hermy, or you are going to be in some deep shit!"

"Please, Marylou, anything you say," Hermy was crying. "I'll even buy you a new car if you want it! Just please come home!"

"We'll see Hermy. I have to think about it for a while." Marylou then hung up the phone.

Marylou no sooner got back to her seat when the phone rang again.

"I'll get it," Marylou said. She walked over to the phone, picked it up and put it to her ear, but she didn't say anything. She could hear breathing and then Hermy's voice came from the other end.

"If that's you bitch, get the fuck home here, or I'm coming to get you!"

Marylou slammed the phone down. She turned to walk away and the phone rang again. Marylou picked it up and slammed it right back down. Then, she took it off the hook and walked back to the bar. "Fatty," Marylou said. "We better leave that phone off the hook or that little weasel will just keep calling here. I'll tell you girls, that Hermy is scaring the shit out of me. The way he's talking, I never heard him so mean before!"

"Let me tell you, Marylou," Patty said. "I don't know what you do to these men, but once you got them, you got them. I wish I had whatever you got!"

"Me, too," Fatty winked at Marylou.

"Fatty, you are such a card!" Marylou said. "Maybe someday," and Marylou licked her lips.

Duke came stomping in the door. "God damn it, who the hell has been on that phone? I told you Fatty. I don't want nobody on that phone for more than three minutes. How many God damn times do I have to tell you?"

"Easy, Duke, it ain't her fault," Marylou said. "I took the phone off the hook because that asshole Hermy kept calling here."

"Oh, then that's o.k.," Duke smiled at Marylou. "That was a good idea."

"Sure," Fatty said. "If I do it, I get yelled at. If she does it, it's a good idea. You know Duke, you are so full of shit!"

"Hey Fatty, never mind all that," Duke said. "Just pour the drinks and they're on me." Duke walked over to the phone and hung it up. "If he calls back, I'll take care of him." Duke started to walk away from the phone and it rang. "Hello," Duke said. There was no answer. "Hello, hello?" Duke repeated. There was no answer, Duke yelled over the phone, "Hermy, if that's you and you keep calling here, I'm going to come over to your place and kick your ass!" Duke slammed the phone down. Duke turned to walk and the phone rang again. Duke picked it up and said, "All right Hermy, little shit, I'm on my way over!" This time, Hermy hung up. Duke started laughing. "Well, I fixed him, but I think I'll leave this phone off the hook in case he calls back. "Come on guys, let's move over to a table. Fatty bring the drinks over and some quarters for the juke box. Hey Patty, how the hell are you? Long time, no see."

Duke and the girls sat at the table drinking. Duke was taking turns dancing with each of the girls, but mostly with Marylou. Yes sir, that Duke was pretty happy again today. Business had been good again, and here he was dancing with Marylou, and hey, that Patty wasn't bad either. Hell, even Fatty looked good to him. Yes sir, old Duke was sitting on top of the world. For now.

It was two in the morning and the party at Duke's was still going on when the door opened and in walked none other than Fox and Bender.

Fox and Bender had met Hunter at Rosie's and by now, were feeling pretty mellow. They were taking the car back to the station when Fox said, "We ought to stop over at Duke's and see if Marylou is there."

"Hey, good idea," Bender said. "We might as well party a little and get some overtime, too. Hell, the place is looking mighty clean lately and the Sarge did say to make friends."

"Yeah," Fox said. "Let's do it!"

Duke didn't quite know what to do when he saw the two detectives walk in. He knew it wasn't closing time yet, there were only two other people at the bar and they were fairly sober. Duke couldn't think of anything that was wrong, so he smiled at the detectives and said, "Hey boys, come on over to the table. How about a drink?" Well much to Duke's surprise, the two detectives walked over to the table, pulled up two chairs and sat down. Not only that, they each ordered a beer and a shot of Wild Turkey. "Whew," sighed Duke. "You guys had me worried, but I see this is a social call right?"

"Half and half," Fox said. "We were out and happened to be in the area, so we thought we would mix business with pleasure."

"That's good," Duke said. "We were just having a little party here and you're more than welcome. Fatty, hurry up with those drinks, will you? You boys know everyone here? This is Marylou, her girlfriend, Patty, and that's Fatty bringing the drinks. It sure is nice to see you guys having a drink in my place."

"Well, don't get too used to it," Bender said. "This is just a one in a million visit."

Marylou said, "Hey man, slack off, will you? Try to be nice and enjoy yourselves."

Everyone at the table was making small talk and then Fox said, "Hey Marylou, want to tell us about last night?"

"Hell yeah," Marylou said. "That was one hell of a night, right Fatty?"

"It sure was," Fatty said. "Tell them about when Hermy grabbed you by the hair and almost pulled you out the car window!"

"Jesus Fatty, you just told them." Marylou told them again, and they all had a big laugh. Marylou told them what happened with her car and all. Fox asked her if she wanted to press charges against Hermy. Marylou said, "No, but I'll tell you what. That little shit scares me sometimes. I'm going to have to watch him."

By now it was close to two-thirty, and Bender said to Duke. "It's getting close to closing time, so why don't you tell those fellows at the bar to drink up and hit the road."

"Sure," Duke said. "Hey fellows, drink up. It's closing time!"

"Hey Duke, since when do you close on time?" Red yelled from the bar.

"Hey Red, I close all the time right at two-thirty, you know that?"

"Bullshit," Red yelled back. "The earliest you ever close is when everyone runs out of money!"

Red and the guy with him were laughing as Duke got up from the table and walked to the bar. He grabbed Red by the collar and pulled him up to his face. Under his breath, Duke said, "You dumb son of a bitch, those two guys are cops!" Duke set Red back on the barstool.

Red grabbed his drink, chugged it down, and said to his buddy, "Man, let's hit the road, it's closing time," and out the door they went.

Duke walked back to the table with a big grin on his face. "Those boys must have been thinking about some other joint that stays open."

"I believe that," Fox said.

"Are you guys going now?" Duke asked the two detectives.

"Hell no," Bender said. "I think we just might have a few more drinks."

"All right," Duke said. "Fatty, bring us all some more drinks. Hell, bring the bottles over here so you don't have to jump up all the time."

My Baby My Baby!

Everyone had a few more drinks and Duke was still dancing with the girls. Duke came back to the table after dancing with Patty and said, "Why don't you guys grab a girl and have a little dance?"

"No," Fox said. "I think we better pass on that one. We'll stick to the drinking."

All three girls decided to go and powder their noses. That left the three men sitting there. "Hey Duke," Bender said. "When's the last time you saw those two hoods? You know, that Big Al and Tony?"

"Hey man, I told you. I don't fool with those kind of guys. They haven't been in here for a long time. No, not since Jimmy died."

"Why don't they come in any more? You quit taking bets?" Fox asked Duke.

"Oh man, just when we're having a good time, you throw shit into the game. I knew it was too good to be true."

"Hell, ain't no problem," Bender said. "I told you we were mixing business with pleasure. Don't get upset. You know how it is. Once a cop, always a cop."

Duke started laughing. "Yeah, I guess you're right, but all kidding aside. I haven't seen those two guys for a long time."

The three girls came back to the table and Fatty was pouring the drinks when there was a loud banging on the front door.

"Open up you sons of bitches! Open the fucking door! I know you're in there! Get outside here you slut! I'm going to drag your ass home! So, get the hell over and open this fucking door!"

"Oh, oh," Duke said. "That sounds like Hermy. I'll take care of him."

"No, no," Fox said. "I'll take care of it. The last thing we want is trouble now." Fox walked over to the front door, unlocked it, and pushed it open. Well, to say the least, when Hermy saw the detective, he was surprised.

"WWWhat the hell are you doing here? Hermy screamed at Fox. "Are you with my Marylou? What the hell are you guys having a gang-bang? God damn it, let me in!"

Fox grabbed Hermy and pulled him away from the door. He pushed Hermy up against the wall of the building. "What the hell is the matter with you?" Fox said to Hermy. "Are you crazy?"

Hermy was struggling like crazy and yelling, "Let me go! Let me go!" He pushed Fox, knocking him to the ground. Hermy took off running down Bridge Avenue screaming "Marylou, where are you?"

Fox walked back into the bar. "What happened?" Bender asked him. "Where's Hermy?"

"That little shit pushed me down and took off running. I wasn't about to chase him," Fox said. "I know where he lives, no big deal."

"I think it's time to break this little party up," Bender said.

"Yeah," Duke said. "Anybody for breakfast?"

"No, not us," Fox said. "But thanks, we got to hit the road. See you all later." Fox and Bender left.

Duke looked at the girls and said, "Well, how about you girls? Breakfast? I'm buying."

"We're going!" Fatty said.

The two detectives headed for the station. Duke and the girls headed for the restaurant.

Fox decided he would drop Bender off at home and pick him up in the morning. They had to be in court at nine a.m. So, it didn't make much sense to go to the station at three in the morning.

Bender said to Fox, "You know, that Duke isn't as dumb as I thought. I thought after we got a few drinks in him, we could get some information out of him."

"So did I," Fox said. "But, as soon as we mentioned those two hoods, he went on the defensive. I think we might have pushed too soon."

"I got that same feeling," Bender said. "What are we going to have to do is stop by his place until he trusts us a little more. Then, maybe he'll open up a little."

"You're right," Fox said. "I sure hate to have people think that we're hanging around that place!"

"Hey, what the hell, it's all in the job," Bender said. "It still beats the shit out of working in uniform."

"You got that right," Fox said. "By the way Bender, I think that Patty had eyes for you."

"Don't start that shit, Fox," Bender said. "I'm a happily married man! Well, at least married."

Duke and the three girls had ordered breakfast and were drinking coffee. Patty was talking about how she had to get home or the baby-

My Baby My Baby!

sitter would have a fit. "I sure had a good time though. Even though, I didn't get lucky," Patty smiled at Duke.

"You're always welcome at Duke's Bar," Duke said. "And there's always someone there to take care of any problem you might have," Duke told Patty.

"That's right," Fatty said. "Any problem can be taken care of at Duke's."

They all had a good laugh over that one. Breakfast came and the four of them were quiet while they ate.

After a while, Duke said, "What did you girls think about those two cops coming into the joint?"

"They seemed friendly enough," Patty said.

"Yeah, but why would they come in there and stay until after closing time?" Duke said. "You know if old Hermy didn't come by, those two were ready to spend the night drinking."

"They were a little high when they got there," Marylou said. "Maybe, they were just slumming."

"That could be," Duke said. "But while you girls were in the bathroom, they started to ask me some questions."

"About what?" Marylou asked.

"Oh, just some little things, nothing important," Duke said. "But, still they were asking."

"Don't get so upset Duke," Fatty said. "You know how cops are. They always ask questions. So, just forget about it."

"You girls just be quiet if they start to pump you for any information," Duke told them.

"Is just plain pumping o.k.?" Patty asked. "I think those two cops are kinda cute."

"Get serious Patty," Marylou said. "One thing you never fool around with is a cop."

They finished breakfast, and Duke took them all back to Fatty's car. "Anyone want to stay at my place?" Duke asked.

"We were all going to stay with you Duke, but you look too tired for us," Fatty said.

"Yeah," Marylou said. "I'm tired too, so let's head home. We can drop Patty off on the way, and I'll stay with you Fatty if that's o.k.?"

"No problem," Fatty said and off they drove.

Duke headed back to his apartment thinking. I just wonder what the hell those cops wanted. I'll have to be careful with them. You know, it's funny. I ain't seen Big Al or Tony for a long time. They don't even stop by to pick up my bets anymore. Oh well, let me think about Marylou again. I gotta try to get her alone so I can talk to her. Maybe, I can get her to go out to dinner with me.

After Fatty and Marylou dropped Patty off at home, they were talking in the car. "Fatty, why do you think those two cops stopped at Duke's?"

"I don't know," Fatty said. "But, I still think they were just out and stopped by. You know, I've known some coppers, and they like to go to out of the way places so they don't get bothered by people. As a matter of fact, if they find a place like that, they usually kind of take it over. Pretty soon, all you got is cops in the joint, which ain't all that bad cause when them coppers drink, they get crazy!"

"Yeah, they like to party," Marylou said. "Maybe, we'll get lucky and that will happen to Duke's."

"I don't' know about that," Fatty said. "But I'll tell you one thing, Duke was pretty nervous about those cops and whatever they were asking about."

"Right," Marylou said. "I got some work to do on that Duke."

CHAPTER 38

Fox and Bender got back from court about twelve-thirty and Hunter called them into his office.

"Late night, uh, boys?" Hunter asked.

"Yes, it was," Fox said holding his head, "On orders from you."

"What the hell does that mean?" Hunter asked him.

"You told us to get chummy with Duke. So after we left you last night, we stopped at Duke's."

"So what happened? Give me the low down" Hunter said.

Fox told Hunter the story with Bender filling in every once in a while.

"What do you think about Duke? Do you think you guys can get him to open up?" Hunter asked.

"I think if we work on him, we'll get some information from him," Fox said. "I think he is still a little nervous. After all, we gave him a hard time before. Now, we stop by and socialize with him. I think it will take a while to gain his confidence. But he ain't all that smart. He'll slip up sooner or later."

"Yeah, I think you guys can do it. You're naturals to hang around a joint like that," Hunter said. "Hell, in a short time, you two will blend right into the crowd."

"Thanks a lot Sarge. All we know, we learned from you," Fox said.

"Oh yeah," Bender said. "We learned this from you too and he threw two overtime cards on Hunter's desk. Bender and Fox walked out of the office.

Hunter called after them, "You guys better be working and not partying in that joint. I'll be checking on you, hear me?"

Fox and Bender were sitting at their desks talking about last night. "What do you want to do with Hermy?" Bender asked Fox.

"I think we should let him sweat for a while," Fox said. "He's probably scared to death waiting for us to come and get him."

"Maybe you're right," Bender said. "But, I hope he doesn't get too crazy. You know that old saying about the worm turning."

CHAPTER 39

Hermy was home sitting at the kitchen table, empty beer bottles on the floor all around him, and a half-gallon of whiskey sitting on the table, half-full. Hermy was thinking to himself; What the hell did I do last night? I must have been crazy, pushing that cop down and then running away. But that damn Marylou, she makes me fucking crazy. If she's with that Duke, I'll kill her! Oh shit! What the hell am I talking about, all I want her to do is come home. Man, what if those cops are looking for me? I've heard what happens to guys that hit coppers. Oh man, they might come here and kill me; well at least, beat me up real bad. Maybe, I should call that cop and tell him I'm sorry. No, that's not a good idea. Hermy took a swig from the bottle of whiskey. He would probably bring that partner of his. Another swig. One guy would hold me while the other guy punched me. Another swig. Maybe, I could handle one of those coppers, but not both of them. Another swig. Shit, maybe I could handle both of them. Yeah, just like on TV. All the time, they do it. Another swig. Hey, I know how to do that. One guy's holding me, I kick the guy that's punching me. I give the guy holding me an elbow in the stomach. He lets go, I turn around, punch him in the face, and both coppers are lying on the floor out for the count. Another swig. Yeah, then I throw them both out the door and yell; "Don't you guys bother me no more, or you get more of the same!" Hermy started laughing. This time, he took a big swallow of whiskey. Yeah, maybe I should just call them two fucking coppers and tell them where I am. Yeah, that's what I'm gonna do!

Lucky for Hermy 'cause then old Mr. Barleycorn got him. He passed out right at the kitchen table. Maybe, that saying is true; God takes care of little kids and drunks.

CHAPTER 40

Marylou and Fatty were getting ready for bed and Marylou was telling Fatty about Hermy. "You know, she said. "Until now, I didn't think Hermy had a mean bone in his body. But now, he scares me. You know, I've heard about people like that. They are so sweet and then something sets them off, and they go out and kill a bunch of people."

"Oh, I wouldn't worry about that," Fatty said. "Right now, he's just jealous and hurt. You know, he thinks you're already sleeping with Duke, so as long as you stay away from Hermy, he's going to continue to think that way."

"Yeah, you're right Fatty. I just don't know what to do yet," Marylou said. "I want to find out what Duke knows and maybe we can make some money. If not, at least maybe I can find out where Noreen is. You know, sometimes I think about her. I sure hope she's o.k.,"

"I think she is Marylou," Fatty said. "I told you those guys planned to sell her. Jimmy knew the whole story. Maybe, that's why he's dead."

"If you are right," Marylou said. "How come Duke is still alive? Does that mean he had a hand in killing Jimmy?"

"Hell, I doubt that!" Fatty said. "You know Duke acts and talks bad sometimes, but ain't that bad. As a matter of fact, he's pretty easy guy to get along with."

"Maybe," Marylou said, "but I got a lot of planning and thinking to do. I just hope those cops don't get in the way and mess things up. Hey, Fatty, wouldn't it be nice to get the twenty-five thousand and Noreen back, too?"

"It sure would," Fatty said, "but for now, good night Marylou. If you get cold, there's plenty of room in here with me."

Marylou woke up the next morning to the smell of breakfast cooking again. I could get used to this, she thought. I wonder if Fatty would let me move in with the kids? If we're going to be partners, maybe we can work something out. I have to get closer to Duke. Just then, Fatty called out, "Breakfast is ready."

Marylou asked Fatty is she could use her car again and Fatty said, "Sure, just drop me off at work and be on your way."

Marylou dropped Fatty off at work and then drove over to Patty's house. It was Friday and the kids were still in school. Patty and Marylou were sitting at the kitchen table drinking coffee and talking about the kids.

"You know," Patty said, "you haven't been spending much time with your kids and they really miss you."

"I know," Marylou said, "but things ain't easy. What with Jimmy dying and poor Noreen still missing. My God, we don't know if she's dead or alive, and now I got all kind of trouble with that asshole Hermy. Patty, I swear I don't know if I'm coming or going."

"But Marylou, I can't take care of your kids forever," Patty said. "I need to have a life of my own, and I just can't do it with all of your kids plus mine. I mean I don't have any time. Hell, all I do is take care of kids!"

"I know," Marylou said, "and I really appreciate what you have done for me. For sure, you are my best friend. Believe me, I won't forget it. If you can help me just a little longer, I think I can work everything out. So, if you will just stand by me a little longer. Please?" Marylou was begging.

Patty looked at her and said, "How can I turn you down? You know I love you and the kids. "But, please try Marylou, at least try and spend more time with the kids will you?"

"Sure, I will. How about tomorrow we take all the kids to the zoo and then you get a baby-sitter for tomorrow night and we can go out again?" Marylou said to Patty.

Marylou, asked Patty. "Do you need anything from the store?"

"No," Patty said. "But, maybe we can do some shopping tomorrow."

"Sounds good to me," Marylou said. "Pick you up around ten in the morning."

Marylou left Patty's and headed for Junkyard Jack's to see what he was going to do with her car. Junkyard was sitting in his office with his feet on an old desk and drinking a can of beer.

"Well, old Marylou. You sure did luck out," Junkyard said. "I checked the car over, and I got enough junk windows and such to fix her up."

"How soon can it be ready?" Marylou asked.

"Well, old Hermy stopped by," Junkyard said. "He already paid me to fix the old heap up, and I got a boy working on her now. It should be ready by Tuesday afternoon."

"That sounds good to me," Marylou said. "I'll pick it up Tuesday."

"Wait a minute," Junkyard said. "I might be able to have her done by Monday," he winked. "You know, maybe if you was good to me."

"Listen Jack. You made your mistake by taking the money from Hermy 'cause you would have had to take it out in trade from me," Marylou laughed.

"Hell, let me give Hermy back his money and then you and me can make our own deal," Junkyard said.

"The deal's done," Marylou said. "So, I'll just pick the car up Tuesday." Marylou walked out the door. As she left, she could hear Junkyard mumbling, "I should have never told her Hermy paid me. That's what you get for being a nice guy."

Marylou drove back to Fatty's house, fixed herself some lunch, and sat down on the couch to watch the soaps. Boy, I haven't done this for a long time, she thought. Marylou didn't have to pick Fatty up until around one in the morning. She thought she might catch a little nap. Then when she went to pick Fatty up, she could have a few drinks with Duke. She still didn't have a plan for trapping Duke, but she knew she would come up with something. Duke didn't have a chance once Marylou set her mind to trap him. Marylou fell asleep on the couch dreaming about getting money from Duke and maybe with any luck, having Noreen back. She missed Noreen, and the rest of her kids for that matter.

Marylou woke up about six in the evening. The news was on TV. She hadn't meant to sleep as long as this. Then, what the heck, she had nothing else to do right now. Marylou went to the kitchen to fix herself some coffee. While she was waiting for the water to boil, her thoughts turned to Hermy. What the hell was she going to do with him? He had always been good to her and he was always a lot of fun, until now. Hell, the way he was acting, she was scared to death of him. At least, he paid to have the car fixed. That was something. Maybe, I should go and see him, she thought. But if he was still drinking, he may be just as nasty as ever. I think I'll just wait a while and let him cool down.

Marylou took her coffee into the front room and sat down to watch the news, but she had too many thoughts going through her head. I might as well go down to the bar and kill some time talking to Fatty. She got to the bar at about eight o'clock, and the place was crowded. She got a stool at the bar and sat down. Fatty brought her over a beer and said, "Can you believe this place? All of a sudden, Duke's Bar is the place to be. I called for Duke to come and help me, but I ain't heard from him yet."

"Hey, how about if I help you out?" Marylou said. "At least until Duke gets here."

"That would be great Marylou," Fatty said. "I sure would appreciate it."

"You got it," Marylou said. "Hell, I ain't worked a bar for about five years."

Duke walked in about an hour later. When he saw Marylou behind the bar, he got a big grin on his face. He couldn't believe the crowd. Duke sat and watched Marylou work. She got along well with the customers. It seemed she knew what she was doing behind the bar. Duke yelled over to Marylou, "Hey babe, you just keep working, and I'll pay you for the night."

"Sure thing Duke," Marylou yelled back.

It was almost closing time before things slowed down at the bar. Duke told Marylou to come over to a table while Fatty took care of the bar. Duke had a big grin on his face. This was another good night and a long way from having only a few customers all day long.

"Hell," Duke said to Marylou. "I don't know why all of a sudden I'm getting all this business, but I ain't asking no questions."

"We sure were busy," Marylou said. "It feels good to sit down."

"Listen," Duke said to Marylou. "How would you like to work here? I mean if business stays like this, I could use the help."

"It sounds good to me," Marylou said. "But let's ask Fatty what she thinks about it."

"Sure," Duke said. "But you know I'm the boss here and what Fatty says don't mean shit to me!"

"Be nice Duke," Marylou said. "After all, there's no sense in making hard feelings. Fatty is a good worker, so let's just ask her to make her feel good; what do you say Duke?"

Duke called Fatty from the bar, "Bring some drinks over here for all three of us, will you? I want to talk to you and Marylou."

"On my way," Fatty hollered back. "Let me take care of these two guys at the bar."

When Fatty brought the drinks over and sat down, Duke reached into his pocket and pulled out a roll of bills. He counted out seventy-five dollars for Fatty and Fifty for Marylou.

Fatty took her money and said, "What the hell Duke, you giving me a raise?"

"Hey babe," Duke said. "As long as business is good, I share. And if business is going to be this good, I've got a deal for you."

"Oh oh," Fatty said. "A deal for me is usually a better deal for you Duke."

"Gimme a break, will ya Fatty? Duke said. "Here's the deal. I'll open the bar in the morning, you two work the bar from two p.m. to closing time. Now, you can split the time. But if the bar is busy, I want both of you here. I'll pay each of you seventy-five dollars a night. Of course, you keep the tips."

"It's o.k. by me," Fatty said. "What do you think Marylou?"

"Well, I'm on welfare," Marylou said. "What about that?"

"Hell, so am I," Fatty said. "But, Duke pays under the table."

"That takes care of that," Marylou said.

"So, we got a deal?" Duke asked.

"O.K. by me," Fatty said.

"I'm in," Marylou said.

"Good, we start tomorrow," Duke said as he raised his glass to toast. "Good health and success to all of us."

The three of them sat at the table and had a few more drinks. Then, Duke got up to close the bar.

When he left, Fatty said to Marylou. "I really think we will work well together. Here's your share of tonight's tips. I split them right down the middle. After all, we're partners, ain't we? I mean in everything, not just working together."

"Sure we are," Marylou said. "Just wait until we find out something. I mean this could take longer than you think. I don't really have any kind of plan yet. We have to play it by ear for a while, but as soon as I come up with something, I'll let you know."

"O.K. by me," Fatty said. "Just as long as we are partners."

Marylou counted out the tips Fatty had given her. "Jesus," she said. "Fifty bucks, I can't believe it! A hundred bucks for the night. Man, my kids are going to have a good time at the zoo tomorrow!"

Duke came back to the table and said, "How about a few drinks to celebrate?"

"Not really," Marylou said. "I'm kind of tired and I have to take the kids to the zoo tomorrow morning. I'd really like to go home. Is that all right with you Fatty?"

"Sure, I'm kind of tired, too. Let's hit the road," Fatty said.

"Go ahead girls," Duke told them. "I'll clean the place up." The two girls left. Duke was cleaning up the bar and thinking to himself. Man, I can't believe this. A week ago that Marylou wouldn't give me the time of day, and now she's working for me. It won't be long before I have that little fat ass of hers in my bed. What a life, only in America! Duke finished cleaning up the bar and went up to his apartment and right to bed.

When Fatty and Marylou got back to Fatty's house, Marylou asked Fatty. "How about fixing us some coffee and having a little talk? I'm really not too tired now."

"Sure," Fatty said. "You go clean up a little, and I'll get us some coffee."

After they had both cleaned up, they sat at the kitchen table talking and drinking coffee. They hashed over the night at the bar and about Duke offering Marylou a job. Then, Marylou told Fatty she would have her car back Tuesday. "I have to find a place to live."

"Hey, you can stay here," Fatty said.

"It's not that easy," Marylou said. "I'm really starting to miss my kids. You know, I haven't been seeing much of them since Noreen has been gone. It seems things happened so fast after she was gone. I also have to get something straightened out with Hermy. I don't want him on my ass all the time."

"I don't know if I can have you and the kids here," Fatty said. "I mean I only have one bedroom here. It might work for a little while until you find something."

"I understand all that," Marylou said. "And, I thank you for even thinking about having the kids here, but they will be fine with Patty until I find out what to do."

The next morning Fatty gave Marylou her car and told her that she would get a ride to work from one of the neighbors. "Don't worry about getting to the bar before seven," Fatty told Marylou. "We won't be busy until then."

Marylou picked up Patty and all the kids and headed for the zoo. Marylou told Patty about taking the kids. Patty told her there would be no problem for her to keep the kids until Marylou decided what to do.

They left the zoo about five o'clock. By then, the kids were ready to go and Patty said, "I'm ready for a couple of cold beers." Patty had hired a baby-sitter and was going as planned with Marylou to Duke's. They got to Patty's house. Patty fixed some hot dogs for the kids and then Marylou and Patty were on their way.

They got to the bar around seven. There were only two guys sitting at the bar, and Fatty was watching TV.

"Hey you guys," Fatty said. "You ready for a cold one after a hard day at the zoo."

"You got that right," Patty said. "Entertaining those kids ain't no easy job. As a matter of fact, it's a mighty thirst-building job," Patty laughed.

"Every job is thirst-building for you," Marylou said. "So keep those beers coming Fatty."

The clock showed about eight when Marylou had to get behind the bar to work. Duke's was jumping again. The place was packed, the juke box was playing, and the people were dancing. Patty was having a great time! All the boys were buying her drinks and asking her to dance.

Patty danced a few times with a guy called Big Red. Marylou noticed after a while that Patty was gone. She looked up and down the bar. She also noticed that Big Red was gone. Marylou smiled to herself. That Patty. Well, she had said a couple of days ago she was hot to trot, and she must be trotting with Big Red. About a half hour later, Patty came back into the bar.

"Marylou, quick, gimme a drink! Now, I know why they call that guy Big Red!!" Patty downed a shot and said, "I ain't gonna let that guy get away for a while. I ain't done with him yet!" Just then, Big Red came back into the bar. He came right over to Patty and said, "come on baby, let's dance."

Patty hopped of the barstool and lead Big Red to the dance floor. There they stayed almost the entire night, taking time out to get drinks and that was about it.

Duke was sitting on a stool at the end of the bar looking like the old cat that swallowed the canary. He still didn't know why business was so good, but he loved it. He was thinking he ought to get a live country band in here for the weekends. Maybe, he could get another barmaid. Hmm, how about that Patty, she looked pretty good. It kind of looked as if Big Red had eyes for her. Well, he looked back at Marylou. Yeah, that's for me. Old Duke was feeling mighty good. Duke liked sitting at the end of the bar watching the door. This way, he could see who came in and best of all, who left with whom. But when the door opened this time, it was none other than Big Al and Tony. Oh shit, Duke thought as he watched the two hoods walk over to him. I thought I was rid of those guys.

Big Al and Tony walked up to Duke and stood on either side of him. "Hey Duke, what's happening?" Big Al asked.

"Oh, nothing much. Where have you guys been?" Duke asked. "I ain't had nobody to pick up my bets, so I ain't been taking any."

"Oh, we got promoted," Tony said. "But not to worry, someone will be in to talk to you next week."

"Yeah," Big Al said. "I hope you will treat him as good as you treated us."

"Sure, sure," Duke said. "Hey Fatty, get these two guys a drink, will you?"

"Duke," Tony said. "Ain't that Jimmy's old girlfriend behind the bar?"

"Yeah, that's her," Duke said. "She needed a job, and I gave her one. You know, feeling sorry for her and all."

"You ain't been telling her anything, have you Duke?" Tony asked.

"Telling her what?" Duke asked Tony.

"Please Duke, don't give us no shit. You know what we are talking about," Big Al said.

My Baby My Baby!

"Hey you guys," Duke said. "As far as I'm concerned, I forgot the whole deal."

"That's smart Duke, very smart," Big Al told him.

Fatty brought the drinks over and Big Al said, "Thanks babe."

Fatty looked at him and walked away. "You should hire some friendlier help," Big Al told Duke.

"Look, guys, I ain't said nothing to nobody about anything," Duke said. "All I'm trying to do is make a living, that's all. As far as what else happened, I forgot all about it. So just send someone around to pick up the bets and that will be it."

"I hope so," Tony said. "Because we sure would hate to see any more suicides around here. You get my meaning Duke?" Big Al and Tony started laughing.

"That's right," Big Al said. "No more suicides!"

Duke was thinking to himself. I know these guys killed Jimmy. Man, if there is ever any way to get even with them, I'm sure as hell going to do it!

"What's the matter Duke? You ain't got much to say," Big Al said.

"Sure, I do," Duke said. "Do you guys want another drink?"

"What do you say Al? One more before we hit the road?" Tony asked.

"Yeah, what the hell," Big Al said. "The price is right and I love the hillbilly music."

Duke yelled to Fatty, "Bring the boys two more." Duke was watching the door as it opened and who should walk in? Bender and Fox. Oh shit! Here we go now, Duke thought. Bender and Fox were dressed in jeans and sweaters, so Big Al and Tony never noticed them.

Fatty walked over to Fox and Bender. "Can I get you guys a drink?"

Bender and Fox ordered drinks. Fox asked Fatty, "Who are those two guys talking to Duke?"

"I'll tell you later," Fatty said.

"Well, well," Fox said. "The two hoods finally showed up."

Big Al drank down his drink and said to Tony, "Come on, let's hit it! This place really sucks."

"O.K.," Tony said. "And don't forget what we told you Duke, my boy. We don't want no more suicides."

With that, they walked out the door. Duke thought, man those guys give me the willies. Duke headed over to see Bender and Fox. Shit, he thought. What do these guys want now?

Duke walked up to Bender and Fox. "Hey guys, nice to see you stop back. What can I get for you?"

"Nothing," Fox said. "We just stopped in for a quick drink. Man, the place is jumping."

"Yeah," Duke said. "I don't know why, but I've been getting a good crowd in here. I was just thinking to myself. Maybe, I should put a live band in here on the weekends."

"Good idea," Bender said. "That ought to draw a bigger crowd. By the way, I see you got a new barmaid! That wouldn't by chance be Marylou, would it?"

"Come on Bender," Duke said. "You know that's Marylou. You sat here and drank with us all night!"

"Just kidding," Bender said. "Well, what do you say Fox! Ready?"

"You guys want one more for the road?" Duke asked.

"No," Fox said. "We have to hit the road. You know, duty calls."

Hmm, Duke thought, What the hell is going on here? Big Al and Tony are here. Those two dicks see them and they don't say a word. I don't understand this shit! "Fatty, give me a drink." Duke walked back to his stool at the end of the bar.

Bender and Fox got out to their car. "I think that was a good move," Fox said. "Not even mentioning those two guys to Duke."

"Yeah, I think you're right," Bender said. "We want it to look like we stopped by the joint for pleasure, not business."

"That's right. The Sarge will be proud of us," Fox said. "Hey Bender, let's take a ride down to Rosie's." Hunter's car was parked there.

"Man, we should have bet that he would be here. We finally would have won one." Fox said.

"Hell," Bender said. "They wouldn't even take that bet in Vegas."

Bender and Fox walked in the door of the bar. Hunter was sitting there talking to Rosie. Hunter looked up at the clock on the wall and said, "I hope you guys are off duty."

CHAPTER 41

Duke was sitting at the end of the bar enjoying watching the crowd when the door opened and in walked Hermy. On no, thought Duke. First those two hoods, then the cops, and now this. If this little weasel starts anything, I'll kill him.

Marylou saw Hermy walk in and thought, trouble is on its way. Hermy went to a barstool and sat down. Marylou walked over to him. At least, he didn't look drunk. "What do you want Hermy?" Marylou asked him.

"Just a cup of coffee please." Hermy was almost whispering.

Well, at least he ain't drunk, Marylou thought as she went to get some coffee. Marylou brought the coffee back and set it in front of Hermy.

Hermy looked up at Marylou and said, "Can I talk to you?"

"Not now," Marylou said. "You can see how busy we are. But, it's almost closing time and you can talk to me then. But, I'm warning you Hermy; if you start any trouble, I'll have to kick the shit out of you!"

"Don't worry," Hermy said. "I'll be good."

Marylou went back to work, but she could feel Hermy watching her.

Duke was watching Hermy, just waiting for him to start something. But, Hermy just sat there drinking his coffee.

It was two a.m. Even though the bar was still jumping, Duke called out, "Last call for alcohol!" Duke didn't want to take any chances of the vice men nailing him for after hours when business was so good. It was almost three o'clock when they got the last customer out the door.

Marylou told Hermy to go sit at one of the tables while she cleaned up. Hermy took a cup of coffee and sat down at the table. When they were all finished cleaning, Duke told Marylou to go over and talk to Hermy. He and Fatty would sit at another table. In case Hermy started anything, Duke would be there to help Marylou. Marylou poured herself a drink, got another cup of coffee, and went over to the table to talk to Hermy.

Marylou put the coffee in front of Hermy and sat down. "O.K., Hermy," she said. "What the hell is going on? Are you crazy? I mean I go out one night, and you make it sound like all I do is whore around. Let me tell you something Hermy. That's the first time I've gone out alone since we've been together. Now, I don't know what your problem is, but I've had enough of your bullshit!" Marylou stared at Hermy. Hermy was just sitting at the table with his head down staring at the floor.

"Well," Marylou said. "Do you have anything to say or what?"

Hermy slowly looked up, and with tears in his eyes said, "Dear Marylou, I'm so sorry. I know I was wrong. But, I want you to come back to me. I promise I will never act jealous again. I just need you to be back with me."

Marylou looked at Hermy. He looked like some little boy who got caught doing something wrong by his mother. He's not such a bad guy, thought Marylou. Maybe I shouldn't be so hard on him. "Look Hermy," Marylou said. "It's not all that easy. Some things have come up that could change the way you think. You may not even want me back."

"Tell me how could anything change? I love you and that's what counts and nothing you can say can't make me love you any less, or make me not want to take you back home."

Marylou thought for a while. "O.K., let me give you the conditions on which I will go back with you."

"Please tell me," Hermy said. He had a big grin on his face.

Marylou looked at him. I've got it made so far with this guy; a little bullshit, and he'll do anything I tell him. O.K. Hermy, she thought, you asked for it.

"Number one, if I come back, my children come with me. Patty is getting tired of watching them. Besides that, I'm really starting to miss them. Number two, I'm going to be working for Duke, tending bar, and some nights I will be coming home late and I don't want any bullshit from you. Number three, If you ever think about hitting me again, forget it. Because next time, I'll kill you! So there's my rules and there ain't no room for any changes to be made by you. One more thing: Tonight, I have to stay at Patty's to watch the kids. She went home with Big Red."

"When will you come back then?" Hermy asked her.

My Baby My Baby!

"Not so fast," Marylou said. "What about my rules?"

"I want you with me," Hermy said. "So I agree with the rules. I don't like you working here or coming home late. But, I will try my best. So, can we just try, please Marylou, please?"

"O.K., Marylou said. "I'll be home around two o'clock tomorrow afternoon. Since it is Sunday, you be ready to take me and the kids to a picnic at Edgewater Park."

"Oh Marylou," Hermy said as he jumped up from the table and grabbed Marylou from her seat. "I love you, I love you. I can't wait until tomorrow. I'll have everything ready for you and the kids. I'm going home to clean up the house for you." Hermy ran for the door. He turned back and blew Marylou a kiss and then was gone out the door.

"Jesus," Duke said after Hermy left. "What the hell did you tell that guy? He looks like he is happier than a pig in shit."

Marylou laughed, "I just told him I was going back to his house to live with my kids."

"That made him happy?" Duke said. "But, what about working for me?"

"I told him about that, too. So, don't worry. Anyhow, why don't you mind your own business, Duke?" Marylou said.

"Hey, don't get mad at me," Duke said. "I ain't done nothing to you yet." He winked. "Now how about a drink, we had a pretty hard night."

"What the hell do you mean we?" Fatty asked Duke. "But, we will take the drink anyhow, right Marylou?"

"Right," Marylou said. "But, just one for me. I got to go. Fatty, will you drop me by Patty's house?"

"Sure," Fatty said. "After this drink, we are on our way." Fatty went to the bar to get the drinks.

Fatty and Marylou left the bar right after they had that drink. When they got to the car, Fatty asked Marylou what had changed her mind about going back with Hermy.

Marylou told her that it really seemed like a good idea. After all, Hermy really treated her good until this one time. She told Fatty she was getting lonesome for her children and even though Fatty had said they could stay at her house for a while, there was a lot more room at

Hermy's. Hermy could watch them while she worked at Duke's and that would keep him busy.

"Hey, hey, what about our little deal?" Fatty asked. "I mean, what are you going to do? Just give it up, or what?"

"No, I ain't, but this will give me a little more room to work," Marylou said. "This way, I have no problem with Hermy. I have someone to watch the kids, and that leaves my mind open to work on Duke. No Fatty, I ain't giving up our little deal. I'm just starting to work on it. By the way, what did those two hoods want?"

"I don't know what they wanted," Fatty said. "But those are the two guys I told you about. They're the ones that Jimmy was talking to about Noreen. They haven't been around for a long time."

"Well, I'll just have to find out what's going on from Duke," Marylou said.

Fatty dropped Marylou off at Patty's and told Marylou. "If you need anything or a place to stay, you just call old Fatty and she will take care of you. See you at work Monday."

Marylou waved good-bye and then went into the house. She sent the baby-sitter home and settled down to await the events of the next day.

CHAPTER 42

Sunday morning, Marylou got up at eight o'clock. The children were already watching cartoons on the TV. Marylou checked Patty's bedroom. There wasn't a sign of Patty and the bed didn't look as if it had been slept in. Marylou hoped Patty would be home by the time she had to go to Hermy's. After all, she did not want to take Patty's kids with her, not this time. Give poor Hermy a chance to get used to her kids first. Marylou put some coffee on and checked the fridge. Good, plenty of eggs and bacon.

Marylou called to the kids, "Hey, all you guys want breakfast?"

"Yeah," they all hollered back. "We're hungry."

Marylou put the pans on the stove and started cooking. She just started to scramble the eggs when the door opened and in came Patty smiling like crazy.

"Hey, you look good," Marylou said. "How was it?"

"Need you ask," Patty said. "That guy is just what I need. He's coming over tonight for dinner."

"Well, good for you Patty," Marylou said. "Just don't do anything stupid."

"Hey," Patty said. "The guy ain't married and he works every day. What more could you ask for?"

"I just don't want to see you get hurt," Marylou said. "Patty, you know you're my best friend."

"I'll try my best Marylou," Patty said. "But, I think I already love this guy."

"You do whatever you have to," Marylou told Patty. "But, in the meantime, I have some news for you."

"Oh shit," Patty said. "Is it good or bad?"

"Just sit down at the table and let me pour you some coffee and get these kids fed. Then, I will tell you."

"Sure," Patty said. "You tell me you have news and then you pour me a cup of coffee and tell me to sit down and you will tell me later. Man, it must be some bad news, right?"

"Heck no, just wait until I get these kids fixed up. It's good news, and you are going to be very happy about it," Marylou told her.

Marylou fixed the kid's plates and took them into the living room so they could eat and watch TV and also keep them out of the kitchen. Marylou went back into the kitchen, fixed herself and Patty a plate, and then sat down at the table.

Patty watched Marylou start to eat. "God damn it," Patty said to Marylou. "Will you tell me the news?"

Marylou looked at Patty and smiled, "Sure, I'll tell you. I talked to Hermy last night and we decided to try again."

"That's good news?" Patty said.

"Wait a minute, will you?" Marylou said. "That's not all the news. I'm going to take the children with me."

Patty just sat there staring at Marylou. "Well," said Marylou, "doesn't that make you happy?"

"I guess it does," Patty said. "But, it seems so sudden. I mean, you know, I've been watching those kids for a long time. It almost seems like they're mine. I mean, oh hell, you know what I mean." Patty had tears in her eyes.

"I know," Marylou said. "But look how I feel. I'm really starting to miss my kids and that Hermy ain't such a bad guy. This way, I will find out how he will be with my kids, and then I can decide if I will stay with him or not."

"You better not let him hurt those kids Marylou, or there will be big trouble, and I mean it," Patty said.

"Don't worry Patty," Marylou told her. "I'll be watching him like a hawk." Marylou and Patty got up from the table and hugged each other. Marylou thanked Patty for all she had done and told her about the deal she had made with Hermy. They both had a laugh over it.

Patty said, "You know Marylou, you are the best. I just don't know how the hell you get away with all the things you do."

"You ain't seen nothing yet," Marylou said. "The best is yet to come."

"You go get cleaned up," Patty told Marylou. "I'll clean the kitchen up."

"O.K., I have to tell the kids what the plans are," Marylou said. "And by then, it will be time to go."

Marylou took the kids into the bedroom and told them what plans she had made. All three of them were happy to be going on a new adventure. At the same time, they were sad to leave Patty's house and the friends they had made. "It's not that far away," Marylou told them. "You can come over here to stay sometimes, and your friends can come to your house." That seemed to make things all right. They went to tell the other kids about going away. Marylou could hear all the yelling and laughing coming from the other room as the kids made plans to visit each other. I sure hope this works out as simple for me as for the kids, Marylou thought. Oh well, I've had it as bad as it can get, I hope. So, let's go on with it. They said their good-byes and started the walk to Hermy's.

CHAPTER 43

It was only about two blocks to Hermy's and Marylou was thinking all the way. I sure hope he gets along with my kids. I hope I'm making the right move here. They turned the corner, and Marylou could see Hermy standing out in front of his place waiting like some goof. As Marylou walked a little closer, she saw he was waving and then pointing at a station wagon parked at the curb. Marylou took a good look at the car and saw it was hers, but it looked brand new. Hermy hollered out, "Hey honey, how does it look? I gave old Junkyard Jack a few more bucks, and he got it done for you!"

Marylou could not believe her eyes. "Why Hermy," she said, "that doesn't even look like my car. It's so pretty."

"Well, let's get those kids of yours and hop in. I got everything ready in the back of the car. Come on kids!" Hermy said. "It's picnic time!"

The kids jumped into the car, yelling and fighting for the window seats.

They had a great time at the park, even Marylou was swinging on the swings and sliding down the sliding boards. Hermy had brought fried chicken, potato salad, pop, and a big apple pie for dessert.

Marylou and Hermy were sitting at the picnic table; the kids were running around chasing each other. "Is this great or what?" Hermy said.

"Yes, it is," Marylou said to Hermy. "The kids are having a lot of fun and so am I.":

"Yeah," Hermy said. "We should have done this a long time ago. You know, Marylou. I think we could have a good family life. Hell, maybe I can open the church backup, and then we could be a real family. What I mean is, Marylou, will you marry me?"

Marylou looked at Hermy and smiled. She then reached across the table and took Hermy's hand saying; "Not right now, Hermy. Let's just wait and see how things work out. If they do,"

"If they do, then what?" Hermy asked.

"Just wait. If they do, then maybe I'll be Mrs. Hermy," Marylou said and they both laughed.

"This is the happiest day of my life," Hermy said. "Let's get those kids and go buy some ice cream."

When they all got home from getting ice cream, it was almost time for the children to go to bed. They walked into the house and Marylou could not believe her eyes. The house as neat as a pin. Hermy told her he had the paint and was going to paint the entire inside of the house starting tomorrow. "I fixed the two rooms upstairs, one for Billy and Joey, and the other room for little Susan. Right now, I just put sleeping bags on the floor. Tomorrow, you can go up on Lorain Avenue and find some beds," Hermy said to Marylou.

"That's o.k.," Marylou said. "The kids will love sleeping in the sleeping bags on the floor a while. You sure fixed this place up nice Hermy, and thanks for being so nice to the kids. Now, let me put them to bed. Come on you guys, tell Hermy goodnight and let's go see your new bedrooms."

Marylou took them upstairs and Hermy sat down in his chair. What a great day, Hermy thought. This is just like I dreamed it would be. Me sitting in my chair, and Marylou putting the children to bed. What could be better? Just then, Marylou came down the stairs.

"Ready for bed?" Marylou asked Hermy.

Now, I know what could be better, Hermy thought and smiled.

"What's the big smile for?" Marylou asked Hermy.

"As If you didn't know," Hermy grabbed her and carried her to the bedroom.

The next morning Hermy got out of bed first and put the coffee on. He crawled back into the bed. But, Marylou said, "Oh no, you don't Hermy. I have to get breakfast for the kids." Marylou jumped from the bed laughing.

The children finished breakfast and had gone out to play. Marylou and Hermy were sitting at the table having coffee. "I'm going to start to paint the rooms," Hermy said. "I think I'll start with the boy's bedroom. Why don't you take a ride and see if you can find some beds and dressers. We can finish one room at a time."

"Good idea," Marylou said. "I'm on my way."

Marylou spent the rest of the morning going from one second-hand store to another. She found two dressers and a set of bunk beds. She loaded the station wagon with her finds and headed for home.

When she got home, she called up to Hermy. "Come on down here and help me with this stuff."

"Be right down," Hermy said. "I'm almost done with this room."

Hermy and Marylou moved the furniture into the rooms.

"Man, it looks great," Marylou said.

"Yes, it does," Hermy said. "They can move their clothes and toys in, but they have to clean their room every day."

"Good idea," Marylou said. "Now, let's go have lunch."

While Marylou made lunch, Hermy took the boys up to see the room. They were all happy and said they would clean the room every day. Little Susie started to cry, "What about my room? It needs to be painted, too, and I don't have a bed to sleep in."

Hermy picked her up and hugged her. "Tomorrow, I'll paint your room and your mom will go buy you a bed."

"Are you sure?" Susie asked.

"I promise," Hermy told her. "Now, let's go have lunch." The boys ran to the kitchen and Hermy carried Susie down to the kitchen.

After lunch, Marylou said, "Hermy, I have to be work at around seven o'clock, so it will be up to you to get the kids in bed, and I'll be home as soon as possible. But, don't wait up for me."

"But Marylou, I stay up late anyway. I wish you didn't have to go to work." Hermy was whining.

"Don't' start that shit Hermy," Marylou said. "This is the first night and already you're starting to make trouble."

"No, I'm not," Hermy said. "It's just that,..."

"Knock if off Hermy. I can leave here again just as fast as I came back here!" Marylou told him.

"I'm sorry," Hermy said as he walked over and hugged Marylou. "Why don't you take a little nap, and I'll clean up the kitchen."

Marylou headed for the bedroom thinking, I hope I didn't make a mistake coming back here. That damn Hermy, starting to bitch and whine already. What the hell am I going to do when I stay out late trying to get Duke to tell me about Noreen? Oh well, I'll cross that bridge when I get to it. Marylou lay across the bed. I have to make a plan to make Duke talk, but she fell asleep before she could start planning.

The next thing Marylou knew, Hermy was shaking her. "Get up Honey," Hermy was saying. "It's time for you to get ready for work."

CHAPTER 44

Marylou walked into the bar and Duke yelled out, "Hey, how was the honeymoon? Did Hermy get it all, or did you save some for me?" Duke lifted his glass in a salute to Marylou and started to laugh.

"I hope you choke on that," Marylou yelled back, "And besides that, nobody gets it all!"

Duke did choke on his drink and the rest of the bar including Fatty, started to laugh.

"Guess she got you on that one," Bid Red yelled out to Duke. He looked at Fatty and said, "Bring us all another drink, your boss spit his all over the bar!"

Duke smiled. Hell, he thought. I can take any kind of ribbing as long as business stays like this. And, I'm glad Marylou said that. Maybe, that means she's still got some for me.

The bar stayed busy until one in the morning, then it started to slow down. "Hey girls," Duke said. "I think I'll go upstairs, how about closing the place up?"

"Sure, no problem," Fatty said. "Me and Marylou can take care of it."

Duke slid off the stool and headed for the door. "See you guys tomorrow."

There were only two other guys sitting at the bar, Big Red and one of his cronies. Marylou and Fatty went to the other end of the bar, so they could talk. "Well, how did it go yesterday?" Fatty asked.

Marylou told her what a good time they had had on Sunday, how Hermy had painted the room, and how she had bought furniture.

"Sounds like a real home to me," Fatty said.

"Yeah, until I mentioned about going to work," Marylou said. She told Fatty how Hermy had acted. "I sure hope he doesn't give me a hard time. You know, this time he had my kids when I'm not there. Man, if he ever hurt them, I would have to kill him," Marylou said.

"How is this going to affect our deal?" Fatty asked.

"Oh, I'll still work," Marylou said.

"Not that," Fatty whispered. "I mean about Duke and getting the money!"

"Don't worry Fatty. I'll think of a plan, but I think we better wait a while. You know, until I get Hermy off my back. I'll go home right after we close now and as time goes by, I'll just get home a little later each night."

After Fatty and Marylou closed up the bar, Fatty said; "Hey Marylou, how about a little drink before we go?"

"Now Fatty," Marylou said. "What did I just tell you about going home early?"

"Oh yeah, you better get home," Fatty said as she laughed, or little Hermy might spank you."

"Funny, funny," Marylou said. "But, you'll be glad I did it this way when all this shit is over with." Marylou went out the door and headed for home.

Marylou parked the car in front of Hermy's place and saw that the lights were on. Just as I thought, Hermy is waiting up for me. Marylou went to the back door. Just as she got there, the door opened. Hermy was standing there with a bunch of flowers in his hand. "For you," he said as he let her in.

"Why thank you, Hermy, but what's the occasion?" Marylou asked.

"Oh nothing," Hermy said. "They're just for you." Hermy kissed her.

"This is really nice of you Hermy," Marylou said. "But, I'm awfully tired, and I just want to go to bed."

"Sure, sure," Hermy said. "Go to bed. I'll be in in a while. I'm going to watch the late movie."

Marylou went into the bedroom and Hermy sat down in his chair. God damn it, he thought. The first night, and she comes home too tired to do anything. Maybe, she got enough at the bar. Oh shit! Why am I thinking this way? I told her I would change, and I'm going to. Hermy sat back in his chair. I have to make myself not act jealous. Hermy dozed off and woke up around four-thirty in the morning. He went into the bedroom and got in bed next to Marylou. Marylou never moved. Sound sleeper, Hermy thought. Anyone could sneak in bed with her. Hermy dropped off to sleep, but kept tossing and turning as he dreamt of a long line of men going into Marylou's bed. She never woke up. As each man left he said to the next one in line, "Sound sleeper."

Marylou woke up and looked at the clock. Shit! It's only eight o'clock. Hermy was moaning something under his breath, but he was still asleep. Marylou could hear the kids out in the front room watching cartoons. She still felt sleepy, but thought to herself, let me get out of this bed before Hermy wakes up and wants to play.

Marylou went out into the kitchen and started the coffee. She yelled into the front room, "Hey, you kids want breakfast?"

"No," they yelled back. "We had some donuts that Hermy bought us last night."

Good, thought Marylou. Maybe, I can have a cup of coffee in peace. Just as she poured the coffee, she heard the shuffle of feet behind her. She looked around, and there was Hermy. He looked awful. "What's the matter Hermy?" Marylou asked. "You look sick, are you?"

"No," Hermy said. "I just slept bad. I was tossing and turning most of the night. Did I bother you?"

"No, not at all," Marylou said.

"You're a sound sleeper," Hermy said, half to himself.

"What did you say?" Marylou asked.

"Nothing, nothing," Hermy said.

Marylou shrugged her shoulders. "Do you want some breakfast?"

Hermy just looked at Marylou and then said, "No, just coffee please."

Marylou gave Hermy some coffee as he sat down at the table. Marylou set the coffee in front of him and thought to herself, what the hell is wrong with him now?

Hermy didn't say anything while he drank his first cup of coffee. Marylou thought he was looking a little better. Then, old Hermy smiled like he was just fine and said, "Hey honey, how about another cup of coffee? I feel a lot better now."

"Sure," Marylou said. "How about a donut too, Hermy?"

"Sounds good to me," Hermy said. "I took the kids to the donut shop last night, and I brought home a dozen for us."

Marylou got the donuts and put them on the table. She thought, Hermy looks fine now, maybe it's just me. I have to relax a little and give Hermy a break. He's trying his best.

Hermy ate two donuts and finished his coffee. He stretched back on the kitchen chair. Ah, that feels better. The bad dreams of last night were fading. "I'm going to start on little Susie's room now. Are you going to get her bedroom set today?"

"Yes," Marylou said. "I saw the set I like at the Salvation Army store on West 25th. There's a bed, a dresser, and a small dressing table, all white with pink trim. It's just the thing for Susie, and all they want is fifty dollars. I have twenty-five now that I will give them to hold the set. Then when Duke pays me tonight, I can give them the rest of the money and pick the set up."

"Wait a minute," Hermy said. He ran out of the kitchen and upstairs. Marylou could hear him up there in one of the closets.

Hermy came back down the stairs with a big grin on his face. "Here honey," he said, and handed Marylou two twenties. "Buy Susie a lamp, too. You don't have to wait for Duke to give you the money," Hermy said. "And besides that, you can pick up the set today."

"O.K., Hermy, I'll take the money, but two things, Marylou said. "One, I'll give the money back to you when I get paid tonight and number two, Duke is not giving me any money. I work for it!"

"O.K., don't be upset," Hermy said. "I meant that you could have the money and pick up the set today. But really, I want to buy the set for Susie, too. Can't we each pay half? I mean, if it's o.k. with you. It makes me feel more like this is my family."

Marylou felt a little bad as Hermy was talking. After all, the guy was trying to be nice. "O.K., Marylou said. "You can pay for half, but I'll take the forty dollars and buy her a lamp, too."

"That's good," Hermy said. "That makes me feel a lot better."

Marylou smiled and thought to herself. What the hell is wrong with me? This guy must have some money hidden upstairs. I should let him pay for the whole thing. I must be losing my touch. I'll just wait for a chance to check that upstairs out.

Marylou went shopping and bought the bedroom set for Susie. While she was at the store, she saw the lamp that would go with the bedroom set and asked the clerk how much it was. The clerk smiled at Marylou and said, "Look honey, you bought enough here. I'll throw the lamp in for free."

Good, thought Marylou. I can put that money away just in case I have to leave Hermy in a hurry.

My Baby My Baby!

The clerk was helping Marylou get all the furniture into the station wagon and was tying the mattress on the roof when he said, "You know, I could bring this stuff over in my truck. It would be a lot easier for you. Then, maybe you and me could have a cup of coffee or something." The clerk stood there with a big grin on his face.

"Look," Marylou said. "If you want me to pay for that fucking lamp, I'll pay for it. But, if you think I'm going to give you a piece of ass for a five dollar lamp, you are full of shit!"

The clerk got a look of fear on his face and stuttered, "Geeze lady, I was just trying to be a nice guy. I didn't mean anything."

"Sure, sure," Marylou said. "I know you just want to help a poor little girl like me. Now, give me that fucking rope. I can tie this shit on my myself."

The clerk tossed her the rope and walked away mumbling under his breath, "Ungrateful bitch."

Marylou thought. All the trouble I got right now and this guy wants to add to it for the price of a used lamp. Men are all the same. They ain't going to give you anything without trying to get in your pants. Marylou finished tying down the mattress and got into the car to head home. Oh well, she thought. I feel better now that I told that asshole clerk off. Best of all, I can kept that extra money Hermy gave me. From now on, I'll take all I can get from him. I'll salt it away and if things work out, maybe I can get Noreen back and we can skip town. Marylou pulled up in front of the house. She could see Hermy in the window upstairs painting. She yelled, "Hey Hermy, come and help me with all this stuff."

Hermy looked out the window, waved, and shouted, "I'll be right down."

Hermy and Marylou moved the set into the front room until Hermy could finish the painting. "Only a little while longer," Hermy said. "And then, we can move everything upstairs."

Marylou went into the kitchen to fix some coffee. While she was waiting for the coffee to perk, she sat at the table thinking about what she would have to do to get the information from Duke. She knew she would have to go to bed with him sooner or later, but that's the breaks. It seemed the only way she ever got anything was to go to bed for it. But the thing that worried her the most was, it was always her luck that the men didn't have to have a one-night stand. They wanted to marry her, or at least, move in with her. I don't need that problem with Duke, she thought. Man, Hermy would go crazy! Why hell, he would probably kill someone. Well, she thought. Maybe, it wouldn't be such a bad idea. I could get Noreen back, plus twenty-five thousand dollars, and Hermy kills Duke. Hermy goes to prison, and I go free from everything. Now, Marylou really felt good and back to her old self. As she smiled to herself, she heard Hermy call, "come up and look at this room. It's a masterpiece!"

Marylou went to look at the room, and it did look nice. They moved the furniture up and Hermy raved about the bedroom set and the lamp he thought he had bought. When they had finished, they had lunch and Hermy told Marylou to go and take a nap while he cleaned up the kitchen. Marylou was just starting to doze when she heard little Susie come into the house and ask Hermy if her room was done. Hermy told her it was and took her up to see it. That was the last thing Marylou heard before she dropped off to sleep.

CHAPTER 45

Marylou got to Duke's Bar a little early. After Hermy had awakened her, Hermy, Marylou, and Susie had gone to look at the room again. Marylou again gave Hermy instructions about the children. She still felt uneasy leaving them with Hermy.

Marylou walked into the bar. Duke was sitting at the end of the bar in the usual place. Fatty was standing behind the bar talking to Duke. There were three customers sitting at the other end of the bar drinking.

"Hey Marylou, you're early," Duke yelled out. "But, that's good. Come on down here. I have something to tell you and Fatty." Marylou went over to Duke and sat down next to him.

"O.K. big boy, what do you have to tell me?" Marylou asked in a sexy voice.

Fatty smiled at Marylou and Duke slide his arm over Marylou's shoulders. "I forgot," Duke said. "I can only think of one thing now."

Marylou took Duke's hand and removed his arm from her shoulders. "You couldn't handle it," she said to Duke and smiled.

"Yeah, just gimme a chance," Duke said. "But anyhow, I want the two of you to be here by ten o'clock tomorrow morning."

"What?" Both girls asked at the same time.

"I have this band coming in to play for us," Duke said. "If they're any good, I'll hire them to play this weekend. I want you girls to hear them. You know better than me if the customers will like them."

"O.K. with me," Marylou said.

"Not me," Fatty said. "I have a doctor's appointment in the morning that can't be changed."

"O.K.," Duke said "Marylou, be here in the morning and let's see how these guys are."

Later when Marylou and Fatty were behind the bar working, Fatty said. "Well, how did I do?"

"Do about what?" Marylou asked.

"About telling Duke I have a doctor's appointment, that's what," Fatty said.

"Well, don't you have one?" Marylou asked.

"Hell no," Fatty said. "I just wanted you to have a chance to be with Duke alone, you know, so you can start to make up to him and get some info. You know our little deal, or did you forget?"

"No, no," Marylou said. "I didn't forget. Good idea Fatty."

Duke's Bar was quiet that night. Duke had left around eight o'clock. Marylou and Fatty were just sitting around talking when Fatty said. "Look Marylou, you have a busy day tomorrow. What with helping Duke and all. Why don't you go home early tonight?"

"Good idea," Marylou said. "It's only ten-thirty now. How about if I leave at eleven-thirty, if it's not busy?"

"Sure," Fatty said. "I want you to have some time to think of how you are going to approach Duke."

"Man, gimme a break, will you Fatty?" Marylou said. "You know you can't force these things."

"I know," Fatty said. "But, it seems like you ain't making no moves at all. Don't you want Noreen back?"

"What's the matter with you Fatty?" Marylou said. "Of course, I want Noreen back. I still don't know for sure if Jimmy did what we think he did. I mean, we don't have any proof."

"Listen Marylou," Fatty said. "I'm sure it happened just the way we talked about it, so you get busy and find out all you can from Duke."

Marylou got into her car to drive home and started to think. That Fatty was going to be a real pain in the ass. She wasn't going to let up on me. Well, maybe that's because I need a little push sometimes. I've got to come up with a plan for Duke. Right now, I have to break the news to Hermy that I have to go to work early and won't be back until after the bar closes. Just then, Marylou had an idea. Let's see, she thought to herself. Eleven forty-five. The kids are all in bed, but I better make sure. Marylou crept all around the house looking in the windows. Sure enough, all she saw was Hermy sitting in the living room watching the old television set. Oh good, thought Marylou as she walked to the back door. When she got there, she put her purse down and started to take off all of her clothes. When she was naked, she knocked on he door. All of a sudden, the porch light went on and Hermy looked out the window. He just stared out the window with his mouth open looking at Marylou without opening the door.

My Baby My Baby!

Marylou screamed, "Hermy, open the fucking door before all the neighbors see me!"

Hermy pulled the door open and Marylou ran screaming in the kitchen. She turned around and looked at Hermy. He was standing there with his mouth still hanging open.

"You dumb shit, shut the fucking door! I'm freezing my ass off!" Marylou screamed at Hermy.

Hermy reached behind his back and swung the door shut, and with that dumb look on his face, he said, "Marylou?"

"Who the hell else would it be?" Marylou asked. Then, they both started to laugh.

"Come on in the bedroom Marylou," Hermy said. "I have something for you."

Later, Hermy asked Marylou, "How come you're home so early?"

"Business was slow," Marylou said. "So, I asked Fatty if she'd mind if I went home early. I felt horny, so I wanted to get home to surprise you."

"Man, that was a nice surprise," Hermy said. I'd like a surprise like that every night."

"You would be dead in a week," Marylou said.

"Yeah, but what a way to go," Hermy said smiling.

"Enough," Marylou said. "I'm going to the kitchen to make a sandwich, want one?"

"Sure," Hermy said. "I'll be right out."

Marylou went to the kitchen and put on some coffee and made two sandwiches. I have it made now, though Marylou. That dumb shit won't think of anything else but what just happened now when I tell him about going in early tomorrow. Hermy came out to the kitchen and sat at the table. "This is living," Hermy said and started to eat his sandwich.

Marylou poured the coffee and sat down. "Oh, by the way, Hermy," Marylou began. "I have to go in early, about ten in the morning, and I won't be home until after my shift."

"No problem," Hermy said. "I can take the kids to a movie. Hey, maybe you can surprise me again tomorrow night!"

"Easy Hermy," Marylou said. "If I told you about it, then it wouldn't be a surprise. But, let me tell you something. If you hear a knock on the back door, open it, and don't turn on the lights!" They both started laughing.

Marylou and Hermy finished their snack and headed for bed. As Marylou was lying in bed, she thought. Man, that Hermy is dumb. Just like any other man. Give them a little and they forget about everything else that is going on around them.

Marylou got up the next morning about nine o'clock and Hermy asked her if she wanted any breakfast. "No," Marylou said. "I'll just have a cup of coffee and be on my way. It's going to be long day."

"Yeah," Hermy said. "For me, too. Do you have any idea when you will be home?"

"Hermy," Marylou said. "I told you I will be home right after work, now lay off!"

"O.K.," Hermy said. "I'll be waiting for you. Do you think you might want something to eat when you get home?"

"No, I doubt it," Marylou said. "If I get hungry, I'll have a sandwich at the bar." Marylou went into the bedroom to get ready. Hermy went into the kitchen for more coffee.

When Marylou came into the kitchen to have some coffee, Hermy looked at her and said, "What the hell are you wearing? Why the hell are you all dressed up like that for? God damn it, you look like some slut!"

"What the hell are you talking about?" Marylou screamed.

"What am I talking about?" Hermy screamed back. "Look at you, your jeans are so tight, they look like they are painted on, and God damn it, your tits are almost falling out of that fucking v-neck sweater! You ain't going to work like that. I'm telling you that right now! If you want to go to work, get your ass back in that bedroom and change your fucking clothes!"

Marylou grabbed the cup of coffee Hermy had poured for her and threw it on him. The coffee was not very hot, but it scared the hell out of Hermy.

Hermy yelled, "What the hell is wrong with you Marylou? You could have scalded me!"

"Fuck you Hermy, you little weasel. If you ever talk to me like that again, I'll kill you. Now, I'm going to work and you better take good care of my kids. Don't you ever tell me what to wear again. Never, do you understand me?" Marylou started for the door.

"Please, honey, I'm sorry. Please don't be mad at me!" Hermy whimpered.

Marylou looked at him with a smirk on her face and walked out slamming the door.

Oh shit, Hermy thought as Marylou slammed the door. What the hell do I do now? Man, what the hell is wrong with me? We had so much fun last night, and then I blow the whole deal by getting jealous again. But God damn it, the way she was dressed! Shit! She's just asking for trouble at the bar. I'm going to have to watch out for her. How am I going to do that? I'll think of some way so she doesn't see me. If she catches me spying on her, it's all over, if it ain't now.

CHAPTER 46

Marylou got to the bar a little after ten o'clock, and she saw a van parked in front of the bar. The van was painted with cowboys and horses chasing a herd of cows. On the hood of the van was a set of steer horns; on the back of the van was a sign that read, THE STAMPEDE BAND. Unloading the van was a lean guy dressed in tight jeans, cowboy boots, western shirt, and a cowboy hat with a snake skin band and a feather sticking out of it. Marylou walked by, and the cowboy looked at her and said, "Hey filly, how about coming in the bar and listening to us play?"

"That's just where I'm headed cowboy," Marylou smiled. "And you better be good 'cause, I'm the one who might hire you."

"I'm always good, on or off stage." He gave Marylou a wink and went back to unloading the van.

Marylou went into the bar and saw Duke sitting at a table talking to some guy dressed just like the one who was unloading the van. Up on the small stage at the back of the bar was another cowboy setting up some speakers. Marylou walked over to the table Duke was sitting at. "Howdy partner," she said. "What time does the grub come?"

The guy sitting with Duke smiled up at Marylou, "Howdy ma'am. We'll be set up in a minute or two, and then we can play a couple of tunes for you all." With that, he got up from the table and walked over to the stage to help set up.

"Hey Marylou," Duke said. "How do you like the band so far?"

"It looks like Dodge City in here," Marylou said. "All three cowboys look the same. What are their names, Darryl, Darryl, and Darryl?"

"Very funny," Duke said. "Let me tell you, these guys are really supposed to be good. Besides that, they have a lot of people that follow them from bar to bar. Maybe, we'll get some new customers this weekend."

"It sounds like you already hired them," Marylou said.

"I did hear how good they are from some of my friends," Duke said. "But, I'd still like to hear them myself. I want you to hear them, too. You know, as they say, two heads are better than one. How about if you get us some coffee while we wait?"

My Baby My Baby!

"Sounds good to me," Marylou said. "But, I don't know how you can have a stampede with just three people," Marylou laughed.

The band played two ballads and one fast song. Duke yelled up to the stage. "O.K. boys, good enough, you're hired. I want you to be ready to play Friday night at eight o'clock sharp. If you guys go good, we'll make it for Saturday night, too."

"Thanks," one of the cowboys yelled from the stage. Is it o.k. if we leave some of our stuff here so we don't have to haul it out again?"

"No problem," Duke called back. "It will be safe here."

"Well, that was fast," Marylou said. "You could have done all this without me."

"Not really baby," Duke said. "Fatty will be late tonight, so maybe you can tend bar and when Fatty comes, I'll take you to dinner."

"Easy Duke," Marylou said. "What makes you think I'll go to dinner with you?"

"Geeze," Duke said. "I just thought it would be nice because you came in early to help me out."

"O.K.," Marylou said, "but don't get any ideas that this is a date or something like that. You know I'm very happy with Hermy."

"Sure, sure," Duke said. "I know how happy you are, but I'm just trying to be nice."

It was about five in the afternoon when Fatty got to work. "Hey Marylou, how are you doing?" She yelled as she came in the door.

"Fine," Marylou said. "Glad you could make it to work."

"It's not like I couldn't think of something better to do," Fatty said.

"What the hell else would you be doing?" Duke yelled from the end of the bar.

"Anything would be better than this," Fatty yelled back. "Duke, that's the same place you were sitting the last time I saw you. You sure that stool ain't growing on your ass?"

"Very funny Fatty," Duke said as he got up from the stool. "See, it's still on the floor."

"It must have rotted off you!" Fatty said.

"Fatty, maybe I can put your act on the stage instead of the band," Duke said. "What the hell do you think this is? The Comedy Club?

So, knock off the smart ass shit and get behind the bar and start working."

"Touchy, touchy," Fatty said.

"Marylou," Duke said. "Tell Fatty about the band while I go up and change. I'll be down in about an hour, then we can go for dinner." Duke headed for the door.

"Now about the band," Marylou said to Fatty.

"Fuck the band," Fatty said. "Duke is taking you out, on a date or what?"

"No, not a date," Marylou said. He's just trying to be nice."

"He's just trying to get in those tight-ass jeans," Fatty said. "Duke never does anything for nothing. I hope this is part of your plan to work on him about Noreen."

"God damn Fatty, keep your voice down. Let's see how far we can get and how soon," Marylou said.

"Yeah," Fatty said. "But be careful. You know you can't push Duke. Just take your time and sooner or later Duke will spill his guts to you."

A little over an hour later, Duke walked into the bar. Everyone turned to look at the door. The smell of after-shave was overpowering. Fatty let out a low whistle and Duke had a big grin on his face.

"Wow," Marylou said as she looked Duke up and down.

He had on his dark pinstripe suit and a white shirt and a red tie. His shoes were shined and looked like glass.

"How the hell can I go out to eat with a guy that looks like a movie star the way I am dressed?" Marylou asked.

"Don't you worry about that," Duke said. "You look just great the way you are. Come on, let's go." Duke opened the door for Marylou. His car was parked out in front of the bar. Duke opened the car door for Marylou and then got in the driver's side. He reached into the back seat of the car and pulled out a bouquet of roses. "Here Marylou, these are for you."

"Wait a minute," Marylou said. "What the hell do you think you are doing? This is supposed to be two people, who are co-workers, going for something to eat, not a God damn date! What the fuck am I supposed to do with these flowers? What do I tell Hermy? Man, you could cause me a lot of trouble!"

"Take it easy," Duke said. "I'll take you to dinner and you can put the flowers in a vase behind the bar. Relax Marylou. Now, how about I take you for a nice big steak dinner?"

"O.K.," Marylou said, "But only if you stop treating this like a big date. So, where are you taking me?"

"I know this great place on West 117th and Clifton," Duke told her. "They have good steaks. It will be nice and quiet and nobody will bother us."

"Good, let's get there. I'm starved," Marylou said.

Duke pulled into the parking lot of the restaurant. "Wow," Marylou said. "This is pretty fancy. I don't think they will let me in dressed like this."

"Oh yeah, they will," Duke said. "You might add some class to this joint." They were both laughing as Duke parked the car.

They walked into the restaurant and the maitre d' asked, "Do you have a reservation?"

"No," Duke said. "We just need a table for two." Duke handed the maitre d' a ten dollar bill.

"Ah," he said. "We just had a cancellation. Let me seat you. Follow me please."

Duke winked at Marylou as they followed him to their table. When they were seated, Duke said to Marylou, "See that, no matter how much class you think they have, they still take the bread."

Marylou laughed and said, "You sure know what the hell is going on Duke. I didn't know you were so worldly." Marylou reached across the table and squeezed Duke's hand.

When the maitre d' had seated Duke and Marylou, they had walked by the bar. Duke did not notice the two guys sitting at the bar. But, Big Al saw Duke.

But Al nudged Tony with his elbow, "Hey Tony, did you see that?"

"What?" Tony asked.

"Did you see who just came in?" Big Al asked.

"No, I never noticed," Tony answered.

"Well," Big Al said. "You sure are going to be surprised when you look over at that table in the corner."

Tony turned from the bar and looked over into the corner. "Holy Jesus," Tony said. "That's that Duke and the fat broad. What the fuck's her name? Marylou, that's it, the kid's mother! What the hell is he doing with her?"

"It looks like true love," Big Al said. "That's all we need is the two of them together. Man, this could spell big trouble."

Duke ordered two martinis, then excused himself to go to the men's room.

Big Al nudged Tony again. "Look, there he goes. He must be going to the men's room."

"So what?" Tony said. "You want to go and hold it for him?"

"Come on smart ass. This would be a good time to talk to him," Big Al told Tony.

Just about the time Duke started to unzip his fly, the door burst open and Big Al grabbed Duke in a full nelson and spun him around.

"What the hell?" Duke sputtered. Then, in the mirror he saw it was Big Al and Tony. "What the hell's wrong with you guys?"

Just then, Tony punched Duke in the stomach. Duke started to double up and Big Al pushed him to the floor. Tony kicked Duke in the side. Big Al bent over and grabbed Duke by the shirt pulling his head from the floor.

"What's wrong with you guys?" Duke asked. "Man, what the hell did I do? Shit, I ain't done nothing!"

"Shut up!" Big Al said. "Now, what the fuck are you doing with that fat bitch?"

"Nothing Al, honest. She works for me, and I'm just taking her out to eat," Duke said.

"Bullshit!" Tony said, "It looks like love to us, and when you fall in love, you start to talk. When you start to talk, you get dead! Understand?"

"Yeah, I understand!" Duke was almost crying.

Bit Al slapped Duke a couple of times across the face. "Now, get the fuck out of here!" He told Duke. "And by the way, some guy is going to stop by to see you. We got a couple of things we want done. Now, get out of here."

Duke got up from the floor and ran out of the men's room.

Marylou was sitting at the table sipping her drink and thinking, That Duke is o.k. He sure tries to be a gentleman. I wonder if he'll try to make the move on me tonight? For dinner in this place, I know what he's gonna want, and it ain't gonna be conversation. Oh well, such is life.

Marylou started to take another sip of her drink when Duke grabbed her by the arm and pulled her from the chair.

"Come on," he said. Let's get the fuck out of here!"

Marylou jerked her arm away from Duke. "What the hell is wrong with you?" Then, she saw Duke's face. It was all red and swollen. He looked scared. "What happened to you?"

"Never mind, let's go now, I'll tell you later!" He grabbed Marylou's arm and started for the door. Duke led her, or more like, pulled her to the door.

As Duke pulled Marylou past the bar, Marylou saw two men standing there smiling. She recognized them right away. Ah, she thought, the plot thickens.

Duke unlocked the car and pushed Marylou through the driver's door and across to the passenger's side.

"Hey, don't get so rough and take the shit out on me!" Marylou said. "I didn't do anything!"

"I'm sorry," Duke said. He pulled out his keys, started the car, and then just sat there.

"Well," Marylou said. "What's the story? What happened in there?"

"Nothing," Duke said. "It was just a small disagreement, that's all."

"Was it with those two guys that were standing at the bar?" Marylou asked Duke.

"What two guys? Who do you mean? You know those two guys?" Duke asked.

"I saw them in the bar a couple of nights ago and you looked shook after they talked to you," Marylou said.

I don't know who the hell you are talking about Marylou. If I were you, I'd forget those two guys, just forget them, you hear me?" Duke slammed the car into gear and peeled rubber out of the parking lot.

Duke drove, or more like raced back to the bar. He pulled up in front, reached over Marylou and opened her door.

"Look," he said. "I'm sorry, but I wouldn't be good company now. So for now, could you just go back to work, and I'll see you later."

Marylou got out of the car and before she could even close the door of the car, Duke was taking off down the street.

Duke drove up to Matt's Deli on Bridge Avenue and bought a six-pack of beer. He drove around thinking. What the hell am I going to do, he thought as he opened the top on a can of beer. Man, I'm scared to death of those guys. I wish they would leave me the fuck alone! I don't care what happened to Jimmy or his kid! Fuck both of them! I just don't want all this bullshit, and now those guys are talking about sending someone else to pick up where Big Al and Tony left off. What the hell am I going to do? Duke headed his car down to Edgewater Park. He parked his car facing the lake. Duke sat there listening to the radio, drinking beer, and staring out at the lake.

Marylou stood at the curb as Duke pulled away. He's a crazy man, Marylou thought. Those guys really shook him up. Oh well, let me get back in the bar and get a drink. Marylou opened the door to the bar and saw that it was about half full. That wasn't bad for this time of night, not too busy. At least, I'll have time for a sandwich.

Fatty looked up and saw Marylou coming in the bar. "Man, that was fast," Fatty said. "But, where is Duke?"

Fatty, gimme a break will y a?" Marylou said to Fatty. "Get me a beer while I fix myself a sandwich and then I'll tell you all about it."

Marylou told Fatty everything that had happened at the restaurant and about the ride back to the bar.

"Duke must have been really shook up," Fatty said. "I mean leaving the place like that and just about throwing you out of the car in front of the bar."

"Yeah," Marylou said. "He was shook all right. I have to find out what the hell those two guys said to him. Fatty, tell me again what you know about those two guys."

Fatty told her just about what she had told before. "I really can't think of any more," Fatty said when she had finished. "But, I'm sure they had something to do with taking Noreen."

"Do you think Duke was in on that?" Marylou asked.

"Yeah, I'm sure," Fatty said. "You know that Jimmy wasn't smart enough to do anything like that by himself. Besides that,

Jimmy and Duke were thick as flies just before the shit hit the fan. Then after Jimmy died, Duke was walking around here in a daze for a while. As a matter of fact, that's when those two guys stopped coming around here all the time and Duke quite taking bets."

Marylou thought for a minute, then said, "I'm going to have to get information from Duke. I have to get him to trust me. You know Fatty, I think a plan is starting to come together. Yeah, the seduction of Duke will begin."

"Good," Fatty said. "And, it's about time, too. Maybe, we can get some money. I sure could use it!"

"Look," Marylou said. "This ain't all about getting you and me some money. How about me getting my girl back? I need to know what the hell happened to Noreen. I want to know if she's all right and if I can get her back! Fuck you and that money!"

"Easy," Fatty said. "You're right. I'm on your side. But, if we can get Noreen and the money, too, that would be all the better."

Duke had finished the six-pack and felt much better. It seems that beer does give you more courage, Duke thought. He did not seem to be as afraid of Big Al and Tony as he was before. Hell, he should have kicked their asses in that shit house. Yeah, that would have given those big shots in the restaurant something to think about. Yeah, kicked their asses and then walked out and had dinner as if nothing had happened. Things would be different the next time those guys come into my bar. I'll give them what for. If they send some little shit to try to take their place, I'll kick his ass, too. Yeah, that's it. I'll kick all their asses, and I'm just the guy that can do it. Now, back to tonight. Shit, I hope Marylou ain't mad at me, or worse yet, think that I'm a coward. Man, I didn't make much of an impression on her. Oh well, I think I'll go have a few drinks and get back to the bar around closing time and see if I can make it up to Marylou. Duke left Edgewater Park and headed out to have a few drinks.

The next time Duke looked at his watch, it was two-thirty. Oh shit, I'm late. He jumped into his car and headed for the bar. When he got there, all the lights were out, but Fatty was still there cleaning up.

"Hey, where's Marylou?" Duke asked Fatty.

"Oh, she left early. By the way, she said she wouldn't be in tomorrow, but she'll be in early Friday," Fatty told him.

"Did she say anything about what happened at the restaurant?" Duke asked.

"No," Fatty lied, "just that she didn't have dinner, that's all she said."

Good, thought Duke. The less people who know, the better. "O.K., Fatty," Duke said. "See you later. Just come in at your regular time tomorrow. I'll take care of things until then." Duke headed upstairs and Fatty locked up and headed home.

Marylou pulled in front of the house about twelve-thirty. She sat in the car for a while thinking. Yeah, a plan was starting to take shape. Marylou thought she would play hard to get for Duke, but not too hard. She wanted to play just enough to keep him interested, leading him on for the kill. She knew she would have to go to bed with him, but she wanted to have complete control over what happened. This is more complicated than a roll in the hay. There was a lot more at stake here; the return of her daughter, Noreen, and like Fatty said, maybe some money. That wouldn't hurt either.

Marylou got out of the car and went to the back door, no surprise for Hermy tonight. Hell, just coming home early was too good for Hermy. She unlocked the door and went in. Hermy was sitting in his chair reading the paper.

He looked up and smiled, "Marylou, I didn't think you would be home this early. I'm glad. Can I get you a cup of coffee or anything?"

"Sure," Marylou said. "Get some coffee while I change my clothes."

Hermy got the coffee and brought it in to the room.

"Thanks," Marylou said. "You're an all right guy sometimes."

"I try," Hermy said. "How come you got off so early tonight?"

"Well, I figured I went in early, so I should get out early," she said. "You know I want to spend more time with you, Hermy."

"I sure like it when you say things like that Marylou. It makes me think you really do love me," Hermy said.

"I took off tomorrow, too," Marylou told Hermy. "Because I have to work longer hours Friday. You know, because of the band and all."

"Oh man, that's great," Hermy said. "We can be home together. I want to talk to you about some plans I have."

"Good, but let's go to bed now. I'm tired, and this will be a good chance to sleep in," Marylou said.

CHAPTER 47

Big Al and Tony ordered another drink. "Well, what do you think?" Big Al asked Tony.

"About what?" Tony asked.

"You know, sometimes I wonder why the fuck I work with you," Big Al said. "What the hell do you mean about what? We just beat the shit out of a guy, and you ask me about what?"

"Take it easy Al. Man, don't get so upset," Tony said. "I'll tell you what I think. I think we did a good job on him. He's scared to death of us. You know we collected bets from him for a long time. Duke never makes any waves, and if he does; well, a few belts in the gut makes him see the way again."

"Yeah, I guess you're right Tony. Even after we took care of Jimmy, he never said anything about it to us," Big Al said.

"Right," Tony said. "Now, you're talking. No problem with that asshole."

"But, one thing," Big Al said. "Since we took that kid, we've had nothing but trouble with the boss. He sends us out of town for a while. Then, we come back and we get the shit jobs like we were just starting out. Besides that, we never did get any money he promised us for the kidnapping job."

"True," Tony said. "But remember what we gave Jimmy instead of money."

"You've got a point there," Big Al said. "We should just chalk that one up as a favor to the old man. It's best we just forget about it."

Big Al and Tony ordered two more drinks and sat at the bar talking about sports and watched the women who walked into the bar. So far, no single ones walked in. "Bad night" Big Al said. Just then, the bartender walked over to them.

"Hey Al," he said. "The man wants to see you in the back room."

"Shit," Al said when he came back to the bar.

"What happened?" Tony asked. "Hell, you've only been gone about two or three minutes."

"Phone call from the boss," Al said. "He didn't even ask what happened, just told me he wanted a meeting with us at three o'clock tomorrow afternoon on the hill."

"Oh oh, do you think we're in trouble Al?" Tony asked.

"Who the fuck knows?" Al said. "But, we might as well get fucked up tonight." Al waved for the bartender. "And make them doubles," he said.

Big Al was sitting in the car while Tony drove. God, he hated going up on the hill. A bunch of old guineas sitting around a table in a room filled with smoke, drinking espresso or whatever that shit was in those dirty cups. They all come there during the day and smoke those God damn cigars acting as if they own the world. But at night, they all headed for their big houses in the suburbs in time for the cocktail hour. Then the boss, well, that's another fucking story. The fucking guy thinks he's the pope, or a little higher. Kiss his fucking ring. That old fucker ought to kiss my ass.

They pulled up in front of the restaurant and parked the car. "Al, Al what the hell are you doing? Daydreaming or what?" Tony said. "Let's go, the old man is waiting for us!"

Al got out of the car and walked to the door with Tony. They opened the door and Sal, the doorman, was standing right inside the door with a cigarette dangling from his mouth. "Hi boys," he said. "The old man is waiting for you in the back room."

Jesus, thought Al, just like in the movies. Sure enough, when Al opened the door to the back room, there it was. All the old men were sitting around the table in the smoke-filled room.

The boss looked up and said, "Hey, mya boys, sita down. Sal, geta the boys a drink. Ah, is so a gooda to seea youse boysa."

Oh fuck, Al thought. The guy's been here sixty fucking years and still talks like that.

"Yousa a boysa did anicea job for me wida that kid. I dona sees a youse a guys that much, too, you know, thank youse."

"No problem Boss," Big Al said smiling.

The boss shook his head and smiled, "An then a when a we have a the trouble with a the father, youse guys take a care of a that, too. Now I a wann a make a good a for youse."

"That's o.k. Boss," Big Al said. "We're as happy as can be. You just let us know what the next job is, that's all."

"No, that's a not a good a enough. Ima gonna give a youse guys a good a reward. Sal give a the boys a here the reward."

Sal reached into his pocket. Oh shit, Al thought. This son of a bitch is going to shoot us! Al didn't move. Sal pulled out a roll of money and threw it on the floor in front of Al and Tony.

The old man sat there smiling and then he said, "And a here youse a guys take a this a here piece a paper." The boss handed Al an envelope. "In a there, youse a gonna fina address. It's a gonna tell a youse a guys where a to go." The old man smiled again and said, "Youse a boys do a this a thing for me. Then, maybe youse gonna come a back an Ima gonna give youse another reward an maybe even a promotion."

The old man started to talk to the other men at the table in Italian as though Al and Tony were gone. Al picked the money up from the floor and motioned to Tony to go. They walked out of the room and shut the door. The old man looked up and said quietly, "If they fuck up again, kill them. Now, the next thing on the agenda," the old man said dropping his accent, "Is, what are we going to do with this Duke fellow?"

Al and Tony got into the car. As they pulled away from the curb, Tony asked, "How much money did he give us?"

"I know it's not enough," Al said. "But, let me count it and see." It wasn't hard to count because there were ten one hundred dollar bills. "One thousand bucks," Al said. "That's it."

"Well, look in the envelope," Tony said. "Maybe there is a check in it."

"Give me a break Tony," Al said. "When the hell did you ever get a check from those guys?"

Al opened the envelope and read the message inside. "Ah, shit," Al said.

"What's the matter Al?" Tony asked.

"Well, we've just been transferred," Al said.

"What the hell are you talking about?" Tony asked.

"Just what the fuck I said, we've been transferred," Al said. "Head back to the apartment. We have to get our shit together."

"You have to be kidding me," Tony said. "Where the hell are we going?"

"To Niagara Falls, that's where the fuck we are going," Al said. "To fucking Niagara Falls. Shit, I can't believe this!"

"When are we supposed to go?" Tony asked.

"When the fuck do you think Tony?" Al said. "You think we're supposed to stick around here for a going-away party? Damn it Tony, sometimes you act like an asshole. We have to leave by tomorrow, so let's go get our shit and blow this town. Hell with tomorrow, we're going tonight!"

"Where the hell we gonna stay when we get there?" Tony asked.

"I don't know," Al said. "It says here we go to this place on Pine Avenue and meet some guy named Vince. That's all it says."

CHAPTER 48

At five p.m., the telephone in the detective bureau rang. "Hey Fox," the office man yelled, It's for you."

Detective Fox answered the phone, "Can I help you?"

"Hello detective, this is the barber. I have some information for you. Can you ride over here?"

"Sure thing," Fox said. "See you in about twenty minutes." Fox yelled to Bender. "Hey Bender, let's go. We have some info to pick up."

Twenty minutes later, the two detectives pulled up in front of the barber shop. The barber was standing at the window waiting.

"Man, I bet that barber knows everything that goes on up and down this street," Fox said.

"Well maybe that will be good for us," Bender told him.

"Nice to see you guys again," the barber said to the two detectives. "You guys want a haircut?"

"Sure," Fox said. "I could use a little trim." Fox got into the chair and the barber put the cover over him. "Well, what kind of info you got for us?" Fox asked the barber.

"Oh yeah, you told me to call if I got any information about those two guys that live upstairs," the barber said. Then, he started to cut Fox's hair.

"Well?" Bender asked.

"Well, what?"

"The information, what the hell information do you have for us?" Bender was losing his cool.

"Oh yeah," the barber said. "Well you see, I was here about four-thirty this afternoon when Big Al and Tony came in. They said they were being transferred out of town and they gave me a fifty dollar bill. They said it was for watching the car lot for them."

"Did they say where they were going?" Fox asked.

"Nope, they just said if they got back in town, they would stop and see me."

"Did they say anything about the car lot next door?" Bender asked.

"Nope," the barber said. "I told you what they said, right to the word, no more, no less."

"O.K., we get the idea," Bender said.

"You're all done Detective," the barber said to Fox and help up a mirror for him to look into.

"Not bad," Fox said. "What do I owe you?"

"It's on the house," the barber said. "What the hell. I just got fifty dollars for free."

"Look," Bender said. "Could you do us a favor and keep an eye on their mailbox? If they get any mail, you can keep it for a few days and then call us. We'll come and check it out."

"Sure thing," the barber said. "I can do that. Next time, it's your turn to get a haircut," he said to Bender.

"O.K.," Bender said. "Next time, you cut my hair; but don't forget to give us a call."

"Looks like you've been bought for a haircut," Bender told Fox and started to laugh.

Bender and Fox headed back to the station to fill Hunter in on what was going on.

"It seems like everyone that might be connected to the disappearance of Noreen is disappearing themselves," Hunter said. "You know, it's been a long time since we've had any good leads in this case."

"You know," Fox said. "Once this stuff gets out of the papers, the public forgets all about it."

"Right," Hunter said, "unless it's your family, it's easy to forget. But, I know some guy down at Rosie's. He's a TV reporter. I think I'll ask him to run a little story on Noreen and see if we can scrape up some leads. In the meantime, when is the last time you guys saw Duke, Marylou, or Hermy?"

"Not too long ago," Bender said. "But we might be down there at Duke's Bar this weekend. He's going to have some hillbilly band playing."

"That's good," Hunter said. "Maybe, you can take your wives with you and make a night of it."

"Not funny, Sarge, not funny," Bender said. "Besides that, we don't take our wives with us when we are working overtime Sarge, overtime."

"Knock it off Bender," Hunter said. "If the city had to pay you two guys off right now, they would go broke."

"Don't worry Sarge," Fox said. "We'll call you at Rosie's so you can turn in a card, too."

"That's my boys," Hunter said. "I need the time. It's almost time to retire you know."

CHAPTER 49

Hermy got up and sent the kids off to school and then brought coffee to Marylou. "Oh boy, it sure feels good to know I don't have to work today," Marylou said as she stretched her arms over her head. "I just think I'll take it easy today. What are you going to do today Hermy?"

"Oh, I thought I would start cleaning and painting the church. I think I'm going to open it back up. The neighborhood could use the church. Some of the old members have been asking if the church was going to open up again."

"Hey Hermy, do you make any money at that church?" Marylou asked him.

Hermy got a big grin on his face, "Well, maybe I do," he said.

"Oh come on Hermy. Tell me about how much. Come on Hermy, how much?" Marylou started to tickle Hermy. Marylou climbed up on top of Hermy and started to grind her body against him. "Come on Hermy, tell me and maybe, I'll give you a little surprise."

"Around twenty thousand," Hermy said as he began to take his clothes off.

After they were done, Hermy lay back on the bed. "Boy are you good Marylou. You make me feel so good, but I lied to you."

"What do you mean, you lied?" Marylou asked.

"It's more like thirty thousand I make." Hermy was smiling.

"Oh man, Hermy, you should have told me. I would have been even better!" With that, Marylou jumped up from the bed.

"Where are you going Marylou?" Hermy asked.

"Where the fuck do you think I'm going?" Marylou said. "I'm going to get that church ready to open. Come on Hermy. We have work to do!"

They spent the day cleaning out the store front and getting the walls ready to paint. "I'll buy some paint tomorrow and start on the walls," Hermy said. "Then, I'll get the seats ready, and I should be able to open, maybe next Sunday. Monday, I have to go to City Hall."

"For what?" Marylou asked.

"Well," Hermy said. "Sometimes, you can get a little money from the city to get started with."

"Like how much?" Marylou asked.

"Oh, about a thousand dollars," Hermy said smiling.

"What do you have to do with the money?" Marylou asked.

"Oh," Hermy smiled and said. "I pay for the paint and stuff to fix everything up."

"Hell, that only costs a few bucks, right?" Marylou said.

"I know." Hermy got the big grin on his face again and said, "The rest is for us."

Hermy and Marylou worked the entire day cleaning and getting ready to paint. They stopped for lunch. Then, they got right back to work. When the kids got home from school, Marylou had them help by taking out all the garbage bags that Hermy had filled up. They worked until seven o'clock when Hermy called down from the ladder, "Hey, how about knocking off for supper?"

The kids and Marylou all thought that was a good idea.

"I'll tell you what," Hermy said. "Marylou, get on that phone and order a big pizza, and it's my treat."

They all went to bed early that night, exhausted. Friday morning, Marylou got the kids off to school. Then, she and Hermy sat down to a nice breakfast.

Hermy left to go get the paint, and Marylou got ready to go to work. She thought she should be there around one o'clock to help get ready for the big opening night. Marylou put on her tightest jeans and the lowest cut v-neck sweater she had. Show a little cleavage for the customers, and some for Duke, she thought. Man, that Hermy ain't gonna like the way I'm dressed. Good thing, he ain't here to see this. He would kill me for sure. Maybe, I ought to take an extra sweater in case he decides to stop by. As Marylou was getting dressed, she thought about Hermy. It's too bad I have to do this thing with Duke. But, the police couldn't find out what happened to Noreen, or Jimmy for that matter! Duke ain't gonna give up any information unless he gets something in return. If I can handle Duke and Hermy at the same time, I might be able to salvage some kind of life for me and my kids. Marylou finished dressing and left for the bar.

When Marylou got to work, she took off her jacket and Duke let out a big whistle and said, "Man, what a set! That Hermy is sure a lucky fellow. What's a guy got to do to be that lucky?"

"You have to be a preacher!" Big Red yelled from down at the end of the bar.

"I don't know about that," Duke yelled back. "But, I can tell you one thing. I'm going to start praying a lot!"

Even Marylou laughed at that one. "Come on Duke," she said. "Let's get busy decorating this place and quit the bullshit."

Everyone in the bar pitched in to decorate the bar, and they were done in no time. "The drinks are on the house," Duke said, and everyone cheered.

"We must be in the wrong place," Big Red said as he slipped his arm around Patty. Patty and Red were going together hot and heavy. As a matter of fact, Red had moved in with Patty, and they seemed very happy.

Duke turned to Marylou and said, "Thanks for all the help. I just hope these guys don't get too stiff before the band gets here. I want to see them all out there dancing, drinking, and spending their money. I want to hear that old cash register just a ringing away!"

Well, it was one hell of a night at Duke's Bar. The cash was flowing and Duke heard the cash register ringing all night. People were dancing and the band playing until one o'clock in the morning. After that, the juke box played until closing time. Duke had to just about kick all the people out at two-thirty in the morning. Then, Duke, Marylou, and Fatty all sat down to have a drink and relax. They all sat there looking at the mess.

"Looks like there was one hell of a party here," Duke said.

They finished the drinks and started to clean the place up. The three of them worked until about four in the morning.

"That's it," Duke said as he sat down in a chair. "Let's knock it off for the night."

"You got my vote," Fatty said as she sat down.

Marylou went to get her sweater. "I have to get out of here and go home before Hermy has a shit fit!"

Fatty handed Marylou her tips. "You ain't going to believe this," Fatty said.

"Why, how much?" Marylou asked her.

Fatty got a big smile on her face and said, "How does one hundred twenty dollars grab you?"

"A piece?" Marylou asked.

"A piece!" Fatty said.

"Hell, you couldn't make that much whoring on the street!" Marylou said.

Duke quickly reached into his pocket and threw a hundred dollar bill on the table and said, "Here baby, you don't even have to go on the street."

"Very funny," Marylou said. "But, you're still twenty bucks short."

Duke started to reach in his pocket again, but Marylou was already at the door. "Too late," she winked at Duke. "I have to get home, but save the money for the right time," she said as she walked out the door.

"That Marylou," Duke said. "She's always teasing me."

"Is she?" Fatty asked.

"What do you mean by that?" Duke asked.

"Hey man, don't give up. Maybe, you can wear her down," Fatty told him.

"I'm sure going to try harder and harder, no pun intended," Duke laughed.

Marylou got home. Much to her surprise, Hermy was in bed sleeping. Good, she thought as she quietly slipped into bed. This will save a lot of aggravation. Marylou fell asleep smelling fresh paint. Hermy must have painted, was her last thought.

CHAPTER 50

Marylou slowly started to open her eyes. That's funny, she thought. That paint smells like coffee. She opened one eye and slowly, the other eye began to open. "What the hell!" She jumped up. Hermy was sitting in a chair next to the bed drinking a cup of coffee. "Jesus," she moaned. "You scared the hell out of me Hermy. How long have you been sitting there? What the fuck time is it?"

"Easy honey," Hermy said. "It's noon, and I thought you might have to get up to go to work. What time did you get home last night?"

"Oh Hermy, I don't know," Marylou said. "It was late, you know, we had to clean up the bar. We had a big crowd in there last night, and Duke is expecting the same thing tonight."

"Well, I stopped painting at two this morning, and I wanted to wait up for you, but I guess I must have fallen asleep. I still have a lot more painting to do," Hermy said. "But, I want you to take a look at what's done when you get up."

"Sure Hermy," Marylou said. "Just let me get some coffee down and my eyes open."

"O.K. honey," Hermy said. "I meant whenever you were ready. I'm going back to paint now. I'll see you later."

Jesus, what a pain in the ass, thought Marylou. He's got to know what the hell is going on all the time. Noon, thought Marylou. Hell, it seems like I just went to bed. Marylou got up and slipped on her robe. I might as well go out and see what that Hermy has done.

"Hey, my Sleeping Beauty is up," Hermy said as Marylou came into the room. "How do you like it so far?" The room was painted a pale green, the walls still had some primer on them where Hermy had not painted yet.

"Looks real good," Marylou said. "That's a nice soothing color."

"I thought you might like it," Hermy said. "Tell me, what color do you think I ought to paint the altar and chairs? I thought a dark green, or else, a pale yellow. What do you think Marylou?"

"I think a dark green would be pretty," Marylou said. "I think you need a little contrast."

"Yeah, me, too," Hermy said. "That's the same thing I thought."

"Well, I have to be at work at six tonight, so what do you want for supper?"

"Anything is o.k. with me," Hermy said.

"Then, it's hamburgers and potatoes," Marylou said. "I'll fix supper around four o'clock. That will give me plenty of time to get ready for work. But right now, I need more coffee. Do you want any?"

"Sure," Hermy said. "Why don't you bring it in here and we can sit and talk." Marylou went to get the coffee.

Hermy and Marylou sat and talked for a while. Hermy did most of the talking, telling her about the church and what he planned to do.

Marylou listened for a while, but was thinking to herself. How the hell am I going to get dressed with Hermy here? If he sees me like I was dressed yesterday, there will be some big trouble here. I can't have that shit. I have too much on my mind. I ain't gonna be like some teenager and get dressed her and have some clothes hidden at the bar. Really, that might be a lot easier than fighting with Hermy every time I go to work. I'll have to think about that one.

"Marylou," Hermy said. "Are you listening to me?"

"Yeah Hermy, sure I'm listening," Marylou lied. "I was just thinking about how hard you are working and how nice it will be when you are done."

"Maybe when you see how nice it is and how well things will go, maybe we can get married. What do you think?" Hermy asked.

"Not right now," Marylou said. "Maybe after everything is done and we see how we are getting along together, well, we'll see, Hermy. Who knows, after a while, you may not even want me around."

"Oh, don't say that Marylou. I'll always want you and the kids with me," Hermy told her.

"Maybe Hermy, maybe. We'll see," Marylou said.

Marylou took the cups back into the kitchen. She told Hermy she had to go to the store and would be right back. "Do you need anything?" she asked Hermy.

"No," Hermy said. "I have everything I need for now."

Marylou went into the bedroom and picked out the clothes she wanted to wear that night and threw them into a paper bag. She took the bag out to the car and left. I'll do this just for now, Marylou thought, just so there won't be any trouble. I guess I can live with this for a while. Marylou drove to the store and bought some potatoes. When she got back, she went in by Hermy. "Come on Hermy," she said. "Let me help you clean up. You've done enough for today. I'll help you tomorrow and I'll be off Monday."

"Good idea," Hermy said. "All I have to do is pour this paint back into the can and wash out the brushes."

Marylou helped Hermy, and then Hermy went into the bathroom to clean up. Marylou went out to the kitchen and started to fry the potatoes and hamburgers.

After they had eaten and the kids were playing outside, Marylou and Hermy sat at the table having coffee. "Well, I better go and get ready for work," Marylou said.

"So soon? I wish you didn't have to go to work," Hermy said. "Will you be late again tonight?"

"God damn it Hermy, don't start. You know I have to go to work and with the band there, I'll be late. So just fucking knock it off!" Marylou headed for the bedroom to get dressed. When she came out, Hermy was sitting in front of the TV sulking.

"Hey Hermy, how about a kiss good-bye?" Marylou asked.

Hermy looked up. Marylou was dressed in loose fitting jeans, flat shoes, and a blouse that buttoned up to her neck. Hermy got a big smile on his face and said, "Sure honey, I got one big kiss for you."

Marylou got in the car to drive to work. Man, that Hermy is so easy. At least, I only have to hide my clothes like this on the weekends. I just hope that asshole Hermy doesn't come down to the joint after I change clothes. Man, he would go wild. Oh well, off to work.

"Just what the hell are you dressed as?" Duke bellowed from the end of the bar when Marylou walked in. "You look like an old hausfrau. You ain't gonna get no tips dressed like that. You know Marylou, you gotta show tits to get tips!" Duke was laughing so hard, he almost fell off the barstool.

"Fuck you Duke!" Marylou shouted back. "You can't give enough tips to see these tits!"

"I got to hand it to you Marylou. You sure got them good comebacks. Did you guys hear that one?" Duke asked the guys sitting at the bar. "Ain't she just great? What the hell you got in that bag? Your lunch? My hamburgers ain't good enough for you?"

"Gimme a break Duke," Marylou said. "I wouldn't eat the hamburgers you make. Hell, they have so much sawdust in them, you ought to call them sawdustburgers." Marylou headed for the back room to change.

Duke was laughing very hard by now, but he managed to say, "Marylou, that ain't sawdust in the hamburgers, it's cereal. So, you can have breakfast and lunch at the same time."

"That's called brunch, you asshole." Marylou called back as she slammed the door.

That just about broke Duke up. "Ain't she something?" He laughed, "Ain't she something?" Duke got off the stool and went to the back room. He pushed the door open and Marylou was standing there in her bra and panties.

"Get out you son of a bitch! Close the fucking door!" Marylou grabbed an empty beer bottle from a case in the store room and threw it at Duke. Duke ducked, but still stood there. Marylou started to throw bottles at Duke with both hands. "Get the fuck out of here before I kill you!" Marylou shouted. The bottles were breaking all around Duke before he had sense enough to close the door.

When he finally closed the door, he leaned against it and announced to the bar, "I just got a glimpse of heaven!"

"What the hell are you talking about?" Fatty asked.

"I just saw Marylou almost naked. It was beautiful, just beautiful."

Just then, Marylou came bursting through the door. "You mother fucker, I should kill you!" Marylou shouted. "You hunk of slime, peeking like a God damn little kid!"

"Hey, wait a minute," Duke pleaded. "I didn't know you were getting dressed in there. You never said anything. Honest, I was just going to get beer to stock the coolers."

"Why the hell didn't you shut the door then, instead of standing there like a big oaf?"

"I was taken in by the beauty of your eyes," Duke said.

"Shit, you never even looked at my eyes!" Marylou said and she started to laugh.

Duke, Fatty, and everyone at the bar started to laugh.

"Really, I'm sorry," Duke said. "Well, not really. I guess the sight was worth getting hit with a couple of bottles."

My Baby My Baby!

Marylou looked in the coolers. "O.K., Duke, I accept your apology. It's a good thing for you these coolers need beer in them, or you would have shit to pay."

Duke went to the back room to get beer. Marylou started to clean up the broken bottles. They were busy getting ready for what they hoped would be another big night.

Saturday night proved to be just as crazy as Friday night was. People were dancing and drinking. The place was full. There was one fight, but Duke broke that up easily. The band played until one o'clock again. When they had finished playing, the juke box started to play. At two-fifteen in the morning, Duke called: "Last call for alcohol! Motel time! Let's drink up."

By two forty-five, the bar was empty. Duke, Fatty, and Marylou were sitting at a table having a drink. Fatty split the tips and there was over one hundred dollars apiece.

"Hey," Duke said. "You girls are making more money than me."

"Bullshit," Fatty said. "You took in three times that much. By the way, we're almost out of beer, whiskey, and snacks. I'll have to place an order Monday. I'll meet you here early so you can pay the beer drivers."

"No problem," Duke said. "I'll open up Monday, and you won't have to come in until around eleven o'clock. By the way, I have a surprise for you girls. I hired someone to clean up this pig sty so you can go home earlier."

CHAPTER 51

"You sure are a jewel lately," Fatty said to Duke. "One would think you're almost human."

"Funny," Duke said. While Fatty and Duke were talking, Marylou was thinking. Hell, I can't go home too early. I want Hermy to get used to me coming home late on the weekends. That way, I can spend more time with Duke.

Just then, Fatty got up from the table and said, "If that's the case, let me get out of here. I still have time to get lucky!"

"O.K. Fatty, see you Monday," Duke said. "How about you Marylou? Do you have to go right away?"

"No, maybe I got time for a drink or two," she said with a wink at Duke.

"Good, I'll mix us a couple of drinks." Duke went to the bar and Marylou went over to the juke box and played some songs.

Duke came back to the table with the drinks and sat down. "Boy, we sure have been busy. This is the best I've ever done in the bar business."

"Yeah, it has been busy. I've never made tips like this any place I've ever worked," Marylou said. "I just hope it keeps up."

"Oh, I think it will for a while," Duke said. "Then, you know how people are. They find a new place to go to. Then, you're back to the old slow business. Sometimes, it's a good time to sell a bar when business is good and you can get the money for it."

"What the hell would you do if you sold this place? You ain't gonna retire, are you?" Marylou asked.

"No," Duke said. "But, if you get enough money, you buy a better place. I doubt I'll ever retire. This bar business gets in your blood. You know that might not be a bad idea. I'll have to give it some thought."

Duke and Marylou sat there making small talk for a while. Then, Duke asked Marylou if she was still mad at him for the other night when they had to leave the restaurant in a hurry.

"No," Marylou said. "But, I sure would like to know what happened. I mean you were fine until you went to take a leak."

"It's a long story Marylou," Duke said. "I might be able to tell you about it some day, but not right now. Hey, that's a nice slow song on the juke box, how about a little dance?"

"Sure, why not?" Marylou said. "I could use a little relaxing, and that might do it for me."

Marylou and Duke just started to dance when the song ended. It was the last song on the box. They both started to laugh. Marylou walked back to the table and Duke went to get some change for the juke box.

"Marylou, you want another drink?" Duke called from behind the bar.

"Bring it over big boy," Marylou called back. "I think I'm in the mood to party tonight."

Duke couldn't believe his ears. He had a big smile on his face and made the drinks a little stronger. Well, maybe a lot stronger.

On the way back to the table, Duke stopped and put some more money into the juke box. He played all slow songs. Then, he walked over and locked the door.

"Duke, what the hell are you doing by locking that door?" Marylou asked.

"Don't get the wrong idea Marylou," Duke said. "The joint is supposed to be closed. I don't want any trouble from the cops. Just when things are going good, I don't want to get busted for having a few drinks after hours."

"Sure Duke, sure," Marylou said. "You really got a line of shit." Marylou got up from the table. "But, you can stop the bullshit for a while and come over here and dance."

Duke just about broke his neck running over to Marylou. They danced a couple of dances. Then, they sat back down at the table for a few more drinks. After sitting at the table for a while, Marylou said, "I gotta get going Duke. It's getting late, and I don't want to get Hermy pissed off."

"How about one more dance before you go?" Duke asked.

"Sure, I have time for that Duke," Marylou said. She got up from the table and walked over to the juke box and pushed her selection. Duke got up and took her in his arms. Duke thought, hell, I might as well make a little pass at her. He started to kiss Marylou's neck. She pressed closer to him. Duke slid his hands up the back of her sweater and started to massage her back. Marylou started to moan a little, but she didn't say anything. Duke pulled back a little and kissed her on the lips. To his surprise, he felt his mouth being forced open by Marylou's tongue and she started to French kiss him. Duke was so surprised he jerked his head back.

"What's the matter big boy, don't you kiss on the first date?" Marylou burst out laughing and pulled away from Duke. "I better go change and make sure you stay out here." Marylou went into the back room.

Duke just stood there. Marylou didn't even close the door. She undressed and changed her clothes right in front of Duke. Duke just stood there staring.

When Marylou finished dressing, she walked out of the room and up to Duke. She reached up and kissed him. She had one hand around Duke. With the other hand, she reached down and started to rub Duke between his legs. She pulled back, but while rubbing him, she said, "You better go take a cold shower Duke. I don't have time to take care of that thing tonight." She kissed him again and headed for the door. She unlocked the door and was gone.

What happened? Was that for real? Duke went to the bar and poured a big shot of whiskey. That happened so fast, I can't believe it, Duke thought. How the hell did she get out of there? I was standing here like a big asshole. Duke poured another drink. She's right, I need a cold shower. He downed the shot and headed up to his apartment. Duke took his cold shower and went to bed. All he could think about was Marylou.

Marylou pulled up in front of the house and checked the time. It was four-fifteen a.m. Perfect, she thought. If I keep getting home about this time on the weekends, Hermy will get used to it. That will give me enough time to screw around with Duke. I might be able to get some information from his faster than I thought. He was so hot tonight. He probably came in his pants before I got out the door. Marylou started to laugh to herself. Well, old Hermy is going to get lucky tonight, because I'm feeling hot myself. Marylou went into the house. Hermy was in bed. She got undressed and got under the covers naked. Hermy was awake and ready for Marylou.

"I've been waiting for you!" he said.

CHAPTER 52

Duke was dreaming about Marylou. He had her upstairs in his bedroom. He had put her on the bed. He was ready to put it to her, but he kept hearing this pounding. Bang, bang. What the hell? Duke was slowly beginning to wake up. Oh shit, someone is at the door. He got out of bed and walked to the door yelling, "I'm coming, hold your horses!" Duke got to the door and yelled, "Who is it?" Just then, the door was knocked right off the hinges smashing into Duke. Duke went sailing across the room landing in a heap against the wall. Before Duke could even look up to see who it was, he was kicked in the stomach, grabbed under his arms, and tossed on the couch. "What the hell?" When Duke yelled, he was punched in the mouth.

Duke lay half on the couch and half on the floor. He didn't move, afraid that he would get hit or kicked again. No one moved or said anything for a few minutes. Then, a voice said to Duke. "O.K. man, sit up. Now that we got your attention, we got some things to tell you."

Duke got up slowly and sat on the couch. He looked around the room and saw one young guy dressed in jeans and a leather jacket standing in front of the couch. There was another guy dressed just about the same way standing behind the couch. "Who the hell are you guys?" Duke asked.

"All in good time, Duke," the guy in front of him said. "All in good time."

He said, "Hey Duke, you got any beer up here?"

"Yeah," Duke said. "It's in the ice box."

The guy standing behind Duke started to the kitchen. "You want a beer Duke?" he asked.

"Yeah," Duke said. "I think I'm gonna need one."

The guy came back with three beers and handed one to Duke, one to his buddy, and popped the top on one for himself. The two guys sat down in chairs facing the couch where Duke was sitting.

"Now that we are all comfortable, here's the score," the one guy started to tell Duke. "This should be nice and simple for you Duke. My name is Nick, and my friend over there is called Dom among other things. The two guys started to laugh.

"Can we knock off the comedy?" Duke said. "Just tell me what the hell you two guys want here!"

"Easy Duke baby, I said it would be simple enough. Now, the two of us are going to be taking over for Big Al and Tony. You know, we are now your contacts."

"Hell," Duke said. "You didn't have to go through all this shit. I've been waiting for someone to show up. My regular bettors have been asking when I was going to start taking bets again."

"Well, there is a little more to it than that," Nick said.

"What else can there be?" Duke asked. "We're going to have the same deal as before, ain't we?" Duke looked at Nick and Dom for a response.

"A little different," Nick said. "We've been watching this place and taking bets ain't enough now. Now, here's what we have in mind for you. Starting next weekend, we'll have two or three girls working out of the bar."

"Oh no, I ain't running a whorehouse out of my bar." Duke shook his head. "No, I never did none of that shit!"

"You ain't got no choice Dukey boy. This plan is all set up for you. Anyway, you'll be getting a cut. That's for you and the man to talk about. Next point, there will be one guy and one broad working in the joint. You don't have to pay any attention to them, but you will see them hanging around."

"What the hell are you talking about? I don't need any more help!" Duke said.

"They ain't gonna be helping you," Nick said. "They will be selling dope either in the rest rooms or outside in the parking lot."

"No, no," Duke said. "None of that shit is going down in my joint. I don't want no part of whores, dope, and that kind of shit! A little booking is my limit. I don't know about none of that other shit, and I don't want to!"

"Look, we're telling you the way it's been planned, so that's it," Nick said. "If you got any complaints, see the big guy. But, if I was you, I'd forget all about doing that. In fact, before we left him to come here, he was talking about how you could be found dead up here in your little apartment. You know, burned to death from a fire that started downstairs in the bar."

Both Nick and Dom got up from the chairs. "So that's the way it is," Dom said. "We'll see you before the action starts this weekend and go over the details with you."

"Nice to meet you Duke," Nick said as he and Dom walked to where the door used to be.

What the hell am I going to do now? Duke went to the kitchen to get another beer. Just when things are looking up, those assholes put this shit on me. I gotta think of some way to get out of this. I don't want to end up in jail! I ought to sell this place. Duke went downstairs to make sure the girl he hired was cleaning the place.

CHAPTER 53

Marylou and Hermy spent all day Sunday working on the church. Marylou had sent the kids to Patty's for the day. Patty was going to bring them back around five o'clock. Then, they were all going to have dinner together. While Marylou was working, she was thinking about how easy it was to con these men. Hermy never even questioned her about what time she got home last night. Hell, she could have stayed out for another two hours. All she had to do was give Hermy a little loving when she got home, and she was in the clear.

Now, about that Duke. She had given him an opening and she was sure it would be hard to keep him away now, not that she wanted to. She did want to control everything. She needed to get as much information as possible without giving too much away.

Marylou felt a little guilty about fucking around with Duke. But, it was all for a good reason. She sure as hell didn't want Hermy to catch her. After all, with the money Hermy said he could make by opening the church and the money he had hidden in the closet, she would be all set. By the way, she had to check that out. It just might be worth her while hanging on to the skinny old preacher.

Marylou and Hermy stopped for lunch. Marylou made some bologna sandwiches for them. "Boy, this sure is great, me and you being together," Hermy said. "With you helping me, we might be able to open this church by next week. Now Marylou, I don't want you to expect a big turnout or a big collection the first week or two. I did have the church closed for some time and you know I had my trouble with the demon rum and such. On Monday, I'll go to City Hall and the printers."

Marylou asked, "The printer, for what?"

"Well, I got a friend of mine that can print up some flyers about the church and what time the services start. By word of mouth and after a few weeks, I should have most of the old flock back."

They quit working around four o'clock. Marylou wanted to go to the store and get something for dinner for Patty, Big Red, and all the children.

"What are we going to have for dinner?" Hermy asked.

My Baby My Baby!

"Oh, I thought I would get some hot dogs and cook them on the old grill you have in the backyard. How does that sound?"

"It sounds all right," Hermy said. "But, I have a better idea. How about you and me going to the store and buying us some nice big steaks to cook on that old grill?"

"That sounds fine," Marylou said. "But, I ain't got the kind of money to be buying a lot of steaks."

"Heck Marylou, you've been helping me and being so good to me, it will be my treat. Now, you just wait here and let me go and get some money," Hermy ran up the stairs.

God damn, Marylou thought. That little pip-squeak must have plenty of money hidden up there. Marylou crept up the stairs. When she was about halfway up, she could see the closet door was opened. Hermy's feet were sticking out from inside the closet. Marylou was afraid to watch too long for fear Hermy would catch her. At least, now she knew the box Hermy was talking about was in that closet. I'll just bide my time, then check it out, she thought. Marylou went back down the steps and into the kitchen. She was sitting at the table when Hermy came down the steps smiling. He had a bunch of bills in his hand.

"Come on honey," Hermy said. "Let's go to the store. I have enough money here for the steaks and all the trimmings."

Marylou and Hermy got into the car and off to the store they went. Sure enough, Hermy had plenty of money. They bought the steaks, plenty of veggies for a salad, and even some mushrooms. "They will be good to fry up and have with the steak," Hermy said.

"I'll bake some potatoes," Marylou said. "This will be a real feast. I'm getting hungry just thinking about all this food."

Marylou and Hermy got back to the house just as Patty and Big Red pulled up. The children jumped out of Red's car screaming and hollering as they ran into the yard to play. Marylou yelled, "Hey, you guys come and help us unload all the stuff we bought for dinner!"

"Wow," Patty said. "What a dinner this will be. Marylou, you must be making a lot of money in tips to be able to buy all this."

"Hermy bought it all," Marylou said. "He's the one with the money."

"That was the end of the money," Hermy said.

What a bunch of bullshit, Marylou thought. Now, I really have to check that closet. She said out loud, "Well, that sure was nice of you to share the last of your money with us."

Hermy looked at Marylou. He heard the sarcasm in her voice. He let it pass. It was better not to say anything.

They carried the groceries into the house. Hermy went out to set up the grill. Red went to the car and brought back a full case of beer.

"I ain't been drinking at all," Hermy said. "But, I guess a few beers won't hurt me." They took the beers into the kitchen.

Marylou saw them come in with the two beers and said, "What the hell do we look like? Two orphans?"

Red laughed, "Does that mean you want a beer?"

"Does a bear shit in the woods?" Patty asked.

Red got the hint and cracked the caps on two more beers. Red gave Patty her beer. Patty grabbed his hand and pulled him closer to her. She whispered in his ear. Red told her, "Sure, go ahead and tell them."

"Attention you all!" Patty held her hands for everyone to be quiet. "I have something to tell you. Me and Red decided to tie the knot." She started to giggle.

"That's great," Marylou said as she went over to hug Patty. Hermy shook Red's hand and said, "Man, that is great. Maybe, we could make it a double wedding."

"Oh boy, that would be great!" Patty squealed. "Wouldn't that be great Red!"

"Hold it! Hold it!" Marylou said. "Me and Hermy talked about getting married, but not for a while, right Hermy?"

"Well, I thought you meant soon." Hermy looked disappointed. "When are you and Patty planning on doing it?"

"In a couple of weeks, something like that," Red told them.

"A couple of weeks, um, Marylou, what do you think?" Hermy asked.

"I think we better stop talking about it right now!" Marylou said to Hermy.

"What do you mean, stop talking now!" Hermy said as he reached under the sink and brought out a bottle of whiskey.

"Now Hermy, please don't start to drink whiskey and beer!" Marylou pleaded. "We don't want to have any trouble, not when Red and Patty want to celebrate getting married."

"That's just what we are going to do, is celebrate," Hermy said as he got glasses for everyone and poured shots for everyone.

Oh shit, Marylou thought. I hope he doesn't get all shit-faced. He's been doing so good lately. Marylou didn't have to worry. The more Hermy drank, the funnier he got. They ate dinner and the steaks were cooked to perfection. So far, so good, Marylou thought. After dinner, Hermy and Red kept right on drinking. Although they were slurring their words, they both seemed to be in a good mood. By the time Patty and Red were ready to go, they had decided Hermy would perform the ceremony in two weeks in the church. After they got the children, Marylou and Hermy walked them to the car. "You be careful driving," Marylou yelled after them as they drove away.

Marylou and Hermy went back into the house. Marylou put the children to bed and Hermy sat in the front room drinking. When Marylou got back downstairs, Hermy had passed out in the chair. I'll just leave him there to sleep it off, she thought and went to bed.

The next morning, Marylou woke up to the smell of coffee. She rolled over and looked at the clock. It was nine o'clock on the nose. Hermy came into the bedroom with a cup of coffee for her and said, "I got the kids off to school, and I have to go to City Hall and to the printers. I might not be home until dinner time. Are you going to work tonight?"

"Now Hermy, you know I'm off on Mondays. You just go about your business today. When you get home, I'll have a nice dinner fixed for you."

"You will?" Hermy asked.

"Sure, why not?" Marylou asked. "I mean, my man is trying his best to get the church started. I have to take care of him you know."

"I thought that after last night, you would be made at me," Hermy said. "When I woke up in the chair, I figured I must have been nasty and pissed you off."

"Hell no, Hermy. You were fine," Marylou told him. "I just didn't want to wake you up. You looked so comfortable sleeping there."

"I promise I won't drink like that again," Hermy said. "I'm sorry I drank so much last night."

"Oh come here, and sit on the bed next to me," Marylou said to Hermy. "Look, you were o.k. last night. Now, just go get everything done and bring me home good news."

"O.K.," Hermy smiled. "Now, I'm ready to face the world!" Hermy kissed Marylou good-bye.

Marylou rolled back over. I think I'll go back to sleep. Marylou slept until about one in the afternoon. That sure felt good to sleep in and not have anyone around, she thought. It's too bad Hermy doesn't have a regular job to go to every day. I sure could get some sleep then. Marylou got up to fix some coffee. I hope Hermy does all right at City Hall. I can always use some extra money. Talking about extra money, now might be a good time to check that box Hermy has hidden.

Marylou went upstairs to the closet and opened the door. She looked on the floor, but there was nothing there but a pile of old clothes. Maybe, it's under the clothes. She moved the clothes, nothing. The floor of the closet was covered with old linoleum. As Marylou sat and stared at the floor, she noticed the left-hand corner of the linoleum was bent up. Ahha, she thought. Under the linoleum and then probably a loose floor board, and voila, the box. Marylou reached down to pull up the linoleum when she heard the back door close.

"Marylou, where are you?"

Oh shit, it was Hermy. Marylou jumped up and ran down the stairs. "Hermy, how come you're home so early?"

"Oh, I'm all done." Hermy looked up the steps. "What were you doing?"

"I was cleaning a little upstairs. How did you make out?" Marylou asked.

"Oh, good. Here are the flyers I had made up," Hermy said. "I'll start to pass them out tomorrow. But, the best news is, I should get a grant for the church by next Wednesday!"

Marylou let out a squeal and gave Hermy a big hug. "I'm so glad you had a good day. Hermy, what are you going to do with all that money?"

"Well, there are some things I have to buy for the church because they come out and check. But, there will be at least half of the thousand dollars left over. Maybe, we can go on a vacation. We'll just have to wait and see."

Marylou noticed Hermy kept glancing upstairs. Oh my god, she thought. Did I close that closet door?

Hermy said, "I have to go upstairs for a minute."

Marylou grabbed Hermy by the arm. "Come on out in the kitchen first. I have some hot coffee on. Let's talk about where we will go on vacation. Oh Hermy, you treat me so good!"

Hermy smiled down at Marylou and let her pull him into the kitchen.

Marylou could see that Hermy had forgotten all about going upstairs. What an asshole, she thought. But, I've got to find a way to get up there and check that closet door.

CHAPTER 54

Duke had gone down to the bar to check on the girl he had hired to clean up. When he got down there, the bar was just about cleaned. He had to admit the girl had done a nice job. Duke was just starting to tell her so when she looked up and saw his face.

"Oh, my god! What happened to you? I heard the noise up there, but I didn't know if I should stick my nose in your business."

"You did the right thing honey," Duke told her. "This had nothing to do with you."

"Just let me get a wet towel to wipe off your face," the girl said.

"I sure would appreciate that," Duke said as he headed for the cooler to get another beer. The girl came back with a wet towel and cleaned the blood off Duke's face.

"Maybe, you should go to the hospital," she said. "You might need some stitches in your lip."

"No, no, I'm fine," Duke told her. "A few more beers and I'll be good as new." Duke sat at the end of the bar drinking beer and watching her clean up. When she was done, Duke paid her and told her to come back next Friday night after the bar closed and she could clean both nights.

"Gee thanks," she said. "I sure could use the money."

After she left, Duke sat at the bar drinking beer. A couple of hours later, he felt pretty good. Hell, he thought. I should call Marylou and see if she wants to come out and play. Yeah, that's a good idea, Duke thought. First, I'll go upstairs and fix the door. Then, I'll clean up a little and call Marylou. Duke fixed the door, or rather, he propped it up against the wall. Duke went into the bedroom to change his clothes. He lay across the bed and fell right to sleep.

The next thing he knew, he heard Fatty calling him.

"Hey Duke, where are you? What the hell happened up here?" Fatty walked into the bedroom. "Oh there you are. Come on, get up."

Duke looked up from the bed. Fatty took one look at Duke's face. It was all swollen and black and blue. "Jesus, what the hell happened?"

"Never mind," Duke said to her. "What the hell time is it? And, what the hell are you doing up here?"

My Baby My Baby!

"It's ten o'clock," Fatty said. "You were supposed to meet me downstairs at the bar. When you didn't show up, I came up here to see if you were o.k. Now, are you going to tell me that happened?"

"Not right now. Maybe later," Duke said. "Right now, I have to get cleaned up."

"You do that," Fatty told him. "I'll go back to the bar and get the beer and everything ordered. Then, I'll bring us some coffee and you can tell me what the hell is going on!"

Duke lay on the bed for a while after Fatty left and tried to get his thoughts together. What the hell am I going to do? Man, those guys mean business. I think I'll tell Fatty about what those guys want to do. Duke got up and headed for the bathroom to clean up.

Fatty came up a short time later with some hot coffee and donuts. She put everything on the kitchen table just as Duke was coming out of the bathroom.

"O.K.," Fatty said. "You just sit down here and tell me what happened."

Duke sat down at the table, took a sip of his coffee, and said to Fatty, "I'm going to tell you a few things, but I want you to keep them under your hat."

"Sure Duke," Fatty said. "You know you can trust me, mum's the word."

Duke told her how the two guys had burst into his apartment and beat him up. He told her about the whores and about the dope. "Hell, you know I did some booking in the joint Fatty," Duke said. "But, you know I never had no whores in here. Or worse yet, I ain't never sold no dope."

"Yeah, I know all that Duke. But, what the hell are you going to do?" Fatty asked him.

"I just don't know," Duke answered. "I guess I'll just have to go along with these guys and see what happens. I mean these guys are serious Fatty. They just might kill me if I tried anything. Now Fatty, I don't want you to tell Marylou about any of this, or no one else for that matter. Let's just wait to see how things work out. Who knows, maybe nobody will pay for the whores or buy the dope. Let's just wait and see."

"You're the boss Duke," Fatty said. "You just get some rest, and I'll be up later to check on you."

"That would help Fatty. Maybe, if I just take my time and think about this, I can come up with something so these guys don't put no more pressure on me. Then, Duke went back into the bedroom and laid across the bed.

Duke thought about all the shit that had happened in such a short time. Man, I wish that fucking Jimmy had never come into my place. That's where all my trouble started and it doesn't look like it's going to be over soon. All that shit with taking Noreen, and I never got no fucking money. Hell, now Jimmy is gone and so are those two assholes who took the kid. I wonder what the hell ever happened to her?

The next time the coppers stop by, I'm gonna ask them if they have any leads. Shit, I better not. They might wonder why I want to know. I still don't trust those two. I could ask Marylou. No, that's not a good idea either. Shit, that's the big problem with Jimmy gone, I ain't got nobody to talk to. Duke went to sleep thinking the only good thing that has happened is that the business is good, and who knows how long that will last?

Fatty went back down to the bar. Wait until I tell Marylou about all this shit. Heck, I wonder if those guys had anything to do with Noreen! I bet that's why Duke has to do whatever they tell him. I'll have to wait for Marylou to come in tomorrow to get her alone and spill the beans to her. Yeah, Marylou will know what to do. She's a pretty cool gal. She'll get to the bottom of all this. She might even get a line on that kid of hers. Then, I might make a few bucks.

CHAPTER 55

Marylou kept Hermy in the kitchen for the rest of the afternoon with talk about how happy she was and about where they might go on vacation.

Finally, Hermy said, "Let's take some coffee into the living room and watch some TV."

"Sure honey, you get the coffee, and I'll go turn on the TV." Now's my chance, Marylou thought as she left the kitchen. She headed for the steps, ran up, and looked in the bedroom door. The closet door was wide open! She went into the bedroom to shut the closed door when she heard Hermy yelling, "Marylou, where did you go now?"

Marylou reached out to shut the door. It slipped from her hand and slammed shut!

Hermy yelled, "What was that?"

Marylou heard Hermy coming up the stairs. She ran for the bedroom window and yelled back, "Nothing Hermy, this window was open and when I tried to close it, it slipped from my hands and slammed shut." By then, Hermy was standing beside her.

"Oh, is that what it was?" Hermy gave her a sideways glance. "You go downstairs and let me check the window," Hermy told her.

"Sure," Marylou said. She walked halfway down the stairs and looked back into the bedroom. She caught a glimpse of Hermy heading to the closet. Boy, that was close, I'll have to be more careful the next time I go up there.

Hermy came down the stairs with a smile on his face and said, "Everything checked out o.k."

"What do you mean by everything?" Marylou asked.

"I, I, mean the window, that's what I mean," Hermy stuttered. "That's all, the window." Hermy sat down on the chair and Marylou turned on the TV.

That old fox, Marylou thought. It's a good thing that closet door was closed.

Marylou and Hermy watched TV for a while. But Marylou could not concentrate on it at all. She kept thinking about Duke and planning her next move. I'm getting a little restless just sitting here when I have so much on my mind. Finally, she said to Hermy. "Hermy, I'm going out to the kitchen to get dinner started."

"So early, the kids ain't even home from school yet?" Hermy asked.

"Well," Marylou said. "I don't know what I'm going to have yet, so I'll just be out there looking to see what I have."

"Sure honey, go ahead," Hermy said. "I have a few things I need to fix around here. I'll just go get my tools."

Marylou went into the kitchen wondering, what the hell is he going to do now? Marylou was sitting at the kitchen table thinking when Hermy stuck his head in the door.

"Well," he said. "That window is fixed good now. It won't slam shut any more. I'll be right back Marylou. I have to run down the street for a minute. I want to give some flyers to some people to hand out."

"O.K.," Marylou said. "Don't be too late or you'll miss dinner."

Marylou was glad to be going to work Tuesday night. Hermy had been gone the good part of the day handing out flyers and talking to people. He seemed to be enthused about getting the church open as soon as possible. Even so, some days a couple of hours with Hermy seemed like a week to Marylou. There was one good thing. On the weekdays, Marylou didn't have to sneak any clothes out. A sweatshirt and jeans were good enough for the regular weekday customers. With the shitty little tips they left, old Marylou wasn't about to show them any skin. Now, those weekends were a different story. Hell, with the money Duke was paying her and the tips she was getting, it was the most money she had ever made. Marylou was wondering how Duke was going to be acting after their little episode. She knew she had to keep him at bay until the weekend. That was the only time Hermy wouldn't raise hell if she came home late. That was the way she would play the game.

Even though Hermy had been gone most of the day, Marylou didn't attempt to open the closet door. She had to check around the door to make sure there weren't any booby traps. She figured she had plenty of time for that. Let things cool down and hit 'em when they least suspected it. That included Duke too. Yeah, that would be part of her plan now, nice and easy. She didn't want to take any chances of screwing up either deal she had going. Right now, things seemed to be pretty easy to handle. She knew it would get more complicated as time went by. Marylou finished getting dressed, kissed Hermy goodbye, and left for work.

CHAPTER 56

Marylou barely got in the door of the bar and Fatty came running out from behind the bar. "Man, do I have a lot to tell you Marylou! You won't believe all the shit that happened! Come over here to the table and sit down. Let me get started!" Fatty no sooner got started when the door opened and Duke came in.

Duke saw Marylou and Fatty sitting at the table talking and he let out a yell, "God damn you two, what the hell do you think you're doing? What the hell do you think I'm paying you for, to sit on your asses and bullshit? Marylou, you get behind the bar and get to work. Fatty, you're done for the day, so get your ass home!" Duke went to the end of the bar and sat on his stool.

"Hey fuck!" Fatty yelled back at Duke. "What the fuck is wrong with you?"

Duke jumped up from the stool and yelled, "God damn you Fatty, get the fuck in the back room. I got some talking to do to you!" They both went in the back room and Duke slammed the door.

Fatty started to yell right away. "Hey man, what the hell's wrong with you? I worked all night last night so you could rest, and this is the thanks I get? Well, no thanks! You fuck me over like this and you can find another asshole to work this bar!"

"I'm sorry," Duke said. "I have so much on my mind. But, what did you tell Marylou? Fatty, I told you this shit was just between you and me. Then, I walk in here and there you are spilling the shit to Marylou!"

"I wasn't telling Marylou nothing about you," Fatty told duke. "Hell, she just walked in the door and we were talking."

"About what?" Duke asked.

"About nothing," Fatty answered. "Just some girl talk. You know, what did you do on your day off? We were talking about that kind of stuff."

"I think you're bullshitting me," Duke said. "But, I'll find out later. Now, just go home and I'll see you tomorrow."

"O.K. Duke," Fatty said. "But damn it, don't be hollering at me like that. I'm not kidding! I can get a job some other place right now. I've had plenty of offers!"

"I bet!" Duke said to her.

Fatty walked out and slammed the door.

"What the hell was that all about?" Marylou asked.

"Oh, that Duke can be such an asshole!" Fatty said. "Listen, as soon as you get off work tonight, call me. Don't call from here. Better yet, try to make some excuse to get off early and come over to my house. I have plenty to tell you."

"I'll see what I can do," Marylou said. "Maybe, I can tell Duke one of my kids is sick, and I don't trust Hermy with him."

"O.K.," Fatty said. "Let me get out of here before that goof comes out of the back room and finds me still here."

It was about a half hour before Duke came out of the back room. It wasn't until then that Marylou saw his face. "Holy shit!" Marylou said. "Duke, what the hell happened to you? Why didn't you call me?"

"Nothing happened," Duke said. "Last Saturday night after you left, I had a few more drinks. When I was going upstairs, I tripped and fell. That's all that happened. That's all there is to it, and I don't want to talk about it anymore." Duke headed for the door. "If you need me, I'll be upstairs."

Marylou watched Duke leave. I have to see Fatty and find out that happened. Marylou knew this was going to be a slow night, as slow as she had ever had in this joint. She was right. The time dragged on. After ten o'clock, there was just one customer sitting at the bar. Marylou was bored as hell. Marylou thought, I'll wait until midnight and if Duke doesn't come down by then, I'll go up and see if he will let me leave. Midnight came, and there was not a soul sitting in the bar.

Marylou locked the door of the bar and went up to Duke's apartment. When she got to the head of the stairs, she saw the door off the hinges. Gee, she thought. I wonder if this is part of the story. "Duke?" Marylou called out. There was no answer. "Duke?" she called again.

"Yeah, what do you want?" Duke answered from the bedroom.

Marylou walked into the bedroom. Duke was lying across the bed with all his clothes on and staring at the ceiling.

"What happened to your door?" Marylou asked.

"Nothing," Duke told her. "I'm just fixing it. Now what do you want?"

"One of my kids is sick," Marylou told Duke. "I don't trust Hermy to take care of him. No one is at the bar. I wondered if I could go home a little early tonight?"

"Do whatever you want," Duke told her. "Go now or go later, I don't care. Just lock the door of the joint." Duke rolled over on the bed and faced the wall.

"Can I do anything or get anything for you?" Marylou asked Duke.

"No, just go," Duke said. "Look, I'll talk to you tomorrow. Just beat it for now, will you?"

"Sure Duke, see you later." Marylou left. She went downstairs and checked to make sure the bar was locked up. She got into her car and started to Fatty's house. This should be good, she thought as she was driving.

Marylou got to Fatty's and knocked on the door. The door opened while Marylou was still knocking.

Fatty said, "Get in here and sit down! I was waiting for you. Man, this night went so slow, and I have so much to tell you! Sit down! I'll get us a couple of beers."

"Fatty, I didn't come here to drink," Marylou said.

"You will when you hear what I have to tell you!" Fatty was right. By the time she finished telling Marylou the story, they had finished a six-pack and were working on a second one.

"Wow," Marylou said. "That's a lot to happen over a couple of days, but I can't let on to Duke that I know all this shit."

"Don't worry about that," Fatty said. "I think he will tell you most of what happened before the weekend. I mean, what the hell, he knows you're going to notice them whores working and all the action in those shit houses."

Marylou and Fatty had a few more beers and talked about how they were going to handle Friday night. They finally decided to wait to see what Duke was going to tell Marylou and work it out from there.

Marylou looked at the clock. "Oh shit Fatty," she said. "Look at the time. It's three-thirty. If Hermy ain't sleeping, he'll be pissed and start bitching!" Marylou jumped into her car and headed home.

My Baby My Baby!

Just as she thought, Hermy was sitting up in his chair watching TV. Marylou walked into the living room and went right over to Hermy and kissed him. Hermy jerked away and said, "God damn Marylou, you've been drinking. I can smell the beer on your breath! Besides that, you're late!"

"Please Hermy, don't start that. I had a busy day and what the hell, I work in a bar. So once in a while, people buy me a drink and it's a policy that we accept. So I just sip on a few beers. Big deal!"

"What other policies do they have at that bar that I don't know about?" Hermy asked.

"Please Hermy, let's not start. I don't want to argue with you," Marylou said. "So, how was your day Hermy?"

Hermy shrugged his shoulders, "It was all right. Maybe, we can open the church next week. I got a lot better reception from the people than I thought I would."

"Oh, that's good," Marylou told him. "What time will be services he held?"

"Well, the first few weeks, we'll just have one at nine-thirty in the morning. Then later if we have enough people, we can have another service at noon. Of course, remember we always have the evening service at seven. People from the morning service almost always come back for the evening service. That's usually the biggest one. After supper, they bring the entire family back to church."

"That's good," Marylou said. "Can I get you anything? I'm going to have a nice cold beer and watch a little TV. I'm still a little wound up."

"No, you go ahead and do whatever you want to do," Hermy told her. "I'm going to bed. I don't want to start drinking now." With that, Hermy stalked off to bed.

The next morning when Marylou woke up, the place in bed next to her was empty. Hermy must be up already. But that's funny, I don't smell any coffee. Marylou looked at the clock. It was eleven-thirty. She got up and went out to the kitchen. No coffee was made, but there was a note on the table. "Marylou," it said. There was no Dear Marylou. "Had to go out, will not be home before you go to work. Will be home to take care of the kids. See you when you get home from work if I am still awake."

It's wasn't signed at the bottom. Marylou thought, he must still be pissed about last night. Well, no time to worry about that now. I have bigger fish to fry. Marylou fixed some coffee and breakfast for herself.

After she ate, she was sitting at the table sipping on some coffee and thinking. Now might be a good time to check that closet. I bet he won't be home until I go to work. That's how his little shit mind works, like he's really punishing me.

Marylou locked the back door. She thought that if Hermy comes home, he will have to bang on the door to get in and he won't be able to sneak up on me. I can always tell him I was in the bathroom. Marylou went upstairs. Let me think now. I have to check this closet out slowly just in case he has tape across the door. Marylou went over the door as carefully as she could. Sure enough, in the upper right-hand corner was a small piece of tape. That sly old fox. It was a good thing I took my time. Marylou took the tape off making sure to remember the exact spot it was on. Marylou got out a bobby pin and began to work on the lock, being careful not to scratch the lock or leave any tell-tale marks. In about five minutes, she had opened the lock. It took longer than I thought. I must be losing my touch.

Marylou carefully opened the door of the closet. I've got to take my time. If he had the outside taped, he could have something inside. Marylou checked the floor, but found nothing that looked like a trap. Slowly, she lifted the corner of the linoleum, being as careful as possible not to tear it. Sure enough, in a hollowed out hole sat a box. It was an old metal box with a broken hasp on it. Before Marylou picked up the box, she looked all around the edges of the hole it sat in. No tape or strings were attached.

Marylou reached into the hold and very gently lifted the box out. Marylou checked all around the cover of the metal box for any tape. She set the box on the floor and slowly lifted the lid. "Jesus H. Christ," she yelled out loud, and closed the lid of the box. Maybe, I was seeing things, she thought. She stared at the box for a while as if she were afraid to open it again. Then, she slowly opened the lid. She wasn't seeing things. Inside the box was money, and it looked like plenty of it.

Marylou started to take the money out and pile it on the floor. The money was wrapped. There were one hundred dollar bills, ten in each pack, fifteen packs in all. At the bottom of the box lying loose, where was another couple hundred dollars in twenties.

Holy shit, where did that creep get all this money? He never told me about it. O.K. Hermy, I can play this game. When the times comes, this is mine. So, I hope you get that church going and add more money to your little old hiding place. Because when I get ready to go, me and my kids are going in style. Marylou began putting the money back in the box making sure she put it back the same way she found it. Marylou replaced the box, laid the linoleum down, closed the door, and replaced the tape. She stood back. It looks perfect to me, she thought.

Marylou went back downstairs and unlocked the door in case Hermy came home. She sat down at the table. This is unbelievable. Who would have guessed that that worm could have so much money? I can't change my plans. After all, I have to find out what Duke knows about Noreen. I'll just have to play it cool. Hey, if worse comes to worse and Duke tells me he has to pay to find out about my baby, well, now I got me some money I can lay my hands on. Whatever happens now, I got it made. Hell, I can grab the money and run. That little worm would never find me. I'll be so far gone, he wouldn't even know where to start to look.

I think I'll get ready for work. I might as well go in a little early, talk to Fatty, and see what's up with Duke, or better yet, see what Duke can get up.

Marylou got to work and Fatty was surprised to see her there so early. "What, you love this place so much you have to come in early?" Fatty said.

"Just came to have lunch with you," Marylou told her. "So, how about fixing me one of those greasy burgers and some soggy french fries? Get me a beer too. I'll probably need a few to wash this slop down."

Fatty fixed Marylou's sandwich and sat down with her. "So, what's up?" she asked Marylou.

"Oh, really nothing much," Marylou said. Then, she told Fatty how Hermy was pissed off at her.

"That guy's a pain in the ass," Fatty said. "You know when he was drinking, he used to come in here. It seemed as though all he did was cause trouble. You know how them little guys are, walking around like bantam roosters, acting tough. Most of the time, they got the shit kicked out of them. Then, he would be gone for a few days and come right back again doing the same thing. He was just a bonafide pain in the ass."

"I don't know about any of that," Marylou said. "But, I can tell you one thing. Sometimes he's a real sweet guy."

"Well, you can think what you want, but I don't like that little creep," Fatty said.

"Oh, let's change the subject," Marylou said. "How's Duke doing?"

"I don't know," Fatty said. "I ain't seen him yet. But, he'll be down sooner or later."

Marylou finished her sandwich and asked for another beer. When Fatty came back with the beer, Marylou said, "Hey girl, when I finish this beer, why don't you go home and give yourself a little break?"

"Gee, thanks a lot," Fatty said. "But, I got me a better idea. I think what I'll do is move to the other side of the bar and have me a little party. You know, I ain't been fucked up for a while, and I'm about due."

"O.K. by me," Marylou said. "This could be quite a day for both of us."

Marylou and Fatty sat there most of the afternoon drinking and talking. The place was dead and usually didn't get busy until about four o'clock. Well, by four o'clock, Marylou and Fatty were shit-faced. Marylou was still able to tend bar, but it was doubtful if Fatty could pour a drink. In fact, most of what she was drinking now was on her shirt.

Big Red and a few of the boys had come in after work. They had managed to get a job putting a roof on, and they were buying the drinks. Marylou slowed down drinking by one pouring herself about every other one that the boys bought her, but she took the money for the ones she didn't pour. After a couple of hours, Red and his buddies left. Red was telling Marylou he had to get home before Patty kicked his ass. "She don't mind if I stop for a few," he said. "But, I have to be home for dinner. Hey by the way, it's getting close to the wedding day. Patty said she can't wait. Tell Hermy I said hello." The rest of the night was pretty slow, but Fatty kept drinking.

Marylou heard some moving around upstairs and looked at the clock. It was nine o'clock. Duke came down to the bar around nine-thirty. He was all cleaned up and his face did not look as bad as it did yesterday. By this time, Fatty was passed out on the table.

"What the hell is her problem?" Duke asked.

"Oh, she was partying a little," Marylou said. "But, she'll be all right."

"How are you doing?" Duke asked. "You look a little fucked up."

"Oh, I feel o.k. I'm just a little tired," Marylou said.

"Come in the back room for a second," Duke said to Marylou. "I have something I want to tell you."

"Sure," Marylou said as she followed Duke into the back room.

When they got in the back room, Duke shut the door, put his arms around Marylou, and kissed her. Marylou put her arms around Duke and stuck her tongue in his mouth pressing against him as hard as she could. When Duke came up for air, Marylou pushed him away. "Easy, big guy," Marylou said. "This ain't the time or the place, so don't get yourself all worked up."

"I'm already worked up," Duke said. "Come on, just some more kissing, that's all."

"Look here Duke. I can tell you're all worked up when you pressed against me, but we ain't got time now." Marylou pushed Duke away. "I'll tell you what. I'm gonna take Fatty home and go home myself. Then this weekend, I can work late." Marylou winked. "Get what I mean Duke?"

"Yeah, yeah, I get it," Duke said shaking his head. "You figure you keep Hermy happy during the week and me on the weekends. Am I right?"

"You are just about the smartest man I know," Marylou said as she pressed against Duke again. Marylou gave him a big juicy kiss. As she pulled away, she dropped her hand and brushed it across Duke's hard-on. "Until Friday night," she said as she walked out the door.

"I'll be ready," Duke sighed.

Marylou walked out to the table and shook Fatty. "Come on Fatty, wake up," Marylou yelled.

"Why? Is somebody buying a drink?" Fatty slurred.

"No, God damn it, just wake up," Marylou said. "I want to take you home."

Fatty raised her head and looked at Marylou. "Yeah, take me home would you? I feel like shit."

"Sure," Marylou aid. "I'll get you home and put you to bed."

Marylou got Fatty out to the car and drove her home. She got her into the house, undressed her, and put her in the bed. "I'll see you tomorrow," Marylou said as she turned out the light and locked Fatty's door.

Marylou drove home. Hermy was watching TV when Marylou walked in the door.

Hermy looked at the clock. It was only ten-thirty. "It's kind of early to be home, ain't it?"

"Well, I told you before Hermy. I would try to get home early during the week because I have to work late on the weekends," Marylou said.

"Yeah, how about last night?" Hermy said. "That wasn't too early, was it?"

"Fuck you Hermy," Marylou said and she went into the bedroom. Marylou got undressed and got into bed. She still felt a little excited after her kissing match, so she yelled out to Hermy. "Hey Hermy, come on in here, I have something for you." There was no answer, but she heard Hermy get out of his chair. Here he comes, she thought. She was wrong. Hermy headed for the kitchen. She heard him open the refrigerator door and pop a cap on a bottle of beer. She rolled over and went to sleep.

At three o'clock in the morning, Marylou rolled over and felt the bed. No Hermy. Marylou went right back to sleep.

The next time Marylou woke up, it was to the smell of eggs, bacon, and coffee. Hermy brought her breakfast in bed. "I know it's very early, but I thought you might like to eat," Hermy said.

"Sure, thanks a lot," Marylou said.

While she ate, Hermy got undressed and got into the bed.

"I'm sorry," Hermy said.

Marylou had all she could do to make him wait until she could finish breakfast. She never did get to her coffee.

CHAPTER 57

After Marylou had left to take Fatty home, Duke was sitting at his usual place at the end of the bar when the door opened. Oh shit, Duke said to himself, and no wonder. In walked Nick, Dom, three girls, and another guy.

They all bellied up to the bar and Nick yelled out to Duke. "Hey fat ass, get over here. You got paying customers."

"Maybe he does and maybe he doesn't," Dom laughed.

Duke slowly walked over to the group and asked, "What do you guys want?"

"Man, is that any way to talk to your customers?" Nick asked. "You know, you ain't gonna get a very big tip if you treat your customers like that. Now, how about we start all over. Here's the idea. You walk over here with a big smile on your face and say, 'May I help you sir?'"

Duke stood there looking at Nick without saying a word. Nick grabbed Duke by the front of the shirt and pulled him across the bar.

"Listen asshole, you want some of the same thing you got the other day? If not, do what the fuck I tell you!" Nick slapped Duke across the face.

Duke stood there with a smile on his face and said, "May I help you sir?"

Everyone at the bar laughed. Duke thought to himself. Why do I let these guys make me look like an asshole? I have to draw the line some place. Maybe, next time.

"That's a lot better," Nick said. "Now give us all scotch and water. Make it the best stuff in the house. We don't drink no cheap shit."

When Duke was done pouring the drinks, Nick said, "Now I want you to meet all of my friends and the people who will be working with you starting Friday night."

The first girl Nick introduced was tall, blonde, and not bad looking. She was dressed in a miniskirt and a low-cut blouse. "This is Bambi," Nick said. "She will be working the bar along with this little cutie." Nick put his arm around a shorter black-haired girl. She was dressed about the same as Bambi. "This is Dawn," Nick told

Duke. "They know their way around, so you don't have to tell them anything, just watch them work. That does it for the two girls working the bar. Now, this girl here," Nick moved over and put his arm around the other girl. "This is Sheri." She was dressed in tight jeans, western shirt, cowboy boots and had her hair tied up in a red bandana. "She'll be working the girl's john. You keep an eye on her Duke, because we want all the sales to be made in the john and not in the bar. This here is Fast Eddy. We call him that because he can sell dope faster than anyone we know. The same applies to him. All sales are to be done in the men's john, none in the bar."

"Now what we want you to do Duke is keep an eye on all these people. If any cops come in, you give them the high sign. You know, tip us off. Got it?"

"Yeah, I got it, but I don't like it," Duke moaned. "This ain't the kind of bar where people buy dope and pay for pussy."

"Bullshit," Dom said. "As soon as the word is out, the dopers will come running and you are going to be surprised when you see who pays for pussy. It might even be you Duke. But, the girls will give you a good discount!"

"Look Nick," Duke said. "I ain't interested in dope or pussy. I don't know if I can handle this shit. All I want to do is a little booking and that's all. You know, there are some cops that come around this place."

"All you have to do is tell us when the cops come in." Dom said. "And we'll lay low until they go."

"Good one," Nick said. "That will be our saying from now on. Lay low until they go. I like that. Maybe Duke will have some tee shirts printed up for us. Anyhow, Duke my boy, if the cops say anything to you, just fix them up with one of the girls here. They will give them some free pussy."

"Yeah, good idea," Dom said. "Some cops may not take any money, but they ain't never gonna turn down free pussy or a blow job!"

"Of course," Nick smiled and said, "that pussy really ain't free, because we'll be taking it out of your end Duke."

"I just don't know about all this." Duke was sweating now. "I mean, I'm telling you guys this shit makes me nervous. If I get caught doing this, I could go to jail!"

"Listen, fat man," Dom said. "You ain't got no choice about any of this. You just do what we say and at the end of the night, we give you your cut."

"Yeah, and how much is that?" Duke asked.

"Ahha, it all comes down to money, doesn't it Duke?" Nick looked at Duke like he was a hung of slime.

"Hey, fuck you!" Duke said getting a little braver now. "If I have to do this shit, then I best get paid."

"On Friday night, we'll let you know how we make the split," Nick said. "Don't worry, we play square. But, I can tell you now it will be on a percentage basis. We could give you a straight salary, so to speak, but we have found out that we all make more money on the percentage. So, that's the way we'll do it."

"Are both of you going to be here Friday night?" Duke asked.

"Hell yes. What the fuck do you think we are, stupid?" Nick asked. "Man, this is business and we have to watch it. You know, we can keep track of how much dope we sell. But, if we ain't here, how do we know how much pussy was sold?"

Duke smiled at that one, then said. "You guys should stay out of the way though. I mean, what the hell, this place will look like it's packed with just all the people who work here."

"You just do what the fuck you do in this joint and don't worry about us, will you?" Nick said. "Now, pour us another drink and you get one too so we can seal the deal."

Duke poured everyone a drink including himself. He even joined in on the toast Nick gave. "To all the partners, even the ones that ain't here."

Nick put the glass down and they all headed for the door. "See you later," Nick said, and out the door they went.

Duke looked down at the bar. The glasses were there, but there wasn't any money for the drinks. Worst of all, there wasn't even a tip.

CHAPTER 58

The next day, Fatty came in to open the bar. She felt horrible. She had a headache, upset stomach; the typical hangover. The only thing she could think of was to get a bloody mary down as fast as she could mix one. Fatty unlocked the door and opened it. She started in the door and jumped back. There at the end of the bar Duke sat, or rather laid. Fatty walked over to him. At first, she thought he was dead. As she walked closer, she could hear him snoring. Fatty grabbed him by the shoulder and shook him. "Get up you drunken bum!"

"What? What? What the hell is going on? What time is it?" Duke said.

"It's time to get your fat ass out of here and go upstairs," Fatty told him. Fatty walked behind the bar and started to mix herself a bloody mary.

"What are you doing?" Duke asked her.

"I'm making a little bit of the hair of the dog," Fatty said.

"Better make me one too," Duke told Fatty. "Man, I need one bad."

"Coming up," Fatty said. "You must have had a bad night. Were you partying alone?"

"Yeah," Duke said. "It was just me and my lonesome. Fatty, when you get those drinks made, come over her and sit with me. I want to tell you what happened last night."

Fatty and Duke had a few drinks while Duke filled her in on what had happened with the visit from Nick and Dom.

"What the hell are you going to do?" Fatty asked him.

"Well, first of all, we have to clue Marylou in on this," Duke said. "It may piss her off, but I have to tell her."

"I could tell her when she comes into work," Fatty said.

"Yeah, maybe she would take it better if you told her," Duke told Fatty. "You can also tell her that this shit may not last too long. If they don't make any money or get too much action, these guys will go and bother someone else."

"Don't count on that Duke," Fatty said. "I think there will be plenty of action here."

"Hell, I don't need all this shit," Duke said. "Why me?"

CHAPTER 59

Marylou came in to work a little early for two reasons; one, to get away from Hermy, who wanted to stay in bed all day and "do it" as he said. The other reason, knowing Fatty had had a bad night, Marylou thought she might want to go home a little earlier.

Old Marylou was in for a surprise. When she got there, Fatty and Duke were drunk as skunks and Big Red was tending bar.

"What the hell is going on here?!" Marylou screamed as she walked in the door.

"Whoa," Big Red said to Marylou. "Don't be pissed at me. Hell, all I did was come in for a couple of drinks, and I found these two all pissy-assed drunk."

"Come over here," Duke yelled to Marylou. "Join the party."

Marylou walked over to the table Duke and Fatty were sitting at and banged her purse on the table. "What the fuck do you two think you are doing? If you think that I'm going to baby-sit this fucking bar every day while you two get drunk, both of you are full of shit!"

"Aw, sit down baby," Duke said as she grabbed for Marylou.

"Keep your fucking paws off me!" Marylou screamed as she jumped back from Duke.

"Come sit down," Fatty said to Marylou. "We have something important to tell you."

Marylou sat down at the table and said, "You better tell me before both of you pass out."

"Hey Red, you better bring all of us a drink," Duke called. "You better have one too" he told Marylou.

"Red, bring me a rum and coke. I might as well join the crew here," Marylou said.

Fatty started to tell Marylou what was going on, hoping Marylou would not let on what she knew. Marylou did a good job of listening. After Fatty told her everything, Marylou told Duke that she would do whatever she could to help him.

Duke was pretty surprised by Marylou's reaction and thanked her for backing him up.

Then, Duke said, "Hey, I have a good idea. How about the three of us going out for something to eat? Red can tend bar. What do you think?"

Marylou thought for a minute and then asked Duke, "Am I going to get paid for this?"

"You got it," Duke told her.

"Let's get out of here!" Marylou said.

The three of them had a great time. Duke took them to a chink restaurant where they drank and had a big meal. After that, they went to a couple of bars that some of Duke's friends owned. The three of them sat in the front seat of Duke's car with Marylou sitting in the middle. Duke either had his hand on Marylou's knee or a little higher, or was hitting her tits with his elbow. Fatty was watching all this. One time, she leaned over and whispered in Marylou's ear, "Just like high school."

"It sure is," Marylou giggled.

"I wish I were driving," Fatty said. Marylou just laughed.

It was around nine o'clock. Fatty was ready to fall asleep in the front seat of the car. "It's time to hit it," Marylou said to Duke. "Let's get her up and go home."

"You got it," Duke said as he headed for Fatty's house.

They got Fatty home and Marylou put her to bed. As Marylou was leaving, she said to Fatty, "We have to quit meeting like this." Fatty never heard her.

Marylou got back into the car with Duke. "Come on baby, sit closer to me."

"What the hell do you think this is, a date?" But, Marylou slid over next to Duke. She no sooner sat closer to Duke, then he was all over her, grabbing her and trying to kiss her. Marylou pushed him away, "God damn it Duke, will you take it easy? Let's wait until we get back to your place before you mug me all up!" Duke started the car. Marylou said, "Be careful of how you drive, you've had a lot to drink."

With all he had to drink and Marylou rubbing his thigh, Duke was trying his best to drive straight.

When Duke got to the bar, Marylou said, "Park all the way in the back. I don't want Red to see us go upstairs. He has a big mouth and might tell Patty."

My Baby My Baby!

"Oh, he wouldn't do that," Duke said. "I have too much on him."

"Yeah," Marylou said. "We'll have to talk about that sometime." Marylou squeezed Duke's thigh.

"God damn, Marylou, that sure feels good," Duke said. "Let's get upstairs."

"Sure thing," Marylou said. "Remember, be quiet." They crept up the stairs. Duke still had not fixed the door.

"Well, at least we won't make any noise opening the door." Duke started to laugh.

Marylou grabbed Duke by the balls. "If you laugh any louder, I'm going to squeeze." They both started to giggle.

When they got in the door, Duke headed for the bedroom. "Hey big boy, how about getting us a couple of beers to take in with us?" Marylou asked him.

"O.K. baby, you got it." Duke walked to the kitchen and Marylou walked into the bedroom.

Marylou was thinking. I have to keep this guy off me. I want to get home early again tonight. I don't want a load of cum dripping out of me! She heard Duke doing something in the kitchen. When he came through the bedroom door, he was buck naked. "What the fuck are you doing Duke?" Marylou said.

"Oh nothing," Duke giggled. "I just brought us a little drink." He handed Marylou a can of beer and sat down on the bed next to her. Marylou started to take a drink of the beer. Duke grabbed her empty hand and shoved it down to his crotch. Marylou jerked her hand away and as fast as she could, she poured the can of cold beer down the front of Duke.

"Holy shit!" Duke yelled as he jumped from the bed. "What the fuck is wrong with you Marylou? God damn it, you tease me, then you pour that fucking cold beer on me. Are you crazy?"

"No, I ain't crazy!" Marylou said. "But, if you think you are going to treat me like some fucking whore, you're the one who is crazy. You think you can just jump in bed with me and stick your old wiener in me, and I'm supposed to go crazy? Man, you're crazy. Don't you know anything about foreplay? If you think grabbing my hand and putting it on your dick is foreplay, you have a lot to learn!" Marylou was up off the bed and heading for the door.

"Wait baby, wait a minute," Duke was whining. "I'm sorry, come on back here."

"Not now," Marylou said. "With all that noise, Red knows I'm up here now."

Duke got up from the bed and walked to the door. "Come on honey, just stay for a little while."

Marylou looked down at Duke's crotch and started to giggle. "That thing of yours must not like cold beer. I gave him a little drink and he must have run off and hid."

Duke looked down. She was right. It was gone. Well, not gone, but shrunk. Duke covered himself up with his hand. He could feel he was blushing.

Marylou gave him a big wink and left running down the stairs. "See you both tomorrow," she yelled up the stairs. Then, she was gone.

That bitch, Duke thought. She is always fucking with me. Then, he started to laugh. Wrong choice of words. Oh well, I might as well go down to the bar and send Red home. Better yet, he can stay. I'll feed him a few drinks and keep him around for company.

Duke went to the kitchen to get his clothes. Shit, he thought. I wish Nick would have stopped by tonight. I could have used one of my discounts on those whores. I might have had that little dark-haired one. What was her name? Dawn, yeah, that's it. I could wake up to the crack of Dawn, or in the crack of Dawn. Yeah, I love it. Duke felt pretty good now. A few more drinks and he would sleep good. A few more drinks and he would pass out. It's the same thing, Duke thought as he headed down the stairs.

Marylou checked her watch. Ah, very good. I'll be home by eleven-thirty. So far, so good. She reached into the glove compartment where she had a small bottle of mouthwash. She had learned when Hermy smelled beer on her breath before. Now, all he would get was a whiff of Lavoris. Christ, I feel like one of those whores. Give a guy a little head, then grab your purse and rinse out the old mouth. Oh well, anything to keep the peace baby.

When Marylou pulled up in front of the house and parked the car, she looked in the mirror and fixed her hair. She wasn't taking any chances. It was all in vain. When she went into the house, the kitchen light was on and there was a note on the table. "Honey," it

My Baby My Baby!

read. "I went to bed early. I worked on the church after you left. I talked to some people, and we will have services this Sunday. Wake me up if you have any surprises! If not, see you in the morning. Love, Hermy."

There ain't no surprise for you Hermy, Marylou thought as she went to the refrigerator and got a beer. Marylou sat down at the kitchen table and started thinking about how she was going to handle everything. One thing was for sure. If she wanted any information from Duke about Noreen, she would have to put out for him. She couldn't keep him out of her pants forever. She had to put out for Hermy, or he would start sulking and making things miserable for her. Man, putting out is all that keeps these stupid men happy. All of their brains must be in their dicks. It's no wonder old Fatty calls men pee brains.

Marylou had one more beer. This should be one hell of a weekend with Hermy opening the church and the new help at the bar. Marylou was ready for bed. She had to sneak in her own bed. What a life!

CHAPTER 60

The next morning Hermy came bouncing into the bedroom yelling, "Marylou, get ready for the vacation!"

Marylou jumped up, "What the hell is going on?"

"The grant, I got the grant!" Hermy was jumping on the bed. "They just called from City Hall and told me the check would be ready this afternoon. They told me I could come down and pick it up if I wanted to. I told them I would come down around three-thirty to pick it up."

Marylou was awake now. Money always woke her up. "That's good Hermy. How much do you think we can keep?"

"Oh, I'd say around seven hundred or so. I'll know better after this Sunday when I see what I have to pay out. You know, we can't go for a while, I mean, I have important things to do for a while."

"Sure, I know," Marylou said. "I'll have to get someone to work for me when we go."

"Maybe, you won't have to work by then," Hermy whined.

"Stop it Hermy," Marylou said. "You know I hate it when you whine like a little baby."

"But, if we make enough money at the church, you won't have to work any more. You can stay home and take care of the kids. Maybe you can help me at the church. You could be the secretary or something like that."

"Sure Hermy," Marylou said. "Are you going to pay me for this?"

"Well, we could be married by then. All the money would belong to both of us," Hermy said.

Marylou thought something sounded a little funny when Hermy said the money would belong to both of us. It sounded as though it was almost difficult for him to say it. I bet that little shit would hide any money he made and then tell me how bad things were. Yeah, I've seen his type before, a pocket full of money and crying that he's poor. No Hermy, she thought. I have some plans of my own. They could change, but I'll just wait and see.

Marylou got out of bed and made herself some coffee. Hermy was busy putting the finishing touches on the church. He told

Marylou he would have to work the next couple of days to be ready to open by Sunday. Saturday, he would have some help from a few of the members.

"They had better be quiet in there Saturday," Marylou said. "Don't forget I have to work late Friday night."

"Oh we'll be quiet as church mice," Hermy said. "Get it Marylou?" Hermy was laughing. "Church mice?"

Hermy left the kitchen to get back to work. Jesus, thought Marylou, that Hermy sure has a weird sense of humor.

Marylou decided she would go into work a little late. Let those two drunks, Duke and Fatty, suffer a little. She took her time having coffee and went into watch Hermy work. She had to admit the place looked good. It was rather soft and calm looking. Hermy might know what the hell he is doing. She fixed lunch for both of them. After lunch, Hermy said he was going to head downtown.

"I don't know when I will be home. I have some things to pick up."

"That's o.k.," Marylou said. "I'll be home to feed the kids. Then, they can stay by themselves for a while."

"See you later baby," Hermy said, and away he went.

Marylou spent the rest of the day relaxing. There are times you need some time to yourself, she thought. It wasn't long until the children were home from school and she had to fix dinner for them. After dinner, when Marylou was getting ready to go to work, she thought this would be a good time to take the clothes she wanted to wear over the weekend. She wouldn't have to worry about Hermy seeing her or catching her taking them out. Marylou went through the clothes she had in the closet. She picked out two of the tightest pairs of pants she had and two of the lowest cut sweaters. Wait until Duke sees me in these, she thought. He'll cream his jeans. I'll hang them in the back room and give old Duke a look of coming attractions.

When Marylou got to work, Fatty was behind the bar. "Hey Marylou, what's going on?" she yelled. "Did you and Duke have a good time after you dropped me off last night?" Fatty gave Marylou a big wink.

"Man Fatty, you have a big mouth."

"Better to eat you with," Fatty retorted and gave Marylou another big wink.

Marylou went behind the bar and said to Fatty. "Fatty, don't be so loud. I don't want anyone to know I went out with Duke."

"Too late," Fatty said. "Everyone knows. It seems that Red heard the two of you up there last night. He said it sounded like there was a lot of action going on up there."

"Shit," Marylou said. "I hope he didn't go home and tell all that shit to Patty. Sooner or later, Hermy will hear about it and then the shit will hit the fan. I'm not ready for that yet. By the way, was Duke down yet?"

"Hell, he was sitting in the usual place when I got here this morning," Fatty said. "Him and Big Red were all drunk up. I told Red to get his ass home and told Duke to get upstairs to bed. Duke was sitting there telling Red how much he loved you and all Red was doing was sucking it up. You can bet he ran home and told Patty all about it. After all, he had to have an excuse for staying out all night. That gossip, plus what he adds to it, will do the trick."

"I'll be right back," Marylou told Fatty.

Marylou walked out of the bar slamming the door and stormed up the steps to Duke's apartment. Marylou went right into the bedroom and saw Duke passed out on the bed. Marylou started slapping him across the face and yelling at the top of her lungs. "You dumb son of a bitch, what the fuck is wrong with you?" She kept slapping him. "If you ever talk about what me and you do, I'll kill you!" Marylou left and went back down to the bar.

Duke sat up in the bed, opened his bloodshot eyes, and thought, what the hell was that all about? It must have been a bad dream. He laid back down thinking, God damn it, my face hurts. Then, he was out like a light.

Marylou came storming back into the bar. "Jesus," Fatty was smiling. "It sounded like you beat the hell out of him. What did he say?"

"He didn't say anything." Marylou started laughing. "Shit, I don't even think he woke up."

Fatty started laughing too. "He probably thinks he was dreaming. Hell, you might have to do it all over again so he knows what the hell happened." Both Fatty and Marylou were laughing by now.

"This calls for a drink," Fatty said as she poured a shot of Jack Daniels for each of them. They clicked glasses and put the drinks down the old hatch. Fatty said, "Well, that's enough for me. The last couple of nights damn near killed me. I must be getting old. Plus, we are going to have one busy weekend! So my good friend, I'll see you tomorrow night."

"So long Fatty," Marylou said. "I'll fill you in later on what happens."

The rest of the night was uneventful. A few people stopped by for a drink or two. Marylou thought they might be saving up for tomorrow night. Man, are they going to be surprised when they see the whores and people selling dope in the johns. This will be very interesting. It was about eleven o'clock when the door opened and who walked in? It was Hermy himself.

"Hi Hermy," Marylou said. "What are you doing here?"

"Oh, I just stopped by to see my baby," he said as he leaned across the bar to give Marylou a little kiss on the cheek. "I got the money. Yep, I got it right here." Hermy patted his pants pocket.

"Have you been drinking?" Marylou asked.

"Hey, I had a little drink with one of my friends, that's all. But, how about a beer?"

Marylou went to get Hermy a beer and was pouring it in a glass when the door opened and in walked Big Red.

Red walked over and sat down on the stool next to Hermy.

"Hey man, how are you doing?" Red asked Hermy.

"Fine, doing fine," Hermy said. "How's about you?"

"I'm good," Red told Hermy and looked over at Marylou and gave her a big wink.

"Honey," Hermy said. "Give my friend here a beer."

Jesus, Marylou thought. I hope this asshole doesn't blow the whistle on me. Marylou brought the beer back to Red and put it on the bar in front of him.

"Man," Red said to Marylou. "After you left last night, me and Duke really hung one on. Hell, Fatty kicked us out when she came in this morning. It's a good thing you've been getting those early quits, right Marylou?" Red winked at her. "That Duke, he treats his help good, don't you think Marylou?"

"Sure he does," Marylou said as she glared into Red's eyes.

Red stared right back at Marylou. Then, he stuck the top of his tongue out and licked his lips. Marylou turned away. Oh shit, she thought. I can see the handwriting on the wall.

Big Red and Hermy sat at the bar talking and Marylou stayed as close as possible without looking as though she was listening to them. Every once in a while, Big Red would look over at Marylou, wink, and lick his lips. Marylou knew she couldn't do or say anything right now. She knew how to get even with Red. One thing, she thought. Red probably didn't tell Patty yet. He would use what he knew to blackmail me.

Just when Marylou thought things couldn't become worse, the door opened and in walked Duke. Hermy and Red greeted Duke and he sat down with them. "Give us all a drink Marylou," Duke said, and the three of them started talking.

Marylou brought the drinks over to them and Duke said, "Get yourself one too and sit with us."

"I'll have the drink," Marylou said. "But, I'm a little too busy to sit and talk to you guys. Somebody has to work you know." Marylou tried to act normal, but inside, she was a nervous wreck. I have to get Hermy out of here before one of those other guys spills the beans.

The decision was taken out of Marylou's hands when Duke called her over and said, "Hey Marylou, give us all one more drink and then you can hit the road if you want to. I'll work until closing time."

"Sure, that would be great," Marylou said. "Hermy, let's go."

"Not until after that drink Duke wants to buy," Hermy said. "You gotta get 'em while the gettings good."

"Before you go Marylou, I have some things I want to show you for tomorrow night. They're in the back room."

"How about if I look at them tomorrow?" Marylou asked.

"No, you better look at them now," Duke smiled.

"Sure, let's do it now while Hermy finishes his drink." Marylou walked, or rather stomped, to the back room. Duke followed her and shut the door.

Marylou turned and said, "What the hell is your problem? Hermy's right outside and you want me to come in here to play grab ass? And what the fuck are you telling Red about us for?"

"Relax," Duke said. "I didn't tell Red anything he couldn't figure out for himself after last night. And, he ain't gonna blow the whistle. So, come on baby and give me a little kiss."

"No," Marylou said. "I told you I take care of Hermy during the week and maybe you during the weekend. But, you have to change your ways." Marylou started for the door. "There are some of my clothes hanging over there. If you want to, you can smell them and whack your willie." Marylou walked out and slammed the door.

She's a real small ass, thought Duke as he walked over to check out the clothes.

Marylou walked over to the bar and said, "Come on Hermy. Let's go."

"Sure," Hermy said. "I'm ready."

Red put his arm around Marylou's waist and said, "I'll tell Patty you said hello." Marylou felt his hand drop slowly from her waist to her ass and then Red gave her a little squeeze.

"You do that," Marylou said as she and Hermy walked out the door.

Marylou and Hermy walked to the car. "Boy," Hermy said, "those two guys are nice."

"Oh yeah," Marylou said as she was thinking. Sure Hermy, how nice would you think they are if you knew both of them wanted to get in my pants, and one of them will.

"What do you say we pick up some burgers on the way home?" Hermy said. "We can sit in the kitchen, have a few beers, and talk about going on vacation."

"Good idea," Marylou said. "How soon do you think we'll be going?"

"Well," Hermy said. "I'll have to wait a while. I mean with the church just getting started up again and all. Oh, I'd say a couple months or so."

"We may both need a vacation by then," Marylou said.

They stopped and picked up some burgers. Marylou could tell Hermy was excited about getting the church going again. When he was in this kind of mood, Marylou could almost see herself getting married to him. But then again, she thought, I better be careful. I've seen him at his worst. Besides that, I ain't making no definite plans until I find out about Noreen. That's what I want to work on now.

Marylou, Marylou," Hermy was looking at her. "Did you hear anything I said? It looks as though you were miles away. What were you thinking of?"

"Uh," Marylou said. "Oh, I was just thinking about how much fun we are gonna have on our vacation."

CHAPTER 61

Oh Friday, Hermy got up early and started working to have things ready for the opening of the church. Marylou walked around the house thinking about work. I wonder how this thing is going to be, what with whores and dopers. This could be one hell of a night. Never mind what could happen between her and Duke tonight. Marylou knew she had to get things moving now, because she knew she could not balance her life like this. It was just getting to be too much. There was Duke, Hermy, Noreen, and now she would have to deal with this asshole Red. Not that that would be any big deal, but it did take some of her time.

Marylou wanted to fix Hermy some dinner, but he told her he was too busy to eat. "Just bring me a sandwich and I'll eat it while I'm working. Some people are coming over later tonight to help me. Don't forget, we'll be working here tomorrow."

"Don't you forget, I'll be sleeping in the morning," Marylou said. "And if you wake me, there will be hell to pay!"

Marylou fed the children early and got ready for work. She put on the loose fitting jeans and a button-up sweater. She went to tell Hermy good-bye. Hermy seemed happy. He checked out her clothes. He didn't say anything, but Marylou could see the smug grin on his face. As Marylou was leaving, Hermy said, "I know you will be late tonight, so I'll be in bed. I have to get up early tomorrow. If we work all day, the church should be done and ready Sunday morning."

"O.K.," Marylou said. "I'll see you some time tomorrow. Don't forget I'll be sleeping, so try to keep the noise down."

Marylou got to the bar and Fatty was there, but hardly any customers. If course, it was only six o'clock. It was still early.

"Where's Duke?" Marylou asked.

"He was down earlier," Fatty said. "He went back up to take a nap. He's hitting the hooch again. He says he's worried about tonight."

"Let him sleep," Marylou said. "But, I think it's too late for him to worry. I mean he picked those guys to fool with."

Yeah," Fatty said. "But, I don't think he wanted all this to happen. You know, I've known Duke for a long time and all he ever did was make some book and sell some hot stuff out of the bar. But, he ain't never dealt in drugs or whores. At least, not in front of me."

"Yeah, well how about what him and Jimmy done together?" Marylou asked.

"We don't know that for sure," Fatty said. "Which reminds me, are you going to try to find something out from Duke, or are you just fucking around?"

"Knock it off Fatty," Marylou was pissed. "I'm doing my best, and I sure as hell don't need no shit from you!"

"I'm sorry," Fatty said. "But hell, I try to tell you everything that goes on. It seems like you tell me nothing. I mean, hell, you been to bed with Duke yet?"

"Shit!" Marylou said. "That's all you're interested in, ain't it Fatty? To see if I went to bed with him or not. You ain't a bit interested in knowing if I found out about my daughter and if she's dead or alive. All you want to know are the details about me and Duke fucking! Well, I ain't gone to bed with him yet, and when I do, you will be the first to know!" Marylou stormed off to the back room to chance.

When she came back, Fatty had a beer ready for her. "I'm sorry Marylou. Hell, I don't want to fight with you. You're my best friend and we have a lot of fun together. Please don't be mad at me."

"Oh hell, I ain't mad at you Fatty," Marylou said. "It's just that I have a lot on my mind. You know, with trying to find something out from Duke and worrying about Hermy finding out about it." Then, she told Fatty about Red.

"That son of a bitch," Fatty said. "I thought he was done screwing around since he started going with Patty."

"I don't know anything about that," Marylou said. "If he tries anything with me, I'll kick his ass! I don't want to say anything to Patty, 'cause she's so happy now. They're supposed to get married in a few weeks."

"Maybe, he was just fooling around and meant nothing by it," Fatty said.

"I'll just wait and see," Marylou shrugged. "If that was just a pat on the ass, I've had plenty of those. Well, hell with it. But, if he keeps at me, then I'll make him sorry!"

The band got there around seven o'clock. By the time they set up and warmed up, it was around eight o'clock. The bar was starting to fill up by then. When Duke came down around nine, the place was starting to jump.

Duke took his place at the end of the bar, looked around, and asked Marylou, "You seen any of those people yet?"

"What people?" Marylou asked.

"You know, them whores and dope sellers," Duke said.

"Not yet," Marylou told Duke.

"Why the fuck don't they work regular hours," Duke said. "You know, in by eight, out by two." Duke smiled to himself. "That's what I'll tell those guys, punch the clock!"

Marylou called Patty and told her to get in to work. Big Red drove her down to the bar. Patty started right to work and Red grabbed a seat at the bar. Marylou walked over to wait on him.

Red smiled and said, "Hey Marylou, how are they hanging?"

"Not as low as yours," Marylou said.

Red let out a big roar. "God damn Marylou, you sure got the comebacks."

"She always did," Patty laughed. "Wait until you get to know her better."

"I can hardly wait," Red licked his lips.

I bet you can't, Marylou thought to herself. Not in your wildest dreams. The place was so busy after that, Marylou didn't have any time to think of Red.

It was eleven o'clock and Duke was getting nervous as hell. No one had shown up. What the hell is going on here? Those guys come in here raising hell and they never show up. I hope they don't come around here either. It would save me a lot of aggravation. That was not about to happen. Five minutes later, Nick and Dom walked in. Behind them came Sheri and Fast Eddy. Oh shit! Now, the shit is going to hit the fan!

Nick and Dom came over and stood behind Duke. Fast Eddy and Sheri took seats at different places in the bar and started to talk to people.

"How about a couple of drinks?" Duke said to Nick and Dom as he waved Marylou over. "Give the boys whatever they want and it's on me," Duke said. Marylou walked away to get the drinks. "Where the hell you guys been?" Duke asked. "Man, I thought you would be here earlier than this."

"Don't fucking worry about us," Dom told Duke. "Just take care of your business and we'll take care of ours."

"Just asking," Duke said. "I don't know what to expect from you guys."

"Don't expect nothing," Nick told Duke. "Just sit back and watch."

Duke watched Sheri first. She was already sitting at a table with two other couples. They were laughing away like they had known Sheri all their lives. It wasn't long before one of the girls at the table went to the john with Sheri. When she came back, her friend followed her out of the bar. Five minutes later, they walked back in. Duke saw the guy who had just come back in hand his buddy something and then the other couple left. In five minutes or so, they walked back into the bar. Duke looked over to where Fast Eddy was sitting. He was talking to three guys.

He watched as all three of them headed for the john. Shortly, they came out and left the bar. In five minutes, they were back and went over to talk to some of their friends. One of the guys who had just come back pointed to Fast Eddy. The guy walked over to Fast Eddy and tapped him on the shoulder. They both walked into the john.

"I've never seen anything like this in my life!" Duke said.

"Yeah, it's something, ain't it," Dom said. "Word spreads like wildfire."

Sure enough, soon neither Fast Eddy nor Sheri came out of the johns, and there was a line waiting to get in.

"Well, if that don't beat all," Duke said. "I know some of those people, and I never knew they were using dope. When are the other girls coming?" Duke asked.

"What's the matter Duke? You got a boner or something for the girls?" Nick smiled at Dom.

Duke smiled and said, "Not right now. I just want to see how they work."

"Oh, you'll like the way they work," Nick said. "By the way, is your door still broken off the hinges?"

"Yeah," Duke said. "Why?"

My Baby My Baby!

"Well, until we get going here and find a place to rent, the girls will be using your apartment."

"What?" Duke yelled. "Are you crazy? Besides that, there's only one bedroom up there!"

"Man, you ain't got to tell us," Dom said. "We've been up there," and he laughed.

"You have one bed and a couch, so there won't be any problem," Nick said.

"You mean, two guys will go up there at one time?" Duke asked.

"Hey, for all we care, they can all fuck at the same time in one bed; just so they pay, know what I mean?" Dom asked duke.

"I hope you have clean sheets for the bed," Nick said to Duke.

"You mean for now?" Duke asked. "I can go up and change."

"No, not for now," Nick laughed. "We mean for later."

"What do you mean for later?" Duke asked.

"Well when those girls get done, if you don't change the sheets, you could be stuck on them for life!" Dom said as Nick laughed.

"Oh hell, they ain't gonna be that busy," Duke said. "Not in his place. Hell, I know most of the people here and they ain't gonna pay for no pussy!"

"Oh sure," Dom said. "Just like they weren't gonna buy no dope and Fast Eddy and Sheri are busier than a one-armed paper hanger."

"Well, that's different," Duke said. "I mean, most of the guys in here are married and they don't have to pay to get pussy!"

"Hey man," Nick said. "Remember those two broads will do it anyway you want and believe me, they can do it some ways that wives don't even know about and ain't even heard about!"

"You got something there," Duke said. "When the hell are they coming to work?"

"Oh, they'll be here around midnight or so," Dom said. "They know how to work these crowds."

It was a little after midnight when Dawn and Bambi walked into the bar. You could see all heads turn to the door when they walked in. The women looked at them with jealousy, and the men looked at them with lust. The two girls sat down at the door and the guys started to buy them drinks.

"See that," Nick said to Duke. "Hell, you'll make more money selling drinks than the girls will selling pussy."

"I doubt that," Duke said as he watched the girls. Man, they do look good, way too good to be hooking, well, out of this place anyhow. Duke watched the girls as they took trick after trick upstairs and came down a short time later. Just as quickly, they had two more and were gone. Duke saw one guy leave his wife at the table and come back about ten minutes later with a big smile on his face. Jesus, thought Duke. I never figured they would get that kind of action in here. Of course, the customers never thought they would get that kind of action here either. It got so the girls didn't come downstairs anymore. The guys knew where to go, and there was a steady stream of customer going up to Duke's apartment.

The band knocked off about one-thirty and the juke box started playing. Duke was enjoying the action and he knew he was making some big bucks. The dope and the whores didn't bother him anymore, at least not after drinking and seeing that the customers were using the whores and buying the dope.

It was getting close to two-fifteen and Marylou came over to Duke. "Hey, you better start getting these people to drink up so we can close," she said to Duke.

"Yeah, you're right," Duke said. He got behind the bar and started yelling. "Let's drink up! It's time to close! Let's go! Motel time! Hey Red, pull the plug on that juke box, will you?"

Once the music stopped, the place emptied out fast. Duke had noticed Fast Eddy and Sheri sitting at one of the table with Nick and Dom, but he didn't see Bambi or Dawn around. Duke looked out the window and saw there were four guys waiting by his apartment door. I can't believe this. They must have done half the guys here, even some of those old winos. Man, they had to spend their last buck.

Shit, I should have locked up all of my valuables. Man, I don't know who the hell was in my apartment. My TV is probably missing! Hell, with this, Duke went outside and yelled at the guys waiting by the door. "Get the hell out of here, the place is closed!"

"Hey man, take it easy," one of the guys said. "We're just waiting here to get a little."

"Come back tomorrow," Duke yelled back. "The girls are done for the night."

Duke walked upstairs. He looked around the living room and everything looked like it was there. Duke could hear some noises coming from his bedroom. He looked in the door and saw both girls in bed with one guy. Jesus, Duke thought. That guy is Little Steve, the roofer! Hell, he just got married, his wife was here about an hour ago. They got into a fight and she left. Man, if she could see him now! He would be in big trouble.

Duke was watching and never heard Nick walk up behind him. Nick grabbed Duke by the arm and Duke jumped. Little Steve never saw him, but Dawn looked up at Duke and smiled. She winked at him and then went back to business.

"Come on downstairs," Nick said. "But next time if you want to watch, we can set up a little peep hole for you." He started to laugh.

"Hey man, I was just checking to make sure all my stuff was still there, that's all. I ain't no peeper!" Duke said.

"Yeah, sure, no need to be embarrassed," Nick said. "Hell, me and Dom see all kind of weirdoes."

Duke was pissed. He didn't say any more. I hope this asshole don't go telling people in the bar that I was standing there watching. Oh well, it did look like fun, Duke smiled to himself. Nick followed Duke down to the bar.

When Duke walked into the bar, Big Red, Patty, Marylou, and Fatty were sitting at a table having a drink. Fast Eddy, Sheri, and Dom were sitting at another table talking and drinking. All of the customers had left.

Nick steered Duke over to the table where Fast Eddy, Sheri, and Dom were sitting.

"O.K.," Nick said. "Time to get the help out of here. We got business to talk over."

"Do you want to wait until they finish their drinks?" Duke asked.

"O.K. by me," Nick said. "The two girls are still upstairs and we can't settle up until they're done."

Duke went over to the other table and said, "Hey, how did you guys like tonight? We were pretty busy weren't we?"

"It sure was busy," Patty said. "Me and Red gotta get going. See you all later."

"Yeah, me too," Fatty said. "We have another big night coming up." Fatty got up to leave. Everyone except Marylou walked out the door.

She looked up at Duke and said, "Well, what's the story big boy?"

"Oh man, baby. I have to settle up with these guys. You want to wait around? Then, you and me can do whatever we want."

"Duke, I ain't go time to wait," Marylou said. "You don't even know how long this will take, and I'm not sitting around until it's too late to do anything." Marylou got up and went into the back room to change.

Duke looked over at the other table and saw they were not paying any attention to him. He walked to the door of the back room and went in. The light was off and it was dark in there. Duke looked, but he couldn't see Marylou. Duke called out low, "Marylou, where are you?"

"Right here," Marylou cooed.

Duke reached over on the wall and turned the light on. Marylou was standing against the wall. His mouth fell open. All she had on was her bra and panties. "Thy cup runneth over," Duke said smiling.

"You mean cups, don't you?" Marylou said as she moved closer to Duke.

Duke started kissing her and running his hands up and down her back. He kissed her mouth, then her neck, and reached down and pulled one breast out of her bra, and began to suck on it. Neither of them heard the door open. Nick stood at the door watching for a minute. Man, what a slob she is, he thought. She's definitely not my type. But man, she sure has some big tits. Then, he said out loud, "Well, well Duke, maybe you can do more than just look!"

Marylou and Duke both jumped. Marylou grabbed her skirt to cover up and Duke yelled, "Get the fuck out of here!"

"Sure," Nick said. "I just wanted to tell you that we are ready to talk business." Nick turned to walk out the door. "Oh, do you want me to close the door?"

"That's it! God damn it Duke. Why the hell didn't you lock that door?" Marylou yelled. "From now on, you get things all arranged or you forget about having sex with me!"

"Oh Marylou," Duke said. "Relax. Stick around while I settle up with these guys and then we can talk."

"Not tonight, Duke. I'm on my way home. I've had enough for tonight," Marylou said as she dressed. "Maybe tomorrow. But right now, I'm gone." Marylou walked out of the bar without looking back at the table where Nick and the rest of the gang were sitting.

Duke waited a few minutes before he came out of the back room. When he did, he walked right over to the table and said to Nick "What the hell is your problem? You guys come into my bar and into my house and take over! Well, this shit is going to stop right now, or else!"

"Or else what?" Nick said. "Remember fat ass, we own you. So, you ain't got no secrets from us. You understand? Now, go lock the door and bring us over some drinks. Then, we can get down to business."

Duke stood at the table staring at Nick. Nick glared back at him and said, "Look Duke, I don't care what the fuck you do around here. If you want to play around with that fat barmaid, that's all well and good. But, I can tell you one thing right now. When it comes to this business, we tell you what to do and when to do it. If you don't like it, we can take you back to the hill and talk to the boss. So make it easy on yourself, understand?"

Duke turned without saying anything and went to lock the door and get the drinks.

"By the way," Dom said. "You ever hear that old saying 'don't shit where you eat?'"

Duke clenched his fists as he walked to the door. God damn it, he thought. What the hell am I going to do? These guys got me good! I got to find a way out of this shit! But, how? Duke got the drinks, pouring himself a double. When he got back to the table, it looked like all the business was taken care of. Fast Eddy and Sheri finished their drinks while everyone made small talk. Fast Eddy and Sheri left, followed by Dawn and Bambi. Duke locked the door behind them. Dom told Duke to bring more drinks over to the table. Duke got the drinks and sat down with Nick and Dom.

"Look Duke, I don't want any trouble from you," Nick said. "But you have to understand. Me and Dom have a job to do. If we don't produce, we get in big trouble with the boys on the hill. I mean, it's just that simple. Everything runs smoothly, everybody's happy. We make money. What the hell more can you ask for?"

"I guess you're right," Duke said. "But, I ain't used to being bossed around. I've had this bar a long time and never had any partners."

"Don't consider us partners," Dom said. "How about associates?"

"Same thing," Duke said. "I guess I'll just have to get used to it."

"I guess you will," Nick said. "Now, let's get down to business. Like we told you before, until we get started, we are going to pay you a flat fee. After a while if things get going good, we pay the rate or a percent of the take, whichever is higher. Does that sound fair to you?"

"I guess," Duke said. "What's the difference anyhow? You guys are going to do whatever you want, right?"

"Come on Duke," Nick said. "Try to be fair about this. We don't stay in business by cheating everyone. The boss keeps close tabs on us, so don't worry about it." Nick reached into his pocket and pulled out a roll of bills. He handed them across the table to Duke. "Count it," Nick told Duke.

Duke counted the money and his eyes lit up. "Six hundred dollars? Is this for both nights?"

"Hell no," Nick said. "We pay as we go at the end of every night." Nick and Dom got up from the table and headed for the door. "Oh, by the way," Nick said. "Don't claim that on your income tax, know what I mean Duke?"

Duke followed them to the door and locked it when they left. He went to the bar and poured a double. Shit, he thought. Not bad at all. Twelve hundred bucks a week and it was that easy? Duke poured another drink to take upstairs with him.

Duke got upstairs and put his drink on the kitchen table. He went into the bathroom and washed up, getting ready for bed. I have to get that door fixed. Duke turned on the lights and his eyes damn near popped out of his head. There lying on the bed stark naked was Dawn. "What the hell?" Duke gasped.

"Surprise!" Dawn said. "Just a little gift from Nick and Dom. Put the drink down, we got champagne chilled and over here." She walked over to the dresser. "We have this." Six lines were laid out on the dresser.

Duke watched as Dawn leaned over to do the coke. Man, what a body, Duke thought and got an instant hard-on.

"Come over here," Dawn said. "Try some of this, it's the best."

Duke walked over to the dresser. "I ain't never done this shit before, and I really don't know if I want to."

Dawn reached up, pulled Duke's head down and began to kiss him. She gave him so much tongue, he could hardly breathe. She whispered in his ear, "Come on Duke, try some for me please." As she was whispering, she was grinding her body into his.

"O.K.," Duke said. "What the hell?"

Dawn gave him the straw and Duke did one line and then the other. Dawn poured the champagne and lay down on the bed. She spread her legs and said, "Come on Duke baby, this thing is all ready for you."

Duke took one look and almost jumped into the bed.

When they were done, they did more coke and finished the champagne. Then, Dawn did things to Duke that he had only read or heard about. The next thing Duke knew it was eleven o'clock Saturday morning. Jesus, Duke thought as he looked around. Dawn must have left earlier. Maybe that was a dream, a wet dream. Duke got up to take a shower. He felt like a million bucks. Maybe, I'll never get that door fixed.

Duke washed up and went down to the bar. The bar was clean as a whistle. Duke checked the johns and found them clean and they smelled good too. That girl he hired did a good job. I'll have to give her a raise. Man, who would think that last night this place was filled with dopers and whores, Duke thought as he fixed a bloody mary. Talking about dope, how about me taking that stuff for the first time in my life. I wonder if I could get Marylou to do some of that? Hey! I wish I could get her to do to me what Dawn did. Jesus, what a broad. Maybe, tonight I could get Bambi. I have to try everything. I don't want the customers to get anything bad. Duke laughed as he mixed himself another bloody mary.

Big Red came in about one o'clock. "Man, what a night!" He said, "Gimme a beer."

Duke got Red the beer and said, "I saw you leave for a while last night, where did you go?"

Red had a big smile on his face. "Well, I told Patty I was going to check on the kids. But, I went upstairs and did that Bambi."

"No shit!" Duke said. "You mean you had the guts to go there with Patty right here?"

"Hell yeah, why not?" Red asked. "What the hell, you didn't even think I went up there, did you?"

"Hell no!" Duke said. "But, I did see a couple of guys do the same thing. If that shit keeps up, there will be some shootings in here. How much did that Bambi charge you?"

"Fifty bucks, but it was worth every cent." Red smiled. "Tonight, I'm going to try that black-haired one."

"Yeah, she's good," Duke said. Aw shit, I didn't want anyone to know, but too late now. "That little Steve did the best," Duke said trying to cover up.

"How's that?" Red asked.

"He had both of them at the same time!" Duke said.

"Oh man, I got to try that!" Red banged his hand on the bar. "Man! Both of them. Wow!"

CHAPTER 62

Marylou walked out of the bar and she was pissed off. She walked to her car thinking. What the hell am I going to do? I can't get that stupid Duke alone to get any information from him. I'm getting no place fast. This shit is going to wear me out. The money is good working, but hell, I don't want to work the rest of my life. That was one thing with that Jimmy around, I never had to work. With welfare and the money Jimmy gave me, I did all right.

Marylou got home around three-thirty. The house was all dark except for the kitchen light. Marylou went into the house and saw a note on the table. I read, "In bed, got to get up early, will try and be quiet. Love, Hermy."

Marylou got a beer out of the icebox and sat down at the kitchen table. It seems I'm spending more and more time sitting at this table thinking. Marylou put her head down on the table and started to cry. My baby, my baby, whatever happened to you? Are you alive? Oh, how am I ever going to find out? Marylou sat there for a while sobbing. Then, it seemed her strength started returning. What the hell am I doing here crying like a baby? I got to get this show on the road. I have to set myself a goal, a time limit. I have to organize my time instead of wasting it. Marylou felt better now. She drank down the beer and hopped off to bed.

At ten o'clock that morning, Marylou got out of bed. Hermy was already up and working. She could hear some people in the church. Marylou made a full pot of coffee and took it out to the church. "Come on boys, take a break," Marylou said to the four men who were helping Hermy. "Here's some nice fresh coffee."

They all thanked Marylou. Marylou went back to the house and Hermy came in right after her.

"That sure was nice of you to bring that coffee out," Hermy said. "I hope we didn't wake you."

"Heck no," Marylou smiled. "Life's too short to sleep it away."

Hermy gave Marylou a hug and said, "Things will be all right." With that, Hermy went back to work in the church.

CHAPTER 63

Saturday night at the bar was a carbon copy of the night before. Everything ran smooth as silk and Duke had gotten into the swing of things. Marylou, Fatty, and Patty were as busy as could be. In fact, they told Duke that if they were going to be this busy all the time, they would probably need another barmaid. "No problem," Duke said. Duke thought the little Puerto Rican broad who cleaned up the bar would make a nice barmaid. Duke was drinking and talking to all the customers and in general, just having a ball. It was two forty-five before Duke got the last customer out of the bar.

After everyone was out of the bar, Marylou and the two other girls sat at one table and Nick and the rest of the gang sat at another table. They were all having a drink, when there was a knock at the door. Duke went over to the door and let Big Red in. Red went over to the table and gave Patty a kiss hello.

"Where the hell have you been?" Patty asked Red. "You left over an hour ago."

"Oh, one of the guys had trouble starting his car, so I helped him," Red told Patty.

Red sat down between Marylou and Patty. They were talking for a while when Patty went to get them one more round of drinks. Red was telling a joke to Marylou and Fatty, when Marylou felt Red's hand rubbing her thigh. At first, she didn't say anything or make a move. Then, Red put his hand right between her legs. Marylou reached down, squeezed Red's hand, and said to him in a nice sweet voice, "Red, could you come in the back room and help me lift a couple of cases of beer? I can't get the ones on top and Duke will have to load the coolers later."

"Sure, I'll be right with you," Red smiled.

Marylou went into the back room and Red came in almost right away. He grabbed Marylou and pulled her up to him trying to give her a kiss. At the same time, he said, "I've been waiting a long time for this."

That's when Marylou kneed him right in the balls. Red doubled over trying not to scream out. "Now, you son of a bitch," Marylou said in her sweet voice. "If you ever touch me again, I'll kick your ass. Not only that, I'll tell Patty that you have been trying to get in my pants and that you've been fucking those whores upstairs." Marylou walked calmly out of the room and went back to the table. "Red will be right out here," she said, giving Fatty a wink. "He has a few more cases to get down for Duke."

It was about ten minutes later when Red came out of the back room. His face was all red and there were still some tears in his eyes.

"What's the matter?" Patty asked him.

"Oh shit, I slipped on the floor in there just as I was reaching for a case of beer on the top. I hurt my neck. I must have pulled a muscle or something."

"Oh, my poor baby," Patty said. "That's what happens when you try to be nice and help other people. Come on home and I'll fix you a nice hot bath and rub your back."

Marylou could hardly keep from laughing. As soon as they went out the door, she couldn't hold back any more. She told Fatty what had happened and Fatty started laughing. "He'll have real blue balls," Fatty roared.

Just then, Duke walked over to the table. "Man, you girls sure are having a good time."

"Sorry if we tore you away from your friends," Marylou said to Duke.

"What's that supposed to mean?" Duke said.

"Well, we figured you're too busy for us. I mean we're just the help," Marylou nudged Fatty.

"God damn it, this is business. Anyhow, Marylou," Duke said. "Come in the back room. I want to tell you something."

"I wouldn't go in there with her if I were you," Fatty started to giggle. "I'll see you later," she said as she left the table laughing.

"What the hell's this all about?" Duke asked.

"Just forget it," Marylou said as she got up to leave. "See you Tuesday."

"Hey, ain't you even going to change clothes?" Duke yelled after.

"What, so you can peek again? No thanks," Marylou said and she was gone. As she walked to her car, Marylou thought, Let him think it over for a while. Hell, Hermy will be in bed when I get home, so he won't even see my clothes.

Duke watched Marylou go out the door. I wonder what crawled up her ass, Duke thought. Oh well, let me get back to business. Duke went behind the bar to get refills for his friends. Duke brought the drinks back to the table and they were making small talk. Twenty minutes later, the girls and Fast Eddy left. Duke locked up and came back to the table.

"Well, how did you like our little present last night?" Nick asked.

"Fine, just fine," Duke said smiling.

Nick gave Duke the money and told him to count it.

"Hell no, I trust you guys," Duke said.

"No, you count it in front of us," Dom said. "That's the way we do business."

Duke counted the money. Sure enough, there was six hundred bucks. "I love America," Duke said.

Nick and Dom got up to leave and Duke followed them right out the door. "Are you in a hurry to get upstairs?" Nick asked Duke.

"Should I be?" Duke asked.

"You better get up there before she starts without you," Dom said. Duke started for the stairs. When he was out of hearing range, Dom said. "What do you think Nick? Do you think we can get him hooked?"

"On pussy or coke?" Nick laughed.

"On the coke man," Dom said. "You know what the boss said."

"Yup, he said to get him hooked and hooked he will be," Nick said. Nick and Dom walked to their car.

Duke got upstairs and went right to the bedroom. Shit, man! Just like last night. Only tonight, it was Bambi. She got up from the bed and said, "come on honey, let's get started with this." She did two lines and handed the straw to Duke.

"What the fuck?" Duke said. "It's all in the game." And he did two lines.

That wasn't all Duke did that night. There was champagne, sex, and more coke. Duke couldn't remember everything they did, but it was better than last night. Man, I have to get these two broads together. Then, he had visions of little Steve, the roofer, on this very bed wrapped up with Bambi and Dawn. Jesus, just thinking about it was great. Next week, that was for him.

CHAPTER 64

Duke woke up and looked at the clock by his bed. It was exactly noon. Duke didn't feel as good this morning as he had yesterday. I probably just need a little drink, he thought. Duke got up from bed and staggered, grabbing on to the dresser. Jesus, I'm a little dizzy, he thought. As he looked down, he saw six lines of coke laid out on the dresser with a note. Duke picked up the note and read it. "This is for being so good last night stud. Love, Bambi." Duke looked at the coke and the straw lying next to the lines. Nah, he thought and he went in to take a shower.

Duke came out of the shower feeling a lot better. He walked into the bedroom to get dressed. As he opened the drawer, he looked down at the lines of coke. Oh what the hell, Duke did two lines. God damn, I feel good now. I think I'll go down and check on the Puerto Rican. You never know, do you stud? Duke was smiling as he started down to the bar.

Duke went into the bar and sure enough, the girl was almost finished cleaning. "Hey, how you doing?" Duke asked as he went over to mix himself a bloody mary. Duke sat at the end of the bar and watched as the girl was cleaning. She had on a loose fitting sweater and tight jeans. Every time she would bend over, Duke could see her tits, that is, all except the nips.

Duke could feel his dick getting hard. Yeah, he thought. That Bambi is right. Stud, that's me. Duke had another bloody mary and said to the girl, "Don't go away. I want to talk to you, but I have to go upstairs for a minute."

The girl looked at him and said, "I won't be done for a while."

Duke went upstairs and headed right for the bedroom dresser. He looked at the coke. Hey man, what the fuck? She left the shit here for me, no sense in wasting it. So old Duke did two more lines and went back to the bar. He fixed another bloody may and sat there watching the girl finish cleaning the bar.

When she was finished, she took all the mops and pails and put them away in the back room. When she came out, Duke said, "Come over here and sit down. What do they call you?"

"Oh, you can call me Margie," she told Duke.

"O.K. Margie, you sure do a nice job around here. How about a drink?" Duke asked.

"Sure, why not?" Margie said. "Could I have a run and coke?"

"Hey, you can have anything you want," Duke said and winked at her. Margie smiled back. Fuck, Duke thought. This will be a snap.

Duke got the drinks. Margie and Duke sat around talking about nothing much. Duke was doing most of the talking. They had about four or five drinks and Duke was feeling pretty high. He knew Margie was too, because every once in a while, she would slip and start talking in Spanish.

Duke went to get them another drink. When he came back, he said, "Listen Margie, you do such a nice job in here. I want to give you a little raise." Duke reached into his pocket and pulled out a twenty. He pulled the top of her sweater and stuck the twenty down between her tits. She looked at him and smiled. So, he didn't take his hand right out, but felt around a little. She was nice and firm, Duke thought to himself. "And another thing, my little Margie, have you ever tended bar before?"

"Oh sure, many times," Margie told him.

"Well, how would you like to work here?" Duke asked her.

"When do I start?" Margie asked.

"Come in tomorrow night and I'll have Fatty, my other barmaid, break you in and show you where things are," Duke told her. "Then, you can work on the weekends. I need another barmaid. The weekends have been so busy with the band and all."

"Oh, that would be good!" Margie said. "You are so good to me." All the time, Margie was rubbing Duke's leg. "Now, let me be good to you."

Before Duke knew what happened, she was leaning over. In one fluid motion, she had his pants unzipped and was taking him into her mouth. This is great, Duke thought. I've had more sex in the last two days, then I have had in the last two months. He leaned back and enjoyed it.

When he was done, Margie jumped up and went to the bathroom to clean up. Duke got two more drinks for them. When she came back, she said, "Next time, you be good to me, si?"

"I can't wait to, si?" Duke said and they both laughed.

Margie got ready to leave and Duke asked her, "Do you need a ride home?"

"Nope," Margie said. "Adios, see you tomorrow."

Hell, I don't even know where she lives, Duke thought. Duke fixed himself another drink, locked up the bar, and went to the apartment. He looked at the clock. Jesus, it was six-thirty already. Man, the time sure does fly when you're having fun. I think I'll go out, have a little dinner, stop by a few bars, and have some drinks. Yeah, that's a good idea. Duke went into the bedroom to get his keys and without even thinking, he did the last two lines of coke.

CHAPTER 65

Marylou got home about three-thirty. Hermy was in bed, which was good. Marylou went right into the bathroom, took her clothes off, and put them in the bottom of the clothes basket. She put her robe on and went out to the kitchen. Hermy had left a note on the table. "Honey, went to bed about one. We got the church ready to open tomorrow. I'll wake you up in the morning to get ready. The first service will be at eleven o'clock. Love, Hermy."

Oh shit. Now, he wants me to be there with him. Oh well, maybe he'll let me take the collection, but I doubt it.

Marylou went to bed right after she read the note. It seemed as though she had just fallen asleep when Hermy came to wake her.

"Come on sleepy head," Hermy said. "Let's get up. Here's some nice hot coffee for you. I'm going out to make us all some breakfast."

Marylou took a sip of her coffee and looked at the clock. It was nine-thirty. Man, if felt like it was the middle of the night. Oh well, she could put up with this for a little while anyway. Keep Hermy happy. That was part of the plan, and the other part? That was Duke. There was time enough to think of that.

Marylou got out of bed and went into the kitchen. The children were already sitting at the table. Hermy was dishing out pancakes, bacon and eggs. Jesus, Marylou thought. It looks like the Cleaver family. Marylou took a seat and Hermy served her.

"You're going to like this," Hermy said. "It's a secret family recipe."

Marylou took a taste of the pancakes. He's right, she thought. They sure are good. "Hey Hermy, when do I get the recipe?"

"When you're family," Hermy said as he winked at her.

When the children had finished eating, Hermy told them to go up and change into the clothes he had laid out for them. "Make sure you wash your hands and face and wash behind your ears too!"

After Hermy had sent the kids on their way, he came and sat down next to Marylou. "Look honey, there are a couple of things I'd like to tell you about what I would like you to do when the church people are here. First of all, don't mention about us living together. Just about everyone knows, but there is no sense talking about it. Try not to lose your temper, no matter what anyone says to you. There are some pretty catty people who go to church. When we go to church, I want you and the children to sit in the front row."

"O.K. so far," Marylou said.

"Now, I'm going to give you a ten dollar bill to put in the offering plate," Hermy told Marylou. "But, what I want you to do is take the ten out of your purse. After they hold the basket in front of you, take your time. Then, put the ten in. Make sure it is not folded and then kind of just lay it in the bottom of the basket so everyone can see it."

"Why you foxy old devil you!" Marylou said.

"You just watch what happens then," Hermy said. "Once those people see you put the ten in, the other people will go back into their pockets to get a five or ten dollar bill instead of the one dollar they were going to put into the basket. Now, just one more thing, wait here." Hermy left and came back a few minutes later with a box. He put the box on the table and told Marylou to open it.

Marylou opened the box and in it was a blue dress with white polka dots, a pair of white panty hose, and a pair of blue low-heeled shoes.

"What the hell! This looks like some kind of costume!" Marylou said.

"It is, it is," Hermy said. "It's the kind of thing the Reverend's wife, or girlfriend would wear to church. So, if you listen to me, we'll make some money from this church."

"You know Hermy," Marylou said. "I believe you. I really think you know what you are doing here."

"You bet I do!" Hermy said. "I'm the best! Now, let me go in and get ready first. I have to be out there a little early to make sure things are shipshape.

Marylou poured herself some coffee and sat at the table drinking it. Hermy came out of the bedroom about ten minutes later. Marylou could hardly believe her eyes. Hermy had on a gray suit and a black dickey, or whatever you call them, with a white collar. "Jesus, Hermy! You look like a real Reverend!"

"Marylou, I am a real Reverend!" Hermy said. "And that's another thing. Let's try to knock off saying Jesus this and Jesus that, at least on Sunday."

"Hermy," Marylou said. "What the hell do you expect me to do, change like that? I'll try my best, but if a Jesus, or damn, or even a fuck you slips out, that's the breaks!"

"Relax Marylou," Hermy said. "Why don't you go get ready and make sure the kids are ready. I'll meet you in church."

"You sure you don't want to check all of us before the flock sees us?" Marylou yelled and then walked into the bedroom slamming the door.

That woman, Hermy thought. I wonder if I'll ever get the rough edges off her?

"Man, I hope this asshole don't think he's going to boss me around just because he's wearing that fucking collar. Marylou thought. I mean, it ain't like he's some real Reverend or anything like that. That little shit got some kind of certificate from a mail order place that says he's a Reverend so he don't have to pay taxes or something like that. Well, I'll just put this shit he bought me on. I'll give him a break, and I'll go to his church. But if he fucks me over one more time, I'll show him the wrath of God!

Marylou got dressed and looked in the mirror. God damn, if I don't look like a preacher's wife and the dress fits good. I wonder how Hermy knew what size to buy? Marylou went out to the kitchen. There sat all the children all cleaned up and in new clothes. "Hey, where did you guys get the new clothes?" Marylou asked.

"Hermy bought them yesterday, but he told us not to tell you. He wanted to surprise you."

Marylou took the children and walked around the front to go into the church. Hermy was greeting people at the door. When he saw Marylou and the children, he got a big smile on his face. He walked over to them. "I'll introduce you to the people who are here after church," Hermy said. "We don't have time right now." Hermy took them down the aisle and sat them in the first row. It was just a short time later when Hermy walked up to the front of the church, got to the podium, and began the service. Just before the sermon, Hermy announced the taking of the offering.

Marylou did just as Hermy had told her and watched the other people. Sure enough, they did just what Hermy had said they would do. They reached back into their pockets and upgraded the amount of money they were putting in the basket.

Hermy began the sermon. Marylou could not believe it was the same Hermy she knew. Hermy seemed like one of those preachers on TV.

There were only about fifteen people in the church, counting Marylou and the children, but they were all paying attention to Hermy, as though he was the most important man they ever knew. To say the least, Marylou was impressed.

After the sermon was over, Hermy walked out to the front door to say good-bye to all the people and invited them back for the night service where there would be coffee and refreshments served. Then, he would introduce Marylou and the children. When the last person had left, Marylou said to Hermy, "What the hell are you talking about serving coffee? Where the hell am I going to get a coffee pot big enough to make all this coffee?"

Hermy smiled and said, "Come back here." Hermy took Marylou to a door on the side of the church. When Hermy opened the door, there was a little supply room there with some more chairs and a big brand new coffee urn.

"Wow!" Marylou said. "That thing should make about thirty cups of coffee!"

"Fifty," Hermy told her. "Now after lunch, you and me will go to the store and buy some bakery to serve tonight."

"Sounds good to me," Marylou said. "By the way Hermy, I sure was proud of you preaching up there. You seemed as though you were someone else."

"Well, I get that from my grandfather. He sold snake oil in the hills and he used to take me with him sometimes. Yeah, that old man sure taught me to work the crowds."

"Talking about working the crowd," Marylou said. "I saw that little trick with the ten dollar bill work like a charm. How much did you collect today?"

Oh, we'll add that up tonight," Hermy said to Marylou. "By the way," he said reaching into his pocket. "Here's a dollar for each of the children to put in the offering." Hermy winked at Marylou. "We'll call the ten our lucky ten."

They all had lunch and sent the children to the show.

"Come on Marylou," Hermy said. "I want to get the bakery for tonight."

They went down to the store and Hermy spent a lot of time picking out the cheapest bakery he could find. "Next week, I'll go to that place on West 25th where they sell that day-old bakery. I just didn't have time this time."

"Man, Hermy, you don't miss a trick, do you?" Marylou said.

"Nope," Hermy told her. "Over the year, I'll save a lot of money buying the day-old stuff. Of course, I still charge the church the regular price."

This is going to prove very interesting, Marylou thought. I wonder what this old goat has up his sleeve? I know one thing for sure. I'm going to keep my eyes on that old fox!

I can see he ain't about to tell me how much money he collects. I'll just have to wait for the right time and check out that little old box Hermy has hidden. Then, we'll see just who the real fox is.

Hermy and Marylou got home and decided to take a little nap. They had plenty of time before the next service. Of course, as soon as Hermy got into the bed, he wanted it. As he called it on Sunday, to shove the wrath of God to her. He did. After he was done, he said to Marylou, "I can't help it. For some reason when I preach, it makes me horny as hell!"

"That's probably just where you are going to go," Marylou laughed.

"Well, at least, I'll be there with all my friends," Hermy replied.

"Not me," Marylou said. "I want to go to Heaven. I'll just make me some new friends up there."

"You ain't never going to Heaven working at Duke's Bar. I can tell you that right now," Hermy said.

"God damn it Hermy! Why do you always have to fuck up a good mood?" Marylou bitched.

"You ain't never going to get there by using that language either," Hermy said.

"Get fucked!" Marylou told Hermy.

"I just did," Hermy said.

"Well, get fucked again!" Marylou laughed as she grabbed Hermy.

"Hallelujah, praise the Lord!" Hermy yelled as he dove under the covers.

My Baby My Baby!

Marylou and Henry were sitting at the kitchen table talking. "How many people do you think will be there tonight?" Marylou asked.

"Oh, I don't know," Hermy said. "Usually, we get more on Sunday night than in the morning. But, most of the people who come in the morning will also show up at the evening service."

"How about the offering?" Marylou asked.

"Sometimes we get more, sometimes we get less," Hermy said.

Real smart answer, Marylou thought as she looked over at Hermy. Hermy was looking at her in that funny way again. Man, he gets that funny look about him whenever I mention any money. I'm really going to have to be careful with him. I sure don't want to screw up a good thing.

"Want some coffee Hermy?" Marylou asked Hermy.

"No, I got to save room for some tonight. I'll just go out to the church and make sure everything is all set." Hermy told her. "Oh Marylou, don't forget our lucky ten when you come to church," Hermy smiled at her and left.

Marylou told the kids to go and get dressed for church. She came out of the bedroom and there were all the kids dressed and ready to go. Hermy has those kids minding him better than they ever did me, she thought. I wonder what his secret is? I'll have to ask him later. She gave each of the kids their dollar and told them how to put it into the collection plate. Off to church they went.

Marylou and the children took their place in the front row of the church. Just before the service started, who should walk in? It was Big Red and Patty. They came right down the aisle and sat in the front row with Marylou and the kids. Patty sat next to Marylou, and Big Red sat on the aisle seat. He nodded at Marylou and sat down gingerly.

Patty leaned over and said to Marylou, "His back is still bothering him."

Marylou shook her head and said to Patty, "That's too bad."

Hermy walked down the aisle and squeezed Red's shoulder as he walked past.

When it came time for the collection plate to be passed, Marylou and the children went into their little act. Even Red reached back into his pocket to get a few more ones. I just can't believe this, Marylou thought. Hermy preached just as good as he had in the morning, impressing Marylou again. She noticed both Patty and Red were paying attention to Hermy almost as if they were spellbound.

Marylou checked to see how many people were there. She noticed that the same people from this morning were there plus ten more. Not bad, she thought. I just hope they're free with their money.

When Hermy was done with the sermon, he asked Red and a man by the name of Myron to help him. They went to the storeroom and brought out a folding table and the coffee urn, which was already filled with coffee. Then, they brought out another table which had bakery on it. "Will you all join me?" Hermy asked.

Marylou walked over to Hermy, who was talking to Patty. Marylou asked Patty, "Tell me, Patty, what the heck are you and Red doing here? I never figured to see either one of you here. The next thing you know, Duke and Fatty will show up."

"I don't know about Duke, but Fatty said she might be here," Patty said. "I guess she got busy doing something. Me and Red were talking and we thought if we were going to be married by Hermy, we better see what kind of minister he is."

"Well, what did you think of him," Marylou asked.

"I'll tell you right now, I was impressed. He sure didn't sound like that little shit Hermy up there. He sounded more like the Reverend H. Weathers."

Hermy was busy introducing everyone to each other, calling Marylou a good friend, who was going to be very active in the church.

Marylou went along with everything Hermy said. It won't hurt anything, and besides that, there ain't no sense in burning bridges.

It was almost ten o'clock before everyone had left the church. Patty and Red were the only ones left. When Hermy asked them to come back to the house, Marylou almost shit.

They were all sitting in the kitchen when Hermy said, "Hey Marylou, get us all a beer, will you? I'm going to change out of this monkey suit."

Marylou went to get the beers and in about five minutes, Hermy was back dressed in a new jogging suit. "Where the hell did you get that?" Marylou asked.

"I bought it when me and the kids were shopping," Hermy said smiling.

"Hey Patty, how do you like the dress Hermy bought me?"

"I think it makes you look like the preacher's wife," Patty laughed.

"That's just what it is supposed to do," Hermy said. "By the way, when are you and Red getting married?"

"Oh, maybe in two or three weeks, right honey?" Red asked Patty. "When do you have an opening Hermy?"

"Let me check with my secretary," Hermy said.

"How much are you going to charge us?" Red asked Hermy.

"It'll be on the house," Hermy said. "And, it's my pleasure to marry our two good friends, right Marylou?"

"Sure," Marylou said. "Our best friends." Marylou gave Patty a hug and a kiss. She said nothing to Red, but that went unnoticed.

The four of them sat and drank beer until one-thirty in the morning when Marylou said, "I have to go to bed. I don't know about you guys, but I'm bushed, it's been one hell of a long day."

They said their good-byes and Marylou and Hermy headed for the bedroom. Hermy got undressed and put on his old robe. He reached into the pocket of the gray suit he had worn to church and pulled an envelope out of the pocket and said to Marylou, "I'll be right back."

Marylou heard him go up the stairs. Then, she heard him in the closet. It was about ten minutes later when he came down the stairs humming, "Rock of Ages."

Hermy took off his robe and got into the bed. Before Marylou even knew what was happening, Hermy grabbed her and started making love to her. Well, not love, it was more like rape. Marylou was more than a little scared, he was like some kind of animal. Hermy finished, rolled over, and went to sleep. Marylou lay there. What the hell, she thought. This guy changes every five minutes. If he's going to treat me like this, half scaring the shit out of me, he's got another think coming. That's all right, Hermy my friend. I'll just mark this one down on my little shit list I have going for you.

Marylou went right to sleep, but she had some bad dreams. The one she remembered in the morning was dreaming Hermy was chasing her down the hall. He was dressed like the devil and was holding this big red snake in his hand. As he got closer, she could see it wasn't a snake, but a big red dick!

CHAPTER 66

Duke got home around three o'clock Monday morning. He staggered up to his apartment thinking tomorrow, I have to get this door fixed. Then again, maybe I better not. How the hell would Nick send my little surprise up here? I could always give him a key. Hell, I could give everyone a key! Well, what the hell would I get the door fixed for if everyone had a key? Duke got a beer from the fridge and went into the bedroom. He undressed and went to bed. He was sitting up in bed drinking his beer when he glanced over at the dresser. Maybe there's a little stuff there, let me see. Duke turned on the light and looked at the top of the dresser. Sure enough, he could see a little white powder on the top of the dresser. He took a match cover and started to carefully scrape the powder together. He divided the powder in half, took the straw, and blew a line up each nostril. "Aw," he said out loud as he fell back on the bed. He started to laugh to himself. Man, I hope they don't find me dead in the morning overdosed on dust! Duke laughed himself to sleep.

Duke woke up the next morning at eleven o'clock. Jesus, I feel like shit. He rolled over in the bed and was facing the dresser. He looked at the top of the dresser. He could see where he had scraped the dresser to get the powder. There wasn't a trace of white left. Well, a bloody mary will do the job for this headache. Duke dressed and headed down to the bar.

Fatty was already there. "Man, you look like shit! What the hell did you do, party all day yesterday?"

"Just about," Duke said. "How about fixing me a bloody mary?"

"How about some coffee and breakfast first?" Fatty asked.

"How about just the fucking bloody mary!" Duke yelled.

"O.K., O.K., you're the boss." Fatty went to fix the drink. Duke sat at the bar with his head in his hands.

Duke spent most of Monday drinking bloody marys trying to get straightened up, but he just got drunk all over again. Duke sent Fatty home at nine o'clock that night. Big Red had stopped in for a drink, so Duke had him tending bar. By now, Duke had switched to beer. He sat there with Red, talking and drinking more beer.

My Baby My Baby!

Big Red told Duke about going to Hermy's church last night. "Man, you should see that guy up on the pulpit. He really is good." Red looked over at Duke and said, "By the way, how are you making out with that Marylou? Are you getting any yet?"

"No, just a couple feels and a few kisses," Duke said. "Personally, I think she's a prick teaser."

"Me, too," Red told Duke what had happened in the back room.

Duke laughed and said, "That's what you get for fooling with one of Duke's girls."

"Yeah," Red said to Duke. "I think we're both better off sticking with the two whores you have working here."

"You got that right," Duke said. "There's no hassle, no problems. It's slam bang, thank you ma'am!"

"Yeah, that's the best way," Red said. He sat there thinking for a while. "Then, he said. "You know as good as Patty is, now that we're talking about marriage, she's getting a little bossy. She always wants to know where I'm going or where I've been. Like tonight, she'll be bitching because I stopped here for a few beers. Oh well, she won't be the first wife I dumped and maybe not the last."

Duke sat there after Red left. He still felt bad. I should call that Nick and get a little more of that powder from him, just enough to pick-me-up a little. Duke had a number to call. When he called it, there was no answer. Duke went upstairs and had a restless night.

Duke finally woke up around noon Tuesday and felt worse than the day before. He got a cold beer and just chugged it right down. That feels better, he thought to himself. He went to take a shower. After the shower, he felt a little better. Something seemed to be missing though. He needed a little something to pick him up. He had another beer before we went down to the bar, but it didn't seem to help. Maybe a bloody mary would help. That's it.

When Duke walked into the bar, Fatty took one look at him and said, "My God! What the hell did you do? Did you stay up all night drinking?"

"Why don't you mind your own business?" Duke snapped at her. "Just fix me a bloody mary."

"My, my, ain't we the crabby one," Fatty said.

"Just get the God damn drink, will you?" Duke said.

Duke sat at the end of the bar drinking bloody marys and thinking about calling Nick again. I think all I need is just one hit and I'll be o.k.

About three o'clock in the afternoon, the door opened and in walked Nick and Dom. Duke jumped off the stool and almost ran over to the two guys. "Hey you guys, I'm glad to see you. Fatty, get my buddies a drink," Duke said. "Come on guys, let's go sit at the back table where no one will bother us."

Duke grabbed his drink from the bar and led Nick and Dom over to the table. They sat down and Fatty brought Nick and Dom's drinks.

"What brings you here?" Duke asked them.

"Oh, we're just checking up on you to see how you are after the big weekend," Nick said. "Tell me, how did you like the way things worked out?"

"Fine," Duke said. "In fact, I think they worked out excellent!"

"Good," Nick told Duke. "The boss was happy too. We stopped by to give him the money and tell him how well things worked out. He was very happy, so he sent you a little present." Nick put his hand into Duke's hand. If felt as though Nick had put a couple of folded bills into his hand.

"Well," Duke smiled. "Tell the boss thank you."

"Don't use it all at once," Nick said. Nick and Dom pushed back their chairs and left the bar.

Shit, I didn't even get a chance to ask them for anything, Duke thought.

Duke walked to the bar calling out to Fatty, "Get me another drink. Duke sat down on the stool and looked in his hand. What the fuck? That ain't money! In Duke's hand were two packets of coke. "Fatty hold that drink. I have to run upstairs!" That's just what he did.

Nick and Dom were sitting across the street in their car. They saw Duke come running out of the bar and up to his apartment.

"Well, well, won't this make the boss happy as a pig in shit," Dom said. "I think we got him hooked!"

"Yeah," Nick said. "He looks like a little old rabbit running for his hole."

By the time Duke got upstairs and into his bedroom, he already felt better. His hands were shaking like crazy, but he managed to get the pack open and poured in out on the dresser. Ah, that's good, I didn't get any on the floor. Duke divided the coke into six lines. Oh man, that's more than I need. I just need one or two lines to pick-me-up, that's all.

Duke picked up the straw and did a line in each side of his nose. Ah, that feels much better. Duke went back down to the bar humming a little tune. "Hey there Fatty," Duke said. "Let me help you clean up here." Duke started to clean the grill.

"Will wonders never cease!" Fatty said. "One minute you're a crab and the next minute mister clean-up!"

About fifteen minutes later, Duke had a beer. About an hour later after a few more beers, he felt pretty good. Then, Duke thought. Man, just a little more would sure put the icing on the cake, so he ran up and did a little more coke. It won't hurt nothing.

Duke went back down to the bar. He sat with a few of the boys who had stopped in. They were talking about the weekend and how much fun they had had.

When one of the guys mentioned how clean the bar was, Duke thought, what the hell happened to Margie? She was supposed to be here last night. Oh well, maybe she'll come in tonight. Man, I hope so. Oh, Marylou will be in tonight. Well, maybe one of them wouldn't show.

CHAPTER 67

Duke sat at the bar feeling pretty good when Margie walked in. She walked over and sat down next to Duke. She put her hand on his knee. "Hi," she said. "I couldn't make it last night, tonight is o.k.?"

"Sure," Duke said. "No problem. Hey Fatty, I want you to meet Margie."

"Hi Margie," Fatty said. "Please to meet you."

"I want you to show Margie the ropes," Duke said. "She'll be working on the weekends. You girls can use the help."

"That's true," Fatty said. "Come on Margie, get behind the bar here and let me show you where everything is. It's not busy on Tuesdays. I'll be going home pretty soon.

Oh shit, Duke thought. I have to get her out of here before Marylou comes to work.

Fatty showed Margie around the bar and where to find things. "That's about all there is to it. Why don't you come in a little early Friday, and I'll get you started working on the tables."

"Si," Margie said. Margie walked from behind the bar and went to sit with Duke.

"How about a little drink?" Duke asked her.

"Sure," Margie said. "I'll have a rum and coke."

Duke was getting a little worried about Marylou coming in and seeing him sitting here with the Puerto broad. I have to get her out of here, he thought.

"Hey Margie," Duke said. "Let's go up to my apartment. I want to talk to you about your pay and clue you in on a couple of things."

"Sure," Margie said as she slipped off the stool and started for the door.

"Fatty," Duke called out. "I'll be back shortly. If Marylou gets here before I get back, don't tell her about Margie. I want to tell her myself, o.k.?"

"Sure, anything you say Duke," Fatty said.

Duke and Margie were no sooner upstairs when Margie was all over Duke. "I miss you very much," Margie told him in between kisses. "Where's the bedroom?"

My Baby My Baby!

Duke glanced over towards the bedroom and let Margie lead him right in to it. She had his shirt unbuttoned and his pants unzipped before he even knew what had happened. She started to suck Duke's cock. When he was good and hard, she jumped from the bed and stripped her clothes off. Duke was on the bed moaning when Margie caught sight of the coke on the dresser. "Hey Duke baby, what you got there?"

"What I got where? Duke said. "Get the fuck back here!"

"Hey, wait a minute porfavor," Margie said.

Duke sat up in the bed. "Come on, we'll have some later."

"No, no!" Margie said. "Before is better!" Margie grabbed Duke by the hand and pulled him from the bed. She took the straw, did a line, and handed the straw to Duke.

Duke did a line and then said, "Come on get back in the bed!"

"O.K.," Margie said. Margie wet her finger and dipped it in the coke.

"What the hell are you doing now?" Duke asked her.

"Just lay down," Margie said. Duke lay back on the bed and Margie grabbed his cock with one hand, took her finger with the coke on it, and rubbed it all over the head of his cock.

"What the hell are you wasting that stuff for?" Duke asked.

"It will not be wasted!" Margie said as she jumped on top of Duke.

"Man," Duke said. "It feels like I could do this all night!"

"You can," Margie moaned. "You can!"

When Marylou got into work, Fatty grabbed her right away. "You ain't gonna believe this. Duke is upstairs with some Puerto Rican broad who's going to start working here on the weekends. It's the broad who cleans up here."

"Slow down Fatty, you're talking too fast. I don't know what the hell you are talking about."

Fatty told Marylou the story. "He told me not to say anything to you, but you can hear them. They're like two animals rolling around up there. I'd sure like to see them up there! Well, Marylou, it's all yours. I'm tired. I need to go home and hit the hay. I don't know when Duke will come back down here. If you want, I could go up and get him," Fatty said as she winked at Marylou.

"No," Marylou said. "Let him enjoy himself."

"O.K.," Fatty said. "Let me know what happens!"

Upstairs, Duke and Margie had finished one round, had a few more drinks, and finished the coke. Now, they were both asleep on the bed.

Marylou never heard any noise coming from Duke's place and wondered if they were still there. This ain't working out like I planned. I got to do something, or I'll never find anything out from Duke with the whores and now this little bitch he's sleeping with. By eleven o'clock, the bar was empty. I bet Duke isn't even coming back here tonight. I should go up there and tell that I am going to close up. She laughed to herself. That would sure shake him up. Oh well, I'll just lock up and head for home. Marylou was home at eleven forty-five.

Duke woke up at midnight. Margie was still sleeping and Duke took a good look at her. She's not bad, he thought. I just might keep her around for a while. Duke got up to get a beer. He brought two beers in and sat on the edge of the bed. Margie woke up and Duke held the bottle of beer out to her. She took a long drink, then said, "Duke honey, you got any more shit? I sure could use a hit."

"It's all gone baby," Duke said. "I wish I had more."

Margie stood up and got her purse. She pulled out a small brown bottle and waved it at Duke. "Here baby, we have enough for a couple more hits." Duke had a big grin on his face.

Margie didn't leave until eight o'clock the next morning. She gave Duke a number to call in case he wanted her to work before Friday. Otherwise, she would not see him until Friday. She told Duke the number she had given him was her girlfriend's and if he called, her girlfriend would get a hold of her.

During the night, Duke had told Margie all about the deal at the bar on the weekends with the whores and the dope. None of it seemed to faze Margie. She told Duke she wouldn't have a problem with any of that.

Duke felt good this morning and thought he would go down to the bar early. When he got there, Fatty was cleaning up the bar.

Fatty said to him, "Man you look better than you have for a couple of days. How about a bloody mary?"

"No," Duke said. "But how about if you fix me some coffee and some breakfast?"

"You got it!" Fatty said. "Welcome back to the real world."

Being in the real world didn't last long for Duke. About two hours after he had breakfast, he started to get that empty feeling again. He was a little light-headed, his stomach felt queasy, and his hands were shaking a little. Jesus, I must need a bloody mary. "Hey Fatty," Duke yelled out. "Fix me a bloody mary, will you?"

"Sure, at least this morning you had something to eat," Fatty said.

"Just get the fucking drink!" Duke told her. "Forget about the sermon." Duke felt bad as soon as he yelled at Fatty. When she brought the drink over, he said, "I'm sorry Fatty, but I just feel a little nervous today."

"That's o.k. Duke," Fatty said. "Maybe you just had a little too much pussy last night."

"You're probably right. But then again, for a stud like me, maybe not enough."

"Well don't be looking this way unless you mean it," Fatty said.

Duke felt better after the drink and a little bantering with Fatty. Duke and Fatty spent some time taking inventory, seeing what they had to replace at the bar. Duke decided he would go to the store and pick up what they needed. By the time Duke had finished shopping, he really felt terrible. He thought if he stopped for a drink, he would feel better. Duke stopped at a bar on Denison Avenue. He had a few beers and bullshitted with the owner, Mike. Even after two beers, he didn't feel all that good. Driving back to the bar, he wondered if Margie had more stuff. He thought he would call that number when he got back. What the hell, he just needed a little pick-me-up.

Duke went into the bar, dumped the groceries on the table, and headed for the phone. Duke dialed the number Margie had given him. On the fifth ring, it was answered by a girl with a very thick accent. After four or five tries, Duke was able to make the girl understand that he wanted Margie to call him. He hung up and hoped that he was able to get the message through to the girl. He got a beer and moved a chair over near the phone.

"It must be an important call if you have to sit right on top of the phone," Fatty said.

"Mind your own fucking business!" Duke hollered back at her. Duke took a sip of his beer. He could feel he was sweating under his arms. Jesus, he thought. I must be getting the flu.

About fifteen minutes and two beers later, Duke was getting pissed off. What the hell's wrong with that broad? She should have called by now. I'll give her a few more minutes before I call again.

Duke waited another fifteen minutes. It seemed like at least an hour to him. Just as he reached for the phone, it rang. Duke jumped back and stared at the phone. On the third ring, Fatty yelled, "God damn it, Duke pick up the fucking phone already!"

Duke gave Fatty a dirty look and picked up the phone, "Yeah," Duke said.

"Hello Dukie, you miss me already?" It was Margie.

"Yeah, I sure do," Duke told her. "I need a little favor from you Margie."

"Sure baby, tell Margie what you need."

"Well, a friend of mine needs a little stuff and my supplier is out of town. I don't want my friend to get sick, you know what I mean?"

"Si," Margie said. "But we used all my stuff last night."

"Well, God damn it!" Duke said. "Don't you know where the fuck to get some more?"

"Easy Dukie," Margie said. "If it is that important, maybe I can get some. But you know, with such notice, it costs more than usual."

"I don't give a shit about that!" Duke said. "Just get it here!" Duke slammed down the phone. He walked behind the bar to get another beer. He went over to his stool and sat down. He just sat there thinking. Man, I feel a little guilty about Marylou. But what the hell, she's living with that asshole preacher and giving him some pussy. It ain't like we're going steady or anything like that. Hell, we ain't even done it yet. A little feeling up don't count for shit. Hell, she shouldn't even be mad at me.

Man, I have to stop thinking like this. I don't owe that bitch anything. I'll get me a little of that shit and I'll be o.k. In fact, I really don't need any of that either, but right now I told that Puerto to bring me some. I might as well use it. Tomorrow, I can quit. I mean, it ain't like I got to use it. It's just a little pick-me-up once in a while that won't hurt you. Hell when I don't want it, I just quit, that's all.

Duke sat at the bar drinking beer like water. It was over two hours before Margie came in the door. She walked over to Duke and sat beside him.

Fatty walked over and said, "Can I get you anything?"

My Baby My Baby!

"Si," Margie said. "I would like rum and coke."

Duke didn't even look at Margie, but said out of the corner of his mouth, "You got the stuff?"

"Si," Margie said. "But, I told you it would cost more."

"How much?" Duke asked.

"One hundred dollars in cash," Margie said and held out a little brown bottle.

"Jesus, don't wave that thing around her!" Duke grabbed the bottle and shoved it into his pocket.

"Hey, don't grab! Give me the money and then we go up to your apartment and you thank me, si?"

Duke reached into his pocket and pulled out a roll of bills. He peeled off a hundred dollar bill and gave it to Margie. "Look Margie," Duke said. "I'd like to take you upstairs, but I have to get this stuff to my friend. Thanks a lot, I'll see you Friday."

"Man, I can tell when I'm not wanted," Margie said. She slid off the barstool and her dress went up over her ass. She had on sheer black panties that hardly covered her ass. Duke didn't even look.

Duke said, "Margie, I am sorry, but I have to go."

Margie left her drink on the bar and walked out the door.

Fatty had watched the entire thing, from Margie giving the bottle to Duke, Duke giving Margie the money, and Margie sliding off the stool. Man, I sure would like to eat those panties, Fatty thought to herself. After Margie went out the door, Fatty said, "Duke, what the hell is going on? What are you going to do with that dope? Man, I hope you ain't on that shit, are you?"

"Fatty, mind your own business will you?" Duke said. "If you have to know, I got this stuff for a friend of mine and he needs it right away, so I have to go. But, I'll be right back." Duke went outside and up to his apartment and into his bedroom. He was shaking so bad by the time he got to the dresser, he could hardly open the cap on the bottle. He got it open and set up two lines on the top of the dresser. He grabbed the straw and did the coke. He lay back down on the bed and waited.

What the hell is this? Did that dumb broad sell me some bad shit or what? He waited a little longer and when he still didn't feel anything, he did two more lines. Duke sat back down on the bed and then he could feel it. Yeah, that was much better. He stopped shaking, his head felt a little light, but man, did he feel good. Oh yeah, shit. I should have told that little bitch Margie to wait for me. Then, I could have brought her up here. Yeah, now I'm ready for that little bitch.

All of a sudden, Duke felt like being busy. Man I should change these sheets on the bed. I think I'll put those satin sheets on that I bought a long time ago. I never had a chance to use them before.

Duke changed the sheets and dusted the bedroom. Hell, I might as well dust the other rooms. When he had finished doing all the rooms, he cleaned the bathroom and the kitchen. Duke didn't realize it, but he was upstairs for three hours cleaning. When he finished cleaning, he looked the place over. Nice, he thought, the place looks real nice. He walked into the bedroom, got the little brown bottle out from under his sock drawer, and did a line. He put the bottle back and went down to the bar.

Duke walked into the bar and yelled to Fatty, "Get me a beer will you? I'm thirsty."

"What the hell were you doing up there?" Fatty asked. "It sounded like you were remodeling!"

"Nope, just cleaning the place up and it looks pretty good if I must say so myself. What time does Marylou come in tonight?"

"Sometime around five-thirty or six o'clock. Somewhere in there," Fatty said.

Duke looked at the clock. It was five-fifteen. "Tell you what I'm going to do. Order us some chink food, set up a table for the three of us. I'll get one of the guys that comes in to tend bar while we have us a little feast."

"Sounds good to me," Fatty said. "I can always use a free meal."

Marylou arrived at work about ten minutes after Duke left. Fatty grabbed Marylou by the arm. "Come on down to the end of the bar. I have plenty to tell you."

"O.K., O.K.," Marylou said. "But where is Duke? Has he been in today?"

"That's what I have to tell you before he gets back," Fatty said. "He went to buy us some chink food." Fatty told Marylou everything that had happened so far today. She told her how Duke had been acting and Margie coming in. "I know that little bottle had coke in it, and I don't know how much Duke paid her." Then, Fatty told her about Margie's panties. "She looked gorgeous," Fatty said licking her lips.

"You are something else!" Marylou laughed. "Do you really think he is taking dope?"

"Man, I don't know," Fatty said. "As long as I've know him, he never did anything like that. Then again, he never ran his business like this either. I guess you and me will just to watch him so he doesn't get fucked up!"

Duke parked his car. He had the chink food and a lot of it. He was hungry and he knew old Fatty could throw down the food, especially when it was free. Duke was walking up to the bar when he thought. Man, I have time to run up and do a line. Hell, the food won't even have time to get cold.

Duke walked into the bar. Actually, he flew into the bar, he was so high. He saw both Fatty and Marylou behind the bar. "Ahha, my little barmaids, I have dinner for us." Duke walked over to the table and started to unpack the food. There were a couple of customers in the bar. One was little Steve, the roofer. "Hey little Steve, how about tending bar for a while, so these girls can have a bite to eat?"

"Sure," Little Steve said, "no problem."

"Fatty, bring me a beer and whatever you girls want to drink. I'll get the knives and forks."

They all sat down to eat and Duke was the life of the party. "Man, you sure are filled with energy," Marylou said to Duke.

"Yeah, well, I've been getting a lot of rest."

"Oh yeah," Marylou said. "What were you doing up there yesterday then?"

"Why hell, I was sleeping," Duke smiled.

"Alone?" Marylou asked.

"Hey, a man gonna do what he gotta do sometimes, you know what I mean?" Duke said.

The three of them finished dinner and had a few more drinks. Fatty and Marylou cleaned up the table and Fatty said, "About time for me to go home."

Marylou went behind the bar to work. Duke sat at the bar to drink with a few with the boys. It was ten o'clock and there were still a few customers in the bar. Duke told Marylou he was going up to fix the door.

Duke went upstairs and started to work on the door. The hinges were just knocked off, so it really wasn't a big job to get the door back on. When Duke had finished, he opened and closed the door a few times. Yes sir, he thought, it works like a charm. I should have fixed that thing before. Hell, as busy as this place is, I should have put in a swinging door. Well, it's time to reward myself. Duke pulled out the little brown bottle and did a line.

Duke went down to the bar. No one was there except Marylou and she was sitting there watching TV. Duke sat down at the bar. "Do you want anything?" Marylou asked Duke.

"Sure, give me a beer."

"Did you fix the door?"

"Sure did," Duke told her. "Do you want to go up and take a look?"

"Duke, you look higher than a kite. What the hell were you drinking up there?" Marylou asked.

"Oh, I got some stuff stashed up there. Come on up and take a look."

"O.K.," Marylou said. "Why don't you go up and fix me a drink and I'll close up down here."

"You have a deal, sweet thing." Duke said as he went out the door.

Marylou cleaned up the bar thinking. Well, I might as well get this show on the road. If that goof is starting to use dope and I don't make my move soon, I'll never fine out anything about Noreen. Sorry Hermy, she thought, but I have to do this. I hope I can get away with this. Then if Hermy doesn't catch me, him and me can be together. Oh well, here goes.

Marylou slowly climbed up the stairs and knocked on the door. "Enter," Duke said in his deepest voice.

Marylou opened the door and went in. She looked around the place. It was all cleaned up. Duke was sitting on the couch. There was a bottle of wine on the table with two glasses. The stereo was playing a Tammy Wynette song.

"Come over here and sit by me," Duke told her. Duke poured the wine and moved next to Marylou. "Listen baby, you ain't mad at me are ya?"

"About what?" Marylou asked him.

My Baby My Baby!

"Aw, you know," Duke said. "I know Fatty told you I had a girl up here last night."

"Well, that's your business Duke," Marylou said. "I mean, hell, we ain't married or anything like that. If we do anything, it's only going to be like an affair. I mean, I ain't figuring on marrying you or anything like that."

"We'll just see what happened," Duke said. "You never know, you may never want to leave here when I get done with you." With that, Duke leaned over and kissed Marylou. Marylou responding by sticking a yard of tongue down Duke's throat. Duke started grabbing her tits and tried to pull her sweater up.

"Jesus, hold on a minute will you?" Marylou pushed Duke away. She stood up in front of him and pulled her sweater up over her head. Duke sat there dumbfounded. Marylou had already kicked off her shoes. She pulled her jeans down nice and slow, then she stood up. She was in just her bra and panties. She was standing only about a foot away from Duke, which put her pussy about a foot away from Duke's face. He could see the black curly hairs sticking out from under her panties. Duke made a grab for her, but Marylou jumped back.

"Hold on big buy!" she said as she reached behind her back and undid her bra. She pulled her bra off. Duke watched as her tits just kept rolling out. It seemed as though they would never stop. Then as she pulled her bra away, Duke let out a sigh. Her nipples were almost a purple color and as bit as silver dollars. They were sticking out just like two little fingers. Duke reached up and took the right nipple in his mouth and started sucking and moaning at the same time.

Marylou pulled away again and said, "Come on in the bedroom. I ain't about to fuck on the couch like some teenager!"

Duke watched her walk to the bedroom. Man, he thought as he watched her ass sway. She makes all three of those other broads look like they have malnutrition. That's what I like, plenty of meat and potatoes; and Hermy boy, I'm going to eat some of your dinner tonight! Duke got up from the couch and took his clothes off.

When Duke got into the bedroom, Marylou was already in bed. The lights were all off and all Duke could see was a big lump under the covers.

Shit, he thought. I should have done a line and rubbed some of that coke on my dick. After all, I have to impress Marylou. I don't want to blow my nuts right away. I've been waiting so long to get her. Oh well, I'll just think of something else. It didn't work. Duke got into the bed and Marylou started kissing him. Hell, he was ready then. Duke jumped on top of her. He got it in and in two pumps, it was all over with.

"Sorry Marylou," Duke said. "The next time it will be better. I just wanted you so much, I couldn't help it."

"That's o.k. Duke," Marylou said. "But, the next time won't be tonight. I just don't have the time to make that thing get hard again. Don't worry, I ain't done with you yet." Marylou pushed Duke off the top of her and went into the bathroom.

Duke watched her go and then turned on the light. He got his bottle and opened it up. He poured the coke out onto the top of the dresser and saw there were only about two lines left. What the fuck! Where the hell did it all go? Jesus, I don't remember using all that. Oh I know, Duke thought. They must not have sold me a full bottle. Yeah, that's it. They only gave me a little bit. Duke did the two lines, put on his shorts, and walked out to the living room.

Marylou was just putting on her bra. "Here, let me help you," Duke said. He walked up behind her and reached around and grabbed her tits. He started to grind up against her.

"Duke, don't start something I ain't gonna finish." Marylou took Duke's hands off her tits and said, "If you want to be helpful, hook my bra." Duke did that and Marylou reached for her sweater.

Marylou slipped the sweater over her head and turned around. She gave Duke a great big, wet French kiss, reached into his shorts, and rubbed his balls and dick. "That's all for tonight." She pulled her hand out of his shorts and headed for the door. "See you tomorrow," and out the door she went.

Duke stood there in his short thinking. It seems like she always leaves me like this, standing here with my mouth open. Duke walked to the kitchen and got himself a beer. He took it into the bedroom and sat on the edge of the bed. As Duke was drinking the beer, he thought, I bought some blow from Margie and those guys gave me some, and I don't even remember using that much. I hope I ain't gonna have a problem with this shit. No, I don't think so, I'm all right. What I'll do is get some more and just use it when I need a little pick-me-up. Hell, a bottle of that stuff should last me a couple of months with no problem. Oh yeah, the duke has everything under control, no problem. Duke lay down on the bed and went right to sleep.

Marylou was on her way home thinking. Man, that was easy. Hell, I won't even count that one as cheating. I feel pretty good, made my move, and I don't even feel guilty. Sorry Hermy, but that's the way it goes.

Marylou got home and Hermy was in bed already. Marylou thought, oh well, maybe I do feel a little guilty. So Hermy, this is your lucky night. Marylou undressed and slipped under the covers naked.

She started to kiss Hermy on the neck. Just then, he rolled over and grabbed her.

"I've been waiting for you. I just hopped in the bed when I heard you coming in the door."

When they were done, Hermy said. "I sure like you getting home early all the time."

"I like it too," Marylou said. "If I work late on the weekends, it ain't so bad."

Then, Marylou thought to herself. Hell, I won't have to work late on the weekends. That Duke is too busy on Friday and Saturday night to have time for me. I'll have to do what I can on the weekdays. Better for me, what with Hermy having church on Sunday. He wants me there all the time. Yeah, this will work out much better. I might be able to get Duke to talk faster this way with more time to work on him. I'd like to get this thing over as soon as possible. Marylou went to sleep feeling she was finally getting some place.

CHAPTER 68

Duke woke up at six o'clock in the morning. Jesus, I'm wide awake, he thought. He got up and went to the bathroom to take a leak. Shit, ain't no sense going back to bed. Duke fixed some coffee and looked around the apartment. It was all clean. There's nothing to do here.

Duke went down to the bar. Fatty wasn't there yet, so Duke put on some coffee and swept the floor. Duke looked at the clock and saw it was only eight o'clock. He fixed himself a bloody mary and sat at the bar.

That's where Fatty found him when she got to work around ten o'clock. "What? Have you been up all night?" she asked.

"Oh no, I'm just getting an early start," Duke said. The bloody marys were making Duke drunk and sleepy. I need a little pick-me-up, he thought to himself. Just a little to get me going. Just one line would do me fine. But, where the hell should I get it? Should I call Nick? Yeah, I got some bets to give him. Oh hell, if I call him, he'll just tell me to give him the bets over the phone like I always do. I could call Margie again. The only problem with that is she gets here and wants to hang around.

Duke had switched to beer and was drinking with a few of his buddies when Margie walked in. She had a dark Puerto Rican man with her. Margie walked right over and sat down next to Duke. The man stood behind them. "Hi baby," Margie said to Duke. "I want you to meet my friend Angel."

"Hello Angel," Duke said without looking at him. "You want a drink?"

"Si," Margie said. "We'll both have rum and coke."

Duke called Fatty over, "Give everyone a drink on me. Now what are you doing here?"

Margie leaned over, stuck her tongue in Duke's ear, then said, "I stopped to see if your friend needs any more blow. My friend Angel here is the one who I got it from last time."

"Now, how did you know I might need some for my friend?" Duke asked Margie.

My Baby My Baby!

"You tell me your man is out of town for a while, so I just tell Angel we stop by and see if Duke needs any help until his man gets back in town."\

"Come on, let's go upstairs," Duke told her. "Too many people are paying attention to us down here."

"Sure, let's go," Margie said.

Duke got up off the stool and fell backwards. Angel was standing right behind Duke and caught him before he hit the floor.

"You o.k.?" Fatty yelled from behind the bar.

"Yeah," Duke said. "I just tripped."

Angel kept hold of Duke's arm and helped him out the door and up the stairs to the apartment.

When they got upstairs, Angel sat on the couch and Margie walked Duke into the bedroom. Duke sat on the edge of the bed. "I felt a little dizzy," Duke said. "I must have drank too much beer."

"Don't worry baby, I got something to fix you up, make you feel like a new man." Margie reached down the front of her sweater and pulled out a little brown bottle. She put two lines on the dresser and did them. She put two more lines down. "For you Duke. Try before you buy, right?"

Duke did two lines and sat back down on the bed. He could feel the coke going right to his head. "Ah," he said. "I feel better already." It seemed he was wide awake now and ready to go. He grabbed for Margie and pulled her down on the bed. Duke reached up under her sweater. "Got any more for me up there?"

"Nope, just me," Margie said.

"That's good enough." Duke grabbed her tits.

Margie pushed his hands away and said, "Not with Angel in the next room, are you crazy Duke?"

"Hey, is he your boyfriend or something?" Duke asked.

"No, just a good friend," Margie said. "But, it don't look right. I mean you just don't leave your friend in one room and go fuck in the other room, it don't look right." Margie walked into the living room.

Angel looked up and said, "si?"

"Si," Margie said. "He wants some. He thinks it is good."

Duke had walked out of the bedroom and was standing behind Margie and shook his head yes.

Angel reached into his pocket and pulled out a packet. He handed it to Duke and said, "One hundred dollars," and he held out his other hand.

Duke took the packet and reached into his pocket. He pulled out the money and gave Angel one hundred dollars.

Angel said to Duke, "When you want more, you call, si?"

"Maybe not," Duke said. "I got my own man."

"But your man not always here," Angel said. "I'm always here, guaranteed. Here I give you my phone number. I be back to you in a minute."

"No thanks," Duke said. "I told you I got my own man."

"Well, you keep the number, just in case," Angel said.

"Sure," Duke smiled. "I'll put it in my pocket."

"Good, is good," Angel said. "Come on Margie, we must go."

Margie walked to Duke and gave him a kiss. "See you Friday," she said and walked down the stairs with Angel.

Duke had watched Angel's face when Margie kissed him, but Angel's face had just been a blank. That guy worries me, Duke thought. I don't trust him at all.

Duke went back down to the bar. When he went into the bar, some of his old buddies were there. "Hey Fatty," Duke yelled as he sat down. "Give us all a beer, will you and have a drink yourself."

"O.K. boss," Fatty said. "You look much better now. What you got hid up in your apartment? The fountain of youth?"

"Just about as good," Duke smiled. "Just as good."

Duke drank with his friends for a while. Then, they decided to go out to eat and play some cards. Duke told them to wait for a minute. He had to get something from his apartment. Duke went upstairs and did a line. Then, he thought, I better take this stuff with me. I may need a little pick-me-up when I play cards. Gotta be awake when you play with these guys. You know that old saying, "if you snooze, you lose." Well, ain't no chance of me snoozing with this stuff.

Marylou came into work at six o'clock. "Little early, ain't you Marylou?" Fatty asked.

"I start early and leave early," Marylou told her. "Where's Duke?"

"He went out with the boys to play cards," Fatty told her.

"Good," Marylou said. "Maybe, I can get out of here before he gets back."

Fatty told Marylou about Margie stopping in with her friend. "He looked like some mean dude! Then, they went upstairs and I'll tell you when Duke came back down, he was a changed man."

"What do you mean, a changed man?" Marylou asked.

"Well," Fatty said. "When he left here with Margie and her friend, he left out of her stumbling and hardly able to stand up. He came back here a while later full of piss and vinegar."

"What do you think made him change like that?" Marylou asked.

"I think he has to be on some kind of dope or something like that," Fatty said.

"I was up in his apartment last night and I didn't see no dope or anything like that. He didn't seem to be high on nothing but the drinks he had," Marylou said.

"You were up there last night?" Fatty smirked. "Tell me! Tell me!"

Marylou told Fatty how she went up to the apartment, but she left out the part about going to bed with Duke. She didn't want Fatty to know any more than she had to, just in case. One never knew what could happen. She told Fatty that they sat on the couch and played some kissy face and that she let Duke suck on her tits and feel her up.

"Didn't you go to bed with him?" Fatty asked.

"No, not yet," Marylou told her. "I have to time this just right. You know, so maybe I only have to go to bed with him a couple of times."

"Good luck," Fatty said. "Ain't no sense giving it away unless you're going to get something back."

"You got that right!" Marylou said.

CHAPTER 69

Duke and his buddies ate and then decided to shoot a little pool instead of playing cards. Duke made two trips to the men's room while they were playing and was feeling wide awake when he looked at his watch. It was ten o'clock.

Good, Duke thought. If I get back to the bar early enough, I can catch Marylou. Yes sir, I might get some pussy from her. "See you guys later," Duke told his buddies. "I have to get back to the bar and take care of some business." When Duke got back to the bar, there were about fifteen people there. Jesus, he thought. It's really busy for a Wednesday night.

"Hey Marylou," Duke yelled over the noise. "What's going on here? You giving something away?"

"Hell no," Marylou said. "They just all of a sudden started pouring in here!"

Duke looked around the bar. He only recognized about two people as regulars. The rest of the crowd were all people he had seen on the weekends. Duke got himself a beer and sat down at the bar. He had been sitting there for about ten minutes when some guy came over to him.

"Hey man," the guy asked Duke. "Is Fast Eddy around?"

"No, not right now," Duke told him. "He only comes around here on the weekends."

"Hey man," the guy said. "We need some stuff."

"Sorry," Duke said. "Can't help you."

"Ah shit," the guy said. "That's a real bummer, me and my buddies over there need some blow. Man, you know what I mean!"

Duke thought for a minute. "Let me see, let me make a couple calls. Maybe, I can help you guys out."

Duke went to the phone and dialed Nick's number, no answer. Damn, Duke thought. It seems that guy is never home. Duke started to walk away from the phone when he happened to think, how about Angel? Let me try that number. Duke reached into his pocket and pulled out Angel's number. Duke dialed the number and on the first ring, the phone was picked up. "Hello," Duke said. Silence. "Hello? This is Duke, is Angel there?"

"Si, this is Angel."

"Angel, I got some people over here at the bar that need to buy some stuff. Can you come over here?"

"You know these people?" Angel said.

"They've been here before," Duke told Angel.

"O.K.," Angel said and the phone went dead.

Well, I guess that means he's coming, Duke thought as he walked back to the bar.

The guy was waiting for Duke and asked, "What did the guy say? Did you get a hold of someone?"

"He'll be here," Duke told him.

"Cool, man, cool." The guy gave Duke a high five and walked back over to his friends.

Marylou had been listening to all this going on. She walked over to Duke. "Duke, I'm going home," she said. "I don't want any part of this here shit. You know, it's one thing when this is going on during the weekends. Then, I'm so busy I don't even see it, but not this kind of shit. No, I have to go home!"

"Come on Marylou," Duke said. "Stick around for a while. After they go, we can go upstairs to my place. What do you say?"

"I say good-bye Duke. See you tomorrow." Marylou walked out the door.

Fuck you, Duke thought as he watched her go. Duke went behind the bar to take care of the customers.

The guy that had talked to him called him over. "Give all of my friends here a drink and have one yourself." He threw a fifty on the bar. Duke got the drinks and gave the guy his change. The guy pushed a five back to Duke. "For you, old buddy."

"Thanks," Duke said as he slipped the five into his pocket. Man, I sure could use a line, Duke thought. He walked to the back room, closed the door, and did his shit. This sure takes the edge off, he thought. Hell, what I ought to do is buy this stuff myself and sell it. It looks easy enough, what with the people coming right here. It's just like they was going to the store. I'll have to think on it. Duke walked back out to the bar.

A short time later, the door opened and in walked Angel. He had another guy with him. They were both dressed in black. They had on big gangster hats. Cigarettes were dangling from their mouths and they had a ton of gold around their necks. Jesus, Duke thought. This looks like a cross between the Mafia, Puerto Rico, and the nineteen forties.

Angel and his buddy walked past the customers and to the end of the bar. Duke walked over to them. Angel held out his hand and Duke shook it. "I want you to meet my friend Jose." Duke put his hand out and Jose shook it. "He will come sometimes when I can't make it."

"Hold it Angel," Duke said. "I told you I already got my man. I just couldn't reach him right now, so I gave you a little break."

"We'll see what happens," Angel smiled. "But right now, we have business to do, si? Now, where is the man you called me about?"

Duke nodded his head towards the guy who had talked to him.

"Go get him," Angel told Duke. "Also, bring me and Jose a rum and coke."

Duke went over and told the guy to go to the end of the bar. Duke went to fix the drinks.

While Duke was mixing the drinks, he kept an eye on what was happening at the end of the bar. He watched as all three of them shook hands. Then, it seemed like they were just making small talk, three old friends bullshitting.

Duke took the drinks over to them and walked away. Out of the corner of his eye, he watched them. The guy reached into his pocket and pulled out a roll of bills big enough to choke a horse. He handed some money to Angel. Duke couldn't see how much. Then, Jose reached into his pocket and handed the guy something.

The guy went back to his friends. As he went by Duke, he waved him over, "Hey man, my name is Ray and you're Duke?" Duke shook his head yes. Ray held out his hand and Duke shook it. "Thanks a lot," Ray said. "Now, bring us another drink will you? In fact, get the whole bar a drink including yourself."

"You got it," Duke said.

Someone put some money in the juke box and the place was starting to move. The regular customers had left, but Duke didn't care, he was making new friends.

Duke noticed that all the guys were making trips to the bathroom, one at a time. Ray called Duke over, "Duke, my man, go into the bathroom. There is a little something for you, but when you leave, set it up for the next guy."

Duke walked into the bathroom. There on the sink was a packet of coke and two lines were laid out. Duke picked up the straw laying there and did the lines. He set up two more lines for the next guy and walked out.

Shit, this is all right, Duke thought. When he got back behind the bar, he yelled out, "O.K. boys, the drinks are on the house!" A cheer went up for Duke and he felt good!

Some of the guys had called girls and by one o'clock, the girls were there and the place was jumping. They all were calling for drinks and Duke had the juke box playing full blast. By then, Duke had made a couple of trips to the bathroom and was feeling great.

Angel and Jose stayed at the end of the bar drinking. Every once in a while, one of the guys would walk over and make a buy.

The party was going pretty good when Duke happened to look at the clock. Holy shit! It was four o'clock in the morning.

Duke unplugged the juke box. "Hey," everyone yelled out.

"Time to go!" Duke yelled back as he started to pick glasses up from the bar. "Let's go, it's four in the morning and I don't need the law in here!"

The place was emptied in a short time. Ray was making one last buy from Angel. As he walked by Duke, he winked and said, "One last hit left for you in there." Duke smiled and waved.

Duke looked down the end of the bar to Angel. Angel held up his hand and said, "One more rum and coke for us and I want to talk to you, si?"

Duke shook his head yes and fixed the drinks. He put the drinks on the bar. "I'll be right back." Duke went to lock the front door. On his way back, he made a slight detour to the bathroom.

Duke got himself a drink and went down to the end of the bar where Angel and Jose were still sitting. "Well, that was a good night," Duke said. "I feel wide awake! Too bad, I had to close, but ain't no sense in pushing my luck. You know, the cops might drive by and we sure don't want them stopping in at four in the morning, do we?"

Angel and Jose just sat there looking at Duke as though they didn't understand a word he was saying. Duke took a drink from his glass.

Angel said to Duke, "If you want us, you just call. Like I told you, we can be here in a short time. You like our service?"

"Very good," Duke said.

"We do very good tonight and those boys, they be back. Now we go, but here Amigo, for you." Angel threw two packets of coke on the bar. Duke let them out the door.

Not a bad night, Duke thought as he fixed another drink. All that free coke and he reached into his pocket and pulled out the tip money. Over seventy-five dollars. Old Marylou should have stayed, but fuck her. This is going in my pocket, that's her bad luck.

Duke walked to the end of the bar and picked up the two packets of coke. He slipped them into his pocket. Now when I get upstairs, I got to find a good place to hide this stuff.

Duke was still pretty high and full of energy, so he stayed at the bar and cleaned all the glasses and swept the floor. When he was all done with that, he still wasn't sleepy. He cleaned all the bathrooms.

When Fatty came in at ten-thirty, Duke was just finishing scrubbing the grill. "Looks like a new bar," Fatty said. "Did you come in early?"

"Hell no!" Duke said. "I've been here all night. I had a busy night. But, I feel wide awake, so I thought I'd get this place cleaned up. I feel a little tired now, so it's all yours Fatty. I'm going to hit the old hay." Duke waved as he went out the door and up to his apartment.

That guy is wired, Fatty thought as she watched him go. I don't know that much about dope, but he's taking it. I'd bet money on that. I have to tell Marylou. She better find out whatever she's going to before this guy really gets fucked up. I gotta watch and see what the hell he's taking. I don't want to see old Duke get hurt or even die from taking that stuff. Then, maybe I'm just imagining it. I'll just talk to Marylou about it. Let her do what she has to do.

Marylou came into work that night and Fatty told her about what was going on. Marylou told her why she had left early the night before. "You know Fatty, I got kids and I don't need to get busted for that dope bullshit. If Duke is on dope, that's his business. I'll do my

My Baby My Baby!

best to find out what I can from him, but you know, I don't even know if he knows anything about Noreen."

"God damn it!" Fatty said. "I told you he knows, trust me!"

Marylou had brought her things to wear for the weekend. I'll be glad when this is all over. Marylou was feeling very depressed tonight. After Fatty left, she only had a few customers the rest of the night. Marylou started drinking blackberry brandy with beer chasers. She sat at the end of the bar drinking, watching TV, and thinking.

Duke woke up around nine o'clock that night. He took a shower. On the way out of the shower, he grabbed a beer. He dressed, laid out two lines of coke, and noticed that his little bottle was almost empty. He went into his sock drawer where he had hidden the packets of coke. He took one packet out and filled the bottle. Duke felt wide awake again. He could feel the coke kick in. He liked that high feeling it gave him. What the hell, the last two packets were almost free. That didn't count like when you had to buy it.

It was ten-thirty when Duke walked into the bar. There were no customers at all. The TV set was on low, but it sounded as though someone was crying. Duke's eyes got used to the light. That's when he saw Marylou at the end of the bar with her head down and crying. Duke walked over to her. He saw the shot glass and the beer glass, still half full sitting on the bar.

Duke walked over to Marylou and put his arm around her. Marylou jumped up, "Oh, it's you!"

"Hey, what's the matter baby? You miss me that much?" Duke asked her.

"Get real!" Marylou answered.

"Well, what seems to be the problem?" Duke asked her.

"Oh shit," Marylou said. "Things just ain't going right. I feel so down."

"Let me get you another drink," Duke said. "What would you like?"

"Give me another blackberry brandy and a beer chaser," Marylou said as she wiped the tears from her face.

Duke got her drink and fixed himself a rum and coke. He brought the drinks back to the bar and sat down next to Marylou. Marylou downed the blackberry brandy and washed it down with the beer. She got up, went behind the bar and got the bottle of blackberry brandy.

She brought it back to the bar and set it down in front of where she was sitting. She turned off the TV, sat down, and poured herself another shot. She drank it down. She went over to the juke box and played some slow songs. Then, she walked over to the front door and locked it. She walked back to the end of the bar and poured herself another shot.

Duke said to her, "I'll be right back." He went into the back room and got out his little bottle. He got the lines ready thinking. What the hell is wrong with this broad now? She must be cracking up. No, she's probably just getting her period or something like that. Duke did his lines and came back out into the bar. Marylou had her head back down on the bar crying. Duke took a big sip of his drink and poured Marylou another drink. "O.K., what's the problem?"

"Just come and dance with me," Marylou said.

Duke took her hand and led her over near the juke box. They started to slow dance. Marylou put both of her arms around Duke and buried her head in his chest. She started to talk, but all Duke could hear was mumbling. "I can't hear a word you are saying," Duke whispered in her ear.

Marylou looked up at Duke, kissed him, and then said, "All I can think of lately is my little Noreen. I need to know if she is safe, dead, or what?"

"I told you one time she's all right, didn't I?" Duke said.

"But, how do you know?" Marylou asked. "I mean, do you know where she is?"

Duke walked back to the bar and left Marylou standing there. "Well? Did Jimmy have something to do with her being gone? Did you help him?" Duke went behind the bar and poured himself a drink. He drank it right down and then poured a double rum.

"Oh hell!" Duke said. He brought the bottle back to where he was sitting.

Neither of them said anything. Duke was sitting there thinking, what the hell can I tell her? Shit, anything I say will get me in trouble. What the hell does she expect me to do? Tell her me and Jimmy snatched Noreen, doped her up, gave her to Big Al and Tony, and then never got the twenty-five thousand. What the fuck! I know damn well that if I tell her any of that shit, she'll start blabbing, 'cause you know she's gonna want her kid back. The next thing you know,

My Baby My Baby!

I'm pushing up daisies right next to Jimmy. Fuck that shit. I got enough trouble the way it is.

Marylou was thinking, what the fuck, I'm half stiff now from drinking this blackberry brandy and beer. I might as well shoot my wad and see if I can get this big prick to tell me something. For sure, he knows what happened to Noreen. Even if he doesn't tell me everything, he might be able to give me a clue. If he just tells me something I can give to those detectives. That's right, come to think of it, I ain't seen them guys for a long time. I got to give them a call. Hell with it! I ain't even interested in that money anymore. Just let me get my baby back. That's all. Maybe then, me and Hermy and all the kids can live like regular people. Marylou really started to cry now.

Duke didn't know what to do now, so he chugged his drink and poured another. God damn, he thought, I'm starting to get hammered. "Hey Marylou," Duke said as he shook her shoulder. "Come on let me pour you another drink. I got a good idea."

Marylou looked up at Duke and said, "What the hell is your good idea?"

"Well, for starters, let's just sit here, talk, and get drunk," he said as he wiped the tears form Marylou's face.

Marylou started to giggle. "That's the best idea I've heard in a long time." Duke poured a shot for her and she said, "Just keep them coming big guy!"

Duke and Marylou sat at the end of the bar drinking, telling jokes, and talking about different customers who came into the bar. The next thing they knew, it was two o'clock in the morning.

"Jesus," Duke said. "We've been sitting her for about four hours and I'm feeling pretty good."

"You think you could get that thing of yours up?" Marylou asked.

"For you, it will raise like a flag," Duke told her.

They both laughed. "But, I don't want the flag. I want the pole!" Marylou said.

"The pole is erect!" Duke told Marylou.

"Let's go upstairs then," Marylou said as she grabbed the bottles of brandy and rum. "You got beer up there?" she asked Duke.

"Sure do," Duke said and they headed for the door.

Once they were upstairs, Duke got out the glasses. They sat on the couch, drinking, talking, and playing a little kissy face. By the time they got ready to go into the bedroom, they were both stiff as billy goats. Marylou went into the bedroom first, undressed, and got into bed. Duke went into the bathroom, did two lines of coke and was wide awake. Just as he was ready to go into the bedroom, he took some coke and rubbed it on the head of his dick. O.K. big boy, that should stop the rabbit act.

Duke walked into the bedroom and Marylou had the drinks poured out. They lay in the bed talking and drinking some more.

Marylou reached for the bottle of blackberry brandy and Duke said, "Hey baby, let's turn out the light and get something going here."

"Let's leave the lights on," Marylou said. "I don't want to miss anything." Marylou pulled the covers off Duke and poured blackberry brandy all over his cock and balls.

"Jesus!" Duke yelled as he tried to jump out of bed. Marylou pushed him back down on the bed and jumped on top of him.

"Now, bad old me. I guess I will just have to clean that up. She slithered down his body and started to lick the blackberry brandy off him. Duke lay back on the bed enjoying every minute of this.

After a while, Marylou raised her head and said, "The pole, she is ready." She jumped up and got on top of Duke slipping his cock right inside her. Duke was in his glory. Marylou's tits hung down in Duke's face. He was busy sucking and Marylou was busy pumping.

They did it every way but loose and when they were done, they lay on the bed exhausted. "How about another drink Marylou?"

"I have to have rum and coke," Marylou said. "I spilled all my blackberry brandy," she laughed.

"I'm glad you did," Duke told her. "But, we might be stuck on this bed forever."

"That's not a bad idea," Marylou said.

Duke fixed the drink. On the way back, he turned the stereo on and the lights off. They lay on the bed. They were both high, but the sex had sobered them up a little.

"You feeling better?" Duke asked Marylou as he sipped on his drink. Marylou was quiet for a while and Duke thought that she was not going to answer him.

My Baby My Baby!

Then, Marylou said, "I don't feel as bad as I did before." She put her drink down on the nightstand and put her arms around Duke. "Duke, you have to tell me all you know about what happened to Noreen. I know you know about what happened and you have to tell me. You just don't understand how it is for a mother not knowing!" Marylou started to cry.

"Look," Duke said. "I can't tell you anything. If I do, I'll get killed!"

"You mean like Jimmy?" Marylou asked.

"Yeah, just like that," Duke said. "These people don't care about killing anyone, it don't mean shit to them. You got to understand Marylou. This is real stuff, these people don't screw around!"

"O.K. Duke," Marylou said. "If you just tell me if Noreen is o.k. or not, I promise I won't tell anyone a thing. It would just ease my mind a little." Marylou started to cry more.

Duke looked down at Marylou. He wanted to tell her everything, but knew he never would. "O.K. Marylou, I'm going to put your mind at ease. Jimmy was hard up for money and he made a deal with a couple of guys to sell Noreen to them. He took Noreen and gave her to the guys and they took her away. Now from what I hear through the grapevine, she is living with some older folks who never had any children and she is just fine. That's all I know."

"Were you involved with this deal at all Duke?"

"No, not at all. This is just what I heard and that's all I can tell you. I don't even know if any of this is true."

"But, you think Noreen is alive and well, right?" Marylou asked.

"Yeah, as far as I know, she is safe and well. By the way, I know for a fact that Jimmy got just a few dollars, not near what he had made the deal for." Duke sat there quiet.

Marylou raised herself up on one elbow and looked at Duke. "And how much did you get?"

"Nothing, nothing. I tell you I had nothing to do with the whole thing!" Duke was almost whining.

Marylou didn't say anything but she stayed propped up on her elbow staring at Duke. All the time, she was thinking. You rotten mother fucker, I know you and Jimmy were in this together. What I'd like to do now is jump on top of you, claw your fucking eyes out, and kill you! But, I won't, I'll be nice. I know I can get more out of you later. She smiled at Duke, "Thanks for telling me that, I feel better now."

"Good," Duke said. "But, please don't tell anyone. I swear they will kill me."

"You're safe," Marylou told him. She kissed him. "I have to go now."

Marylou got home at six in the morning. Lucky for her, Hermy had gone to bed early. She undressed and crawled into the bed. Hermy never moved.

After Marylou left, Duke went into the bathroom to take a leak. He also did a couple of lines. He walked out thinking, I'm wide awake again. I have to find something to make me sleepy. Oh well, maybe some more rum and coke will do the job. Duke was sitting at the table when it dawned on him. What the fuck did I do? I told her all that shit. What the hell was I thinking of? Jesus, what if she tells those coppers? I'm in some deep shit. Hell, I'm dead, that's what I am, dead! What the fuck was I thinking of? I know that ain't gonna be the end of this, she'll keep after me now. Yeah, I know it will be nag, nag, nag. Then, she'll probably try to blackmail me. Man, I should have kept my mouth shut! All for a piece of ass! Well, it's her word against mine. I'll see if she keeps her mouth shut, 'cause if she don't, I'll tell Hermy he's got a whore for a girlfriend.

CHAPTER 70

Duke was up the rest of the night, unable to sleep. He kept drinking. Then, he would do some lines and be wide awake again. He had the bar opened and all cleaned up when Fatty got there in the morning.

"Hell," Fatty said. "If you are going to be here every day this early, I ain't coming in until later. You know, I put long hours in this joint, and I could use some time off."

"Fatty, don't give me no shit," Duke said. "You know, I pay you more than anyone else here, so just get me a bloody mary and keep your mouth shut."

"You know Duke," Fatty said. "You ought to lay off that fucking shit you're taking, because it's making you one big crab."

"What the hell are you talking about?" Duke asked her. "What shit? Fatty, you ought to mind your own business."

"Listen Duke," Fatty said. "I don't want to see you get fucked up, but you know I been around and I' ain't blind. I can tell you're using coke."

"Yeah, you're right Fatty. I been doing a little. You know, I just do it when I need a little pick-me-up and that's all. I can take it or leave it, don't make no difference to me."

"Well, you're wired now right?" Fatty asked.

"I got to get down from this high. But not now, we got a busy night, Friday night. After today, I won't use the stuff anymore, just tonight, you know, to keep me sharp."

"I don't know what to tell you," Fatty said. "But, you do whatever you have to do. Me, I think you need some help."

Duke went back upstairs to his apartment and lay across the bed. He dozed off, but kept dreaming about Big Al and Tony. They had a big needle and were trying to hold him down and stick the needle into him. You had to talk right? You had to talk and all for a piece of ass. Hope it was good. Duke woke up in a cold sweat.

Duke looked at the clock on the dresser, seven o'clock. Seven o'clock! Holy shit! Duke jumped from the bed. Man, I got to get downstairs. Duke jumped into the shower. When he was finished and drying off, he thought. I have to check to see how much stuff I got left. I just need enough for tonight and then that's it, FINITO! Yeah, no problem with that. Duke went into the drawer and got the packet. Only enough left for two lines. What the hell happened to all that stuff? I couldn't have used that much. Man, I got to booby-trap this drawer, somebody must have been here and took some. That's it, I've been robbed!

Duke did the two lines and headed down to the bar. Hell, I can get some stuff from Fast Eddy. In the meantime and in between time, I'm cool.

Duke opened the door to the bar and was surprised to see the place was already busy. All three girls were behind the bar and Margie was working the floor. He looked around. There was no sign of Nick or any of his other people. Oh well, it's too early for them. Duke went to the bar, "Hey Marylou, how you doing?"

"Just fine, how about a drink?" she answered.

"Sounds good to me, make it a rum and coke."

Marylou got Duke's drink and handed it to him. Duke turned from the bar and ran right into Margie. Margie gave him a kiss on the cheek and said, "How you doing big boy?"

"Doing just fine Margie, doing just fine." Duke went over to sit at the only empty table near the back room. The juke box was playing, the band wouldn't start for another half hour or so. People were dancing and drinking. It looks like another good night, Duke thought and sipped his drink.

It wasn't long before Nick and Dom came in. They came over to the table and sat down with Duke.

"Hey man," Nick asked. "How's it going?"

"Just fine," Duke replied.

"See you got a new girl working," Nick said.

"Yeah," Duke said. "Had to put a new girl on to work the floor."

"Puerto broad, eh?" Dom asked. "You get any of that yet?" Dom said with a sneer on his face.

Duke didn't answer him. Soon after, Fast Eddy and Sheri walked in. They stopped by the table, said hello to everyone and then were off working the crowd.

Bambi and Dawn got there at eleven o'clock and came over to the table. "Hey Duke," Bambi said. "We went upstairs to put some stuff there and the door is fixed and locked. Are we working someplace else?"

"Hell no, come on. I'll unlock the door for you." Duke took the girls upstairs and unlocked the door. The girls headed right for the bedroom. Bambi took some coke out of her purse and put some lines on the dresser. "Come on Duke, a little treat for you." Duke did two lines.

Bambi and Dawn did a couple of lines and started to comb their hair. "Hey Duke," Bambi said. "How about a quick blow job before we start to work?"

"Sounds good," Duke said. "But how about later when I can have a slow one?" The girls giggled.

Duke went back down to the bar. When he walked in, he noticed there were about ten Puerto Ricans in the bar. They must be some of Margie's friends. Duke called Margie over to the table and ordered drinks.

Nick leaned over and whispered into Duke's ear, "You're going to have to get rid of that Puerto broad."

"Why the hell would I do that?" Duke asked.

"Why? Jesus, look around!" Nick said. "See all them Puerto Ricans in here? They ain't nothing but trouble. Next thing you know, a couple stabbings, then maybe a shooting or two, and man, you're out of business. Hire yourself some nice hill cranker, you know, tight jeans, high heels and a beehive hair-do."

The band was playing and Duke could see Fast Eddy and Sheri were doing a good business. The two girls were up and down from the apartment. It looked like the drinks were flowing pretty good. Duke looked over by the juke box and saw all the Ricans were hanging around in that area. Margie was over there talking to them. Duke could just about make out, over the band playing. They were speaking Spanish. Duke yelled for Margie. When she came over, he said, "Bring us another drink and work the tables, don't stay over them with all the Ricans."

Margie gave Duke a look that could kill and said, "Hey gringo, those are my amigos!" And she walked away.

"See what I mean?" Nick said. "Nothing but trouble!"

Man, maybe he's right, Duke thought. I sure as hell don't want those Ricans hanging around. Shit, they can't even talk English. I need a hit and I got no shit. Just then, Dawn walked over to Nick and whispered in his ear. Nick tapped Dom on his arm and nodded towards the door. They both got up without saying a word to Duke and walked out the door.

"What the hell was that all about?" Duke asked.

"Well," Dawn said. "I was on my way down to get another trick and some Puerto stopped me and asked if I wanted to buy some blow."

Oh shit, Duke thought. I hope that ain't that Angel guy, that's all I need. "Hey Dawn, you got any stuff on you?" Duke asked.

"Sure baby, you want a little hit?"

"Yeah," Duke said. "Come on in the back room." The two of them went into the back room and each of them did a couple of lines. When they came back out, Nick and Dom were sitting at the table.

Duke sat down and Nick said, "You are a fucking asshole Duke."

"What the hell are you talking about?" Duke asked.

"I told you these Puertos are nothing but trouble. Some asshole was out there trying to sell coke to the people coming in here. We went out there to get him, but he was gone."

"Yeah, we find him and he's dead," Dom said.

"I want that broad fired now! Tonight!" Nick said to Duke.

"Let her finish the night will you?" Duke asked.

"O.K.," Nick said. "But, let me tell you something. If we come in her tomorrow and she's working here, there is going to be some shit hitting the fan around here. Got it?"

"Sure," Duke said. "No problem."

The band stopped playing and the juke box went on. Fast Eddy and Sheri were sitting at the table with Duke and the rest of the guys. Things had slowed down. Bambi and Dawn were upstairs turning what should be their last trick.

Duke told Margie to pull the plug on the juke box and turn the lights up. It was two-fifteen. Duke got up and went behind the bar yelling "Motel time! It's all over! Drink up!" In a short time, the bar was empty of customers. The two girls came down from upstairs and sat at the table. Duke locked the front door and had Marylou bring drinks for everyone there.

They were sitting there drinking when Nick leaned over to Duke and said, "Duke you might as well tell that broad that she's fired."

"Right now?" Duke asked.

"Yeah now," Nick said. "Get it over with here," Nick handed Duke a packet. "Maybe, that will help you get up the nerve."

Duke took the packet and went into the back room. That son of a bitch, Duke thought. I don't need this shit to get my nerve up. All the time, he was laying two lines out.

Duke did the two lines and laid out two more. He went back out into the bar to get Margie. He had an idea. Duke grabbed Margie by the arm and whispered in her ear. "Come on in the back room." Margie smiled and walked with Duke to the back room. Of course, this didn't go unnoticed by anyone. Nick and Dom smiled at each other. Fatty nudged Marylou and said; "Looks like Duke is going to get some p.p."

Marylou smiled at Fatty and then Patty asked, "What the hell is p.p.?"

"Puerto Rican Pussy!" Fatty said and Marylou laughed out loud.

When Margie got into the back room and saw the coke on the table, she jumped up and kissed Duke. "We party, si?"

"Do the coke," Duke told her.

Margie did the lines and Duke said, "Sit down, I got something to tell you. I don't want you to say anything until I'm all done."

"Si, si, senor," Margie said.

"You know, someone was outside the bar tonight selling dope to people in the parking lot while they were on their way into the bar. Was it Angel?"

"I don't know," Margie said. "I don't keep track of him, but what the hell, you sell drugs in here. What's the difference if someone sells outside, same thing, si?"

"No, it is not the same thing!" Duke said. "You don't realize who the people selling drugs inside are, do you?"

"No, but I don't know what you are talking about," Margie said.

"Listen Margie, these are bad people. They will kill you in a minute."

"Hey man, Angel can take care of himself. There's enough out there for everyone," Margie said.

"That's where you are wrong," Duke said.

Margie just shrugged her shoulders.

"Who were those other people in the bar who you were talking to?" Duke asked.

"Those are my friends, my amigos, some are my cousins and some of them lived in the same town with me in Puerto Rico. They come to see me at my new job."

"I really don't think you are paying any attention to me," Duke said. "I'm going to make it very simple for you. Those two guys out there will kill Angel if they have to, no problem. They do not want you to work here anymore. They want me to fire you."

Margie spit on the floor. "Fuck them, I get my friends and they beat the shit out of them before they get to their car, maybe they get cut up a little so they have nice scar on the face to remember me by."

"Will you wait a minute?" Duke said. "Here is my plan. You go on cleaning up on Friday and Saturday nights."

"I make much more money working in the bar," Margie said.

"Will you wait until I get done?" Duke asked. "What I will do is pay you double what I was paying you before."

"You mean you pay me double for doing the same job I do before?"

"That's right, double. What do you say?" Duke asked.

"Can we still party? I mean, you and me up in your place?"

"Hell yes," Duke said. "No problem. But, you would have to go along with my plan."

"Si," Margie said as she lifted her dress. "Now, we fuck?"

Duke started to laugh. "You come by later, maybe Sunday morning. Now, here is what I want you to do."

Margie came storming out of the back room and slammed the door. She walked right over to the table Nick and Dom were sitting at. "Fuck you!" she said to Nick. "And, fuck you too!" she said to Dom. Then, she spit on the floor and yelled in Spanish at them. She spun around and walked out the door.

Duke was watching. Perfect, he thought. He walked out of the back room and over to the table. "What the hell did you do to her?" Nick asked.

"I fired her," Duke said smiling.

Duke sat down at the table. "You do nice work Duke," Nick said.

"Yeah, I know." Duke felt good, like he had put one over on the boys. They ain't all that smart, he thought.

"Fast Eddy says there was a guy out there selling drugs. You know who he is?" Nick asked Duke.

"Nope, I got no idea," Duke said.

"You sure you ain't trying to two-time us?" Nick said. "Maybe you and the Puerto broad got something going. That guy out there was a Puerto. Maybe, you're trying to pull a fast one. Going into business for yourself?"

"Hey man, I don't know nothing about selling and I ain't got nothing to do with Margie," Duke said. "So, just forget about all that shit will you?"

"Well just so you understand Duke my boy, 'cause shit like that will get you dead," Nick told him.

Fast Eddy and Sheri got up to go. "See you tomorrow night."

"Good," Nick said. "And Eddy, don't worry, there won't be nobody outside selling tomorrow. Me and Dom will take care of that."

"Good," Eddy said. "It cut into some of our business and the boss don't like that."

"Not to worry," Dom said. "We got it covered for tomorrow night."

Bambi and Dawn got up to leave. "We're going upstairs to straighten things up. See you later Duke?" Dawn asked.

"Yeah, in a little while," Duke said.

Marylou, Fatty, Big Red, and Patty left telling Duke they would see him tonight. That left Duke, Nick, and Dom sitting at the table.

Nick pulled out the money and gave Duke his six hundred dollars. "Oh, by the way, the boss sent this over for you," Dom said as he handed Duke two packets of coke.

"Jesus!" Duke said. "How come so much?"

"The boss likes the way you operate and he takes care of the guys he likes. You know, like a bonus," Nick said.

"That's good," Duke said. "But, I don't use that much of this stuff."

"For your friends too," Nick said. "Give some to your friends. Oh, by the way, when you go upstairs, leave me the keys to the joint. Me and Dom got to wait here for a while. Someone is going to meet us here."

"No problem," Duke said. "When you get done, just make sure you lock the place up and put the key under the mat upstairs."

As Duke walked to the door, Dom yelled out, "Have a good time tonight Duke. You know, double the pleasure."

All right, Duke thought as he walked up the stairs to his apartment. This must be the night, and it was. When Duke walked into his bedroom, the light was on. There were about ten lines of coke on the dresser. Dawn and Bambi were in the bed naked and kissing. They both looked up. "Had to start without you," Bambi said.

"Yeah," Dawn said. "Why don't you just sit in that chair over them and let us put on a little show for you."

Duke did a line first and then sat down. The two girls did things to each other that Duke had never even heard of. Duke sat there watching for a while and then his dick got so hard he thought it would burst. He stripped off his clothes and jumped into the bed. In between doing coke, they did about everything in bed you could imagine.

When Duke left the bar, Nick said to Dom, "What do you think, is that dude needing his fix?"

"Yup, he's hooked," Dom said. "Hell, I bet he don't even know how much of that shit he is doing."

"We'll see," Nick said. "The boss says as soon as we know for sure the guy is hooked, we start to charge him for the stuff and also after tonight, no more free pussy. He pays just like everyone else pays."

"Poor guy," Dom said. "There goes his weekends."

There was a knock on the door of the bar. "Good, they're here," Nick said and went to open the door. He let the guys in. They were both Puerto Rican. Nick brought them over to the table and introduced them to Dom. "I called the boss earlier," Nick told Dom. "You know after we heard about the guys selling in the parking lot. These two work for the boss. They know everything that goes on in the Puerto neighborhoods and they keep the boss informed. So, what did you guys fine out?"

The one Puerto, the tall one, the one that would do all the talking, while the shorter one just stared through hooded eyes said, "There was no problem. The one selling the dope is called Angel. His sister works here at the bar."

"No more." Nick said. "She got fired."

The Puerto shrugged his shoulders and went on. "He's a small time hood, deals in small quantities mostly selling on the corners. But word has it, he was selling to the guy who owns this joint and was soon going to be selling here on the weekends."

"What the fuck are you talking about?" Nick asked. "You mean he was selling to Duke?"

"If that's the name of the guy that owns the joint, then that's the dude," the Puerto said.

"Well, that's good in a way," Dom said. "That means our boy must be hooked."

"O.K.," Nick said. "What did the boss say to do about this asshole Angel?"

"That's between us and the boss," the Puerto said. "So, you do your business and we do ours." The two Puertos got up and headed for the door. Nick unlocked the door for them and as they were leaving, the big Puerto said, "Don't worry. After tomorrow night, you never have to worry about Angel again."

Nick stood by the door for a minute thinking. Looks like these guys are going to waste that goof. Oh well, ain't no skin off my nose. He called, "Hey Dom, come on. Let's get the fuck out of here. It's late." Nick ran the key upstairs and put it under the mat. By the time he got back down, Dom had pulled the car up to the front of the bar. Nick got in. "Man, you should hear all the noise up there, sounds like a slaughter house with all the squealing going on."

CHAPTER 71

Duke woke up Saturday morning, or rather noon Saturday. The girls were gone. Duke had no idea when they had left. He looked over on the dresser and there were still a couple of lines of coke there. That was great. Duke had always dreamed of being involved in a threesome, and now he had. That was the best time he had ever had by far. Yes sir, his dick was getting hard just thinking about it. Oh well, it was all over for now. I need to change these sheets and take a shower. This place smells like a whorehouse. Duke got out of the bed and grabbed the straw on the dresser and did two lines of coke without thinking about it.

Duke took a shower, changed the sheets, and cleaned up the bedroom. I have got to take these sheets to the laundromat. When Duke had finished cleaning, he needed a reward for all the work he had done. He took out one of the packets Nick had given him. He never opened any last night; the girls had supplied everything. Well, they supplied everything but the sausage. He laughed to himself. He did a couple of lines and hid the coke in the sock drawer. He put the rest of the open packet into the brown bottle and slipped the bottle into his pocket. Duke opened the door and found the key to the bar under the mat. I wonder what time those guys left the joint?

Duke opened the door to the bar and almost shit. The place was a mess. That fucking Margie never came to clean this place up. Oh shit, now I'll have to clean. Duke went to the phone and dialed the number Margie had given him. After three rings, someone answered the phone, "Si?"

"Hello? Is Margie there?" Duke asked.

"Si, this is Margie. Is this Duke?"

"Yeah, how come you ain't here cleaning this place up?"

"I oversleep. Don't forget I worked last night. But, I come right down to clean up, si?"

Duke hung up the phone without answering. That dumb shit, overslept, my ass. She was probably partying all night with them fucking spics. All the time he was thinking this, he was laying out a line right on the bar. He picked up a straw and did the line. Duke walked to the cooler and took out a beer and popped the top. He took

My Baby My Baby!

a big swig. I feel good. I might as well start to clean this place up. I'll give that spic a hand. Duke started to sweep the floor.

Fatty walked into the bar at two o'clock. "What the hell are you doing?" she asked Duke. "I thought you had someone to clean this place."

"Yeah, I thought I did too, but that stupid spic overslept."

"You mean Margie?" Fatty asked.

"Yeah, that's who I mean." Duke then told Fatty about how and why he had to fire her and the deal he made with her to clean the place.

"Well, Jesus, give her a break?" Fatty said. "I mean what the hell, she worked last night, and we worked hard."

"Well, she could have been here by now. Shit, I got half the place cleaned up myself!"

Just then, Margie walked in the door saying, "Oh Duke, sorry I'm late. I had some things to do first. You go sit down, Margie will take care of this, si? Then, Margie take care of Duke!" Margie licked her lips.

Duke smiled and sat down at the bar. "Gimme a beer," Duke said to Fatty as he thought to himself, I'm the stud of Bridge Avenue. That's for sure.

Margie finished cleaning the bar and went over to Duke. She sat down next to him. Duke told Fatty to bring him another beer and a rum and coke for Margie. Margie took a sip of her drink and put her hand on Duke's leg. She whispered in his ear, "Let's go upstairs, si?"

"No," Duke said. "Tomorrow when you get done cleaning, you come up to my place. I got too many things that got to be done today."

"You need to buy some stuff?" Margie asked.

"God damn it!" Duke yelled. "I told you I got my own man. I hope you told Angel not to come around here tonight!"

"He does what he wants!" Margie said. "I told him. He sent a message. 'Fuck those guys!'"

"Well, that might be what he thinks; but like I told you last night, these guys are nobody to fool with!" Duke said.

Margie shrugged her shoulders. "Fatty, give us another drink." Margie and Duke sat there drinking until around five-thirty. Margie was feeling no pain by now. She slid off the barstool and said to

Duke, "Hey Amigo, if we ain't gonna fuck, then I got to hit the road Jack!"

"Hit it!" Duke said. "I told you I had things to do."

"See you tomorrow Dukie," Margie slurred as she left.

Duke told Fatty to bring him another drink.

Marylou and Patty got to work at seven o'clock. "Duke, if we get busy like we were last night, you'll have to work the floor," Marylou said.

"Not me," Duke said. "Don't any of you girls know of anyone who wants to work?"

Red said to Duke, "Hey man, I'll work behind the bar if one of the girls will work the floor."

"Good deal," Duke said. "Who wants to work the floor?"

"I'll do it," Patty said. "That way I can boss Red around."

"You ain't gonna boss shit!" Red told Patty.

"Jesus, don't start fighting before you start to work!" Duke said.

"Just kidding," Patty said. She winked at Red and Red winked back.

"I got her trained good, don't I?" Red said to Duke.

"Yeah, she's trained," Duke said. "They're all trained, at least that's what they make you think."

By eight o'clock, the bar was jumping. Nick and Dom walked in the door. Fast Eddy and Sheri were already working the crowd. Fast Eddy stopped by the table and asked Nick, "There won't be anyone stealing out customers tonight, will there?"

"Don't you worry about it," Nick told him. "All you got to do is mind your business and sell your wares. We take care of the other shit!"

"Sure," Fast Eddy said. "But how the hell you gonna take care of all that other shit sitting in here on your ass?"

"Just do what you're paid to do!" Nick said. "Now, get back to work!"

Duke sat at the table with Nick and Dom. They had a few drinks when Dom said to Duke, "I never noticed that girl who's working the floor. Is that the same one who was working behind the bar?"

"Yeah, that's her," Duke said.

"What's her name?" Dom asked.

"Her name is Patty and that's her boyfriend working behind the bar," Duke told him.

"I didn't ask you who the fuck was working behind the bar," Dom said to Duke. "Hey," he called over to Patty. "Come on over here."

Patty walked over to the table. "You guys ready for another drink?" she asked.

"I'm ready for some of this," Dom said as he slipped his hand between Patty's legs.

Patty jumped back, "Hey mother fucker!" she yelled.

"Hold it! Just hold it!" Duke said. "Dom, look. I don't want no trouble here, so just take it easy, will you?"

"Look Duke," Patty said. "You know I don't go for that shit!" Then, she looked at Dom and said, "Look man, if you're so horny, why don't you go fuck one of them whores you got working for you. 'Cause if you grab me one more time like that, I'll kick your ass!"

"Oh, I love a broad with spunk!" Dom said. "But, I can wait baby. Sooner or later, you'll be begging for it."

Patty turned and walked away. What a pig, she thought.

"Leave the help alone, will you?" Duke said. "I mean what the hell, she's right. Why cause trouble? You can fuck any one of those whores, right?"

"It's none of your business what I can or can't do! By the way, Nick, I think it's time we told this fat ass about the other shit!"

"You're right Dom," Nick said. "Duke, let's go into the back room. We want to talk to you in private." They all got up from the table and Duke led them to the back room.

Duke opened the door and switched on the light. Before he knew what happened, Dom grabbed him from behind and Nick punched him in the stomach. Duke doubled over, but was held up by Dom. "That's just to get your attention," Nick said.

Dom pulled him up and Nick hammered Duke in the stomach again. "That's for what you did!" Dom pulled Duke up again and Nick hit him in the stomach. "And, that's so you don't do it again!" Dom let Duke slip to the floor.

"Now, as soon as you catch your breath, I want you to sit in the chair and we will have a little chit chat."

Duke crawled to the chair and Nick reached into his pocket and pulled out a packet. He put it on the table next to Duke. "You're going to need this!" Nick said.

Duke got up from the chair. He was having a little trouble breathing. "What the fuck is wrong with youse guys?" Duke sputtered.

"Well, for starters," Nick said. "Who the fuck is this guy called Angel?"

"I don't know what you are talking about!" Duke stuttered.

Dom slapped him across the face. "Listen Duke, you want to make this hard or easy? It's all up to you. Let me tell you something Duke. We know what the fuck is going on, but the way we play the game is like this. We ask the questions and we see if you come up with the right answers. That's all there is to it. Now, let's start all over. Who is this guy Angel?"

"He's a friend of Margie's," Duke answered.

"That's close enough," Dom said. "O.K., let's try the next question. Why are you buying shit from this guy?"

"I never bought anything from him," Duke said.

Nick slapped him across the face. "Oh, I forget to tell you. If you answer wrong, you get this prize!" Nick slapped him again.

"O.K., O.K.!" Duke said. "One time a friend of mine needed some stuff, and I tried to call you guys, but I didn't get an answer."

"Sure," Nick said. "How did you find this guy?"

"I told Margie that the guy I bought my stuff from was out of town and my friend needed some stuff right now. So, Margie brought Angel here and he sold me the stuff. That's all there is to it. No big deal."

Nick slapped Duke again and said, "You asshole. I'll tell you what's a big deal and what's not! So, you say that's the only time you called him?"

"Yeah, that is the one and only time I called him," Duke said.

Nick slapped Duke again. "Maybe you don't understand this game we're playing! You see the object of this game is for you to tell the truth!" Nick slapped him again. "Now, let's start again. That's the only time you called this guy?"

Duke was getting scared now. "I called him one other time when some guys were in here looking for Fast Eddy. I didn't know where to get a hold of Fast Eddy, so I called Angel and he came down to sell this kid some stuff, and that's it! I swear Nick, that's all I did!"

Nick looked at Dom. "What do you think Dom? Is he telling the truth or what?"

"Yeah, maybe." Dom smiled and backhanded Duke in the face. "That's just in case you're lying," Dom said.

"Now, one more question," Nick said to Duke. "Did you ever tell that fucking Angel he could sell in this joint?"

"I swear to God, Nick, I never told that guy nothing like that. As a matter of fact, I told him not to come here anymore! Honest, Nick. I don't want no trouble!"

"Well, you got plenty of trouble right now!" Nick told Duke.

Dom pulled Duke from the chair and punched him in the stomach. Duke fell to the floor gasping for breath. Nick kicked him in the side.

"That's all we got to tell you for now Duke," Nick said. "See you at the table." Nick and Dom left the room and shut the door.

Duke got up from the floor and sat back into the chair. He sat there trying to catch his breath. I guess I'm in the big leagues now, and there's no way to get out. Shit, what the hell am I going to do now? Duke reached over and opened the packet of coke. He poured the coke out on the table and divided it into six lines. He did two lines and sat back in his chair. He closed his eyes. He could hear the band playing a slow love song. Duke sat there for about fifteen minutes and let the drug have its effect on him. He felt the jolt from the coke, and he felt much better. He leaned over and did two more lines.

Duke stood up and fixed his clothes. He combed his hair and wiped his face with his hanky. Duke opened the door and shut the light off. He walked over to the table where Nick and Dom were sitting. Duke smiled at them as he sat down. Duke called Patty over to the table and told her to bring all of them a drink.

After Patty left, Nick put his hand on Duke's shoulder. "No hard feelings, huh Duke? You know we got a job to do and that's the way it is. Hell, the old man wanted to do worse than we did to you; but me, I couldn't see it. I'm going to tell him that you told us everything with no problem and that you just made a little mistake, that's all."

"Thanks," Duke said. "You know, just like I told you. I don't want no trouble."

"Sure, I know," Nick said.

The rest of the night went by without incident. Duke, Nick, and Dom sat at the table. Nick and Dom made small talk while Duke sat there without saying much. Closing time came and Duke got everyone out of the bar as quickly as possible.

Fatty, Marylou, Big Red, and Patty told Duke they were going out for breakfast and asked if he wanted to join them.

"Hey, that's not a bad idea," Nick said.

Fatty looked at Nick and Dom, "The invitation don't include you two grease balls!"

"Hey, watch your fucking mouth!" Dom said.

Fatty gave him the finger and said to Duke, "If you want to come, you know where we will be. I'll save you a seat."

Duke locked the door after they left. "Hey Duke," Nick yelled. "Bring some drinks back here to the table, will you?"

Duke walked past the table and into the back room. He did the two lines he had left on the table. Duke walked back out and up to the table. "Look guys, I think I'll go have breakfast with my friends. There's no time for drinks. How about you give me my cut and we'll call it a night."

Nick looked up at Duke standing by the table, "Sit down, mother fucker!" Duke knew Nick meant what he said and sat down.

"Me and Dom ain't ready to go yet. Besides, we have to meet someone here in a little while, so just give us the keys and we'll lock up when we go. So, you are free to go meet your friends."

"Good, just give me my money," Duke said as he threw the keys on the table.

"Oh yeah," Nick said. "That's another thing I got to tell you Duke. The boss said no cut for you tonight or next week. He says that should make up for what Fast Eddy and Sheri lost in sales last night."

"That ain't right!" Duke said.

"I ain't done yet!" Nick growled. "The boss also said no free pussy until he gives the o.k. and if you need any coke, you gotta buy it from Dom or me. You understand? 'Cause if you pull any more Angel shit, you become an Angel!" Nick and Dom started laughing.

Duke just sat there looking at them. Finally, he said, "Would you unlock the door for me? I got to go."

"Hey Duke, no problem," Nick said. "Just don't be pissed at us, huh? It's only business!"

Nick let Duke out the door and locked it up. Nick went behind the bar and got a bottle of V.O. and a glass of ice. He brought them back to the table. Dom asked Nick, "What do you think Duke will do?"

"Shit, he ain't gonna do nothing. He's scared to death. You see he never made no fuss about getting paid. But, bet on one thing, he'll be making a fuss when he runs out of that dope I gave him."

"Did the boss really tell you not to pay him?" Dom asked.

"Nope," Nick said as he reached into his pocket. He counted out three hundred dollars and handed it to Dom. "That was my idea."

"Man, what if the boss finds out?" Dom asked.

"How the hell is he going to find out? Are you gonna tell him Dom?"

"Hell no, not me! I like this deal!" Dom put the money into his pocket and then poured a drink for him and Nick.

"Hey Nick, who we got to meet here?" Dom asked.

"Nobody, I just made up that bullshit."

"I got to hand it to you Nick. This is all right. You know, just like our own private club."

"That's right, Dom, our own private club. God damn! That gives me an idea."

"What you got in mind now?" Dom asked.

"Well, you know, Three Fingers Rudy is always looking for a place to run those card games of his. That back room is plenty big enough. Here's what we do. We tell Duke the boss says he has to let Rudy use the back room for the card games. Then, we charge Rudy rent. You know, a percent of the pot, something like that."

"Sounds like a good idea to me. Do you think we should cut Duke in for some of the action?" Dom asked.

"Fuck no," Nick said. "Well, on second thought. That we could do is let him sell sandwiches and drinks to the guys playing cards. That way, we don't have to hang around here. You know, if the game gets busted, fuck it, let Duke take the rap." "Sounds better and better," Dom said.

CHAPTER 72

Duke walked out of the bar and went upstairs to his apartment. The keys were in the lock of the door. He walked into the bedroom. The bed was made. Unlike the other weekends, there were no girls waiting for him. Things do change fast. He went to the kitchen and took out a bottle of rum from the cupboard. He took a glass of ice, some coke from the fridge, and sat down at the kitchen table. He poured himself a good stiff drink. Duke didn't feel like meeting anyone for breakfast. He just felt like being alone. Hell, even with all the money I'm getting now, I wish it was like the old days. Hell, I always had enough money to do what I wanted to. Best of all, I didn't have any problems. I just lived day by day. That's all there was to it. Jesus, now I get kicked out of my own place. Not only don't I have a say in my own business, but my own apartment. Shit. I got whores sleeping in my bed with their tricks. Who the hell knows what some of those bums got on their bodies! Lice, crabs, who knows. Jesus, I have to get that shit off my bed. Duke went into the bedroom and stripped the bed, throwing the sheets out the bedroom window.

Duke went back into the kitchen and poured himself another drink. I'm going to do something about this. I ain't sleeping in a whorehouse. Let those guys rent a room for those girls. Duke went back into the bedroom, got a packet out of his drawer and set up the lines on the dresser. He did a couple of lines and kept thinking about how those guys were giving him such a shitty deal. I'll just go tell those two assholes to get the fuck out of my bar. Duke went running down the stairs. The door was locked. He looked in the windows. Nobody was there. He ran back up the stairs and looked under the mat. The key was there. Good thing for those guys. They don't know how lucky they are that they left. Man, I was ready to kick ass. Duke poured another drink. The next time they come here, they're going to get you know what! Duke went back into the bedroom and lay across the bed. There he passed out, fully clothed, laying on the stripped bed, just like a bum.

The next thing Duke heard was pounding at the door and someone yelling in a mix of Spanish and English.

CHAPTER 73

Marylou, Fatty, Big Red, and Patty were all sitting in a booth at the Egg Restaurant talking. "Well," Fatty said. "You think Duke will show up?"

"I doubt it," Red smiled. "He's probably up in his apartment with one or both of them whores!"

"Shut up Red!" Patty said as she kicked him under the table. "I'm surprised you ain't up there, if you already ain't been up there?"

"Oh, come on sweetheart. You know, I ain't been cheating on you. Hell, we're going to be getting married soon."

"I doubt if that would ever stop you!" Patty said.

"Stop fighting you two," Fatty said. "We're talking about Duke. Did you see these two greasers take Duke into the back room?"

"Yeah, when I worked the tables," Patty said. "I walked by the door and tried to listen. All I could hear was low mumbling. I couldn't hear what they were saying. When Duke came out of the room and ordered those drinks, his face was all red and had little welts on it, like when you slap someone."

"Well, I can tell you. Those guys didn't take Duke in there to play patty-cake with him," Red told the girls. "As a matter of fact Patty, maybe you ought to quit working in that place. It could start getting rough."

"I know that Red, but the money is really good. I mean there ain't another bar that pays as good as Duke does. But, you're right. If it starts to get too rough in there, I'm gone!"

"You know," Fatty said. "I was a little worried Friday night when all them fucking spics was in there. I thought for sure there would be a stabbing or two, but then, they didn't show up tonight. Maybe, that's the end of them." Fatty then told them about Margie coming in the afternoon.

"Man, Duke would do well to stay away from that broad," Red told the girls. "She looks like a tough one."

Marylou looked at her watch. "I got to go, it's late, and I have to be up for church in the morning."

"Hell, sleep in," Fatty said. "Let Hermy take care of the church."

"Hell no," Marylou said. "He likes me going to church. Besides that, it keeps him off my back."

"O.K. girl, me and Red will see you in church. Are you going?" Patty asked Fatty.

"You never know," Fatty said. "But if I ain't there in the morning, I'll be there for sure at the evening service. I think I can make that one."

Marylou got into her car to drive home. Jesus, it's five-thirty in the morning. I hope Hermy is sleeping. As Marylou was starting to get out of her car at home, she realized she forgot to change her clothes. Jesus, if Hermy sees me dressed like this, I'm in big trouble! She looked in the windows, but couldn't see Hermy anywhere. That's good, he must be in bed. Sure enough, Hermy was sleeping. Marylou undressed and crawled into bed.

Hermy woke Marylou around nine a.m. He had coffee ready and told Marylou he had to leave a little early to get things ready. "I'll see you later."

"O.K. Hermy, we'll be there."

Marylou sat drinking her coffee. She still felt a little sleepy, but not too bad. She was thinking about Duke and all the trouble he seemed to be in now. I'll have to talk to him and see if he'll tell me what's going on.

The children came downstairs all ready to go. Marylou went into the bedroom to get ready.

CHAPTER 74

Duke looked at the clock, it was seven-thirty. Jesus, who the hell is at the door? Duke yelled, "Hold it, I'm on my way!" The pounding continued. Duke slipped on his pants and went to the door. "Who is it?"

"Open the door you son of a bitch! Open the fucking door! I kill you!"

Duke thought it sounded like Margie. He opened the door a crack and looked out. Sure enough, it was Margie and she was crying. The tears were running down her face.

When she saw the door open, Margie threw her body against it. The door pushed Duke to the floor and Margie came bursting through. She threw herself on top of Duke and tried to scratch his face. Duke grabbed her arms but not before she had scratched him.

"What the hell is wrong with you?" Duke yelled.

"You fucking son of a bitch! You kill him! You murderer! You kill my brother!" Margie was screaming, kicking, and spitting in Duke's face.

"God damn it!" Duke hollered. "Cut it out!" Duke slapped her across the face. Margie grabbed her face, rolled off Duke, and lay on the floor sobbing. "Now," Duke said. "What the hell are you talking about? I didn't kill anyone!"

Margie lay on the floor sobbing. She didn't say anything. Duke went over to her and knelt down next to her. He put his hands on her shoulders and said, "What happened? Who got killed?"

Between sobs, Duke could hear her say, My brother, my brother, Angel. You killed him!"

"Angel? Angel is your brother? I didn't know that."

"Would that have made any difference?" Margie asked.

"What the hell are you saying?" Duke asked her. "Come on, get up. Sit on the couch and tell me what the hell is going on." Duke helped Margie up off the floor and over to the couch. Then, Duke went out to the kitchen and fixed a rum and coke for Margie and himself. All the time, he could hear Margie sobbing in the front room. He took the drinks over to Margie and held one out for her. She looked up and took the glass. She took a big drink and set the glass on the coffee table. Duke sat down next to her. "Now, tell me what happened?"

Margie took another drink. Then, she asked Duke, "Did you kill him? Did you kill my brother Duke?"

"No," Duke said. "I don't know nothing about it. Now, you just try to calm down and just tell me what happened."

"Yesterday after I leave you at the bar, I go home. Angel is there with a bunch of his friends. They are all having a big party, all kinds of drinks, beer, food, everything. Angel tell me he make big score selling outside the bar. I tell him what you told me. I tell him the people are very bad and he should not go back there. He says, 'I told you what to tell them before, tell them fuck you!' We party some more and then about eight o'clock, Angel tell me, 'O.K. Margie, I got work to do.' I beg him not to go back to the bar. Duke says those guys will kill you! They very bad! Angel say, 'fuck them, they never catch me. I make a lot of money last night and I make more tonight.' So, Angel leave and the party is over. It is late, so I go to bed."

"Two-thirty this morning, the police come knocking at my door. They say, 'you know a guy a guy named Angel?' Yes, I tell them, that is my brother. The police say, 'you have to come with us.' Where? I ask them. They say, 'to the morgue to identify his body.' They take me in the car and I go into this room. The man pulls a bed out of the wall and pulls a sheet off this body. 'Is it him?' he asked me. I look, and there is Angel laying there. I say yes, that is my brother. "O.K.' the man says and he covers Angel back up and slides the bed back in the wall. The police tell me, 'come with us.' They take me into a room and ask me all kind of questions. I ask the police what happened? They tell me that they find Angel in a parking lot at Edgewater Park. He still had money in his pocket and the police found packets of cocaine in the car ready to sell. They told me it was a drug-related killing." Margie started to cry again.

Holy shit, Duke thought. I bet Nick had Angel bumped off. There's not a doubt in my mind. Man, I bet those cops will be here to ask me some questions. I better find out what the hell Margie told them. Duke went into the bedroom and got a packet from his sock drawer. He brought it out to the front room. He put a couple of lines on the coffee table and did them. He laid out two more lines and gave

Margie the straw. Margie did the lines, then leaned back on the couch.

"Feel better?" Duke asked her.

"Yeah, a little better. I'm sorry I come breaking in here. I know you didn't kill Angel. You tried to warn him."

"I know." Duke put his arm around Margie. "Now, tell me what you told the police."

"O.K., but can I have another rum and coke?"

"Sure, I'll get it for you." Duke took the glasses out to the kitchen and fixed the drinks.

When he came back into the living room, Margie was doing more coke. She looked up when Duke came in. "Don't worry, I got plenty of that shit in my purse. This was just handy."

"Well, don't hog it all!" Margie laid out two lines for Duke.

"Now," Duke said. "Tell me what you told the police."

"The police ask me if Angel was selling dope. I told them I don't know about dope or anything like that. They asked me where he lived, and I told them he lived in the house with me. They asked if they could come and search his room. I tell them yes. You see, I know Angel don't keep nothing in his room, so they can't find nothing. Then, they take me home and go through Angel's room. But, they don't find nothing. Then, they ask me if I work any place, and I tell them that sometimes I work at Duke's Bar. Then, they tell me. You have to make arrangements for your brother. I say, what do you mean? The police say, 'Well, he can't stay at the morgue. You have to bury him.' Then, they walk out the door."

"That's it?" Duke asked.

"That's all they ask me," Margie told him.

Duke sat there thinking. Those cops will come and see me sooner or later to check on Margie's story. Well, that's all right. I'll just tell them she works here cleaning up, that's all I know. They got no way to tie me into what happened to Angel. Hell, there were enough customers in here last night to vouch for me. Come to think of it, Nick and Dom got the perfect alibi, too. Me!

"O.K. Margie, I'll help you make the arrangements for Angel. We'll go see Marylou and Hermy after a while. Hermy is a Reverend. He can call the funeral home and set everything up for you."

"But Duke, I don't know if I got enough money to have a funeral."

"Don't worry," Duke told her. "We'll work things out."

CHAPTER 75

Marylou pulled her ten dollar bill trick again in church. And darn, if it didn't work. Patty and Red were there. About ten minutes after the service started, Fatty walked in. After church, they had coffee and cookies in the hall. About an hour later, everyone was gone. Hermy asked Red if he would help him set up for the night service and Red told him he would.

While the men were working, Marylou said, "How about if you girls come back to the house, and we'll make some lunch."

"Good idea," Fatty said. "I ain't never got nothing to do on Sundays, but sleep and I'm wide awake now."

They went back to the house and Marylou got out all the fixings for sandwiches. Fatty was drinking beer, while Marylou and Patty were drinking coffee. The two men came in about an hour later. Red looked at the beer Fatty was drinking and said, "Man that sure looks good. I think I'll have one too."

Hermy said, "I sure would like to join you, but I got services tonight."

"How about if we have a party after you get done?" Red suggested.

"It's a date," Hermy said.

At two-thirty in the afternoon, there was a knock on Hermy's door. Hermy got up from the table to answer it. When he opened the door, he was shocked to see Duke standing there with some Puerto Rican girl, who was crying. The tears were streaming down her face.

"Come on in. Marylou, get some chairs for these two."

Margie and Duke sat down at the table. "Jesus," Marylou said. "What the hell is wrong with Margie? Do you guys want a drink?"

"We sure could use one," Duke said.

Marylou got them all a drink and Margie was starting to calm down. "Now, tell us what's wrong," Hermy said.

Duke told the story to everyone, then turned to Hermy. "Hermy, you can see we need your help to make all the arrangements."

"Sure, that's why I'm here," Hermy said. "So, let's get started." Hermy called Mr. Sauers at the funeral home and made arrangements with the funeral home to have the body picked up. They would have a showing on Tuesday and Wednesday. A service would be held at Hermy's church on Thursday. Hermy then told Margie what he had done. Margie thought everything would be fine. Duke told Hermy he would pay for the funeral. They all sat around the table talking about what had happened.

Hermy said, "Maybe, you two would like to stay for the services tonight?"

"Yes," Duke said. "I think we'll go back to my place first and get cleaned up a bit."

"Si," Margie said. "We can stop by my house first, and I can pick up some clothes."

"You can stay with me," Fatty said to Margie.

"Thank you," Margie said. "But, I'm going to stay at Duke's for a while." Fatty, Marylou, Red, Patty, and Hermy all looked at one another.

Duke and Margie left. "Well, what do you think?" Fatty asked.

There was silence for a while and then Marylou said, "You know, maybe Red is right. I see nothing but trouble coming at that bar."

"I told you so," Red smirked. "I could see it coming. Now, Duke is going to have that spic hanging around and then more spics will be at the bar. Then, there will be big trouble. Patty, you ain't gonna work there no more!"

"God damn it Red," Patty said. "Don't' tell me what I'm going to do! Marylou and Fatty, what do you think? What are you girls going to do?"

"Well," Fatty said. "I'm just going to go about my business. I've worked at some bad places and some good places. Duke's is a little better than most places I've worked."

Marylou said, "I think I'll work a little longer and see what happens. The job pays real good with the tips. Besides, that, I don't want to leave Duke in a bind right now."

"Well, I hope you guys all know what you are doing," Red told them. "And, I hope you all get out before it's too late."

Red and Patty got up from the table to leave. They told Hermy they would be at the evening service.

"Good," Hermy said. "And, then we are going to party after. I feel like hanging one on."

My Baby My Baby!

"Oh boy, I'll bring that bottle of V.O. I've been saving," Red told Hermy. "Ain't often you get to hang one on with the preacher."

Hermy was just as impressive as usual when he was up on the pulpit. Red and Patty were there, as well as Fatty, Duke, and Margie.

Hermy introduced Margie to the people and told them how her brother had been killed last night, maybe by some drug-crazed person who he had gone to help. He made Angel sound like a martyr. "Now my good people, now is the time when the Lord is watching you. Now is the time to show your generosity. You see my good people, Margie has no money to bury her beloved brother. Mr. Duke said he will help as much as he can, but Mr. Duke is a poor man, too. Marylou and I are helping as much as we can, but we still need more. I'm going to have the ushers pass the basket once more. Remember as you give, the Lord is watching you!"

When the service as over, Hermy took Margie to the door with him and introduced her to all the people there. It had been a good turnout with about fifty-five people. All of them offered to do something for Margie including bringing food for the people after the funeral. Hermy had told the people they were forgoing the coffee hour so they could donate the coffee to have after the funeral. In reality, Hermy couldn't wait to get in the back and start partying.

After all the people had left, Hermy, Marylou, Big Red, Patty, Fatty, Duke, and Margie went back to the house. Big Red had brought the bottle of V.O. just like he said he would. Hermy told Marylou to get out the beer. Red took the cap off the bottle and threw it away. "Won't be needing this!" Red winked. He poured a shot for all who wanted it.

Hermy downed his and said, "I'll be right back. I got to take care of the offering for the church."

Hermy went upstairs and opened the closet door. He took out the box, took the offering from the church, and counted it. He then put the box back. Next, he took out the special offering for Margie. He counted it. Four hundred and fifty dollars wasn't too bad, he thought. Let's see with my, or rather the church's cut, that leaves Margie with two hundred dollars. Hermy put the two hundred and fifty dollars into his pocket. He smiled to himself and went back down the stairs.

Marylou could hear Hermy rooting around in the closet upstairs and was thinking to herself, I got to check that box again. Hermy has been adding to it. I just like to keep tabs on what he has up there. Just then, Hermy came back into the kitchen smiling.

"Well Margie, it seems by flock took to you. To show they want to help, they were mighty generous." Hermy had an envelope in his hand. He handed it to Margie. "Yeah, they done pretty good giving to a stranger. There is two hundred dollars in there. I know you can use it. By the way, there won't be any charge for the funeral, for me, or the church."

"Thanks a lot." Margie went over and kissed Hermy on the cheek.

"Oh hell, that's the least we can do for our friends," Hermy smiled.

That little weasel, Marylou thought. I know there was more than two hundred dollars in that basket.

They all sat around the kitchen table drinking and talking. It wasn't long until the bottle was gone and no one was feeling any pain. Duke made a few trips into the bathroom, but no one really noticed. They all thought the beer was going right through him. Little did they know that every time he went into the bathroom, he was doing a line.

Fatty finally said, "Jesus, will you guys look at the time. It's two o'clock in the morning and I have to go to work early, right Duke?"

"I'll tell you what I'll do," Duke said. "Why don't you come in late tomorrow. I'll open up and take care of the drivers."

"Thanks," Fatty said. She turned to Margie and said, "You sure you don't want to stay with me?"

Margie looked over at Duke. Duke put his hand on Margie's knee and said to Fatty," No, Margie is going to stay with me. We got some things to talk over."

"I bet," Fatty said.

They all decided to leave. By the time all the good-byes were said, it was two-thirty. Hermy said to Marylou, "I'm going to have one more beer, you want one?"

"Yeah," Marylou said. "I'll have one more, too."

Hermy got the beer and sat down at the table. "That was nice, relaxing, sitting around with some friends, drinking and talking. That was too bad about Margie's brother. Not that I knew him or her that matter until today. Sometimes, a little party takes your mind off the bad things that happen to you."

My Baby My Baby!

"I guess," Marylou said. "Partying always makes you feel better. That sure was nice of the people to give money like that to someone they don't even know. But, I thought there was more than two hundred dollars in that basket."

Hermy slammed the beer bottle down on the table and shouted, "Are you saying that I took some of the money? Don't you ever question me about the church or the money! Do you understand me? Never again, do you ask about it. That's my business what goes on with that basket! I don't got to account to you for it!" Hermy downed what was left in the bottle of beer and got another one. "Now, you listen to me Marylou. I didn't mean to yell at you, but you have to understand. The church is like a business. If I give all the money away, then I don't have any, you understand?" Marylou shook her head yes. "Good," Hermy said. "So from now on, I don't expect to hear anymore about it, right?"

Marylou shook her head yes, but she thought, Fuck you, you asshole. I'm going to check that box upstairs; and if I decide to take off, you shithead, that box will go with me. Then, you can start all over.

"O.K. Marylou," Hermy said. "Let me finish this beer and go to bed, 'cause I feel like making wild love to you!"

Hermy did make wild love that night. That preaching sure do make this man horny!

On Monday, Hermy left after breakfast. "I have some things to do downtown, so I won't be back until four or so."

"O.K.," Marylou said. "Try not to be later than five. I'll have dinner ready for you.

Hermy kissed her and was gone. Marylou waited for about half an hour to make sure Hermy wasn't coming back. Then, she went upstairs.

Marylou went through the same ritual as before, checking for any traps that Hermy might have set. She didn't find any. That's odd, she thought. Then, she knew why. The box was gone. There was just the empty hole, nothing else. What the hell? If he knew I was up here before, you think he would have said something. Maybe he just moved it to be safe, but why would he do that? That shithead. He must have known I was up here.

CHAPTER 76

Duke drove Margie to her house to pick up some clothes. When they got there, the lights were on in the house. "Does someone else live in the house?" Duke asked.

"No, but my brother, he had all kind of people going in and out of the house, sometimes they sleep there and sometimes they just hang around."

"Don't you have any other family?" Duke asked her.

"My mother and father, they are both dead. I had one other sister, but I don't know where she is. I have some cousins here, but that's all."

"You want me to go in the house with you?"

"No, you better not," Margie said. "I don't know who is in there and they might not be too friendly to a gringo right now."

"O.K., I'll wait in the car, but if you need any help, just let out a holler."

Duke sat out in the car watching as people went in and out, none staying too long. Then, he saw Margie coming to the car. She was carrying a suitcase and a small make-up case. She opened the car door and threw the cases in the back seat.

"You gonna leave the lights on in the house?" Duke asked her.

"There are still some people in there."

"Do you have any other things in there? If you do, we can come back tomorrow and get them."

"No, that's all I take," Margie said. "I don't want to come back here anymore."

"I'll have to have Fatty take you shopping and buy you some clothes."

Margie didn't say anything all the way to Duke's. Duke parked the car and took the bags upstairs. He took the bags into the bedroom and laid them on the bed. "There are a couple of empty drawers in the dresser and you can hang the rest of the stuff in the closet."

Margie started to unpack her things while Duke stood in the doorway of bedroom watching her. Margie reached down to the bottom of the big suit case and tossed Duke a package all wrapped up in newspaper.

"What's this?" Duke asked.

"Unwrap it," Margie said.

Duke took the newspaper off the package. "Holy shit!" It was the largest packet of cocaine Duke had even seen.

"We have to cut it first and then, we can sell it," Margie told him. "That's what all those people were looking for at the house. But, I knew where Angel had hidden it. So, maybe, we have a little trouble, but I think it will be well worth it."

"What do you mean a little trouble?" Duke asked. "You know I don't want to be in the middle of some fucking war!"

"Don't worry about it, si?" Margie went on. "I know what to do and I know how to handle my people."

"I'm not kidding Margie," Duke said. "I don't know nothing about selling this stuff, and I don't want to get involved in this. Man, you know they kill people over this shit!"

"You just relax, my little gringo, and Margie take care of everything." Margie pulled a handful of little packets from the case and laid them on the dresser. "This, my lover, is for us to use now, so why don't you fix some while I go freshen up?" Duke did a couple of lines before Margie came out of the bathroom.

When Margie came out of the bathroom, Duke was already in bed and under the covers. Margie went over to the dresser and did the lines Duke had set up for her. Duke watched her. She had on a short red nightie. When she bent over to do the coke, Duke could see her bare ass. Man, he thought, I hope she ain't grieving too much to give me a little of that. Duke didn't have to worry about that. She no sooner jumped into the bed and was all over him. She sure is a hot little bitch, Duke thought.

When Duke looked at the clock the next morning, it was nine in the a.m. He remembered he had told Fatty to come in late. He would have to do the ordering today. Margie was still sleeping. I'll just let her sleep. He walked to the dresser and did a line of coke. That sure wakes a guy up. I feel good!

He went down to the bar and opened the door. The place smelled of stale beer. Shit, in all the excitement yesterday, no one had thought to clean up the bar. Duke started to clean the place up. I'll just do this cleaning up now, it won't take too long. While he was working, all the beer drivers came in and took the orders from Duke. He was just about done when two guys walked in. Duke could tell they were policemen right away.

"Hey!" one of them called out. "Your name Duke?"

"Yeah, what can I do for your guys?"

They both pulled out their badges. "Homicide Unit," one of them said. "We need to ask you a few questions."

"Sure," Duke said. "You guys want a cup of coffee or something?"

"Nope, thanks, but we just need a little information from you."

All business, Duke thought to himself.

"You got a Puerto Rican broad by the name of Margie working here?"

"Yeah, she cleans up here on the weekends."

"You know her brother, Angel?"

"I saw him once or twice," Duke said. "He came to take Margie home, that's all."

"Did you see him Saturday night at all?"

"No, I never saw him. He don't hang around here."

'O.K., that's all we wanted to know." The two detectives walked out the door.

That was easy, Duke thought.

"Ain't that the guy Bender and Fox were checking out? You know, I think he was involved with that little girl who's missing."

"Yeah, I'm pretty sure it is," the other detective said. "We'll have to give them a call." The two detectives got into their car and drove off.

It was close to noon when Margie came down to the bar. "Why did you let me sleep so long?"

"I got up early. There was no sense in both of us being up. Let me get you some coffee," Duke said. "I just finished cleaning the bar. You know, we forgot all about it yesterday."

"Oh, I'm so sorry," Margie said. "I never thought about cleaning the bar. For sure, you should have got me up. I feel so bad now."

"Don't you worry," Duke said. "It's all taken care of now. You just enjoy that there coffee."

At one o'clock, Fatty made her entrance into the bar. "Boy, what a night! I slept in this morning, first time in a long time." She walked behind the bar to get a cup of coffee. "Everything go all right? You got all the beer ordered?"

"Jesus, Fatty! I've been in this business for a long time. I know what the hell to do," Duke said.

"Yeah, but you ain't done nothing in a long time," Fatty laughed. "And, how are you doing this morning?" Fatty asked Margie.

"Oh, I'm fine, so far," Margie said. "Duke let me sleep in this morning. He is so good to me."

Just then, the door opened and in walked two Puerto Rican men. They walked up to where Margie was sitting at the bar and stood on either side of her. They started to talk in Spanish. Duke walked over and asked, "Can I help you?" One of the men waved his hand at Duke to go away. "Is everything all right?" Duke asked Margie.

"Si, these are some of my cousins. They want to know about the funeral arrangements."

"O.K.," Duke said and walked away. He went over and said to Fatty, "I don't like those guys! Every time those people talk in Spanish, it sounds like they are fighting."

The two guys left. Margie was sitting at the bar starting to cry. Duke walked over to her. "What was that all about?"

"They wanted to know about the funeral. Also, they wanted to know why I was staying here with you, and if I am sleeping with you."

"Hey! That ain't none of their business. Hell, you're old enough to do whatever you want. I should go out and see if I can catch them two and give them a piece of my mind!"

"No, no! Just leave it alone. Let them cool down. It will be all right. But one thing Duke. I don't think you should go to the funeral home, but you can go to the church."

"Yeah, maybe you're right." Duke then thought to himself. Man, I don't want to get knifed at the funeral home by some crazy spic.

Duke and Margie left the bar. Margie had some things to do and Duke had offered to drive her around. They went to Sauers Funeral Home and Margie took care of what she had to do. She had Duke drive her to two houses where she said her cousins lived. She told Duke to stay in the car.

Duke has having a great time. At each house, he sat in the car and did coke until Margie came out. He was pretty high by the time Margie was finished with all of her errands.

"Hey Duke," Margie said. "How about giving me some of that stuff before you inhale it all?"

Duke laughed, "No problem baby, we got plenty." Margie did some and then Duke said, "You know what I got a taste for?"

"What?" Margie asked.

"Some hot dogs from the Hot Dog Inn. What we'll do is get a six-pack of beer and six hot dogs."

"With the works?" Margie said.

"Yeah," Duke said. "And then, we'll go down to the park and have us a little picnic."

CHAPTER 77

The two Homicide detectives investigating the Angel murder who had talked to Duke returned to their headquarters and were working on their reports.

"Hey, did you ever talk to those two detectives from the Second District who were working on that little missing girl case?"

"No, I never did," the other detective said. "But, I'll take care of that right now. Hey Weaver," he yelled across the room.

"Yeah?"

"You know those two guys who were handling that missing kid in the Second District?"

"Yeah? What about it?"

"Well, we might have some information for them." He told Weaver the story.

"Good," Weaver said after he heard the story. "I'll get the information to them."

Weaver called Bender. "Hey, how about if I meet you, the Sarge, and Fox at Rosie's tonight. I have something to tell you that may help on that missing kid case you guys got."

"You mean Noreen?"

"Yeah, that's the one. I'll meet you guys about nine tonight."

"We'll be there."

Weaver walked in the back door of Rosie's. There were a few guys sitting at the bar, but they were all policemen. Hunter, Bender, and Fox were sitting at the bar talking to Jerry, who was tending bar.

"How you doing Jerry?" Weaver asked. "Give us all a drink will you?"

Jerry went to get the drinks and the guys moved over to a booth so they could talk in private. They made small talk for some time and then Bender asked, "Well, what have you got for us?"

Weaver told them what the Homicide guys had told him, and then added, "We talked to the Narcotics guys and they said one of their snitches had told them that Angel was selling drugs outside Duke's Bar. He also said that a lot of drugs were being sold inside the bar. He thought there might be a connection between the bar and the killing."

"When is the last time you two were in the bar?" Hunter asked Fox and Bender.

"It was before they started having the band there. We really haven't had much time with the case load we have now," Fox said.

"I'll tell you, that would be a big change for Duke," Bender said. "I mean, all he ever did was a little booking in the place. He just seems like the type of guy who wouldn't be selling drugs."

"That's not all that's going on in that joint," Weaver said. "This guy said they also have whores working out of the bar. They're taking the tricks upstairs to Duke's apartment."

"Jesus!" Fox said. "This should be worth looking into. We haven't had any leads in this case for a long time. The leads we had are stale as can be."

"Here's what I want you two guys to do," Hunter said. "Stop in the bar tomorrow night, just for a drink. Try to see what's going on. You know what to do."

"One more thing," Weaver said. "The First District vice guys are going to start watching the place."

"I'll stop that with a phone call. How about the Narcs?" Hunter asked.

"I don't know about them," Weaver said. "You know everything with them is a big secret."

"I'll give them a call too and see what they tell me," Hunter said. "I have a good buddy up there. Maybe, I can tell them to lay off for a while. Just until we find out if any of this shit at the bar is connected with our case."

Hunter called Jerry. "Bring us all drinks, Jerry. Hell, we might as well party for a while." They all sat there drinking and talking about the possible connection between the news about the bar and the case of missing Noreen. "You know," Hunter said. "I still say that girl is alive and well. Let's give this thing one real good last shot!"

The next morning when Bender and Fox went in to work, Hunter was already there. "In a little early, uh Sarge?" Fox asked.

"Yeah, you know the story about the worm. So, get your coffee and come into my office."

Bender and Fox got some coffee and donuts. They went into Hunter's office and sat around Hunter's desk.

"O.K.," Hunter said. "I called the Narcotics Unit and talked to that asshole in charge. After I explained everything to him, he tells me they have information on the place that they can't tell us. It's being watched tonight and they can't help us. So, I went to our Captain, told him what Weaver told us, and what the Lieutenant in Narcotics told me. The Captain made a call and chewed some ass, and we have two weeks. That's two weeks that none of the other guys can come near the joint. When we are done, we have to give them everything we find out. Not a bad deal, huh? Also, the Captain says forget all the other cases you have right now. Work the two weeks on the missing girl case. So, we have to bust our asses on this thing!"

"Are we going to be working overtime?" Fox asked.

"Every day for two weeks," Hunter said. "So, let's get started."

Bender and Fox went to their desks and started pulling out all the files on the case. They went over all the interviews looking for something they might have missed before. They checked out all the reports made by the other detectives looking for clues. They spent the entire day going over reports. Finally at seven o'clock, Sergeant Hunter came out of his office and said, "We're going to Rosie's for dinner. She has it ready for us. So, bring all the information with you. We'll talk in a booth while we eat."

They had finished eating and going over reports by nine-thirty. "Now, here is what I want you guys to do. Go to that bar, have a drink or two, then park outside for a while to see if anything goes on. Come back here and let me know," Hunter told them. "Oh, by the way, don't take one of our cars. I don't want anyone to see the detective car parked outside the bar. Take one of your own cars."

"O.K.," Fox said. "Are we going to make Rosie's our headquarters for this case?"

"You got that right," Hunter said. "No sense going back to the station, too many interruptions there. See you later." Fox and Bender left.

Fox and Bender went back to the station to pick up one of their cars. "We can take mine," Fox said. "I have the old station wagon that I drive to work and it will fit right in the neighborhood."

They got to the bar around ten-ten. When they walked into the bar, there were no customers. Marylou was sitting behind the bar watching TV. "Well, well," she said. "I ain't seen you guys for a long time. To what do we owe this honor?"

"Oh, we just stopped by after work to have a drink or two, you know, unwind a little before we go home," Fox said.

"Glad you're here," Bender said. "We wanted to talk to you."

"So talk," Marylou said as she poured them a drink.

"We haven't had any clues for a long time on Noreen. To tell the truth, we are at a stand-still in the case," Bender said.

"I wondered why none of you guys ever call me."

"You know," Fox said. "Our Sergeant thinks your daughter is alive, don't you?"

"Yeah, I know what he thinks," Marylou said. "He thinks I was in on the deal to kidnap her!"

"Well, were you?" Fox asked.

"No, I was not and I don't know where she is!"

"Have you heard anything new that might help us?" Bender asked her.

"Maybe I have, and maybe I haven't," Marylou said.

"Well, If you have, don't you think you should tell us?" Fox said. "I mean, we could use all the help we can get. Besides, we could follow up on any leads better than you, don't you think?"

"Maybe, maybe not," Marylou said. "Maybe I got a way of getting information that you can't get, or don't know how to get. I don't want to talk about this anymore. You guys want another drink?"

"Yeah, hit us again," Bender said. "And how about one for yourself?"

"Well, I wasn't going to drink tonight, but I guess one won't hurt," Marylou said. She went to get the drinks.

"How are things going with that band?" Bender asked her.

"I'll tell you, business is great," Marylou said. "No problems at all. Duke is very happy with the way things are going. Hell, he even had to hire extra help on the weekends."

"That's good," Fox said. "We'll have to stop by and check things out."

"Sure," Marylou said. "Anytime."

"Time to hit it," Bender said. "We have to be at work in the a.m. Tell Duke we said hello."

"Will do," Marylou said. "I'm going to clean the place up and close. It's pretty slow tonight."

Bender and Fox got into the car. They drove away from the bar around the block. They pulled up three doors from the bar and parked on the other side of the street.

They were sitting there for about ten minutes when a car pulled up in front of the bar. One guy got out of the car and the other guy pulled the car behind the bar and parked it. He got out of the car and went into the bar. Then, they saw Marylou come out of the bar and go upstairs to Duke's apartment. In a minute or two, Duke and Marylou came down and went into the bar.

Bender and Fox sat in the car watching. Ten minutes later, Marylou came out of the bar, walked to the parking lot, got into her car and left. Ten minutes after that, Duke came out of the bar and went back upstairs. "What the hell do you think is going on?" Bender asked Fox.

"Damned if I know, but those other two guys are still in the bar."

At midnight, another car pulled up in front of the bar. Two guys got out and the third car pulled the car in the back and parked it. All three of the guys walked to the door of the bar and knocked. The door opened and they all went in. Fifteen minutes later, the same thing happened.

"That makes eight guys in there," Fox said.

"What do you think they are going in there?"

"I don't know, but we'll know shortly," Fox said. He reached into the back seat of the car and pulled out a beat-up old leather jacket and an old baseball hat. He got out of the car and walked down the street weaving as if he had been drinking. Fox walked up to the front of the bar and looked in the window. He tried the door. Next, Bender saw Fox walking toward the back of the bar. Bender sat there waiting for Fox to come out from behind the building. He had the window of the car open, but he couldn't hear anything. Bender was getting a little nervous. Fox had been gone for almost fifteen minutes and Bender was just getting ready to go after him when Fox came staggering out from behind the bar. He got into the car and drove away.

"Well?" Bender asked.

"They got a card game going on in the back room. I couldn't see who any of them were, because the shade on the window is halfway down. All I could see was up to the table, just enough to see what they were doing. But, I got the license numbers of the cars in the back. We'll run them for a check later."

CHAPTER 78

The two detectives had just left and Marylou was wiping up the bar. The door opened and those two assholes, Nick and Dom, walked in.

"Sorry, I'm closing up," Marylou said to them. The last thing she wanted to do was sit the rest of the night with those two creeps.

"You can go home," Nick told her. "We'll take over now."

"Hey, I don't work for you guys and you don't tell me what to do!"

"Then, go get the boss and he'll tell you what to do," Nick said. "But before you go, get us drinks."

"Get them yourself," Marylou said. She went out the door and up to Duke's apartment. She knocked on the door and Duke answered. She told Duke about Nick and Dom in the bar. Duke went back to the bar with Marylou. As soon as they got in the door, Nick told Duke to send Marylou home.

Nick told Duke to sit down. He wanted to talk to him. Duke sat down and Nick told him about the card game they would be running in the back room.

"God damn it! This is my place!" Duke yelled. "I decide if there are any card games in the back room!"

"You don't decide shit!" Dom said.

"You better go back up to your apartment," Nick said. "We'll figure out the details later."

Duke stormed out the door and back upstairs. He headed right for the bedroom, did some lines, and sat down in the chair. Margie asked him what was wrong. "Nothing, just get me a beer."

Bender and Fox headed for Rosie's. "Think Hunter will be there?" Bender asked Fox.

"Does a bear shit in the woods?" Fox asked.

"Yeah, I guess you're right," Bender said. "Rosie ought to make him pay rent. He does everything but sleep there."

"Hey, I've seen him do that, too," Fox said. Sure enough when they got there, Hunter's car was parked right next to the bar.

They went into the bar. Hunter was sitting there talking to some cops from the Mounted Unit. He saw Bender and Fox walk in and waved them over to the booth. "I didn't expect to see you guys so soon."

They told Hunter what had happened at the bar. "Get the listings on the plates," Hunter told them.

"You mean now?" Fox asked.

"Hey, why not? Hey Jerry, can Bender use the phone?"

"Sure," Jerry said.

It took almost twenty minutes to get the listings on all three plates. Bender came walking back to the booth.

"Well, what have we got?" Hunter asked.

"Car number one listed to a Nick Conti of South Euclid. Car number two listed to Sal Lucci in South Euclid. Car number three listed to a Rudy Dober who lives on the South side."

"Tomorrow, get record checks on all of them and we'll see what we have," Hunter told them.

"You sure you don't want us to get them tonight?" Bender asked.

"Don't be so fucking sarcastic," Hunter said. "Come on up to the bar, the drinks are on me. You guys did a nice job."

Bender and Fox were at work at seven the next morning. They got all the record checks and were sitting in Hunter's office drinking coffee when Hunter got to work. "Hey Sarge, rough night?" Fox asked.

"My boy," Hunter said. "When you get as old as me, all nights are rough." Hunter sat down in the chair behind his desk. "Now, what do you boys have for the old Sergeant?"

"We got the record checks for all the names who owned the cars. By the way, on my way to work I drove by the bar and cars are still parked there," Fox said.

"Sounds like a big time game, you guys think?" Hunter asked.

"I think you're right," Fox said. "Wait until you hear this list. The first car that came there listed to Nick Conti who's a small time hood with a couple of assaults. He served nine months; shoplifting, no time; three moving violations, and ten outstanding parking tickets. He picks up bets for the guys on the hill. The guy with him has to be Dom Santanio. He's the guy he always hangs with who has about the same record. Two punks. The next car is listed to Sal Lucci, who has a couple of moving violations and five outstanding parking tickets. He owns a small printing shop on Euclid Avenue. The third car is listed to Rudy Dober, AKA Three Fingers Rudy, who lives on Tremont Avenue on the South side. He's a small time gambler, runs some floating crap games, but likes to run the big card games with heavy players. He got a couple gambling busts, but no other record."

"That leaves four guys we don't know anything about," Hunter said.

"Right," Fox said. "The way we figure it is Nick and Dom ain't playing in the game. They're just there to make sure everything runs smooth. You got Three Fingers, a bodyguard, and one player in that car. Then, you got Sal, the printer, and two of his friends, all players."

"I want that place watched, or better yet, I'll tell you how I want this done," Hunter said. "Until the weekend, you can check the bar around eleven o'clock or midnight. Then, on the way into work in the morning, check the lot behind the bar again and see if there are any cars there. Maybe, we can get a couple of the vice people to hang around on the weekend and see what's going on inside."

"Sounds good to me," Bender said.

Fox and Bender went back to their desks and the tedious job of going over reports on Noreen.

"You know, Hunter thinks that Duke is tied in with this missing girl," Bender said.

"Yeah, I know. He thinks that Marylou is too, but I don't know about that though," Fox said. "If she knew where Noreen was, you would think after all this time, she would have gone to see her."

"Could be," Bender said. "But, remember, we haven't been watching her for a while."

"True," Fox said. "We have kind of let this case slide."

"Well, that's what happens when you run out of clues. Then, you get a little line on things and away you go. Besides that," Bender said, "Hunter really wants this case solved, just to show everyone he was right."

"I hope he is," Fox said. "It sure would be nice to find that little kid safe and sound!"

The phone rang. "Hey Fox, it's for you. One of the guys yelled from across the room.

Fox picked up the phone. It was Weaver. "I just wanted to let you guys know, the funeral for that Angel guy is going to be at THE MASTER'S TOUCH."

"Jesus, that's the church Hermy has."

"Right," Weaver said. "And, let me tell you another thing. Angel's sister, her name is Margie, just moved in with your buddy who owns the bar."

"You mean Duke?"

"You got it good buddy!" Weaver hung up.

Fox told Bender what Weaver had said. "Man, this thing seems like one big mess," Bender said. "But, it sure seems like one way or another, everything is tied together. We better tell Hunter about all this shit."

CHAPTER 79

Wednesday night, Margie had just left to go to the funeral home. Duke was sitting upstairs thinking about how pissed off that fucking Nick made him last night. He could hear those guys downstairs in the back room playing cards. He had finally fallen asleep around three-thirty in the morning. He got up around nine and they were all gone. I hope this shit ain't gonna happen every night, he thought. What the hell, I got plenty now. I don't have to get any shit from Nick. This way, he doesn't know I'm using it. I think I'll go down and talk to Marylou for a while.

Duke went down to the bar. There were a few customers at the bar. Duke said hello to them and told Marylou to give everyone a drink on him. Marylou got all the drinks and then brought Duke and herself drinks.

"You know Duke," she said. "I don't know what the hell is going on, but I will tell you one thing. I don't like it! I don't care what you do in this place. I mean, what the hell, it's your place. But, just the same, I think you are losing control. I don't want any part of this shit. Hell, you're selling dope in here, running whores, and now, you got a card game going on in here all night. Don't you think the cops are going to get wise pretty soon? Oh, by the way, just before those two asshole buddies of yours came in, the two detectives, Bender and Fox, just left."

"Shit," Duke said. "What the hell did they want?"

"They said they just stopped in for a drink after work. But, I don't believe that. They asked how you were doing on the weekends, and I told them good. They said they would stop in to see you."

"Man, that's all I need," Duke said. "That's all I need."

Between waiting on people, Marylou was getting drinks for Duke and talking to him. "You know Duke," Marylou said. "I'm going to try and work maybe two or three more weekends and then I'm going to quit. Hermy doesn't like me working here. Besides that, I'm getting a little scared."

"Yeah, I can understand that," Duke said. "I just got to find a way to get that Nick and Dom off my back. I don't know what to do. Do you have any ideas?"

"No, not really. Maybe, if you stop the band on the weekends, the people would stop coming. Then, there would be nobody to buy the dope or go with the whores."

"Sure, that sounds like a good idea, but what the hell do I tell Nick?" Duke asked.

"Can't you do whatever you want? What the hell, you own the joint, don't you?"

"You don't understand Marylou. These guys don't play that kind of game. Once they get their hooks in you, you're fucked!"

"What do they have on you?" Marylou asked him. Duke just sat at the bar staring. "Come on Duke, you can tell me. Is it about Noreen?"

Duke got up and walked to the back room. He took out the little bottle from his pocket. He did a couple of snorts and went back out to the bar.

Marylou had given him another drink. "Duke, God damn it, will you tell me about Noreen? I know you know where she is!"

"I swear! I don't know where she is!" Duke told her.

"But you do know who took her, don't you?"

"Duke lifted his glass and took a sip. Marylou kept at him, trying to get him to say something about Noreen that would help her, or at least give her some kind of clue. All the time, Duke was thinking, I should tell her what I know, or maybe even tell the cops. I could make a deal with them. Oh, what the hell am I thinking about. That Nick would have me killed.

Marylou said, "For the last time Duke, why the hell can't you give me some kind of help? I have to find my baby!" Marylou started to cry.

Shit, thought Duke. This is all I need. "Look Marylou, give me a little time to figure something out, will out?"

"O.K., I'm going to give you some time, but I swear Duke. If you don't come through with something to help me, I'm going to drag the police back into this thing!"]

"Don't do that Marylou. Just wait a while, will you?"

Marylou walked away. "I have to go to the back room. Watch the bar."

When Marylou came out of the back room, she was back to her old self. She walked behind the bar and got drinks for Duke and herself. She set the drinks on the bar, looked Duke right in the eyes

My Baby My Baby!

and said, "One more thing Duke, our little affairs is all over. You got that broad living with you now, and I ain't taking no chances of getting stabbed by some spic broad!" Duke didn't say a word. He could see Marylou meant business.

Just then, Margie walked in the door. She came right over and sat next to Duke. "Hi," he said. "Everything go all right?"

"Si, everything o.k. I have a rum and coke please Marylou?"

"Sure thing," Marylou said.

"Duke, I hope you don't get mad at me. Some of my cousins, they are going to stop here for a drink."

"Margie, you know I don't want any trouble in here. You told me they were mad at me. That's why I didn't go to the funeral home with you."

"I know that Duke. But, I tell them how good you are to me and how you pay for the funeral. I no think there will be any trouble." The door opened and in walked five guys and five women. Oh shit, thought Duke. This has got to be trouble.

Margie introduced everyone to Duke. The ones who could speak English thanked him for taking care of things. Duke had Marylou get drinks for everyone. Marylou gave them their drinks and called Duke down to the end of the bar.

"Duke, I'm going home. This place is packed with spics. It makes me nervous."

"Yeah, sure, go ahead, beat it," Duke told her. "See you in church."

Marylou smiled. On the way out, she stopped to talk to Margie. "I have to go Margie, but I'll see you at the service tomorrow."

"O.K.," Margie said. "Thanks for helping me."

Marylou walked out the door. I sure hope old Duke ain't going to have any trouble in there tonight, she thought.

Duke sat at the end of the bar watching Margie talking with her family. Jesus, he thought. I don't know how the hell they understand each other, they talk so fast. One of the men called for Duke to give everyone a drink. Duke got up from the end of the bar to take care of them.

They were all sitting there drinking rum and coke. They were really starting to throw the drinks down. Duke would just about get the drinks served and someone else would order another round. Hell with this, Duke thought. I should have Marylou stay here. Just as Duke was taking some drinks to the bar, he saw one of the guys laying out some coke on the bar. "Hey, hey," he yelled. "What the hell do you think you are doing?"

The guy looked up and smiled at Duke. He held out the straw to Duke and motioned him to do the lines. Duke took the straw. He called Margie over. "Margie, tell this guy he can't do that shit right here at the bar. What if some coppers walk in here? Tell him to do that shit in the bathroom."

Margie told him in Spanish. The guy looked at Duke and smiled. Then, he walked into the bathroom. He left the stuff on the bar. Duke looked at it and thought, hell, no sense in letting it go to waste. He leaned over and did the coke. Duke heard some cheering and clapping. When he looked up, he saw everyone was watching him. Duke had a big smile on his face and said, "That's what's called snorting up the evidence." Those who understood English all laughed.

Somebody put some money in the juke box and the place settled down a bit. Duke fixed himself a drink and went down to the end of the bar. Pretty soon, some of the couples were dancing and the loud talking had become whispers. Margie came down to the end of the bar and sat next to Duke. "I'm sorry they were so loud when they first came in, but they were excited."

"That's o.k.," Duke said. "Man, they must have a lot of stuff with them. There's a steady stream going back and forth to the bathroom."

"Most of them are dealers and users," Margie said. "So, when something bad happens, they always got enough blow to make everybody happy." She took Duke's hand and pulled him off the stool. "Come on in the back room." She pulled a packet from her blouse. Duke went with her and they both did some coke.

When Duke came out of the back room, he yelled. "The drinks are on me!"

Around midnight, Nick and Dom walked in the door. They took one look around and Nick almost ran to the end of the bar where Duke was sitting with Margie.

"What the fuck is this?" Nick screamed. "What the fuck is going on here?"

Just then, the door opened again and in walked five white guys. They took one look around and walked right back out the door.

My Baby My Baby!

"Holy shit!" Nick said. "Dom, get out there and stop them guys! Tell them everything is o.k.! Duke, tell these fucking spics to get the fuck out of here now!"

"No can do," Duke said. "I don't kick paying customers out!"

Nick headed for the door, but not before saying to Duke, "You're in some deep shit now, my friend. I'll be back shortly!"

Nick ran around to the back parking lot. Everyone was still there and Dom was talking to them. "O.K.," Nick said. "No problem. We can go in the back door."

"Get fucked!" Three Fingers Rudy said. "You know me better than that. You think I'm going to take my people into that place to play? Hell, them spics will have us robbed before we can get in the back room! No, no, my friend Nick. I will call the game off for tonight. That's it! But, my friend, you will pay me. You know my time is worth money. I made plans for tonight and now we can't play. I don't like this kind of business. You want me to come back here again? You make sure we are the only ones here. Just like last night. Now, my friend, good-bye!"

Nick and Dom stood in the parking lot as the other two cars pulled away. "That mother fucker!" Nick said.

"Who, Duke or Three Fingers?" Dom asked.

"Both of them! God damn it!" Nick screamed. "Both of them! Come on!" Nick said. We're going back in there and kick that fucking Duke's ass!"

Nick and Dom walked back into the bar. Duke was still sitting at the end of the bar. They walked down to him and sat on the stools. "Give us a drink," Nick said.

Duke got up, went behind the bar, and fixed them a drink. Nick and Dom chugged their drinks down. Nick slammed his glass on the bar and said to Duke, "Come on in the back room. We got something to discuss with you!"

"Fuck you!" Duke said. "I ain't going in the back room with you guys, not after last time."

Nick looked at Duke. "What the fuck is your problem? Are you cracking up? When I tell you to do something, you better fucking well do it! Maybe you been doing too much of that shit we've been giving you! What do you think Dom?"

"I think what I always thought," Dom said. "This here guy is a real asshole! I say we grab his ass and haul it into the back room, or if he wants, we can kick his ass right out here in front of all his fucking friends!"

"That sounds like the best idea," Nick said.

Duke leaned on the bar with both his elbows, looked Nick right in the eyes, and said, "For your information, all these here dudes just came from the funeral home, where old Angel is laid out. Now, if you want to grab my ass, I'll just let it be known that you're the two guys who had old Angel knocked off."

Nick and Dom looked at each other and then around the bar. The juke box was still playing, but none of the spics were talking. They were all just starting down to the end of the bar. Nick got up from the stool. "See you later Duke," he said and slowly walked toward the door. Dom was right behind him.

"Nick didn't say anything until he was in the car and had started it. "That son of a bitch!" he said as he banged on the steering wheel. "That son of a bitch!" He peeled the car out of the lot.

Bender and Fox were parked down the street and had seen most of what had happened outside the bar. "Something got everyone pissed off," Fox said. "I wonder what the hell happened?"

"You got me," Bender said. "But, there sure is a lot of action, people going in and out."

"Time for my little act again," Fox said as he reached behind the seat. Bender watched as Fox staggered down the street. He's good at this, Bender thought. Of course, he has had a lot of practice, and he laughed to himself.

Fox got back into the car. "Well, that explains it all. The place is filled with Puerto Ricans!"

Duke kept the bar open until two o'clock and then he told Margie to tell everyone to drink up. The police were here last night, he told her. I don't want them to cite me for after-hours. Margie told her cousins to drink up. They all raised their glasses to Duke and toasted him.

Duke said to Margie, "If they want to have a few more drinks, why not invite them up to the apartment? I'll bring up the rum and coke and we can party."

My Baby My Baby!

"Oh, you are so good to me," Margie said. Then, she yelled something in Spanish. Another cheer was hollered out and everyone headed for the door to follow Margie. Well, at least, they took their glasses, Duke thought as he grabbed up a couple of six-packs of coke and a couple bottles of rum. I hope this was a good idea, he thought as he locked up the bar.

When Duke got upstairs, Margie had turned on the radio and they were already starting to party. Duke took the booze into the kitchen, set it on the table, and walked back into the living room.

Margie waved him over to the coffee table. He looked down. Sitting in the middle of the table was a fruit bowl of cocaine. One of the women handed Duke a small spool and said, "Enjoy!"

Duke stood there looking at the spoon. "Like this," Margie said as she took some in the spoon and snorted it.

Duke did the same. "I like it," he said. "I like it! I got to get me a spoon."

The woman who had given him the spoon said to Duke, "It's yours to keep."

"Thank you." Duke was like a kid with a new toy. He watched as the men used spoons snorting the coke like it was nothing. The women used one nail they had let grow way out. That fascinated Duke as he watched them.

Between the rum snorting, Duke was pretty high and lightheaded. He thought he would lay down for a few minutes. H e went into the bedroom and laid across the bed. When he woke up and looked at the clock, he couldn't believe his eyes. It was nine o'clock in the morning. Man, I got to be at the church by eleven, he said to himself. He got out of bed and went into the living room. The place had been cleaned. You could never tell there had been a party there last night.

Duke went into the kitchen and on the table was a note. "Dear Duke, had to go to the funeral home. I didn't want to wake you up. See you at the church. Love, Margie."

Duke took a shower and had a cup of coffee. He went into the bedroom and got out his best suit. Well, it was his only suit. After he dressed, he took a packet from his sock drawer, took out his new spoon, smiled and snorted the coke out of the spoon. He slipped the spoon into his pocket. I'm ready now, he said to himself, and off he went.

Duke got to the church at ten after ten. Red was getting the tables and chairs set up. "Glad you're here Duke. I sure could use some help.

"You got it," Duke said as he took off his suit coat and started to help Red.

"Hermy went to the funeral home to say a few words over the stiff. Patty and Marylou are in the back getting the food ready. You should see all the stuff the people brought!" Red told Duke. "We're going to have a good old time after the funeral!" Red was happy as could be.

CHAPTER 80

Everyone got to the church at eleven-fifteen. The casket was carried by six of Angel's cousins. Hell, Duke thought. All these spics must be related. They set the coffin up at the front of the church and all the pallbearers took their seats. Duke was shocked by the number of people in the church. Duke judged there were about one hundred. They were standing against the wall since there weren't enough seats.

Bender and Fox were parked across the street about half a block from the church. They could easily see the front door and were watching to see who was going in. "What a mixture of people," Fox said. "We got whores, pimps, dope peddlers, and dope users."

"Yeah," Bender said. "Reminds me of one of them old gangster movies you see on TV."

"Let's get some of the license numbers. We can check them out later," Fox said.

"Right, make us look just like the F.B.I.!" They both laughed.

Hermy went to the pulpit and gave a sermon about dying. He didn't have much to say about Angel. But, two of his cousins had asked to say a few words. Hermy introduced them and they both made short speeches in Spanish. When they were finished, the six pallbearers got up and carry the casket outside. They put the casket in the hearse and Mr. Sauers drove it away. The body was going to be cremated.

As soon as the hearse pulled away, Marylou got some of the men to start putting up more tables. Some of the women helped carry the food from the back. Hermy told Marge that they couldn't have any alcohol in the church. So, Duke told her that after everyone had finished eating, they could go back to the bar and he would spring for some booze.

"Don't' tell them about the booze for an hour or so after the funeral, or no one will eat," Duke told Margie. "They would all head for the bar." After Duke had some food, he and Fatty went back to the bar to get things set up. "You better get Patty to come with us," he said.

After it looked as though everyone finished eating, Hermy made an announcement drinks would be served at Duke's Bar. Hermy had hardly finished the announcement then the church was empty. Hermy told Marylou he would supervise the cleaning up and she could take Margie to the bar. "I'll meet you there later."

Marylou told Margie to come back to the house for a minute. She got her clothes to wear for the weekend at the bar. She had Margie carry the bag of clothes out to the car. This way, Hermy would think it was Margie's bag and not question her.

CHAPTER 81

When Margie and Marylou got to the bar, it was already crowded. Duke, Fatty, and Patty were working behind the bar. Duke told all the people he would supply the beer, but they would have to pay for the booze. The juke box was playing and the men's room had a line waiting. They sure are starting early, Duke thought. Just then, one of Margie's cousins waved to him. He told Duke he was next. Everyone in the line by the bathroom gave Duke the thumbs up. Oh well, Duke thought, Angel would have wanted it this way.

Hermy came into the bar around four o'clock. He had some bags with him and told Marylou to send someone out to the car. There was more food out there. They set up some tables against the wall and filled them with food.

The party lasted until eight o'clock. Then, it started to slow down. Most of the people had gone, the good was gone, and most of Duke's beer was gone. "We'll have to call for more beer in the morning," Duke told Fatty, "or we won't have enough for the weekend."

"Right," Fatty said. "I think I'll go home now. I'll be in early in the morning and get things ordered."

Duke asked Margie if she was ready to go upstairs. "Yeah, I'm pretty tired," Margie said.

"Can you and Patty hold the fort down for a while?" Duke asked Marylou.

"Sure can," Marylou said. "But when it slows down, will it be o.k. if we close up?"

"Sure," Duke said. "See you tomorrow."

Patty, Red, and Hermy were sitting at the bar. Marylou was serving drinks. Marylou wasn't charging for them. "Hey, the party is still going on for the help!" she joked.

Duke and Margie went upstairs. When Duke opened the door, he couldn't believe his eyes. The place was a mess, the cushions from the couch and chairs had been cup up and the filling was all over the floor. They went into the bedroom. The drawers from the dresser were all emptied on to the floor and the mattress was slashed. The clothes from the closet were thrown all over the floor.

"Oh shit!" Duke said as he looked through the socks on the floor. "They got the stuff I had hidden there! How about that stuff you had Margie? Did they get that too?" Margie turned and went into the kitchen.

She opened the cupboard door under the sink and pulled out the wastepaper basket. She pulled the garbage out along with the empty cans. At the bottom, there was a package wrapped in tin foil. "Here it is!" she said as she held the package over her head.

Duke followed Margie back into the bedroom where Margie hid the package inside the slashed mattress. "They won't look for it there!" she said.

"What makes you think that's what they were looking for?" Duke asked.

"I don't think that's what they were looking for," Margie said. "But, if anybody comes back, they won't look where they already looked."

"Pretty smart," Duke said.

"Si, now we do this." Margie reached down the front of her blouse and pulled out that little brown bottle. They both had a hit.

"You call the police?"

"Hell no. They didn't take anything but the dope, and I sure as hell ain't going to tell the police about that. As for the furniture, I needed new stuff. We'll just go to the Sleepy Bear Motel for the night. In the morning, we'll come back and get the place cleaned up. Then, we'll go out and by some new furniture. Let's go back down to the bar and have a couple of drinks with Marylou and the other guys. Then, we'll head to the Sleepy Bear."

Duke and Margie stepped from the doorway of the apartment when they were grabbed. One guy threw Margie against the wall and said, "Just stand there spic. This has nothing to do with you, but if you scream or try to run, big trouble for you!" The other two guys took Duke around the corner of the building.

Duke was pushed up against the building face first. "This comes straight from the hill asshole! No more fucking spics hanging around the bar! You fucking got that!" Duke was hit in the side. "From now on, the bar closes at ten o'clock except on Friday and Saturday. You got that?" Duke was hit again. "When you close the bar during the week, you don't show your ugly fucking face until the next morning, you got that?" There was another hit. "You understand everything I told you?" the guy asked Duke.

"Yeah," Duke whimpered.

Then, he was turned around. Before he could see who was talking to him, he saw the fist coming right into his face. The punch would have knocked him down, but the second guy was holding him up. Shit, Duke thought. I've been here before. The guy hit him a few more times and then the guy holding him let him slip to the ground. Duke got ready for the kicks, but they never came. Instead, one of the guys leaned over and said to Duke, "Next time, we use a knife and your face will look just like that mattress of yours."

Margie could hear Duke getting hit, she could hear some talking, but she couldn't hear what was being said. The guy holding her against the wall never said a word after he had warned her. She didn't know how long the guy was gone, but she didn't feel him near her anymore. It was almost like he had just melted away. She stood for a minute or two without moving. Then, she slowly turned around. Not a soul was in sight.

"Duke," Margie whispered. "Duke, are you all right?" No answer. "Duke," she said a little louder. "Are you all right? She heard a moan. Margie walked around the corner of the building and saw Duke laying on the ground. Margie ran to the bar yelling, "Help! Help! They kill my Duke!"

Big Red jumped from the stool, "What's the matter?"

"Go help my Duke! I think he's dead! Around the corner on the ground!"

Red and Hermy ran out of the bar and to the side of the building. Duke was just getting to his knees. "You o.k.?" Hermy asked.

"I don't 'know, just help me into the bar."

Red and Hermy took him under each arm and dragged him into the bar.

Once Duke was inside, they dragged him to the table. "What the hell happened?" Big Red asked. "Was somebody trying to rob you or what? Marylou, get him a shot of whiskey!"

Patty went to the back room to get some rags.

Marylou brought a bottle over to the bar and poured Duke a shot. He drank that and Marylou poured him another. Duke drank that one and said, "I don't' feel too bad." He felt his chest and side. "Doesn't feel like any broken ribs. Fuck, those guys are wimps. Are you o.k. Margie?"

"Si, they only push me against the wall so I can see nothing."

"Do you know who they were?" Hermy asked.

"No," Duke said. "I don't know who they were, but I sure as hell know who sent them!"

Duke told them about the apartment, but left out the cocaine.

"I'm going to call the police," Hermy said and started for the phone.

"No, no," Duke said. "I don't want the police here. As a matter of fact, that's the last thing I want!"

"Well, what the hell are you going to do about all of this?" Patty asked. "I mean, you can't let it go by without doing something about it."

"I have to think this over," Duke said. "But right now, all I want to do is have a few more drinks." Duke poured another shot.

"Can't let the poor man drink alone," Fatty said as she went and got shot glasses and beer for everyone.

They sat around drinking. Then, Hermy said, "I told you Marylou. I don't want you working here. It's getting too bad. Somebody is going to get hurt here!"

"Look Hermy, I told you before. I don't want you telling me what to do, where to work and where not to work and all that shit! We ain't married, you know!"

Hermy didn't answer, but just sat there. Marylou could tell he was in one of his sulking moods.

After a few more drinks, Hermy got up from the table and said, "Time for me to go home. Someone has to take care of the kids." He gave Marylou a dirty look.

"I'll just go with you," Marylou said.

"No, you stay here with your friends, I'll see you later." Hermy started for the door. Margie jumped up and walked with him.

"Thank you very much Hermy. You give real nice sermon for my brother." She gave him a kiss and a hug.

"That's o.k. Margie. I'm always glad when I can help someone." With that, Hermy left.

"Oh shit," Marylou said as the door closed. "I'm in for some shit tonight. Keep your door unlocked Fatty. I just might be there!"

"Anytime Marylou, anytime. The bed will be warm, just slip in beside me."

"Well, if I'm going to get yelled at," Marylou said, "I might as well make it worthwhile." She poured everyone another drink.

Bender and Fox pulled up across the street from the bar at midnight. The signs were still lit in the windows, so they knew the bar was still open. Bender told Fox there was no sense going through the drunk act. He would just run across the street and peek in the window.

"Go, my man, go!" Fox said.

Bender jumped out of the car, ran across the street, and peeked in the window of the bar. Then, he ran back and jumped into the car.

"Well?" Fox asked.

"Six people sitting at the back table; Duke, Marylou, Fatty, and three of their backs to me."

"The bar is still open," Fox said. "I think we should stop in."

Bender and Fox walked into the bar and sat on two stools near the door. When they walked in, everyone sitting at the table looked towards the door. Oh shit, Duke thought to himself. This is just what the fuck I need. Duke recovered and yelled over to the two cops, "Hey, don't be anti-social. Come on over and join us. Red, pull up two more chairs. Fatty, get the boys a drink and put some money in the juke box."

Bender and Fox walked over to the table and shook hands with Duke. Duke introduced them to Big Red. They already knew Patty. "And this here," Duke said, "is my little Margie."

Fatty brought the drinks over to the table and sat down. When everyone was taking a drink, Fox asked, "What happened to your face Duke?"

"Well," Duke said, smiling the best he could. "Just about an hour or so ago, I went upstairs to fresh up a bit and on my way down, I tripped and fell all the way down the steps. Hell, it was a good thing Margie was with me," Duke winked, "or, I still might be laying out there. She came into the bar and got some help for me. I must just be getting old. Them steps is just getting too much for me." Duke glanced from Fox to Bender. They bought it, Duke thought.

Bender and Fox each had two drinks and when they tried to buy a round, Duke told them their money was no good in here. Bender and Fox said their good-byes and left.

"Jesus," Duke said as soon as they left. "I never expected them to be stopping here."

"Well, I told you they were here the other night," Marylou said.

Duke turned to Margie. "Let's get out of here and head for the motel. Fatty, fix me a bag with some booze and beer in it. I still got a giant thirst and they ain't got no room service at the Sleepy Bear!"

Fox and Bender got into the car. "What do you think Bender?"

"Do you mean about Duke's face?"

"Yeah, Duke's face. Now, I know neither one of us believes that story about him falling down the steps," Fox said. "But, I will tell you one thing. Those cuts and bruises are fresh."

"I think you're right about that," Bender said. "I just wonder who the hell would beat him up like that?"

"What do you think about the broad?" Fox asked.

"That must be the spic whose brother was killed. Duke never made any mention of that."

"No, I don't think old Duke ever wants to tell us too much," Bender said.

"Who does?" Fox said. "Let's just sit here for a while and see what happens. See if there is any more action around here."

They only had to wait a few minutes when they saw Margie and Duke come out of the door of the bar. They walked to the back parking lot and got into Duke's car.

"Let's follow them," Bender said. "Did you notice Duke was carrying a bag?"

"Yeah, I saw it. Let's see where they go."

They didn't have to follow Duke very long. Down the street, they saw him pull in the lot of the Sleepy Bear. They parked across the street and watched. Duke went into the office, came out, got Margie and the paper bag, and they went up the stairs to a room.

Bender and Fox stayed put for about an hour. When nothing happened, they left. "Take a ride by Rosie's and see if the Sarge is

there," Bender said. He was there, so Bender and Fox went in and told Hunter what had happened.
"Good work boys, now let's have a couple of drinks."
"Oh boy, another late night," Fox said and smiled.

CHAPTER 82

After Duke and Margie had left the bar, the rest of the gang had a few more drinks. "It's two-fifteen," Marylou said. "It's time for me to go. Who wants to give me a ride home?"

"We will," Patty said.

"You guys go ahead," Fatty said. "I'll clean the bar and lock up. See you all tomorrow night."

Big Red and Patty took Marylou home. "Want us to come in with you?" Patty asked.

Marylou thought for a minute. "You know that might not be a bad idea."

They all walked to the back door. There was a light on in the kitchen. Marylou opened the door. Hermy was sitting at the kitchen table. There was a bottle of whiskey in front of him and a half bottle of beer. "Hey, come on in you all," Hermy said. "I hate it when I got to drink alone." Marylou could see that Hermy was happy again.

"Well, that looks like it just might hit the spot," Red told Hermy. "You sure do set a nice table."

Hermy laughed, "The centerpiece came from Duke." He pointed at the bottle of whiskey.

They all sat down at the table. Marylou knew it would be a late night, but what the hell. It was better than she had expected.

They were drinking and talking about what had happened to Duke.

"It's been one hell of a day," Hermy said.

"You can say that again," Patty said. "And one hell of a night."

They were all pretty well drunk by now. "I got something to tell you Marylou," Hermy said. "Now, don't be getting mad at me."

"Go ahead Hermy, tell me what you got to tell me."

"Well, some of the people who come to the church said that they don't think it's right you being my girlfriend and all, well, they…"

"Come on, damn it Hermy, spit it out!" Marylou said.

"Well, they don't think it's right for you to be working at the bar. They tell me there is whoring and dope selling going on down there. They just don't think that it's right."

"Fuck them!" Marylou yelled. "Want to know how they know about the whores and dope? Well, let me tell you!" Marylou was yelling now. "It's because I've seen some of your flock fucking! Yes, Hermy dear. Some of those assholes that are holier than thou. I've seen them going upstairs with them whores who are working there! What the hell do you think they were doing up there? Having a bible study? So, what do you think of your fucking flock now?"

Patty and Red were laughing. "Now, what the hell is it?" Patty asked. "A fucking flock, or a flock fucking?"

Hermy started to laugh and Marylou seeing everyone laughing, started to laugh herself.

"You're a God damn poet!" Red told Marylou.

At six-thirty, Patty and Red decided it was time to go home. "Sure, I knew you would be ready to go now," Hermy said as he pointed to the bottle. "You see, it's empty."

"Good thing," Red told Hermy. "I don't think I could drink another drop."

Patty and Red left. Marylou and Hermy headed right for the bed. Marylou was thinking, Good, he should go right to sleep with no problems. Marylou was right. In just a few minutes, they were both sound asleep.

CHAPTER 83

Margie and Duke got back to Duke's apartment a little after two o'clock the next morning. The first thing Margie did was look in the mattress for the coke. "Ahha!" she said. "Just like I told you, nobody find the stuff here!"

"Where are you going to put it now?" Duke asked her.

"Oh, don't worry Duke," Margie said. "I got just the place for it. But, let's clean this place up."

Duke and Margie spent until five-thirty cleaning the apartment. "We can stay here tonight. Tomorrow, we can go look at new furniture."

"Sounds good to me," Margie said.

Duke took a shower. When he came back into the bedroom, Margie had fixed a couple of lines for him. "This will pick you up," she said. "If you need more tonight, it will be ready for you, si?"

"Thanks baby," Duke said as he did the lines. "That sure hits the spot. Now, remember what I told you. Stay here and don't let in anyone but me, o.k.?"

"Sure Duke, no problem. I want to cut this stuff up so we can sell it."

"Do you really think that's a good idea?" Duke asked her.

"Si, I know where to get rid of it with no problem."

Duke went down to work and Margie went to work at the kitchen table.

Duke walked into the bar. Fatty was working behind the bar. "Hey Duke, how you felling tonight?"

"Oh, probably better than I look."

"Oh, you don't look that bad. That eye is mighty black, but not too swollen."

"It'll get better," Duke said as he sat down at the bar. "How about a drink?"

About an hour later, Marylou came in. "Hi Duke," she said as she sat down next to him. "How you doing?"

"O.K. Marylou, just sitting here thinking."

"About what?"

My Baby My Baby!

"Oh, I don't know, but there has to be some changes made here. I can't stand all this bullshit."

"Well, you just think about it," Marylou said. "Because, like you said before. These guys ain't nobody to fuck with!"

The bar was starting to fill up and was crowded by the time the band started to play at eight o'clock. Duke moved to the table he usually sat at and waited for Nick and Dom to come in.

Patty was working the floor and Red was behind the bar with Fatty and Marylou. Tomorrow night, Duke thought, I'll have Margie work again. Fuck what them WOP's say. Duke reached into his pocket and pulled out his little bottle. He reached in with his spoon and did some. Hell, what do I care if anyone in here sees me, all that comes in here is a bunch of dopers.

It was about nine-thirty when Nick and Dom walked into the bar. They came right over to the table and sat down. "How's it going?" Nick asked as he slapped Duke on the shoulder.

"Keep your fucking hands off me!" Duke said.

"My, my a little touchy ain't we?" Dom said.

Duke made no reply, but waved for Patty to come over. "Patty, get these guys a drink on me and then start a tab for them." He got up from the table and took a seat at the bar.

Nick and Dom sat at the table laughing. "That asshole thinks we're going to pay for drinks," Dom said. "Man, he's got another thing coming."

"Well," Nick said. "It looks like the old Duke goes another week without getting paid."

"That sure sounds good to me," Dom said.

Fast Eddy and Sheri walked into the bar. Duke called them over to where he was sitting. Nick and Dom were watching. "What the fuck you think he's talking to them about?" Dom asked.

"How the hell do I know?" Nick said. "What the hell do I look like, a mind reader?"

Fast Eddy and Sheri walked over to the table and sat down.

"What did that asshole tell you?" Nick asked.

"He told me and Sheri to get out of the joint. If not, he was going to call the cops. Man, I don't need this kind of shit. Hell, me and Sheri can set up shop any place. Don't make no difference to us, do it baby?"

"Hell no," Sheri said. "They all follow us, no matter where we go."

"You just get to work," Nick said to Fast Eddy. "I don't care what he told you. We run this place and that's all there is to it!"

"Look" Fast Eddy said. "I don't want to be in the middle of this shit, so the first sign of trouble, me and my lady are out of here, you dig?"

"Just get busy!" Nick said. "Me and Dom will handle this whole thing." Fast Eddy and Sheri left the table and started to work the crowd. Duke watched them and smiled.

Duke sat at the bar drinking. Every once in a while, he would reach into his pocket, pull out his bottle, and do some coke.

Nick and Dom sat at the table watching Duke and ordering drinks from Patty. "See, I told you, he wouldn't do anything. The man's a chicken shit!" Nick said to Dom.

"Yeah, I guess you were right," Dom said and he waved Patty over for another drink.

At eleven o'clock, Bambi and Dawn walked into the bar. Duke called them over and was talking to them. "What the fuck!" Nick said. "What the hell is he doing now?"

"We'll find out in a minute," Dom said. "Here come the girls now."

Dawn and Bambi sat down at the table. "What's the story?" Dawn said to Nick. "Duke says we should beat it, we can't work here anymore. He says if we start to work, he will call the cops."

"God damn it Dawn!" Nick said. "You two worked for me long enough to know that whatever that asshole says don't mean shit! I'm the boss, so go to work." Dawn and Bambi shrugged their shoulders and went to work.

It was just a short time before Dawn picked up a trick. Duke saw her head for the door to go upstairs. Duke laughed to himself. Let's see what they do now, he thought. Two minutes later, Dawn came storming into the bar and went right over to the table Nick and Dom were sitting at. "O.K.," she said. "What the fuck kind of game are we playing?"

"What's the matter now?" Nick asked.

"The fucking door to the apartment is locked and the key ain't under the mat! What the hell am I supposed to do? Fuck the guy in the hallway?"

"Just hold on a minute," Nick said as he got up and headed for Duke. He grabbed Duke by the arm and hissed in his ear. "Where the fuck is the key to the apartment? The door is locked and the key ain't under the mat! What the fuck are you trying to pull?"

Duke looked Nick right in the eye, "Get your hands off me! Look asshole, the place is a mess, the mattress is all cut up, and I didn't have time to buy a new one." Duke turned away from Nick.

Nick stood there for a minute, then walked back to the table.

"Well?" Dom asked.

"Shut the fuck up!" Nick said to him. Then, Nick called Dawn and Bambi over to the table. "You girls take the rest of the night off," he said as he reached into his pocket and gave each of them a hundred dollar bill.

Shit, that don't cover it!" Bambi said.

"Look, just get the fuck out of here!" Nick said. "I'll talk to you later about it." The two girls walked out the door. Duke watched smiling.

Nick said to Dom, "This guy is going to pay, and I mean big!"

At midnight, the band stopped playing. Marylou went to plug in the juke box. Duke got off his stool and went over to Marylou.

"Don't plug that thing in."

"What are you talking about?"

"I'm going to close early tonight," Duke told her.

"You think these people are going to go this early?" Marylou asked.

"Hey, they got to do what I say! I own the joint!" Duke said as he walked behind the bar. "Last call for alcohol, motel time, let's go!" Duke hollered out. Everyone in the bar including Fatty and Patty looked at Duke surprised.

"What the hell is he pulling now?" Nick asked.

"Who knows?" Dom said. "I think the guy is cracking, too much dope."

Surprisingly, the place emptied out pretty quickly. There was a lot of mumbling as they went out the door, but that was about it.

Duke looked around. The place was empty, except for the people working. Duke walked over to the band leader and was talking to him.

"What the hell is he doing now?" Dom asked Nick.

"Who knows? I think you're right Dom," Nick said. "That guy is nutty as a fruit cake!"

The guys in the band left. Duke looked over and saw Nick and Dom were sitting at the table. He walked over to the table. "Hey! Didn't you guys hear me? The joint is closed, everybody out!"

"Are you shitting us?" Nick asked.

"No, I ain't shitting you. I said out! Patty get the check for this table."

Patty brought back the check and laid it on the table. Nick picked up the check, looked at it, and slowly tore it up. When he was done tearing it up, he threw the pieces into Duke's face. "Come on!" he said to Dom. "Let's get the fuck out of here! By the way Duke, you ain't got no cut for tonight!"

Duke watched as Nick and Dom walked out the door. Seems like that might have been a little too easy, he thought. Oh well, I made my move, now I got to follow through.

Duke walked over and locked the door. Tomorrow, I'll have the lockman come in and put new locks on the door. In the apartment, too. That should do it, he thought. The next move will be up to them.

Duke called everyone over to the table. "Bring us all drinks," Duke said. "Bring enough so you don't have to be getting up and down." While Duke was waiting for everyone to get settled, he thought. I better go up and get Margie. She should know what is going on here. "I'll be right back," Duke said and he went up to get Margie.

Five minutes later, he was back down with Margie. They all sat down at the table. Fatty was the first to say anything. "Tell us what the hell is happening here, will you Duke?"

"Sure," Duke said. He told them that he knew it was Nick and Dom who had torn up his apartment. He was sure it was them who had beaten him up the other night. "They act like they own this joint. I've been working for myself for thirty years and those punks have pushed me too far!" Duke said. "At the beginning, I thought the money would make things all right. But all it got me was started on dope and thinking about getting my money every week from them bums." Duke took a big swig of his drink and held his glass out for a refill. Marylou made Duke another drink. "Over the last few days, I found that there are a lot more important things than money. Besides, I'm afraid that if I keep up with this, one of us will get hurt, or worse yet, killed. I sure don't what that on my conscience."

"Maybe, you're making things bigger and worse than they really are," Fatty said.

"You know, I tried to tell Margie about these guys and she didn't listen to me and you see what happened to her brother?"

"Shit, you think those guys had something to do with killing Angel?" Red asked.

"I'm telling you, they might not have pulled the trigger, but you can bet your sweet ass they put somebody up to it," Duke told them.

"How the hell did you ever get involved with these guys?" Patty asked Duke.

"It's a long story," Duke answered. "But now, I got a plan. Maybe, I can get out of this mess."

Duke started to outline the plan for them. "First of all, if any of you don't want to be involved in this, tell me now." No one said anything, they just sat there looking at Duke. "I take that to mean you all are going to stick with me?" There was a murmur around the table that resembled a yes. "O.K., to start with, I told the band to come in early tomorrow and get their stuff together. I told them I would pay them for tomorrow night, but they were through working here. Second," Duke went on. "I'm going to have the locks changed on the doors, including my apartment. No one will have to worry about that because I'll be staying here all the time until this shit blows over."

"I ain't got no work for a while," Red told Duke. "So, if you like, I can hang around with you. You know, kind of like a bodyguard."

"That's o.k. by me," Duke said. "I'd appreciate that. Let's all have another drink. Duke made everyone a drink. "Now, tomorrow night, I want everyone to come into work. I think it will be busy until they find out there ain't no band playing. Fatty, I want you to call the police station in the morning and tell them you would like to have two men in uniform working here tomorrow night. Tell them, it's just for one night and I'll pay them fifteen dollars an hour each in cash to work from six o'clock to midnight."

"Sure," Fatty said. "I know a couple of guys who will take the job. I'll call them first thing in the morning."

Duke poured some more drinks. They all sat around drinking and talking until well past three o'clock in the morning. Then, they all left. Everyone headed for home.

When Marylou got home, Hermy was sleeping in bed. She was pretty wound up, so she woke Hermy. Hermy came out to the kitchen and sat at the table while Marylou told him everything that had gone on at the bar.

"Jesus," Hermy said. "Do you think you ought to go back to work there?"

"You bet I do," Marylou said. "We ain't gonna let Duke try this shit alone." Besides, Marylou thought, if Duke is getting all this religion, maybe he'll tell me about my baby.

"I'll tell you right now," Hermy said. "You ain't going to work at that place without me being at your side!"

"Thanks Hermy," Marylou smiled as she took his hand.

Red and Patty talked about the events of the day all the way home and later as they were in bed. "I can't wait for tomorrow night," Red told Patty. "But, if things start to get out of hand, I'm going to tell you to leave and I want you to do just that, o.k.?"

"Sure," Patty said. "If that's what you want me to do."

Fatty went straight home. She went into the kitchen and opened a beer. She took it into the bedroom with her and sat on the edge of the bed. She reached over and turned the TV on. She really didn't pay much attention to what was on. She sipped her beer thinking, that damn Duke sure got his ass in some trouble now. But, I ain't gonna run out. Hell, I've been working for Duke about ten years now, and I ain't gonna let no bums chase me out. No, I'll just stick by Duke and see what happens. She lay back on the bed. Before she knew it, she was sleeping.

Duke and Margie went up to the apartment. Duke shut and locked the door. Then, he got a chair and wedged it under the door knob. He checked all the windows and pulled the blinds. Margie went into the bedroom and brought a couple of packets of cocaine. "Look Duke, while you were downstairs working, I got all this shit cut up, weighed, and packaged. Let's try some, si?"

"No," Duke said. "I'm going to quit doing that shit right now."

Margie looked at Duke. She could see he wasn't kidding. Then, Duke said to her, "Margie, I want you to stay with me. But, I got no room in my life that that shit. So, if you want to stay with me, you have to get rid of all that stuff." Margie stared at Duke, but didn't say anything. Then, Duke said to her, "If you want to stay, I want you off that shit. If you don't think you can do it by yourself, I'll help you. If you need to go some place to dry out, I'll help with that too."

"I'll try," Margie said. "I'll really try."

Margie took the packets back into the bedroom and put them in a drawer. She came back out into the living room and sat on the couch with Duke. Duke pulled her over to him and held her. "We can make it," he told her. "But, now let's go to bed."

CHAPTER 84

Dom and Nick left the bar. They got into their car and headed for another bar they had some hookers working at.

"Well, what do you think of the way old Duke is acting?" Dom asked Nick.

"I'll tell you right now. I don't like it one bit."

"What do you think we should do about it?" Dom asked.

"Can't you ever think of anything?!" Nick asked Dom.

"Hey man, you're the boss. I don't get paid to think of anything, or to make any decisions, you know what I mean?" Dom asked.

"Yeah, I know," Nick said. "I'm the boss."

"That still don't answer my question," Dom said. "What are you going to do?"

"I think what we will do," Nick said, "is nothing."

Dom looked over at Nick. "What the fuck do you mean, nothing? Man, that guy is shitting all over us!"

"I think the guy is just a little pissed off," Nick said. "I mean, what the hell, his apartment just got trashed and he got the shit kicked out of him. He's pissed, that's all."

Dom thought for a while, then said, "You mean you think that he'll be back doing business with us? Is that what you are trying to tell me?"

"That's it pal."

"Well, I think you are wrong. This guy ain't done with us yet. That's what I think!" Dom said.

Nick pulled the car up in front of the joint they were going to. "Remember, you don't get paid to think." Nick parked the car.

Bender and Fox pulled up in front of Duke's Bar. "The place looks dead," Fox said.

Bender looked out the window of the car. "It's deader than a door nail. What time is it?"

Fox looked at his watch. "It's one o'clock."

"Go into your act," Bender told Fox.

Fox came back to the car after staggering around for a while and looking into the window of the bar. "It's just Duke, Patty, Red, Marylou, Fatty, and that spic broad sitting at a table drinking. No one else is in sight."

They watched the bar for about half an hour and left.

CHAPTER 85

Duke and Margie got up the next morning. Duke could hear some noise down in the bar. He looked at his watch. Hot damn, he thought, ten-fifteen, gotta get up. He looked over at Margie. She was just waking up. "Come on sleepy head. Let's hit the floor. We have a lot to do today!" Duke headed for the shower. When he got out of the shower and came back into the bedroom, Margie was sitting on the edge of the bed. She had a packet of coke, sitting unopened on the top of the dresser, and she was staring at it. Duke walked over to the dresser and picked up the packet. He opened the dresser drawer and put it inside. He turned and said to Margie, "Come on baby, take a shower and then we'll go have breakfast."

Margie smiled at Duke, "It ain't going to be easy, si?"

"I know," Duke said. "But we gotta try."

Margie and Duke went down to the bar. The guys from the band were moving their stuff out. Fatty was behind the bar. Duke paid the band off. The leader told Duke anytime that he wanted them back to give them a call.

"Thanks," Duke said. "Sorry, we had to let you guys go."

"I called them two cops," Fatty said. "They're going to be here at six."

"Good," Duke said. "You're on the ball and so early in the morning." Duke told Fatty he and Margie were going to get something to eat and go look at new furniture. "We should be back in a couple of hours. Then, you can take a break if you want."

"Oh, I'll just have a sandwich here and wait for the action tonight. I don't want to miss anything, you know."

Duke and Margie had breakfast and looked at furniture. They bought a living room set, a kitchen set, and a new bedroom set with a water bed. The man at the store said he could have everything delivered Thursday afternoon.

"Great," Duke said. "We'll be home waiting."

They got into Duke's car and headed for the bar. "Oops," Duke said as he turned the car around. "I forgot something."

"What did you forget?" Margie asked. "We got everything brand new."

My Baby My Baby!

Duke didn't say anything until he pulled into the lot of the appliance store. Then, he told Margie, "I'm going to buy you the biggest TV they got in this place!" And, he did.

Duke looked at his watch as they headed back to the bar. It was three-thirty. Duke stopped and got a bucket of chicken. He told Margie they could sit at the bar with Fatty and all have chicken for lunch.

"Good idea," Margie said. "But you got enough chicken there to feed all my cousins!"

They got back to the bar and Fatty told them nothing new was going on. Duke put the chicken at the bar. Fatty got some paper plates, napkins, and a pitcher of beer. They all dug in. "Best lunch I've had in a long time," Fatty said.

"Hey, you can't beat home cooking," Duke told her.

They finished eating and sat at the bar talking. Only a few customers came in, mostly the wine heads that came in, got drunk and gone, and passed out some place by seven o'clock.

Duke said to Fatty, "I like it this way, just like the old days."

"Yeah," Fatty said. "Just like the old days, no business and no tip!" They all laughed.

The customers started coming in around seven o'clock. They didn't notice anything because the band didn't start playing until eight. But by then, they were asking Duke where the band was. "Oh, they quit," he would tell them. The customers would have a drink or two and then slip out the door, going somewhere else to look for the action.

Duke had the two cops standing on each side of the door. The people coming in threw nervous glances toward them and shifted uncomfortably in their seats.

Nick and Dom came in at eight-thirty. When they walked in the door and saw the two policemen standing there, they almost went crazy. They walked over to where Duke was sitting at a table.

"What the hell are you trying to pull here?" Nick asked, keeping his eyes on the cops.

"It was starting to get too rough in here," Duke said. "So, I thought we could use a little protection."

"Where the hell is the band?!" Nick yelled.

"They quit last night," Duke told him.

"You know, I don't believe this shit. Dom, get out in the parking lot and try to catch Fast Eddy and Sheri before they come in here. Fast Eddy will have a heart attack if he walks in here and sees them two coppers standing over there!"

The word must have traveled fast about the band not being there and about the cops at the door. Hardly anyone was walking in the door. Those who did left as soon as they saw the cops.

Dom walked back into the bar about fifteen minutes later. "I saw them," he said. "I told them about the cops. Man, was Fast Eddy pissed. He told me to tell you he wouldn't come back to this place anymore and if you want him to work another joint, you better have things worked out better than this."

"We'll settle with him later!" Nick said. Nick got up from the table. "Come on Dom, let's get out of this place! As for you Duke my boy, you are fucked!" Nick and Dom walked out the door.

The whole gang at Duke's was sitting at the bar including Hermy when Bambi and Dawn walked in. It was ten-thirty and the two cops were sitting at the end of the bar. Bambi and Dawn both smiled at them and they smiled back nudging each other with their elbows.

Bambi and Dawn walked over to Duke. "Man, what happened here? Where the hell is everybody?"

"Didn't Nick get a hold of you girls?" Duke asked.

"Nope," Dawn said. "Was he supposed to?"

"Yeah," Duke said. "As you can see, there ain't no business in here anymore. The band quit, and I ain't hiring any more bands. I'm going back to the old style bar I had, no fuss, no muss. Just some regular customers coming and going."

"No fuss, no muss, and no us!" Dawn said to Duke. The two girls said their good-byes and headed for the door. They stopped by the two cops, said something, and the cops laughed. Then, the two girls walked out the door.

"One thing for sure," Duke said. "Those two girls won't be out of work long. I'd be willing to bet money on that."

Duke and his friends sat there drinking. There were only a few customers at the bar and Fatty was taking care of them. Duke called the two coppers in to the back room and paid them for the night.

At eleven-thirty, Bender and Fox pulled up in front of the bar. "Man, the place looks dead again," Bender said. Just then, the two cops came out the door.

Fox stopped them, "You guys have some trouble in there?"

"Hell no!" the one cop said. "We were just working off-duty."

"Man," the other cop said. "That Duke pays well."

Bender and Fox both looked in the window of the bar. They sat Fatty working behind the bar and a few customers. Duke and his friends had moved to a table.

"Let's go in and see what the hell is going on," Bender said.

"Good idea, let's go." Fox and Bender walked in the front door.

Duke waved them over to the table. "Sit down boys, take a load off."

Bender and Fox sat down. "Duke, what happened to the big crowds and the band? Me and Bender decided to stop after work and we were ready to party. But, it don't look like any party is going on here."

"There is going to be one right now!" Duke said. "Hey, Fatty, bring over a couple bottles. The rest of the night, the drinks are on me!"

They all partied well into the morning. It was about four a.m. when Hermy said, "I got to go, I have to preach in the morning."

"Come on," Marylou said. "I'll go with you now." They left.

"It's time for us to go too. It's pretty late," Bender said to Fox. They walked out the door with Red, Patty, and Fatty.

Duke and Margie sat there for a while. "You think everything will be all right?" Margie asked Duke.

"I don't know," Duke said. "I don't think these guys will let me go that easy. Then again, who knows?"

Duke and Margie locked up the bar and went up to the apartment. Duke opened the door. "Just think, by Thursday, this place will look like a different apartment."

"I can hardly wait," Margie said. "This will be the nicest place I ever lived in." Margie felt good, better than she had in a long time, until she walked into the bedroom. All she could think about was the cocaine in the dresser drawer. She stood in the doorway like a statue. I sure could use a couple of lines, she thought.

Duke walked up behind her and put his arms around her. He whispered in her ear, "I know what you're thinking. Come on out in the kitchen and we'll have a little night cap."

Duke and Margie sat in the kitchen talking about what had happened the last few days. "One thing for sure," Duke said as he held Margie's hand. "We have to get rid of that stuff!"

"I know just the place to get rid of it," Margie said. "But, I'll have to go tomorrow night."

"Good, that will solve part of the problem," Duke said. "You know, out of sight, out of mind."

"I hope it is that easy," Margie said.

Duke and Margie went to bed. They spent one bad night, tossing and turning. At eight o'clock, Duke was up out of bed. He went to the kitchen and put on a pot of coffee.

A little later, Margie came in, "Smelled the coffee," she said.

"Good," Duke said. "Sit down." They sat in the kitchen drinking coffee. "Margie, what do you say we go over to Hermy's church?"

CHAPTER 86

Nick picked Dom up at ten o'clock Sunday morning. "We got plenty to do today," Nick told him. "I got a call from the old man last night."

"Yeah, so what did he have to say?"

"He said Duke had to go and he wants it done now!"

Dom smiled. He enjoyed this part of the job. A lot of guys, even like Nick, got a little jumpy when the old man wanted someone killed, but not Dom.

Nick looked over at Dom and saw he was almost in a trance. Nick knew how much Dom liked to do this shit. Nick didn't say anything to Dom, he just let him sit there thinking to himself.

Dom was wondering how they wanted Duke killed. I hope they want to blow the mother fucker up! I haven't done that in a long time. Dom sat there thinking about different people he had killed. Dom could feel himself getting excited. He would have to have a girl tonight. He had a hard-on now. I got to quit thinking about this now, or else I'll come right in my pants! He started laughing, first to himself, then louder and louder.

Nick looked over at him. Man, this guy is scary, he thought.

Dom quit laughing and looked over at Nick, "How do they want it done?"

"Any way we want to, just so there are some drugs involved, but not an overdose."

"Good," smiled Dom. "We got to make a couple stops. I got stuff to get and we can do the job later tonight."

CHAPTER 87

Duke and Margie got to the church and were surprised to see not only Fatty there, but also Red and Patty. After the service, they stood around talking and drinking coffee. Marylou invited them back to the house for lunch. But Duke insisted that he take all of them, including Marylou's children, out to lunch, his treat. Duke took them to this little restaurant he knew called "Georgies." They sat down and ordered. Everyone was talking and having a good time. After dinner, Duke got ready for his little speech.

He thanked all of them for sticking by him last night. Then, he told them, "I'm going to close the bar for a couple of weeks. Margie and I are going away tomorrow morning. When we get back, we'll all meet again and I will tell you what I've decided to do."

They all wished Duke and Margie good luck and thanked Duke for lunch.

As they were leaving, Duke pulled Marylou aside. "When I get back, I have something to tell you. I should have told you before, but more than anything, I was scared. When I get back, I'll clear everything up for you. That's all I can say right now."

"I've waited this long Duke, I can wait a little longer. Why don't you and Margie come back to the service tonight?" After the service, we'll all go back to the house and have a little going-away party for you and Margie."

Duke told Marylou that Margie had something to do and they had packing to get done. But, he would call her as soon as they got back.

Duke and Margie went home. They got back to the apartment around four-thirty. They took a shower and jumped into bed for a little nap. Margie told Duke she would leave around seven o'clock and get rid of the stuff. "I know the contact Angel had and where to find him. There will be no problem. You know this stuff is worth a lot of money."

"I really don't care," Duke said. "Just get rid of it."

At six-thirty, Margie got out of bed. "I have to get dressed and get going."

"You can't go Duke."

Duke sat back down on the edge of the bed and looked up at her. "I'll wait in the car."

"No, they will never let me make contact if they see you. They don't know you they just know me."

"I don't like this at all," Duke told her.

Margie told Duke that she would be safe. "After all, I will be dealing with my own people, all Puerto Ricans. If I can't trust them, who can I trust."

At seven-fifteen, Margie was on her way out the door. "Be home by nine gringo." Margie threw Duke a kiss and was gone.

CHAPTER 88

It was eight-fifteen. Duke was in the bedroom packing. He hadn't told Margie where they were going. It was to be a surprise. Duke had a friend who owned a cottage in Erie right on the lake. He told Duke he could use it, free of charge for the next two weeks. Duke felt pretty good. But, he thought, I sure could use a little pick-me-up. But, I ain't taking none of that dope. Then, he laughed to himself. I ain't got none to take. Duke went to the kitchen to get a beer.

Just as he passed the front door, there was a light knock. Good, she's home early, Duke thought as he opened the door. "Hi baby," Duke said. "Glad!…

"What did you say sweetheart?" Nick said.

Duke tried to slam the door, but Nick and Dom pushed the door right into Duke's face. Duke flew across the room and fell on the floor. Nick and Dom were on top of him before he could move.

Duke had a feeling this wasn't like the last time. No, they weren't here to beat him up this time. They're going to kill me!

Duke fought as hard as he could, but to no avail. Nick and Dom soon overpowered him.

They snapped a pair of handcuffs on him and pulled him to his feet. They dragged Duke into the bedroom and threw him across the cut-up mattress.

"What do you guys want from me?" Duke screamed.

"Where's that spic bitch?" Dom hissed in Duke's ear.

"She left me! She ain't staying here no more!" Duke said.

"I can understand that," Nick said. "What the hell does she want a fat ass like you for?"

Duke stopped struggling and lay on the bed. He saw Dom reach into a small bag and pull out a syringe and a vial. Dom stuck the needle into the vial and pulled it out. He aimed the needle up in the air and Duke saw the stream of liquid gush out of the end. Oh no, Duke thought. They must be going to kill me with an overdose just like they did to Jimmy. Dom came towards him with the needle. Duke felt like he was hypnotized. Duke started to struggle again. But, Nick punched him. At the same time, Duke felt the prick of the needle in his arm.

Duke could feel the hot liquid running through his veins. If felt nice and warm. It felt good. Duke felt his entire body starting to swim. Not bad, he thought, not bad.

"There you go," Duke heard someone say, but he didn't know the voice. He felt the handcuffs being taken off his wrists. They don't want to hurt me, Duke thought. These guys are all right. All I want to do now, is lay back on this bed and enjoy this high. Man, I wonder if they'll give me some of this stuff to take with me? Margie would love this stuff.

Nick watched Duke while Dom went into the kitchen. Dom went over to the stove. Ahha, good, he thought, gas. Dom blew out all the pilots, then turned the jets on top of the stove wide open. He then opened the over door and turned on the gas to the oven. Dom placed a small box inside the oven and called out to Nick, "Let's go!"

Nick and Dom ran down the stairs, jumped into the car, and pulled away. "Push it! Push it! Nick yelled to Dom.

"Wait, wait," Dom said.

Nick could see the look on Dom's face. He watched as Dom leaned back in the seat of the car. Dom's eyes rolled back into his head and then Nick saw him push the button. Dom shuddered. Nick looked down and saw a wet spot on Dom's pants between his legs.

Duke felt good, he tried to raise up off the bed. He could sense there was no one in the room with him. Those two are nice guys, Duke thought. Duke was half out of the bed when he heard a loud roar and saw a flash. He felt himself being lifted into the air. I'm flying, then the pain came, but only for a second, and then nothing.

When Dom pushed the button, Nick looked out the back window of the car. He saw a huge flash and then heard a loud explosion. Windows in the bar and the building next to it blew right out into the street. Nick felt the car rock. Man, this is just like being in the war. Nick floored the car and headed away.

The fire department was there in a matter of minutes. But, the building was an infero by then. The police got there and helped rope off the street. They shut the street off to all traffic.

CHAPTER 89

Margie had taken Duke's car. She was driving back to the apartment. It was nine-thirty. She had made the deal with the contact with no problem. She knew Duke was going to be surprised at the amount of money she had. Duke would never have to work again if he didn't want to.

Margie was a little later than she had intended. She had stopped on the way home to buy corned beef sandwiches. She knew how much Duke liked them with a nice cold beer.

Margie could see the flames in the sky as she was driving. Wow, must be a big fire, and close to the bar. I wonder if Duke can see it? Margie wanted to turn on Bridge Avenue to get to the apartment. A policeman stopped her, "Sorry," he said. "But you can't go down that way. There's a big fire and no traffic can get through."

"What's on fire?" Margie asked.

"I think some old bar, Duke's Bar. I think I heard someone say."

Margie sat in the car. Oh my God, she thought. Duke! Margie was smart enough to know she didn't want to park the car and leave all the money in it. If it was Duke's on fire, she didn't want to be walking around with all that money on her. If Duke was inside the building and was hurt or dead, the police would want to talk to her. She had to get away from here. She headed right for Marylou's place.

Marylou, Hermy, Fatty, Red, and Patty were sitting in the kitchen drinking. They had been laughing just a minute ago about this becoming a Sunday ritual, when they had heard this big explosion. They heard sirens and thought, maybe one of the factories in the Flats had blown up. No need to run outside, they would see it all on the news.

Margie banged on the door. "Come on in, it's always open!" Hermy smiled.

They all looked surprised when they saw Margie walk in the door.

"What the hell, I thought you were going to be busy tonight? Where is Duke?" Marylou asked.

Margie collapsed into a chair. That's when they all noticed how ashen her face was. She looked as though she was in shock. "What's the matter?" Fatty asked her.

Margie just sat in the chair. She looked at each one of them. "Duke, Duke, I think he might be dead."

They all sat there looking at each other. Finally, Fatty said, "What makes you think Duke is dead?"

"The policeman, he told me there was a big fire. I asked him where? 'Duke's Bar,' he said. He say, 'you can't go down there, big fire!'" Margie started crying and screaming, "Duke! My Duke!"

Hermy reached across the table and slapped Margie across the face.

Margie's head snapped back. She laid her head on the table and started to sob. "Hermy," Margie said between sobs, "Would you go to the bar? I'm afraid to go."

Hermy and Red got up from the table. "You girls stay here," Hermy told them. "Me and Red will go check this out."

Hermy and Red got into Hermy's car and headed for the bar. They only got part way down Bridge Avenue before they were stopped by a policeman. They pulled the car around and parked down a side street. The two of them walked towards the bar. The street was packed with people, all walking around and talking, asking each other if they knew what had happened. Red and Hermy got close to the bar and could see the fire was just about out. The building was flattened. "Jesus!" Hermy said. "If old Duke was upstairs in the apartment, he's goner now!"

"Let's check the crowd, see if he might be here," Red said.

Hermy and Red searched the crowd and found nothing. They saw some of the old timers who hung around the bar and asked them if they had seen Duke. None of them had. Hermy went up to one of the firemen and told them they thought that Duke might have been in the building. The fireman went to get the Assistant Fire Chief. He asked Hermy, "What makes you think there was someone in there?"

Hermy told him, "Duke lived upstairs. He was planning on going away and was home packing."

The Chief told Hermy that it would be some time before they could search through the building for anything. He also told Hermy that by the time the Fire Department got there, the building was such an inferno that it would have been impossible to get anyone out.

Hermy and Red walked back to the car and headed for home. "Damn," Hermy said. "Now, we got to go home and tell the women that Duke is probably dead."

When the two men got home, the women were still sitting around the kitchen table. They were drinking coffee now. The party mood had long been gone. Hermy and Red walked into the house and sat down at the table. Neither of them knew what to say, or who should say it, so they just sat there, one waiting for the other to speak.

Marylou looked at each man and then said, "You didn't find Duke, did you? He didn't make it, did he?"

"There still could be some hope. He could have left the apartment to get something from the store," Hermy's voice faded off. They all knew there was no chance of that happening.

CHAPTER 90

The phone was ringing at Bender's house. Bender raised up from the bed and looked at the clock. Midnight, who the hell is calling at this time? "Jesus, answer the phone, will you?" Bender's wife said as she gave him the elbow.

"Hello?" Bender said into the phone. "What? Are you shitting me? No, I'll be right down as soon as I get a hold of Fox."

Bender called Fox and told him he would pick him up right away. Then, Bender called Hunter, taking a chance he would be home on a Sunday night. Sure enough, the phone was answered by Hunter, who told Bender he would meet Fox and him at the station.

The three detectives sat around Hunter's desk drinking coffee.

"What the hell do you guys think happened?" Hunter asked.

Bender told them he had talked to the Fire Chief and they still weren't sure if Duke had been in the apartment. It would be a while before they could search through the ashes. That's about all there is now. But the Chief had talked to some people at the fire and they felt that Duke had been up in the apartment.

"Did the Chief have any idea what started the fire?" Hunter asked.

"Not yet, but from all the interviews so far, it seems there was an explosion, maybe a gas leak or something like that," Bender said. "You never know about those old buildings."

Bender and Fox told Hunter they had stopped in the bar Saturday night. There was no band. In fact, it was quiet in the place. They told Hunter they sat there drinking and Duke was in a good mood.

"Hold on a minute!" Hunter said. "What the hell about that spic broad who was staying with Duke? Maybe, we have two bodies in there?" Bender and Fox looked at each other. "I think you guys better go interview Marylou for starters," Hunter told Bender and Fox.

Bender and Fox thought they would wait until morning to talk to Marylou. Hunter said he wanted it done now. So at four a.m., they headed for Marylou's, or rather Hermy's house.

Much to their surprise, when they got to Hermy's house, they saw the lights were on. Sitting around the kitchen table were all the people they wanted to talk to including Margie. They were all drinking beer now.

Marylou let the two detectives in and told them to sit down. "Coffee or beer?" Marylou asked. They both took coffee, admitting it really was a little too early for cocktails.

"We know this is a bad time to ask questions, but that's the way things go," Bender said. "We have to get as much information as possible and as soon as possible."

Bender and Fox told them that they wanted to know what had happened from the time they had left the bar Sunday morning to the present time.

"Of course, we still don't know for sure if Duke was in the building, do we?" Fox asked.

Margie put her head down on the table and started to cry. "He was there when I left to go out!" she sobbed.

"Hold on," Bender said. "Let's start at the beginning."

They all sat around looking at each other. Marylou asked, "Who do you want to start?"

"How about if you start?" Bender said.

Marylou told them she and Hermy had left the bar, came home, and went to bed. They got up for church. Duke and Margie had come to church and then Duke had taken them all out to lunch. Duke had told them he and Margie were going away for a while. He had left the restaurant with Margie and that was the last they saw of them. Well, until Margie had come to tell them about the fire.

Big Red, Fatty, and Patty told just about the same story and really had nothing more to add.

Now, it was Margie's turn. She told them Duke and her left after the bar after everyone was gone. They had gone up to the apartment and went to bed. They got up the next morning and went to church. They had gone to the restaurant. After that, they had gone back to the apartment and had taken a nap. She had taken Duke's car to go pick up some clothes at her old house for the trip. Margie told them what the policeman had told her when she tried to get back to the apartment and she had come right to Marylou and Hermy's.

Hermy told the two detectives how he and Red had gone to the fire and searched the crowd for Duke. "We asked a lot of people who we saw in the crowd who knew Duke if they had seen him after the fires started. But, they all said no."

"O.K.," Bender said. "But, let's get back to your story Margie. We want to know what time you left the apartment, where you went, and what time you got back."

"Si," Margie said. "I leave the apartment about seven-fifteen at night and I take Duke's car." Margie was thinking to herself. I can't tell them where I go, but they gonna check on whatever I tell them.

Margie told them she had gone to her old apartment to get some clothes. "I spend some time there getting all my things ready for the trip. Then, I go to the Deli to get some corned beef sandwiches for Duke. Oh, they are still in the car. I get back to the apartment at nine-thirty. That's when the policeman, he tell me I can't go to the apartment and then I come right here."

"Did Duke say he was going any place, or maybe to the store to get something for the trip?" Bender asked Margie.

"No, he just said he was going to pack."

"That means that at this time, we can believe he was in the apartment," Fox said.

"Let's not jump to any conclusions, let's wait until the Fire Department searches the ashes," Bender said.

Fox and Bender got up from the table. "As soon as we hear anything, we'll let you know," Fox told them.

When the two detectives left, Marylou went to get more beer. She thought, I'm not going to say anything yet about Duke telling me something when he got back from the trip, at least, not until we know for sure he's dead. Then, I'll have a little talk with them two detectives.

CHAPTER 91

Bender and Fox went back to the station. They talked with Hunter and told him all they had learned. Hunter told them he had talked to the Fire Chief again and they would start searching the ashes this afternoon. He said we were all welcome to assist in the search. "I'll be at Rosie's, so you two better go home and get some old clothes. I expect a first-hand report."

Bender and Fox got to the scene about one in the afternoon. The scene was marked off with yellow ribbon marked "Crime Scene." There was a large crowd outside the markers and also some policemen to hold the crowd back.

"Amazing, how many people hang around to see how much gore they can see, isn't it?" Fox asked. It was a question that did not need an answer.

Bender and Fox reported to the Fire Chief. He told them they could look around, but his men would do the actual sifting through the ashes. If the detectives saw anything, they were not to touch it, but were to call one of the firemen over.

Fox and Bender were just as glad. They didn't want to be finding any body parts. They walked around the scene peeking here and there and watching the crowd. They were looking for any familiar faces or anything that would catch their eye.

The Red Cross had set up a wagon for the searchers. Bender and Fox made their headquarters there, drinking coffee and munching on donuts.

At three-thirty, one of the searchers called the Chief over to where he was searching. Bender and Fox started over to where the Chief was. The Chief waved them to hurry and they ran over to him. "Find something?" Bender asked.

The Chief smiled and pointed under a charred board. At first, Bender and Fox couldn't see anything. Then, the Chief put his light so it shone under the board. Both Bender and Fox jumped back.

"Jesus!" Bender yelled.

There was Duke's head smiling at them. Fox started gagging and the Fire Chief started laughing.

"Is that the guy you're looking for?"

"Shit, that's him, but where the hell is the rest of him?" Fox asked.

"Oh, we'll find him, in bits and pieces. Just like a jigsaw puzzle," the Chief told them. "It takes a little time, but my boys get all the pieces that can be found."

Bender and Fox walked away. "Don't call us if you find any more pieces, just put it in your report," Bender told the Chief.

The Chief and all the firemen were laughing as Bender and Fox got into the car and headed for the station.

The Sergeant wasn't there, but Fox and Bender knew where he could be found. They made some of the reports that they had let go for a while and then headed down to Rosie's.

When they walked into the bar, the Sergeant was sitting there eating a pork chop sandwich. He looked up, saw Fox and Bender and yelled out to Rosie. "Fix the boys a sandwich. Oh, put some cheese on it, make that head cheese!" Everyone in the bar started laughing.

Bender and Fox looked at each other. "All right, who told you about it?" Bender asked.

"The Chief told me. I stopped down at the scene to see how things were going and I must have just missed you boys."

"Did they find anything else?" Bender asked.

"Oh yeah, they found a couple of Duke's fingers." Hunted called out to Rosie. "Maybe the boys would like some hot dogs instead of pork chops." Hunter started laughing again.

Fox and Bender sat down at the bar. They didn't think any of this was funny, but Hunter was having such a great time, they didn't want to say anything to him. Bender ordered a beer for him and Fox. "Oh, and give Jackie Gleason there a drink, too." He pointed to Hunter.

After Hunter finished eating, he told Fox and Bender to come and sit at the table with him. Hunter used the table as an office sometimes.

Hunter told them that the searchers had found enough of Duke's body to see if there were any drugs or alcohol in him before he was blown up. "The Chief said they thought the fire was an arson, but they ain't sure yet. The Chief thought they would have a complete report in a few days. The way things are now, we know for sure Duke is dead and so far, it looks like his is the only body that was in the place."

"What do you want us to do now?" Bender asked.

Hunter laid out what he had planned. "We didn't release any information to the press yet, and Homicide said they won't either. So until all the reports are back from the lab, no one will know whose body was found."

"Marylou and that gang she hangs around with will know for sure who was found," Hunter said.

"I don't even want you to talk to them," Hunter said. "And if they call and want to talk to you, you're not in."

Hunter told them to check up on Margie's story. "See if you can come up with anybody who saw her out that night and give you some times."

"You know," Bender said. "I just thought of something. When we left Marylou's in the morning and walked by Duke's car, I looked in the window. Margie said she stopped by to get some clothes. Well, I didn't see any clothes in the car."

"The clothes could have been in the trunk," Fox said.

"Maybe, but just some clothes and nobody else in the car. It seems like you wouldn't bother to open the trunk," Bender said.

Bender and Fox left the bar. Each were trying to think about the case and if this whole thing was tied together. But so far, they didn't even know for sure if Duke had been killed, or if it was an accident. There really wasn't much they could do until the reports came back and Hunter let them start talking to Margie and the rest of them.

When they got back to the station, they had messages from Marylou, Fatty, and Patty. "Let's get out of here before they start coming to the station," Bender said to Fox.

CHAPTER 92

Margie stayed at Marylou's house the night of the fire. She knew well enough that Duke was in the apartment and was dead. Margie lay in the bed that night thinking about what she should do. She had a little over one hundred thousand dollars from the sale of the cocaine. She and Duke would have had a good time with all that money. She thought they would have been able to stay together with no problem. Margie knew she could stay here and become part of the drug scene, but she really didn't like that idea. She decided she would get on a plane the next afternoon and fly back to Puerto Rico.

Margie decided she wouldn't tell anyone she was going. She fell asleep and dreamed about she and Duke on vacation. They were having a good time making love in a huge bed, when all of a sudden, Duke started screaming, "Help me! Help me! I'm on fire!" Duke began to melt right before her eyes.

Margie woke up with a start. At first, she didn't know where she was. Then, it all came back to her. She looked at the clock and saw it was six in the morning. Margie got up and went out in the kitchen. She put the coffee on and was drinking a cup when Marylou came from the bedroom.

"I smelled the coffee," Marylou said. "But, it's kind of early to be up ain't it?"

"Si, but I could not sleep. I was having a bad dream and it woke me up."

"What do you think you are going to do now?" Marylou asked.

"Oh, I just go back to my old place and start all over."

They sat there drinking coffee and talking about what had happened. Marylou told Margie she could stay there for a while if she wanted to. But, Margie said she still had the house, so she might as well move back there. "I will come back to see you Marylou."

Marylou got up from the table to go to the bedroom. Margie reached into her purse and took out two one hundred dollar bills. She slipped the bills under Marylou's coffee cup, got up from the table, and walked out the door.

Marylou came out of the bathroom and saw Margie was gone. She called out to her, but there was no answer. That's strange, she thought. Oh well. She picked up her coffee and saw the money underneath. What the hell?

Margie got into Duke's car and headed for the airport. She found out there was a flight leaving for Puerto Rico at eleven o'clock. She parked Duke's car in the long-term parking garage. By eleven-thirty, she was up in the air and headed for home.

Marylou looked at the money and thought, well, that's the last we see of old Margie. Marylou stuck the money in her bra. This will come in handy.

Hermy came into the kitchen and Marylou poured him a cup of coffee. "Margie left," Marylou told him. Hermy didn't say anything, he just sipped on his coffee.

Hermy was thinking, I have to think of a way to keep Marylou home now. I don't want her to get another job, at least not in some God damn bar. He looked at Marylou and smiled.

Hermy got up from the table without saying a word. Marylou watched as he went back into the bedroom. She sat at the table drinking coffee and wondering what bug was up old Hermy's ass.

Hermy came back into the kitchen with the black box in his hands. He put the box on the table and opened it. Marylou could see the box was filled with money all neatly tied into little bundles.

"What's this?" Marylou asked.

"Well now," Hermy said. "This here is our future, that is if you want it? Here is my plan. First of all, you will never have to work again, we get married, I adopt the children, and we live happily ever after. What do you say?"

"I say, I got one thing to clear up and then I will give you my answer. And Hermy, it ain't gonna be the money that will make up my mind."

Hermy took Marylou by the hand and they went back to bed.

Afterwards, Marylou was laying in the bed thinking, I wish those detectives would call me back. I have to tell them that Duke knew what happened to my baby. I'll tell them about the two guys hanging around the bar. I just bet they killed Duke. Maybe, the police can make them talk and tell them about my baby and where she is. The tears were rolling down Marylou's face. If I can get this straightened out, then I will give Hermy his answer and I think it will be, oh hell, I know it will be yes!

CHAPTER 93

Bender and Fox were sitting at their desks at the district. Every time the phone rang, they refused to answer it for fear it would be one of the people they were trying to duck. The office man was getting pissed at them because he had to keep making up excuses as to why they were not returning the calls.

It had been three days after the fire and the detectives were getting antsy waiting for the reports to come back. The news media still had not released Duke's name, at least they were working with the department, for once.

They were just getting ready to go to lunch when Hunter yelled from his office, "Bender, Fox, get in here!"

They went into Hunter's office and sat down in the chairs by the desk.

"I got the reports by phone," Hunter said. "The Fire chief says that the fire was arson. They found evidence of plastic explosives on the oven door. It looks like it was a professional hit. The coroner says there were traces of cocaine in the body, but get this. There was enough heroin in the body to make him be off in dreamland. There will be a press release this afternoon. You guys can get back to work now."

Bender and Fox headed for Marylou's hoping to catch Margie there.

When they got to Marylou's, they knocked at the door. Marylou answered, "Where the hell have you guys been?" I've been trying and trying to get a hold of you."

Marylou let the two detectives in and told them to sit down. "I have so many things to tell you guys, things I probably should have told you a long time ago."

"Wait, before you get started, let us fill you in on the details we have now," Bender said to her. He started to tell her what they had when Marylou interrupted him.

"Could you guys wait a minute? Let me get Hermy and I'll call Fatty to come over here," Marylou said. "This way you only have to tell the story once and Fatty can help me tell you and Hermy my story."

"Sure, we can do that," Bender said. "In fact, I have a good idea. How about if Fox and I go out and get some sandwiches for all of us. Fox and I haven't had lunch yet."

That's what they decided to do. Fox and Bender got out to the car and Bender said, "What do you think?"

"I think that it's confession time!"

"Think we ought to get the Sergeant?" Bender asked.

"Let's give him a call and tell him what's going on. Let him decide what he wants to do," Fox said.

Bender called Hunter and told him what had happened. Bender told him they were going to pick up some lunch and go back to Marylou's.

"Good," Hunter said. "Stop by the Hot Dog Inn and get a bag of dogs with everything on them. Then, stop and get a case of beer."

"What the hell are we going to do?" Bender asked. "Have a party?"

"Yes, we are. If this works out like I think it will. We are going to have a big party!"

Hunter hung up the phone and sat at his desk. He leaned back in his chair and smiled to himself. Maybe, this is the break I've been waiting for. I know I'm right about that girl. I bet we find her now. Yes sir, we might clear up a lot of things. He got up and went to his car. He drove slowly over to Marylou's house almost as if he was afraid that it would all be over soon. By the time he got to Marylou's, he felt relaxed but ready to hear the story.

Hunter knocked on the door of Marylou's. Hermy opened the door. Let the Sergeant in and pointed to a chair at the table. Bender, Fox, and Marylou were already sitting down. They all had a beer in front of them.

"Sit down Sergeant," Marylou told Hunter. "We still have to wait for Fatty."

"How about the other girl Margie?" Hunter asked.

Marylou handed Hunter a beer and said, "She was here, but she left. I doubt if we'll see her again." Marylou did not mention anything about the money.

Hunter said to Fox, "Call the boys at the airport and have them check all the parking lots. See if they can find Duke's car. Also, check and see when the flights to Puerto Rico were."

Fox smiled at Hunter, "Already got the ball rolling. I called the airport as soon as Marylou told me what had happened."

Fatty walked in the door, "Hey, what the hell is going on here? Are we having a party?"

Fatty sat at the table and they all ate hot dogs and drank beer. No one mentioned a thing about Duke or Noreen. When they were finished, Hunter took a big swig of beer, set the bottle on the table, and said, "O.K., let's get started here. Marylou, I understand you have something you want to tell us?"

Marylou looked at Fatty and then at Hermy. "I have some things to tell and I hope Fatty will help me."

Fatty seemed to know what Marylou was going to tell, so she just let out a sigh, smiled, and said, "O.K., do whatever you have to do and when you are done, I'll add whatever I can."

"Thanks Fatty," Marylou said. "But if Noreen is still alive, there is no chance of me finding her now that Duke is dead without help from the police."

Marylou told the story Fatty had told her and everything she could remember that Duke had told her, leaving out the part about going to bed with him. When she finished talking, she looked over at Fatty.

"I think she covered it all," Fatty said. "I really ain't got anything to add."

They all sat there looking at each other. Then, Hermy said, "You mean you would have gone to bed with him?"

"Thank God, it never came to that!" Marylou lied. She thought, what the hell is a little white lie now? There ain't no way to say I did. She reached over the took Hermy's hand, "I really don't know if I would have or not. But, if I would have had to, it would only have been to find out where my baby was."

Hermy squeezed her hand, "Let's not even think about that now, that part is all over with."

Hunter hadn't said one word or asked one question during the time Marylou was talking. When she was finished, he still didn't say a word. He watched the little scene between Hermy and Marylou. Then, he drank what was left in his beer bottle and got up from the table. He looked at Fatty and said, "You know, it's people like you that fuck up our investigations. It's hard enough to do our work. Then, there are people like you who don't give us the information they have! Do you know that had we known half of what we were just told, that little girl might be home right now?"

Hunter walked out the door.

"What the fuck is his problem?" Fatty asked. "What the hell was I supposed to do? Squeal on Duke? I didn't even know for sure what the hell was going on myself."

"Relax Fatty," Bender said. "Sometimes, the boss gets a little emotional."

CHAPTER 94

Hunter got into his car and drove away from Marylou's. He knew he was going to Rosie's to tie one on. He thought about the story Marylou had told. It really wasn't any different from what he thought in his own mind all the time. Hunter was a little disappointed. There still was no real proof of anything. Hunter had hoped Marylou or Fatty would have been able to give them something concrete to work on. Oh well, he thought. This is the way detective work was, you just had to keep plugging away, then sometimes when you least suspected it, the case was solved.

Bender and Fox sat at the table at Marylou's for a while. They decided it was time for them to leave to meet Hunter.

When they got into the car, Bender asked, "What do you think?"

"Damned if I know." Fox said. "But, I'll tell you one thing, the boss was pretty pissed off when he left."

"Yeah, you're right. Think we should go to the office or head right down to Rosie's."

"We might as well go to the bar. That's where he'll be."

They went to Rosie's. Sure enough, Hunter's car was parked in the back. Bender and Fox went into the bar. Hunter was sitting at the table waiting for them.

The minute they sat down, Hunter said, "The only way we can find this girl now is to find Big Al and Tony and make them talk!"

Fatty, Hermy, and Marylou sat at the kitchen table after Bender and Fox left. This whole story had come as a shock to Hermy. He had never had a clue about what was going on. Fatty, in her own mind, was a little pissed off. She was thinking that by Marylou talking, she was screwed out of some money.

Marylou felt somewhat relieved. She was glad she had put the burden of the investigation back to the police where it belonged.

Hermy got up from the table to get another beer. He brought the beers back to the table and said to Marylou, "Where does this leave us?"

Marylou looked at Hermy, "If you will still have me, I'd like to get married and settle down with you Hermy."

"Does that mean that you are finished playing policeman?"

"All done. I just want to be a housewife now, or at least as close to one as I can be."

Fatty got up from the table. "It's time for me to go. I have to look for a new job and get on with my life." Fatty walked to the door. She turned around before leaving and said, "See you guys in church."

Hermy and Marylou sat at the table drinking beer and planning for their future.

CHAPTER 95

Bender, Fox and Hunter stayed at Rosie's until three-thirty in the morning.

They were all back at work at nine a.m. "How the hell does the Sergeant do it? He stays out all night and looks so good in the morning?" Bender asked Fox.

"Maybe he looks good on the outside, but inside he has to be hurting, just like me," Fox said.

Hunter called them into his office. They all knew they had a lot of hard, boring work in front of them. This was not going to be easy. To find Big Al and Tony might prove to be the easiest job. To get any information from them could prove to be impossible.

"I talked to the Captain and told him what we had so far," Hunter said. "He told me you guys should spend as much time on the case as you have to. We just have to keep him posted." Hunter looked down at some papers on his desk and started signing them. Bender and Fox took that for a sign of being dismissed.

They went to their desks and sat down. Neither of them said anything for a while, both thinking about where to start. They both knew the colder the trail got, the harder it was to follow, and this trail was cold.

Then, Bender said, "Hey, you know what we should do? We got to get to that playground and see if we can find that creep Porky."

"Man, you're right. I forgot all about him!"

Hunter happened to be looking out the door of his office when he saw Bender and Fox go flying by. He could see they both had grins on their faces. Ha! Hunter thought. They must have come up with something good.

Bender and Fox got into the car. "Fox, stop at the bank on West 25th, will you?"

"Sure, no problem," Fox answered. "But, what do you need?"

"I know that Porky. This might cost us more than the usual ten bucks. So, I'll just get some paper from the bank and save time."

Bender and Fox got to the playground around noon. "I think it's a little early for Porky, but let's hang around a while and see," Fox said to Bender.

They were just sitting in the car keeping an eye on the people going in and out of the playground. They had been there for about forty-five minutes when some guy walked over to the car.

"You coppers looking for something or someone?"

"What's it to you?" Bender said without even looking at the guy. "If you got some kind of problem, tell us. If you don't leave before you have one!" Bender slowly turned his head until he was looking right into the guys' face.

"Jesus, man, take it easy. I just thought I could help you guys out. I mean like you talking to the messenger man. Otherwise, known as the pigeon. That's like carrier pigeon. You dig?"

"How much is it for you to carry the message?" Fox asked.

"You gotta tell me, where, when, who, and all that shit before you gets the price!" the dude told them.

"Here, seven tonight, Porky. That's all the shit and here is the price," Bender said as he handed the guy a fiver.

The guy looked at the five, "Man, you ain't getting no air mail for this!"

Bender looked at his watch and then up at the guy, "You got about five hours to deliver the mail, pigeon, 'cause when we get back at seven and our package ain't here, the five bucks comes out of your ass! Get it?"

"Man, watch this pigeon fly!" The guy ran from the car and through the playground flapping his arms like wings.

Bender and Fox drove away. They went to Lorain Avenue to check on the car lot. The sign B.A.T. Auto Sales was still there. The lot itself was empty. They drove by the barber shop and they saw the barber standing at the window with his hands behind his back just staring out the window. They went back to the office and got out more reports on the case. They were going over everything once more, just in case there was just one little thing they had missed.

Hunter walked out into the office. He had been out to lunch. Bender told him what had happened at the playground. "Sounds good. After you meet the guy or whatever happens, meet me at Rosie's."

Hunter went into his office and closed the door. I sure hope that snitch knows where those two guys are, Hunter thought.

My Baby My Baby!

The day went slowly for Bender and Fox as they read reports and waited to go back to the playground. Bender pushed back his chair from the desk, looked at his watch, and said, "O.K. Fox, let's hit the road. It's six-fifteen."

Fox looked up from the report he was reading. He had a look of relief on his face. "Man, that was the longest few hours of my life. Let's get the flock out of here!"

They were at the playground by six-thirty. They sat, watched, and waited. It was six forty-five and nothing. Seven o'clock, nothing, Seven-fifteen. "I'll kill that fucking pigeon!" Fox said.

At seven-thirty, the back door of the police car opened and in slipped Porky. "Come on! Get this fucking car out of here will you?" Porky said to the cops. "What the fuck is wrong with you guys?"

"Hold it!" Fox said to Porky. "What the hell is your problem?"

"God damn it, I'll tell you my problem! You fucking guys are going to get me killed!"

"What the hell are you talking about?" Bender asked him.

"Man, the pigeon, you tell him you want to meet me. Jesus. Why didn't you just wait until night time to come and see me? You know, I ain't gonna be here during the day."

"We thought the pigeon took the messages and delivered them," Bender said.

"He does, then every once in a while, some pusher gives the pigeon fifty bucks and asks who he got messages from lately and the pigeon tells him!" Porky said. "That's how they try to catch the finks."

Bender pulled the car away from the playground. Porky had ducked down in the back seat. Seemed a little corny for all this cloak and dagger, but Bender and Fox knew when it came to the drug world, things could get violent over the smallest of things.

"Where to?" Bender asked Porky.

"How about Edgewater Park?" Porky said. "But, first stop and get some beer will you guys? Man, I could use a drink."

Bender pulled into a Mini Mart and Fox went in to get some beer. Then, they headed for the park.

Bender pulled into the parking lot and went way to the back where they were no cars parked. He shut off the lights and the motor and turned to look in the back seat.

Porky was just getting up off the floor. "Gimme a beer, will ya?"

Fox reached into the bag and pulled out three beers, one for each of them. Porky popped the tab on the beer and chugged it. He opened the car window and threw the can on the grass. He held out his hand for another beer. "O.K., now what the fuck do you guys want?"

Porky sat back in the seat of the car and took a sip from a can. Bender looked at him and thought, why the hell do we have to deal with slime bags like this?

"Remember those two guys we asked you about a while ago?" Fox asked. "You know, Big Al and Tony?"

"Yeah, what about them?" Porky asked. "Man, I gave you the info, right?"

"Sure, you did," Fox said. "But, we want to know where they are now."

"Man, I don't know if I can find that kind of shit out. I mean, what the fuck do I look like, 411?"

Bender reached into the back seat and grabbed Porky by the shirt. He pulled him almost into the front seat. "Listen, you little mother fucker. I've had just about enough of your shit! You remember, we're the cops and you are fucking garbage! So talk nice before I throw you in the can! Got it!"

Bender threw Porky back into the seat. Porky picked his can of beer up from the floor and patted down his collar. He just sat in the back seat and didn't say a word. No one said anything for a while. Then, Bender reached into the bag and handed Porky another beer.

"Look," Bender said. "I didn't mean to grab you like that, but sometimes you get me so pissed off!"

Porky looked at Bender. He smiled and said, "Shit, that's the same thing my old lady tells me!"

They all laughed and the tension was gone. Bender and Fox both knew that Porky was off his high horse and back where he belonged.

"We're looking for those two guys. We got some questions to ask them," Bender told Porky.

"I'll try my best," Porky said. "But, if these guys are buried some place, I may have to pay to find them."

"Do what you got to do," Fox said. "Here's a hundred for starters." Fox handed Porky the money.

Porky just sat there looking at the hundred dollar bill.

"What's the problem?" Bender asked. "You think it's a phony?"

"No, it ain't that," Porky said. "It's just that's about what I got to pay the pigeon to keep his mouth shut. Man, I'm sorry guys, but that's how much he wants."

Fox gave Porky another hundred dollar bill. "You better come up with some good shit!" Fox said. "Or, I'll tell you what me and Bender will do. We go back to the pigeon and give him a few bucks to set your ass up, but good! Got it!"

"Hey man, you know I always do right. Don't even say things like that!" Porky whined. "Look, meet me here tomorrow night, say ten, ten-thirty, somewhere around here." Porky opened the back door of the car and slid out. "I'll just get out here. How about a couple beers for the road?"

Fox handed him the bag with the rest of the beers in it.

"Hey man, thanks," Porky said. "Bring some more beer tomorrow night and some more money, too!" He ran away from the car laughing.

"Jesus, what a creep," Fox said. "But, I bet he comes up with something."

"Yeah, he does all right," Bender said. "But, just once, I'd like to kick his ass until his nose bleeds."

Bender and Fox left the parking lot and went to see Hunter. They told him what Porky had said and that they would meet him tomorrow night. "You want to go with us?" Fox asked Hunter.

"Hell no, I had enough of that shit and scum when I had to work the streets."

The next day, Bender and Fox got into work around noon. Hunter called them into his office. "What? You guys think your working the afternoon shift?"

"Hey Sarge, give us a break, will you?" Bender asked. "You know we're not as tough as you."

"How well I know," Hunter said. "It says right on the bottle, Not Made for Kids!"

"You know, Sarge, I'm starting to believe that shit!" Fox said.

"O.K., now down to business," Hunter said. "I've been trying to find out any information on those two guys, but so far, nothing."

"I think anything we are going to find out about those two guys, we're going to find out on the street," Fox said.

"Well, let's hope this Porky guy comes up with some information tonight," Bender said.

Bender and Fox spent the rest of the day in the office again reading reports. They both made phone calls to other snitches they knew, but so far, they came up with a big fat zero.

Later in the afternoon, Hunter called Bender and Fox into his office. "How you guys making out?"

"Nothing," Bender said. "We haven't found one thing."

"I just got a call from Homicide. It seems they're looking for two guys who were hanging around Duke's Bar, a Nick and Dom. You guys ever hear of them?"

"Those might be the two guys who were doing all the hustling down at the bar," Bender said.

"What the hell," Fox said. "We got plenty of time to kill before we meet Porky. Let's stop by Marylou's and talk to her about these two guys."

"Good idea. Maybe, she remembered something else that will help us," Bender said.

They went to Marylou's. When they got there, they found Marylou and Patty sitting in the kitchen. Big Red and Hermy were doing some work in the church, Marylou told them.

Marylou fixed them some coffee and they all sat around the table. Yeah, Marylou knew who Dom and Nick were. "They were the bosses, or at least, Nick seemed to run everything."

"What do you mean by everything?" Fox asked. "You mean the bar, too?"

"It was getting pretty close to that," Marylou said. "But, not yet. I mean, they were telling them two whores what to do and Fast Eddy and his girl when to sell drugs."

"Sounds like you guys were doing all right," Fox said.

"Hey, how come you guys are asking all these questions?" Marylou asked. "Just about two hours ago, the Homicide guys were here asking the same questions. What's the matter, don't you guys talk to each other?"

"Most of the time, no," Bender said.

My Baby My Baby!

They spent some time drinking coffee. Marylou told them the same story she had told the Homicide guys. Then, she asked, "Do you guys think that Dom and Nick had anything to do with killing Duke?"

"You know, you could have something there, but we ain't handling that case, so we really don't know what Homicide is doing."

"That figures," Marylou said. "No God damn wonder you guys couldn't come up with anything on my little girl. Hell, one part of the Police Department don't know what the hell the other part is doing!"

"We agree with you Marylou. But, you have to believe that we are doing our best. In fact, I shouldn't tell you this, but we have a meeting tonight that might shed some light on your case."

"Really?" Marylou asked. "Will you guys tell me right away if you find out anything?"

"We sure will," Fox said. "Oh, by the way, did Duke ever say what happened to Big Al and Tony?"

"All I remember," Marylou said, "is him telling me that they had gone out of town, but I don't think he ever told me where they went."

Bender looked at his watch and motioned over to Fox that they had better go. They left Marylou promising her that whenever they found anything out, they would let her know.

CHAPTER 96

Fox and Bender made a stop at the Mini Mart to pick up the beer for their meeting and headed for the park. They got there at ten o'clock on the button. They pulled into the same place they had parked the night before. They sat there waiting. "God damn it! The same shit as last night, wait, wait, wait," Bender said. "Give me one of those beers, will you Fox?"

Fox gave Bender a beer and took one for himself. At eleven o'clock, there was still no Porky. Fox opened two more beers. It always seemed that when you were waiting on a stakeout or waiting for a snitch, there was never anything to talk about. Just sit in the car watching the clock.

At eleven-thirty, the back door of the police car opened and in came Porky. "Man, what the hell are you guys doing? The heat is on heavy about this here Big Al and Tony," Porky said. "But, let me tell you guys something. If it ain't for the connections I got, you never find out nothing about these two guys."

Fox handed Porky a beer. "Tell us what you found out."

"Before I start, let me give you the damages on this here caper." Porky thought for a minute, like he was adding up a list. "That hundred you gave me covered the pigeon. The next hundred almost got me the info, but I had to add another hundred, and then a hundred for me. That makes, let's see, you guys owe me two hundred smackaroos."

Fox reached into his pocket and gave Porky two one hundred dollar bills. Porky took the money and looked at Fox like he couldn't believe Fox had given him the money. "Oh yeah," Porky said. "There was another fifty bucks for some expenses I had."

Fox looked at Porky, "Don't push your luck. You're overpaid now."

"Can't blame a guy for trying," Porky said. "I mean you gave me the two hundred so easy, I figured another fifty ain't gonna hurt."

"Come on Porky, give us what you got," Bender said.

"O.K., here goes. I guess these guys got the big man pissed off somehow. Now, not enough to get themselves killed, but got him

My Baby My Baby!

mad enough to take the chain of joints they were collecting from and then having their asses sent out of town."

"Come on Porky, where's out of town?" Bender asked.

"As far as my contacts could find out, they were sent up to the Falls to stay with some guy named Vince. The best I know is the guy lives on Pine Avenue. I couldn't get the address."

Fox handed Porky another beer. "I'll tell you Porky, you done good."

Porky had a big smile on his face. Most of the time when you gave these guys any information, it wasn't enough or not the stuff they wanted. Porky was already thinking about how much he could get next time. Maybe, double his price. "Oh, by the way," Porky said. "The word on the street is that those are the two guys who snatched that little girl, I forget her name."

Bender and Fox looked at each other. "Who the hell told you that?" Bender asked.

"Man, you know better than that!" Porky said. "It's one thing to trade a little info for some money, but you know I ain't never gonna be giving one of my sources away."

"What's the chance of this story being one hundred percent?" Bender asked Porky.

"I tell you guys right now," Porky said. "This is no rumor. When this here guy that told me this shit tells me something, it's the genuine thing and no less."

"Here, have another beer," Fox told Porky. "Maybe, we can still do a little more business here before you leave."

"I don't know about that," Porky said. "You know, I been busy tonight and I still got more work to do."

"Like what?" Fox asked. "What the hell do you have to do? You got a job or some place you have to be?"

"Well, like I said, I been real busy. I mean, that's why I was late. I was talking to Weaver from Homicide. I had some info for him."

"Did you tell him about these two guys?" Bender asked.

"No, but what they wanted to know about was who murdered that Duke guy. The only thing I could tell them was Duke was involved in snatching that kid."

"What did Weaver say about that?" Bender asked.

"All he said about that was that he would talk to me later about the kid getting snatched." Porky opened the car door and jumped out. "Look, I'll talk to you guys later, see youse." Porky took off running.

Bender opened his door to chase Porky.

"Let him go!" Fox yelled. "We got all the info from him that we are going to get for now."

Bender got back into the car. "You're right. It's just that I would like to catch that little fucker and kick his ass!"

"Yeah, I know," Fox laughed. "He's just the kind of guy who makes you want to do things like that."

Bender looked at his watch. "It's almost twelve-thirty. Let's go see Hunter."

When they got to Rosie's, Hunter was sitting at the table by himself. "I've been waiting for you guys. What happened?"

They told him the story and also about what Porky had said about talking to Weaver.

"Don't worry about that," Hunter said. "I'll take care of that later." Hunter ordered a round of drinks and sat there not saying a word.

"Something wrong Sarge?" Bender asked. "You seem so quiet."

"Ah, nothing, just thinking. By the way, the guys from the airport called. They found Duke's car in one of the lots. It seems like Margie parked the car and took a flight out that same day."

They all sat at the table not saying much of anything. Then, Hunter said, "Here's what I want done." He took a big swig of his beer. "First thing tomorrow morning, I want you to send a teletype. No, fuck it, call the Niagara Police Department, talk to someone in the Detective Bureau and tell them who we are looking for. We'll wait until the morning. I don't want to get some asshole desk man that forgets to tell anyone we called until a week later." Hunter called for more drinks. He was back to his old self now, talking a mile a minute about the case.

It was three in the morning before they left the bar. No one was drunk, but they were high on the case and thinking about what would happen in the morning.

Hunter told them to be in the office by eight o'clock, but he didn't want to make the call until about nine. That way, they could probably talk to a boss.

They all went home. None of them could sleep. At seven o'clock the next morning, they were all sitting around Hunter's desk having coffee.

Eight-thirty was as long as they could wait. They had decided the night before that Bender would be the one to make the call. Hunter would stand by in case they wanted to talk to a supervisor.

At eight thirty-one, the phone in the Niagara Police Department rang. Bender said, "This is Detective Bender from the Cleveland Police Department. Could you please connect me with your Detective Bureau?"

Bender told his story to the detective on the other end of the line. Hunter and Fox could tell whoever was on the other end of the line was listening and not saying a word. Bender told the entire story without mentioning Big Al or Tony's name. At the end of the story, Bender said, "So that is why we are looking for these two guys, Albert Walsh and Anthony Russo." Bender waited for some response from the other end of the line. Nothing. "Hello?" Bender said, "Hello?"

The voice on the other end of the line finally said, "You better hang on a minute."

Bender looked at the other two and said, "The guy put me on hold!"

It was about a minute before Bender heard someone pick up the phone. "Yes," Bender said. "Yes sir, Walsh and Russo, yes sir, yes, how about my Sergeant, he's right here."

Bender held the phone out to Hunter. "It's their Captain." Hunter took the phone.

Hunter sat at his desk with the phone up to his ear and hardly said one word, except for a grant or a no shit, he was quiet. Then, he said, "Yes sir, we'll be waiting for your call." He hung up the phone.

Hunter sat back in his chair and looked up at the ceiling. "Jesus, you guys ain't gonna believe this shit!"

"Come on, tell us," Fox said.

"They got Tony in jail and Big Al is dead."

They all sat there for a minute, not quite believing what had just been said. Then, Hunter unfolded the conversation he had had with the Captain. "Evidently, Big Al and Tony had gone into a bar to hold it up. The bartender pulled a gun from behind the bar and Big Al shot and killed him. Unlucky for Al and Tony, an off-duty policeman came out of the bathroom just as they were pumping lead into the bartender. The copper killed Big Al, and Tony dropped his gun and gave up."

"When the hell did this happen?" Fox asked.

"Yesterday afternoon," Hunter told them. "The Captain up there told me he would call me back as soon as they got everything straightened out. So now, all we can do is wait."

Bender and Fox went out to their desks. Hunter went to tell the Captain what was happening.

Lunch time came and Hunter sent the office man to get lunch for everyone. No one wanted to leave the office in case the call from Niagara came.

"I bet you a hundred dollars Hunter sent the office man to the Hot Dog Inn to buy lunch," Bender said to Fox.

"No bet," Fox said.

Sure enough, about twenty minutes later, in came the office man preceded by the smell of hot dogs with the works.

They ate lunch sitting around Hunter's desk and waiting for the phone to ring.

At two-thirty in the afternoon, the phone rang. The office man picked it up, said a few words, and then yelled, "Hey Sarge, it's for you, Niagara Police."

Hunter took the call. Bender and Fox stood next to his desk listening.

Hunter got off the phone. He had a big grin on his face. "Pack your bags boys, that guy Tony wants to talk to us!"

Hunter headed for the Captain's office to tell him the news. About a half hour later, he came out of the office all smiles. "Bender, Fox, take my car over and get the oil changed and gassed up. We're leaving for Niagara in the morning."

They took the car to get it ready. Hunter called the Niagara Police back to make all the arrangements.

When Bender and Fox got back to the office, the office man told them they were to meet Hunter at Rosie's.

They met Hunter at the bar and it was like a party. The three of them were so wound up, it would have been impossible to go home to bed. But, by ten-thirty, Hunter was saying goodnight to everyone.

"You guys better go home and get some sleep. I'll see you at six bells sharp."

"Wow, that's the earliest I ever saw him leave here," Rosie said. "Must have a big date, uh?"

Bender and Fox both left about an hour later. All of a sudden, they were both feeling a little sleepy.

At six a.m., they were all at the office ready to go. Bender was driving. Hunter and Fox fell right to sleep. Great, thought Bender. This is going to be a long four hours. He turned the radio on hoping to wake Fox or Hunter up. No such luck.

They pulled into the Niagara Police Station at ten a.m. The three of them were taken to the bureau and introduced to the Captain. The Captain took them into his office and sat down behind his desk. "Coffee gentlemen?" he asked.

The detectives really didn't want any coffee. All they wanted to do was see this guy Tony, but, they had to play the game.

The Captain had coffee brought into the office. After they had settled down with the coffee and made some small talk, the Captain got down to business.

"We have that guy, Tony Russo, booked here for a murder of the bartender," the Captain told them. "After you called, we talked to him, and he said he would like to talk to you guys. We never mentioned about the case you're working on. We just told him that you wanted to talk to him. He still doesn't have a lawyer, but I guess he still wants to talk, at least he did last night."

"There's only one way to find out," Hunter said. "Let's go see him."

The Captain picked up the phone. "Have that Russo fellow taken up to one of the interrogation rooms, and we'll be right up." The Captain hung up the phone, got up from his desk, and motioned for the three detectives to follow him. He took them up to the next floor and down a hall. They came to a metal door and the Captain knocked. The door swung open and they could see Russo sitting at a table.

Tony looked up, "Hey, come on in you guys, have a seat."

They all walked into the room and sat at the table. Tony looked at them one by one. "Don't I know you two?" he said as he looked at Fox and Bender "Yeah, I seen you guys at Duke's place, right?"

"Could be," Fox said. "But, that's not why we're here."

"I know what you want to talk about. What happened, that fucking Duke turn me in?"

"No, he didn't turn you in, he's dead," Fox said. "But what do you think we want to talk to you about?"

Tony looked at Fox, "Look, I don't want to play no fucking games! I want to make some deals!"

"What kind of deals are we talking about?" Fox asked.

"Man, I'll make it easy for youse guys. Let's start with that little kid, Noreen, you remember her?"

The detectives didn't say anything nor did they show any emotion. Tony looked around the table in disbelief. "Man, ain't you guys something? You mean, you are going to sit there and pretend you forgot that little girl? Man, I can tell you right where she is!"

"Sure," Hunter said, "we heard all that shit before."

"Hey man, who the fuck are you?" Tony asked.

"Easy," Fox said. "That's our boss. Can't make no deals without him."

"O.K., youse three guys from Cleveland stay here. I want to talk to youse. The rest of youse leave. I got nothing to say to you right now."

The Captain shrugged his shoulders and motioned for the other Niagara Detectives to leave. The Captain pointed to a button on the wall. "When you're done talking to this piece of shit, push the button." Tony gave him the finger as he walked out the door.

"These guys are something else," Tony said. "Everything's a big deal with them. Know what I mean?"

"Yeah, that's the way it goes," Fox said. "But, let's get down to business, shall we?"

"O.K., here's what I want," Tony leaned back in his chair. "I want that murder charge against me dropped. Let them charge Big Al. What the fuck, he's dead anyway right? In return, I tell you where the little girl is. They can close that case, saying, Big Al, Duke, and Jimmy did it," Tony smiled.

"Blame it all on the dead, right?" Bender said.

"Hey man, they ain't got shit to lose," Tony said. "What the hell. A guy gotta watch out for himself, know what I mean?"

"You're asking an awful lot," Hunter said. "You know, to start with, we can't make any deals up here. What the hell, you ain't in

Cleveland. Besides that, if the kid is out of Ohio, the F.B.I has to make the deals and you know how hard it is to deal with them?"

"Yeah, I know all about that shit too," Tony said. "But, I got a deal for them too, a deal they can't refuse." Tony started laughing.

"Tell me one thing," Hunter said. "Do we need the Feds here?"

"Go get 'em. Yeah, we gonna need 'em," Tony said.

The three detectives walked out of the room and Hunter went right to the Captain.

About an hour later, two F.B.I. agents, Brooke and Franki, came to the Captain's office. Hunter gave them the scoop. The agents said they wanted to talk to Tony alone. They were taken to the interrogation room.

Hunter sat in the room with the Captain, and Bender and Fox were talking in the other office with some of the Niagara detectives.

About an hour later, one of the F.B.I. agents, Brooke, came back to the Captain's office. "Look," Brooke said. "This guy has to go with us. If you guys are going to give me a hard time, we go over your head and he goes with us anyway."

"What about the charges we have on him?" the Captain asked.

"No problem," Brooke said. "What I'll do is type up a report for you saying that you handed this guy over to the F.B.I and we take all responsibility for him."

"What about us?" Hunter asked. "We have a stake in this, too. I mean what the hell, he told us right off he knows where the little girl is."

"That also is no big problem Sergeant Hunter," Brooke said. "In fact, I think you will have your case cleaned up in a few days. What I want you detectives to do now is go back to Cleveland and wait for us to call you. You have my word it will be no longer than three days."

Hunter knew he had no other choice. The best thing he could do was act like he was cooperating one hundred percent and that's just what he did. Hunter thanked the Captain for all the help and told him he would see him in a couple of days. "Right?" Hunter asked as he looked right at Brooke.

Brooke smiled back at Hunter and said, "You have my word on it."

Hunter walked out of the office and waves at Bender and Fox to come on. Bender and Fox followed Hunter to the car. They could tell by the way he was walking, he was pissed off. When they got to the car, Hunter got in the back seat. Fox was going to drive back as Bender had driven up.

Hunter told them what the agent had said. "Those guys always piss me off," Hunter said. "They sure think their shit don't stink."

The rest of the trip back to Cleveland was spent telling stories about what assholes the F.B.I are and what they thought Tony was going to do.

They came down Route 90 and as they hit the innerbelt, Hunter said to Fox, "Don't you drive by Rosie's without stopping."

"You really think this car could do that?"

Lucky for them, Rosie had made a big batch of pork chops.

Hunter was in his glory as he drank beer and ate pork chop sandwiches.

CHAPTER 97

The next morning, they were all at the office early. Hunter spent about two hours in the Captain's office telling him what had happened back at Niagara Falls.

None of the detectives wanted to leave the office for fear that the call from the F.B.I. would come. Finally, about six o'clock, Hunter told Bender and Fox to go home. He was going to stay a while longer. Then, he would head down to Rosie's for dinner.

The next day was spent about the same as the day before. Only today, Hunter was pacing the office, yelling at everyone, and drinking coffee until he must have been pissing brown.

When Hunter was just about to leave the office, Bender and Fox said they would stay late. The phone rang and the office man picked it up. "Hey Sarge," he yelled. "The F.B.I. wants to talk to you."

Hunter went into his office and shut the door. He was in there for about five minutes. Bender and Fox sat at their desks not saying a word. Hunter came out of his office and without even looking at Fox or Bender, he walked right into the Captain's office.

Three minutes later, Hunter walked out of the Captain's office. He waved for Bender and Fox to follow him. They followed him right down to the garage. Hunter got into the back seat of his car. Fox got in behind the wheel and Bender got in on the passenger's side. As soon as the doors were closed, Hunter let out a yell. "They know where she is! She's alive and safe!" Hunter was laughing, tears running down his face. "What do you think about that?" he said. "Just what the fuck do you think about that?!"

Bender and Fox both let out a cheer. They reached back and shook Hunter's hand. "You were right all the time!" Fox said. "No one believed you, but God damn it, you were right!"

"O.K.," Hunter said. "Let's go get a drink, and I'll tell you what we have to do."

Fox drove to Rosie's. On the way, he checked the rearview mirror and saw Hunter just sitting back in the seat, with a big grin on his face.

They sat at the table drinking beer. Hunter outlined what they were going to do. "We have to go tell Marylou she has to leave with us at six o'clock tomorrow morning. We have to meet the F.B.I. at the Niagara Police Station around eleven."

"We better go over to Marylou's and tell her now, so she don't go out and we can't fine her," Bender said.

"Yeah, that's a good idea," Hunter said. "Let's go there now."

They got some beer and went to Marylou's. They knocked on the door and Marylou opened it.

She took a look at the three detectives standing there and jumped right into Hunter's arms. "You found her! I know it! You found her, right?"

Hunter hugged her and said, "right, we found her and she is safe and sound."

Marylou said, "Come in, sit down!" Then, she screamed for Hermy. "Hermy, get in here! Hurry!"

Hermy came running into the room, "What the matter?"

"Sit down Hermy!" Marylou said. Then, in a calm voice, she said, "Hermy, they found my baby!"

Hermy looked at Marylou, then at the three detectives. He just smiled and then held out his hand to Hunter.

Fox opened some beer and said, "This really should be champagne, you know?"

"I guarantee it will be tomorrow night," Hunter said.

Hunter told Marylou they would have to leave by six a.m. to make sure they were in Niagara by eleven. Marylou asked if Hermy would go. Hunter told her no, the F.B.I. had already said only the three detectives and Marylou could go.

It was eleven-thirty when Hunter said, "We better call this a night. We'll be back in the morning to pick you up."

"I'll be ready," Marylou said. "In fact, I'm ready now!"

Fox dropped Hunter off at his apartment and then took Bender home. He would pick them all up in the morning, so no one would be late.

CHAPTER 98

At six-fifteen the next morning, they were on their way to Niagara. They stopped for some breakfast. When they ordered, it was about the most talking that had been done on the trip so far.

When they got to the Police Station, Hunter went right into the Captain's office. Brooke and Franki were already there. A half hour later, the door to the Captain's office opened. Hunter came to the door and called Bender, Fox, and Marylou into the office. Hunter introduced Marylou to everyone.

"The reason I called you in here is so we can pull this thing off with no problems," Brooke told them. He looked over at Hunter. "Who will be driving the car?"

"Fox can drive."

"O.K.," Brooke said, and then he handed Bender a radio. "This is on the same wavelength as the one in our car. Here is what I want you to do. Fox, you follow us. When we get in front of the house, we will tell you on the radio. You park the car right in front of the house. Got it?"

"Got it."

"Now, we sit there until you see the little girl," Brooke told them. "When and if you can identify her, you give us a yes or no over the radio. If you give us a yes, all of you sit in the car until we come over to you. If you give us a no, we all drive away. That's all there is to it."

"O.K.," Brooke said. "Let's go."

They followed the F.B.I. car for about fifteen minutes when they pulled down a side street. They were about ten houses from the corner when the radio crackled and Brooke's voice said, "See that little white house with the fence around it and the sandbox in the yard?"

"Yeah, we got it."

They pulled the car up in front of the house and Fox parked. No one was in the yard. They could see no one moving in the house.

"Maybe, no one is home," Marylou said. "God, I don't know how long I can wait here."

"Take it easy Marylou," Hunter said. "You've waited this long, a little longer won't hurt you."

They waited about ten minutes longer. All of a sudden, the front door to the house opened. A thin woman about fifty or so walked out the door followed by a little girl.

"I can't see her! I can't see her!" Marylou was jumping around in the back seat.

"Sit still, damn it!" Hunter said. "Just sit there until you can see!"

The little girl and the woman walked over to the sandbox. They played for a bit. Marylou still could not see the little girl's face.

The woman got up, gave the little girl a hug and a kiss, and walked back to the house. Before she went in the door, she turned and waved at the little girl.

The door to the house closed. Just then, the little girl in the sandbox looked right at the car.

Marylou took a deep breath and all of a sudden, all hell broke loose in the car.

Marylou started screaming, "MY BABY! MY BABY!" She was struggling to get out of the car. Bender was trying to get to the radio, but it had fallen on the floor. Hunter let Marylou go. Bender got the radio up to his mouth and was ready to call Brooke. Hunter grabbed Bender's hand and said, "Wait!"

Marylou jumped from the car like she was shot from a gun. She ran to the fence and the little girl looked up.

"Hi Mommy," she said and walked over to the fence.

Just then, two cars came skidding to a stop in front of the house. Brooke jumped from his car screaming, "I told you to stay in the car!"

The other F.B.I. agents burst through the gate, ran to the house, and started banging on the front door.

Marylou grabbed Noreen and ran for Hunter's car. One of the agents helped her to the car. She got in and the agent stuck his head in the window. "Follow me!" he told Fox and ran to his car.

They all got back to the Police Station. Marylou and Noreen were sitting in the corner of the office playing. Hunter and the two other detectives were in the Captain's office when Brooke and Franki came storming in.

"What the hell were you guys trying to pull down there?!" Brooke was screaming.

"Hey, go fuck yourself!" Hunter said. "Just tell me what you want us to do now."

Brooke looked at Hunter and shook his head. "Take that kid, her mother, your detectives, and get your ass back to Cleveland. That's all I want you to do."

Hunter got up from the chair smiling. "Come on boys, I think we just did one hell of a job!"

They pulled up in front of Marylou's house about seven that night. Hermy had the place all decorated with balloons and ribbons. Parked in front of the house were all the news vans from the local stations.

Fox pulled the car to the curb. "Looks like somebody told the news media," he said.

"Marylou, you and Noreen get out. We'll talk to you later."

"Ain't you guys coming in?"

"Nope," Hunter said. "We'll see you on the news."

They went to Rosie's. They got stiff as billy goats, but not before they saw the news.

CHAPTER 99

Two weeks later, Hunter had just finished talking to the F.B.I. on the phone. Bender and Fox walked into the office.

"What did they have to say?" Fox asked.

Hunter pushed his chair back from the desk, leaned back and put his feet on the desk.

"Yeah," Bender said. "What are they going to do about those people who had the kid?"

"Hey, how about Nick and Dom?" Fox asked.

Hunter put his hands behind his head, smiled, and said,

"That's another story."

THE END

ABOUT THE AUTHOR

Earl S Kratzer was born in Cleveland, Ohio, and became a member of the Cleveland Police Department in 1962. He worked in almost every district in the city, as well as the Mounted Unit, Juvenile Unit, liaison man with city hall and finally as a detective sergeant in the Detective Bureau. He worked closely with the detectives on many cases—some large, some small, but all interesting.

Earl S Kratzer currently resides in Stuart, Florida with his wife, Michele, who is a retired Captain from the Cleveland Police Department. He is the father of three daughters who also reside in Florida.